Ashes of Evil

A Tale of Three Women

Jan Gallagher

PublishAmerica
Baltimore

PublishAmerica has allowed this work to remain exactly as the author intended, verbatim, without editorial input.

Hardcover 978-1-4512-1633-2
Softcover 978-1-4512-1726-1
PUBLISHED BY PUBLISHAMERICA, LLLP
www.publishamerica.com
Baltimore

Printed in the United States of America

This novel is dedicated to the precious people in my life, my family and my friends.

Acknowledgements

If it hadn't been for the support of my friend and fellow writer, Lori Baskin, I might never have finished this novel. I thought the diagnosis of Parkinson's disease meant the end of my writing career. Over lunch at poet Arlene Webber's home, Lori, and Barbara Deming, writer and mentor of writers, encouraged me to get back to work.

To all the friends, family and colleagues who listened as I read half-formed chapters, thank you for your patience and for you valuable suggestions.

Special thanks to Victoria Featherstone, Davina Hecht and Paige Osborn.

Prologue

Modern-day U.S. Highway 101 begins in San Diego, California, and runs north through Oregon to Olympia, Washington. It follows the general route of the original mid-eighteenth century trail known as El Camino Real—the King's Highway.

The Southern Oregon section of 101 rushes through wild costal landscapes, occasionally slowing long enough to provide the main street for towns with names like Harbor, Brookings, Port Oxford and Gold Beach. These towns cling to 101 like barnacles to a gray whale. They are dependent upon the trucks and cars rumbling north and south on the highway's potholed surface.

But somewhere in that temperate region there is a place of abundant rain, lush green ferns and towering trees, a place where the cacophony of traffic is no longer audible. Instead, the roar of white capped billows crashing against a rock studded coast provides background music for the drama of everyday life.

Highway 101 once ran through the middle of the village of Tamlin. Logging trucks rolled through the center of town, and the economy thrived—until the big storm of 1950. Longtime inhabitants of Tamlin still tell stories about the time it poured for three days, dumping more than twenty inches of rain. On the second day of the storm, the main highway, several access roads and a bridge washed out. By the morning of the third day, folks in low-lying areas were clinging to their roofs, praying to be rescued.

Highway engineers decided not to repair the old thoroughfare, but instead rerouted Highway 101 twenty miles to the east. Without easy access, Tamlin was frozen in time.

It became a haven for artists and recluses, but things are changing. The rural beauty of the town has recently been discovered by retirees and young families.

* * *

It is the custom of old-timers to gather at the big table in the back of Tamlin Café, where they drink strong coffee and gossip. This morning George from the filling station; Deputy Sheriff Doug Simpson; Annie, a grocery store clerk; Bertha, owner of the Café and her husband, Jake, the mailman, are discussing some of the changes taking place in Tamlin. Alice, coffee pot in hand, moves around the table filling cups.

"No more for me." George drops his cigarette stub into the dregs of his coffee with grease stained fingers. "I gotta get back to work." He throws two rumpled dollar bills on the table and shrugs into his rain slicker.

"Give me a warm-up and get me one of them Danishes." Bertha holds up her half full cup, and hitches her chair closer to the table.

"Get it yourself, Ma. I'm busy," Alice says and hurries over to hand menus to a gray-haired couple seated in one of the booths.

"Sure a lot of strangers in here lately," Bertha says.

"That's the couple bought old Maude Weiss' wreck of a mansion— gonna make it into a bed and breakfast," Doug says. "Should be good for your business."

"No good ever comes from strangers," Jake growls. "You ain't so dumb as to have forgot that crazy Ruby—we never had anyone like that in Tamlin before strangers started movin' in. A serial killer in Tamlin, and all because of strangers. "

"Must'a' been some night, and me off on a fishing trip. Did you hear about how…?" Doug begins.

Jake interrupts saying, "Things began to go downhill when Charlie showed up with that pregnant girl a year or so ago. Since then there's been nothing but trouble."

Bertha gives a "humph" and dabs at a spot on the table with her napkin. "It started way before that. Remember how I told you there was something unnatural about the way Tomasina—'course they call her Ma Tom, now—appeared out of nowhere and put a spell on poor Gus. To this day nobody knows for sure where she come from."

"Alls I can tell you is she sends a money order to Mexico every month." Jake lowers his voice to a dramatic whisper. "I'm not sayin' it's underhanded or anything …"

"You better not let Ernest hear you talking about his family like that." Doug gets to his feet and walks out saying. "I don't like it much either; they're good people."

"Wait for me, Doug." Annie grabs her umbrella. "Past time for me to open the store," she says. "Besides, I like Ma Tom."

Bertha heaves her bulk out of the chair and waddles behind the counter for a Danish, muttering, "Definitely something evil about Tomasina. She gets off the bus, marches in here and hypnotizes Gus. I seen it with my own eyes. And that baby boy born eight months after they was married didn't look anything like Gus; that's for sure."

Book I
Tomasina

Chapter One
Tomasina

Tomasina Rosita Sanchez trudged along the dusty track toward her family's home in the village of Agua Dulce, in Sonora, Mexico. Chickens skittered out of her way and a thin brown cow pulled at tufts of dry grass. It was a golden October afternoon in 1968. Though her hands were empty, Tomasina moved as if she was burdened with a weight.

She had just turned seventeen, but a stranger would have thought she was an old woman. Her thin back was permanently stooped from years of carrying heavy buckets of water, and she was in the habit of draping her black shawl over her face in an attempt to hide her crooked nose, however her lucent eyes glowed with intelligence; her full lips were sensuous. Her hair, when unpinned from its tight knot, cascaded down her back like a sparkling blue-black waterfall.

It was a sad day. When the government opened the school and medical clinic for the children two years ago, Tomasina was proud to be hired to help the nurses care for the sick *niños.* Her job at the clinic elevated her from the status of unmarried daughter of a poor farmer to that of a professional woman earning a wage.

Today, an important man from the government came to visit. The children learned a song to greet their guest. They assembled on the wide porch in front of the school.

The man got out of his big black car. His face was hard as he listened to the children's singing. Then he began to speak. "There is no more money for this school and clinic," he told the students, and staff.

Some of the children began to cry.

"The children must go back to their families or the orphanage," the man continued. "There is no more money," he repeated, then turned and walked to his waiting car and driver.

The car sped away in a cloud of dust. Tomasina tried to comfort the children, but she wanted to cry along with them. With his words she had become *nada*, an ugly spinster, a burden to her family.

* * *

For one year Tomasina worked in the garden and helped Mama in the four room adobe house. She didn't expect to marry. Her life was set in a pattern, until the day a car pulled up next to the low mud brick wall that encircled the house. Two men got out. One wore khaki pants and black tee-shirt, and had a gun in a holster on his hip; the other looked like a cowboy with boots and a fancy shirt.

Tomasina stepped into the swept dirt yard to see what business the men had at her home. Mama and the two babies remained inside the house, listening and peeking out through the small window.

"Is there anyone here willing to work hard for a good wage?" The men were not Mexicans; the cowboy spoke to Tomasina in a strange sort of Spanish which made her think he was, perhaps, from Texas.

"My father and brothers are in the fields working, sir," said Tomasina. "They will be home in the evening. I will tell them what you said."

"I'm looking for workers to come to California in the United States. The wages are good, twenty dollars a day. Housing and transportation are provided," the cowboy told her.

The man with the gun did not speak, but his narrowed eyes kept looking all around as his hand caressed the butt of his gun.

Tomasina knew the business of these two strangers was to recruit men and women from villages and streets, and to arrange for their transportation to migrant camps. What she did not know was that the bosses of the big ranches and farms needed the strong backs of the migrant workers only during the harvest season. When the vines and trees were bare, the pickers would be forced to move on in search of other harvests—other employment of any kind no matter how menial.

"I will go to the United States to work," Tomasina blurted out. To be employed would lift the shame of spinsterhood from her head.

"No, Tomasina, no," Mama cried from the house.

"What must I do?" she asked the cowboy, ignoring Mama's warning.

"Bring a small blanket, a jar of water and a few tortillas—that's all. We will come for you at sunrise in two days." He held up two fingers as one would do for a child.

The men started back toward their car. "We won't wait if you're not ready," the cowboy called as he shut the car door.

That evening Papa urged Tomasina to reconsider. "You can stay at home and take care of us when we are old, if you don't find a husband," he said.

She knew that although Papa said to stay, he wanted her to go. He loved her, but an unmarried daughter was a heavy burden.

Two mornings later the whole family: Tomasina, her Papa, Mama, two grown brothers and two baby sisters, stood together in the gray dawn watching for the car. When they saw the dust cloud in the distance, Mama covered her face with her hands and moaned. Tomasina kissed each of them. "I'll send money when I get paid," she promised.

Tomasina was relieved to see three women in the back seat of the rusty Cadillac. The cowboy took her bundle and tossed it in the trunk. She got in the back seat with the others. The cowboy climbed into the front seat, and they were on their way.

She twisted around to watch Mama, Papa, her brothers and the girls growing smaller and smaller as the car sped down the track. "I may never see them again!" she cried, and reached for the car door handle

A slender woman who would have been pretty if not for the wine colored birthmark across the right half of her face moved closer to Tomasina. "I'm sad also, but I must go to *El Norte* to work." She pulled Tomasina's hand away from the handle. "My family needs the money I will make. My poor father is sick and cannot work."

"What is your name?" whispered Tomasina, allowing the other woman to hold her hand.

"Aurora, just call me Aurora," she whispered back, giving Tomasina's hand a reassuring pat before releasing it. "And you?"

"I'm called Tomasina. I also want to earn money for my parents and my little sisters. Perhaps my family can use the money I send to buy another piece of farm land. My poor brothers can't support wives unless our family has more land to farm."

"Why do you whisper?" asked a large woman with strong looking arms. "We aren't in church, are we? And by the way, my name is Carmen, and I can out-work any two men," she said with a laugh.

The forth woman looked to be the oldest of the group. There was a silver streak in her hair and slackness to the soft skin under her chin. She had not yet spoken, but now she smiled in the direction of Carmen as if acknowledging the big woman's courage and strength. Then she said firmly, "Carmen, Aurora, Tomasina, I am called Maria. I say we make a pact to stick together like sisters. One person alone is weak, in many there is strength."

The other women nodded in agreement. "Now we aren't strangers, but have become sisters," Maria continued, "we need to get to know each other. I'm a childless widow from a settlement so small it has no name. I lived with my brother and sister-in-law for three years after my husband died. Ah, that woman, what a tongue in her head. Like a machete."

"Look at me." Aurora put her hand to the birthmark. "My father is old and I have no brothers. If I don't make this trip to *El Norte* I'll end up begging in front of the little church. My father must have medicine, and we have no money."

Carmen lifted her hands and let them drop to her lap. "My family begged me to stay, lazy bastards. Ha! What do I care for them? My mama died a year ago. Even she had trouble keeping my father and six brothers out of the cantina. Now that she's gone they drink and fight while I farm our piece of land. It is enough. Without me they will work or starve; I don't care which."

The sun was low in the western sky by the time the car turned off the main road and bumped down a rutted dirt lane to where a dilapidated van was parked in a gully. In shadows cast by spiny cactus bushes, fifteen men waited. They squatted on their haunches, and remained so still they seemed part of the landscape.

The coyote, their smuggler, was a surprise to the women; he was a young man of about sixteen years. His round shiny face looked smooth and soft.

"I didn't know I was to transport women," he grumbled. "This is very bad, very unlucky."

"Women or men, it's all the same, a strong back and a pair of hands. The same as burros, jack or jenny, no matter," said the cowboy. He threw the women's bundles into the van then got into his car and drove back down the rutted lane.

The coyote approached the four women, "Ladies, for the love of God, don't continue on this journey. I myself will get my cousin who lives near here to give you a ride to the bus stop."

"But we must go on," Carmen said. "Men aren't the only ones to have need of good wages."

Stepping closer the coyote continued in a barely audible voice, "Young ladies are often forced to work as *putas*. It is very bad for young ladies at the camps. I beg you to pay attention to my warning."

"Don't worry about us, *Señor* Coyote," said Maria. "We will go to the camp together as sisters and God will protect us."

Shrugging his shoulders, the coyote began to motion to the men. "Let's go—let's go," he called clapping his hands and whistling.

The waiting men and the four women climbed into the back of the van. The coyote pulled pieces of cardboard over the windows so the migrants couldn't see out, or be seen. It was very hot inside the van. The women crouched together in one corner. They no longer whispered, and the fifteen men soon ceased mumbling to each other. They endured the heat and thirst in silence for many hours.

When he van stopped and the back door was opened, they were in what seemed like a vast wilderness of desert. Several of the men fell when they climbed out and tried stand on cramped legs. The coyote ignored them, but he assisted the women down from the van and gave them a jug of water to share.

"We made it," he said. "You are standing in California, the United States of America. Try to be inconspicuous; a bus will pick you up very soon." He handed the bundles of belongings out of the van, then climbed into the vehicle and drove away.

The women seated themselves beside a rock. They must have driven all night; toward the east the sky was turning gray and a crimson fringe outlined the tops of the hills. A new day was beginning.

"We should eat a bite," Carmen said. "It's important to keep our strength so we will be ready for work." She pulled a package of tortillas from her bundle and divided them among her new sisters.

Several hours later a green bus drove into the clearing. Two men got out. One was a mean looking fellow with a pockmarked face. He pointed a rifle toward the workers. The other man was very fat. He held a shining machete and said nothing. The driver of the green bus remained inside. In a few minutes a white truck pulled up next to the bus, and a small man in dirty overalls got out.

"Stand up and form a line," yelled the small man, gesturing with a pistol. He jerked one of the waiting workers to his feet and shoved him toward the bus. "I told you donkeys to line up!"

The four women moved into the line. "Stay close together!" said Carmen. In one hand she held her bundle. She placed her other arm around Tomasina's shoulders.

The small man stood by the door of the bus. After thrusting the gun into the holster that hung beneath his soft round belly, he reached into the bus for a clipboard. "I'm Mr. Seligman. You'll be working for me and I don't like no trouble."

The workers began to mumble to each other and shuffle to their feet.

Mr. Seligman shouted, "Shut up and line up. Give me your name then get on the bus."

The workers looked confused. What did the man want them to do? Tomasina had learned English at the clinic in Agua Dulce. Her voice trembled as she translated the man's words for the others.

When Tomasina, Carmen, Aurora, and Maria reached the man he looked them over with his pig-like eyes. Gesturing for the women to turn around, he inspected their figures. He motioned Maria and Carmen into the van, then studied Aurora and Tomasina. With one grimy hand he grasped Aurora's chin and tilted her face toward the light; when he saw the birthmark he gave a snort of disgust and pushed her roughly toward the bus. Holding both hands over her face, she stumbled up the steps.

Then it was Tomasina's turn. The man tore the shawl from her face and tossed it into a clump of cactus. He smiled as his hand trailed over her face then cupped one of her breasts. She stared impassively into Mr. Seligman's cruel face, mesmerized by his evil blue eyes.

"You just might be the one. How would you like a cushy job in my office?"

"I'll work in the fields with my sisters," she answered in a quavering voice.

After a week in the fields you'll be beggin' to be my office woman," he said giving her buttocks a slap as she hurried into the bus.

Chapter Two
Tomasina

The green bus kept to a dirt road through California Indian land until Buckman Springs, where it turned onto the smooth pavement of west bound I—80. Except for occasional detours on the rutted side roads which circumvented Border Patrol stop points, they proceeded at a rapid speed.

If comfortable seats had ever been a part of the green bus, it was in the distant past. Hard wooden benches lined the sides. The migrants faced each other across a middle aisle piled with shovels, rakes, trimmers, bags of chemical fertilizer and bottles of insect poison. The air reeked of a combination of chemicals, exhaust fumes, urine and sweat.

Some of the men amused themselves by staring at the women and muttering suggestive remarks. Tomasina ignored them and turned in her seat to gaze out the dusty windows.

At Pine Valley the bus headed north on Highway 79. It climbed higher and higher on narrow roads, before it began to descend. Passing by the outskirts of Ramona, it rolled through Escondido, a pleasant little town snuggled in a green valley surrounded by purple mountains.

Tomasina thought this was the prettiest place she had ever seen and wished with all her heart they could stop and rest there, but the bus sped by brightly painted houses, stores with windows gleaming in the sunlight, shade trees, palm trees and flowers of every color with no sign of slowing down.

Who could have guessed that there were so many shiny cars and big trucks in the entire world? Tomasina stared at the excess of wealth evident on all sides.

On the northern edge of Escondido the bus rolled onto broad, smooth Highway 395 where it picked up speed and seemed to fly along the pavement. Tomasina leaned against Carmen, closed her eyes and slept.

She woke-up many hours later when the bus stopped in the desert town of Mojave for gas, then drove onto a side road. The sun glinted on the diamond sand. This was a place so hot and dry that trickles of sweat no longer dripped from the migrants' flushed faces. The shimmering pastels were lovely, but Tomasina was too thirsty to appreciate the landscape.

The driver turned off the engine and motioned everyone out. The reason for the stop became obvious. "I don't want none a you pissin' in my bus," he shouted.

The men stood with their backs to the road and urinated into the weeds. The women took turns spreading their skirts to make a little area of privacy for each other before they relieved themselves.

Tomasina and Aurora walked about, feeling the circulation come back into their legs. Carmen and Maria stood nearby talking through heat-cracked lips.

"I wish we had a tortilla or some morsel to eat," said Maria. "We finished the last of the food this morning."

"I am so thirsty," said Aurora. "Can we have a little drink?"

"How much water do we have left?" Carmen asked.

"I think just a few sips each. One of us must ask the driver to stop at a place where we can fill our jars," replied Maria.

"My God!" cried Tomasina in a frightened voice. "Who would dare go to a man such as that with a request?"

"I'll go," said Carmen, smoothing her skirt front with mannish hands.

Tomasina watched in awe as the big woman walked past the men. They made cat calls and kissing noises. Carmen ignored them.

The driver squatted on the ground smoking. He was a handsome young man, a thin Hispanic version of Elvis Presley. His oily hair swooped up into a high curl which hung onto his forehead in front, and folded elaborately into a duck tail in the back. Long sideburns framed a perpetual sneer.

"Hey, *amigo*, we need to get some drinking water."

"What is that to me?" the driver replied with a smirk.

"You won't collect your fat wages if you deliver corpses and *Mexicanos* so sick they are unable to work. Also, I notice that to drive you must turn your back to us." Carmen paused for a moment and then added, "I wish you good health and prosperity *amigo*."

Head high, Carmen walked toward the waiting women. She boldly returned the stares of the men who raked her with their eyes as she passed by them.

"*Mojados*, pah." The driver spit on the ground, whistled and clapped his hands, motioning for the migrants to get back into the bus. He drove a bit farther, and then pulled the bus in behind a rundown gas station and convenience store. "Stay here and keep quiet," the driver said in a dramatic voice. He swaggered toward the store in his high heeled cowboy boots.

In a few minutes he returned with a fresh pack of cigarettes bulging in the pocket of his tight black shirt, and a large plastic jug of water in each hand. He moved down the cluttered center aisle until he reached the four women. With a mocking bow he handed Maria and Carmen each a jug of water before resuming his seat at the front of the bus.

Soon the green bus was on the road again. "He didn't give the men water," Aurora said in a low voice. "They must also be very thirsty."

The men watched through narrowed eyes as each woman in turn tilted a water jug and drank. Carmen held first one jug, then the other up to show that they were still almost full. She passed the jugs to the men.

"*Gracias, señoritas.*"

"*Muchas gracias.*"

The men lowered their eyes and each man thanked the women in a respectful voice for his portion of the water.

"I am called Ernesto." The gray haired man sitting next to Tomasina introduced himself, "and these are my four *hijos*—Felix, Jose, Sam and Gabe—good workers all."

"Pleased to meet you," Tomasina's smile was shy. "So many good workers, you will soon be rich."

"Not so rich, just enough to return to our village and buy a piece of land big enough to support my boys and the families they hope to have."

"I'm sure you will realize your dream before many months go by," replied Tomasina. She returned to looking out the window. Once across the desert, they came into a fertile land with acres of fruit trees, fields of feed grains such as corn and alfalfa, and vast expanses of scrubby little plants with white cotton bursting from the blossoms.

They passed through Bakersfield on I—99 and continued north through the central valley of California. In one place Tomasina saw many cattle crowded together in a field. There was no pasture and the dejected animals were standing on a mountain of their own dung.

Tomasina didn't understand this land. Was it a paradise of plenty or a hell where cows stand in their own manure while waiting to be slaughtered and thirsty women must beg for a drink of water?

Darkness was closing in, making the bus seem like a little world of its own. Although it had only been two days and one night since Tomasina left her village, she felt as though she had been traveling forever.

"We're almost there," the driver called.

He turned off the highway and drove east for several miles. Easing into a private road on the right, he followed a winding dirt lane through acres of grape vines. To Tomasina it seemed as though the big round harvest moon was painting the fences and vines with gold dust. Then the moon hid its light behind a cloud.

It was very dark when they pulled into a wide clearing. The beam of the headlights fell on a gray cement block building about twenty feet by ten feet and a single outhouse. Tomasina rubbed her tired eyes. She had seen painted houses, grand stores, and bountiful fields, but, it seemed that migrants like her were not destined to have a share in the richness.

The newly arrived workers remained in the bus waiting to be told what to do next. A truck pulled into view, illuminating the clearing with its headlights. Mr. Seligman got out on the driver's side.

"Did they all make the trip okay?" he asked the driver of the bus.

"Yah, yah, no problems," said the driver holding out his hand to receive a fat envelope.

"Get out! Get out! This is your new home," the driver called into the green bus and the migrants climbed out into the glare of the headlights.

"Horst, you didn't tell me there were females," exclaimed a woman as she got out of the truck. She hurried over to Carmen, Maria, Aurora and Tomasina. "Oh, my dears, what an ordeal this trip must have been for you," she whispered to them.

The woman had kind eyes. Tomasina could see Mrs. Seligman was nothing like her husband.

"Anna, you are here to feed the workers not to socialize with them," said Mr. Seligman.

"Yes dear, of course. Just let me get set up."

The woman returned to the truck, and reached in for a large black kettle. She struggled with the weight of it, and the bus driver sidled over to take it from her. "That's too heavy for you, Mrs. Seligman. Let me get it. I'm very strong."

"Thank you, Juanito," she murmured.

The bus driver set the steaming kettle on a stump in the middle of the clearing and removed the lid. The spicy fragrance of boiled beans and chili peppers wafted into the clearing. Mrs. Seligman followed Juanito carrying a cardboard box full of pie tins.

"This is your supper," she called to the migrants in English.

Juanito repeated the woman's words in Spanish, and added importantly, "Line up, line up, no shoving."

Mrs. Seligman ladled boiled beans into the pie tins and handed one to each migrant worker in turn. Carmen, Maria, Aurora and Tomasina stood together. Ernesto and his boys joined them. They slurped down the rich liquid and then used their fingers to scoop the beans into their mouths.

"The only thing wrong with these beans is there is not enough," said Carmen smacking her lips. "The *señora* is a good cook."

"Save your plates for tomorrow," Juanito told them. "You ladies will be glad to know there is a water faucet at the end of the building." Laughing as if his words were very funny, he got into the bus and continued up the road.

Mrs. Seligman pointed toward the gray building and said in English, "You'll sleep in the little house. Tomorrow I'll bring blankets to make a private section. "

After lifting the empty kettle into the truck, she walked back to where the four women stood. "I do hope you'll be alright. I hate to leave you like this."

"For gawd sakes Anna, let's go, it's almost midnight," Mr. Seligman bellowed.

"Yes dear, of course dear." She scurried toward the truck.

The truck made a u-turn and headed back up the road, taking the light with it. The migrants clutched their small bundles of belongings and huddled together. The house was a forbidding shadow in the darkness and the air was growing cold.

Tomasina was glad her Mama and Papa couldn't see her in this place. She moved closer to Carmen's bulk in search of comfort.

Chapter Three
Tomasina

Ernesto had a flashlight in his belongings. Gabe pulled the door of the cement building open. Leaning in, Ernesto flashed the beam of his light all around the room. "Nothing to hurt us, just rubbish, a few old tin cans and newspapers," he called.

The men crept into the dirt floored room, and settled themselves to sleep. After pausing a few seconds, the women followed. The air was musty.

"It smells of mice in here," whispered Aurora.

The women stretched out on the floor close together, using their bundles as pillows. At first Tomasina didn't think she could relax on the cold hard ground, but she quickly fell into a deep sleep.

There was a loud pounding on the door. To Tomasina It seemed only a few minutes since she had closed her eyes.

"Who is there? What do you want?" several of the men called out.

"Four o'clock, time to go to work." It was Juanito's voice.

The workers stumbled out into the dark clearing. The green bus was waiting to take them to the vineyards.

Juanito pointed at Tomasina. "You wait here. I'll be back for you."

"No, we stay together," said Maria.

"Mrs. Seligman wants that one to trim the hedge along the drive to the big house. I'll bring her back here tonight," Juanito promised. "Now get into the bus."

In a short while Juanito returned. This time he was driving a battered truck. "Hurry, we haven't got all day," he called to Tomasina as she climbed into the back of the truck.

Tomasina had never used hedge clippers. "Look, hold them this way," Juanito demonstrated. Pointing up the impossibly long driveway which was bordered on both sides by thick hedge, he said, "Trim all the way to the top on this side before you start on the other side." After giving his brief instructions, he got in his truck and drove away, leaving her alone.

The clippers were heavy and hard to open and close with enough snap to cut the tough branches of the hedge. The sun was still low in the eastern sky, but Tomasina's back ached between her shoulder blades, and already the skin was rubbed off her hands. Little rivulets of blood dripped between her fingers.

"You aren't going to make much money at that rate." Juanito, a cigarette dangling from his lower lip, pulled up in his truck. He got out and stood watching Tomasina work for a few minutes. Then he reached in the truck and found a plastic bottle of water which he handed her.

"*Gracias*," Tomasina murmured. The water was cold and delicious.

When she handed the bottle back to Juanito, he caught her wrists and turned her hands over. He whistled when he saw the open blisters.

"Tomorrow I'll bring you gloves, for now pull your sleeves over your hands and work like so." He showed Tomasina how to protect her hands. As he got back into the truck he said, "Tell the large lady that I am looking after her little sister," and drove away laughing.

At sunset Tomasina limped back along the road to the camp. By the time she got there some of the men had swept the floor of the gray house using branches as brooms and Mrs. Seligman was hanging tattered blankets to make a private place in one end of the room.

Although Mrs. Seligman had brought tortillas, oranges and another kettle of her good beans for supper, Tomasina and many of the others were too tired to eat.

"You must eat; then you can sleep," said Carmen giving first Tomasina and then Maria a rough shaking to wake them up.

"Tomasina, they weigh the grapes we pick and write it in a book. We must carry the full boxes to the scale and they are so heavy," said Maria rubbing the middle of her back. "You're lucky to be chosen to help Mrs. Seligman."

"Perhaps," replied Tomasina. "I'm fearful when Mr. Seligman is around. His little blue eyes follow me all the time. I don't want to be his 'office woman.'"

The workers were on the green bus each morning before the sun was up in order to be in the fields at first light. They returned to the clearing when there was no longer enough light to see the ripe grapes.

Tomasina was the exception. As the others were getting onto the bus, she was walking toward the big house. It took her three days to trim the hedge. When that was done, she helped Mrs. Seligman in the garden and sometimes in the kitchen.

Mr. Seligman was often at the big house. He said nothing to Tomasina, but he stared at her. He didn't care that Mrs. Seligman was close by. With his mean little blue eyes he showed disrespect to both his wife and Tomasina.

"The work is good and Mrs. Seligman is kind," Tomasina told her friends that night. "But, even if the boss did not look at me, I would rather be in the fields with the others. Poor Juanito is no longer one of us, but he is not American either. I do not wish to become like him."

On Friday Mrs. Seligman said, "You have worked hard the whole week, Tomasina. Tomorrow is Saturday. There is always only half a day for the workers on Saturday, because payday is in the afternoon. There is no work on Sunday. You and your friends will have a nice rest."

Mr. Seligman was waiting for the workers when the bus pulled into the clearing on Saturday afternoon. The dirty man with the rifle and the machete man were beside him. Juanito was also there. When Mr. Seligman spoke, Juanito translated the words into Spanish.

"Come up one at a time when your name is called, *amigos*," said Juanito.

As the workers received their envelopes an angry murmur, like the buzz of a swarm of bees, began amongst them. The armed men stood with their feet spread and their guns pointed at the hostile crowd. Mr. Seligman spoke to Juanito.

"The boss wants me to explain," Juanito said to the group. "Only very experienced workers can earn twenty dollars a day. The pay is fair according to how much work you produce, and there is a charge of $2.00 a day for sleeping in the gray house, $3.00 a day for transportation to the fields and $3.00 a day for food. If you don't like it—leave."

Juanito was not smiling or laughing now. When he stepped back to stand by Mr. Seligman and the men with the weapons, he kept his eyes on the toes of his fancy boots.

After handing out all the pay envelopes, Mr. Seligman and his two helpers drove away in their truck, leaving Juanito behind.

"Don't blame me," Juanito told the sullen men, "I work here the same as you." Then he brightened, "Good news, the sellers' vans will soon arrive with all sorts of things to buy with your money."

Juanito beckoned several of the young men to follow him away from where Carmen, Maria, Aurora and Tomasina stood. He told the men something in a whisper and they responded with whistles, whoops and bursts of excited talking.

Just then a dilapidated red van pulled into the clearing. The driver was a round faced Hispanic woman who looked to be in her forties. "Come and see what I have for you my friends," she called in a pleasant voice.

Maria went to bargain with the vender. Each of the four women contributed five dollars to the shopping fund. Maria was able to get six dozen tortillas, a large jar of peanut butter, a box of plastic knives and forks, six cans of fruit cocktail, two cans of tuna and a can opener. She also got a large bag of Oreo cookies and a flashlight.

The workers had been told that Mrs. Seligman would not bring dinner on the weekends. The vender had ready-to-eat hotdogs, so Maria purchased four of them for a payday celebration dinner.

Even though the pay for the week had been small, Tomasina felt a sense of wellbeing as she sat on the ground in front of the gray house talking to her friends, and admiring Maria's purchases.

Eight dollars after expenses was all Tomasina had to show for a week of hard work. It was not much, but she would ask Juanito to purchase a money order with it to send to her family. Perhaps the next paycheck would be larger.

One of the venders sold beer. The women could hear the men's voices getting louder and bursts of excited laughter. Ernesto came over to sit with them.

"Another sort of vender is due here soon. He will have whiskey and women for the men to throw away their money on. It would be well for you ladies to remain inside the gray house until tomorrow morning," he told them.

"We aren't afraid. These men are our friends—although none is so good a friend as you Ernesto," Maria told him.

"Please go behind the blanket in the gray house and do not come out until tomorrow. I am so sorry to tell you this, ladies, but I fear for your safety."

"Thank you for your concern; we'll remain in the gray house as you suggest," replied Maria.

It was a pleasant evening. The four friends fixed up a makeshift pantry for their purchases in a broken box Aurora had found. Despite the noise outside the gray house, they went to sleep early and slept soundly.

The pale light of dawn was coming in through the crack around the door when Tomasina opened her eyes. All about her she heard steady breathing and snoring. Surely even Ernesto would think it was safe to be up and about.

Tomasina stepped out of the door. Orange and purple streaks colored the sky to the east. "God has sent us a beautiful Sabbath day," she said out loud, stretching her arms above her head.

A hand clamped over her mouth and a knee pressed into the middle of her back. It felt as if she would break in two. She smelled the stench of whiskey and tobacco. When the assailant grabbed a fistful of her hair, instinct took over and Tomasina fought fiercely to escape. She sunk her teeth into the hand.

"You little whore. I'll teach you to bite me!" The hand jerked away and Tomasina gave a loud high scream.

A fist smashed against the side of her face. She saw pinwheels of light behind her eyes as she fell. A weight pressed her into the ground, and the front of her blouse made a ripping noise when it was torn away. Rough hands pushed her skirt up. A piercing pain—no—this was not happening to her. It had to be a bad dream. The rank smell and the body pushing again and again could not be real.

From somewhere above Tomasina heard a dull thud; the heavy body on top of her went limp. She could not breathe; darkness closed over her.

Chapter Four
Tomasina

The weight was lifted; Tomasina could breathe again. She felt someone helping her up. She opened her eyes and saw Carmen fighting to break free from the restraining hands of Sam, Gabe and Jose. Carmen's eyes were wild and she held a bloodied whiskey bottle like a club. The three men struggled to control the big woman as she kicked, squirmed and tried to bite their hands.

Aurora and Maria supported Tomasina between them. They pulled her skirt down and brushed dirt out of her hair with their hands. Ernesto draped his poncho over her torn blouse.

A man lay in the dirt. Blood oozed from a wound near his left temple; his overalls were around his knees. It was Mr. Seligman.

"Look," Ernesto said angrily. "That drunken pig drove his truck into a ditch." Ernesto spat into the dirt. Across the clearing in the irrigation ditch Mr. Seligman's truck rested on its side. "He must have seen Tomasina come out of the little house. He was always looking at her. Thank God, Carmen heard her scream."

The commotion startled the migrants out of their sleep; even those who had indulged heavily in whiskey the night before. The men emerged from the gray building. Blinking against the brightness of the morning light, they milled around in the clearing.

"We have to run away. They'll put us in their jail," said one man hysterically.

"Where will we go?" asked another, "The whiskey man got all my money last night."

"We'll say the boss was drunk. He fell down and hit his head," said Paco, a tough looking man who rarely spoke. A scar ran from the corner of Paco's left eye to the corner of his mouth making it appear as if one side of his face was smiling while the other side frowned.

By grasping Carmen's wrist and twisting her thumb, Paco was able to pry the whiskey bottle from her grip. Walking to the outhouse, he opened the door, and threw the bottle down the hole. It made a sucking splash.

"Someone's coming,'" Gabe motioned up the road. A cloud of dust could be seen headed toward the clearing from the main road. The workers watched it draw closer with pounding hearts. Was it the police? Was it the men with the guns, or the Border Patrol?

In a few seconds, Juanito's old truck came into view. He was on his way back to the ranch after a night in town. Brakes screeched and the truck stopped in the clearing.

"What's going on?" Juanito called in a raspy voice. He peered out from the curtain of greasy black hair which hung over his face. "*Madre Dios, mi cabeza*," he said putting one hand to the side of his head as he got out of the truck. His black satin shirt was wrinkled and mostly unbuttoned. "What happened here?"

"The boss was drunk. He fell down," said Ernesto.

Juanito's bloodshot eyes took in the truck in the irrigation ditch, Mr. Seligman's inert figure with his pants around his knees, Tomasina's torn clothing and bruised face.

"He was drunk alright," said Juanito bitterly, "but he hit his head when he drove into the irrigation ditch. Help me."

Juanito took one of Mr. Seligman's arms and several men stepped forward to help carry the boss to his wrecked truck. They stuffed him in behind the wheel.

The jostling roused the intoxicated man. "I'm gonna kill that bitch. I'm gonna have my fun with her, then I'm gonna kill her real slow," he babbled before he passed out again.

Leaving the others to finish with Mr. Seligman, Juanito went back to his old truck, and pulled out a black denim jacket. Grasping Tomasina by the shoulders, he looked directly into her dazed eyes and spoke slowly, "Put my jacket on then get into my truck. Crouch down so no one can see you. Do you understand?"

Tomasina's eyes were huge in her pale face, but she nodded her head yes and, with Aurora's help, did as he told her.

Juanito returned Ernesto's poncho to him and said, "Wait fifteen minutes, then go to the house and tell Mrs. Seligman you just found her husband unconscious in his wrecked truck."

Tomasina crouched on the floor of Juanito's truck. She cried, and she shook so hard that her teeth chattered. When Juanito gave her a worried look; she tried to smile. "I am so glad for the warmth of your coat," she said.

"Are you okay?" Juanito asked gently as they sped along the highway, "He didn't—you know—hurt you?"

"He"—"that man"—she couldn't go on. Tears ran down her cheeks; she wiped them away and said, "Someone saved me; I don't know who."

"I think it was Carmen," said Juanito, "but you must never tell anyone. I'm going to take you to the bus station in Willowbrook, twenty miles north of here. Take any bus going north. If Mr. Seligman and his thugs look for you, and I don't think they will—at least until tomorrow—they'll figure you headed south back to Mexico.

* * *

Twenty minutes later they pulled up to a busy bus depot. "Remember, Tomasina, go north. Do you have any money?"

"No, I left everything behind."

"Here, it's all I have." He thrust a wad of bills into her hand. She got out, and stood on the sidewalk watching the battered little truck until it turned at the intersection and disappeared.

Although there were people all around, Tomasina felt alone and frightened. She worked up the courage to go into the bus station, but was afraid to stand in the line at the ticket window. Instead she went into the ladies room and scrubbed her hands and face. She had lost her hairpins and couldn't fasten her hair into the usual knot at the nape of her neck. After running her fingers through the tangles, she made a thick braid. The bruise on her face was beginning to turn purple, and one eye was swollen almost shut.

Next to her, a respectable looking gray haired Hispanic matron in a black pants suit with sparkling buttons dabbed a powder puff over her nose. The woman caught sight of Tomasina's bruised face in the mirror. "*Pobrecita*," the woman said.

The lady's long silver earrings swung back and forth, as she strode toward the door to the waiting room. Tomasina took a deep breath and followed close behind the kind lady. Without warning, the stout little woman moved backward, bumping into Tomasina and almost knocking her down.

"Do you have a green card?" the woman hissed in Spanish.

"No *señora*," replied Tomasina.

"In here quick!" The woman pushed Tomasina into a toilet stall. "Stand on the seat so your feet don't show." The woman shut the door and slid the bolt.

Tomasina heard voices, "Show me your identification. Do you have a green card?"

There was a loud knock on the door of the stall.

"Oh," the woman groaned, "What is it? I have a problem with my bowels."

"Do you have a green card?" the voice demanded first in English then in Spanish.

"Just a moment," the woman opened the door a crack and showed her green card; at the same time she loudly expelled a cloud of gas.

"Holy cow! Never mind!" The footsteps moved away.

Tomasina and her new friend waited until the commotion in the restroom had subsided, and then the lady peeked out. "All clear," she said.

"*Gracias señora,*" was all Tomasina could say.

"It was nothing." The woman beamed at her. "You are so much like my daughter Anita. We have a little apartment in Willowbrook, with a television and everything so nice. I take care of an old lady in Crescent City during the week. Her children stay with her on Saturday and Sunday, and I go home to Anita. Did I tell you Anita works in a nursing home? She's a very bright girl—yes—oh—Manuela—I am called Manuela. Where are you going child, and what terrible thing has happened to you?"

Tomasina had never heard anyone talk so fast or so much; she found the stream of words comforting. "I am Tomasina and I must go north to seek work."

"Well, give me ten dollars and I'll get you a ticket to Crescent City, that's north of here. Mrs. Lori, my lady, will love to meet you. Tomorrow we'll go to the Salvation Army Thrift Store and find some American clothing for you, and we'll look in the newspaper for jobs."

It was early evening by the time the bus reached Crescent City. Tomasina helped carry Manuela's bulging string bags as they walked up a road edged with small colorful houses. Only a few flowers still bloomed in the autumn gardens, but the trees and bushes were decorated with gold and orange leaves.

"Hello, Manuela. Is that your daughter?" a man looked up from trimming his rosemary hedge.

"Did you have a good trip?" a lady called from a porch. "Mrs. Lori will be glad to see you, those kids of hers …."

They stopped in front of a pink cottage with white trim. Tarragon, oregano, cilantro and mint flourished in terra cotta pots on the porch. In the driveway a sporty black car reflected the last rays of the setting sun.

"Ah, the son is still here. We'll go in through the kitchen and you can stay in my room until he leaves. My lady has three children and they all want her to give up this house and go to live with them. They worry— ah well—they don't realize it would kill her to give up her house."

Manuela took Tomasina into a pretty room with many pictures and knickknacks adorning the walls and furniture tops. In the middle of a rose patterned carpet stood the biggest bed Tomasina had ever seen. It was covered with a rosy blanket of nearly the same pattern as the carpet.

"Look, you take a shower and wash your hair." Manuela motioned Tomasina into a small bathroom and showed her how to use the shower. The shower curtain had a pink and red rose design. "Leave your clothing outside the door so I can put it into the washing machine. Here is a robe for you," she added, handing Tomasina a pink terry cloth robe with embroidered rose buds.

Tomasina was combing her hair with Manuela's wide toothed comb when Manuela poked her head into the room. "Mrs. Lori is waiting to meet you. Come on."

After wrapping her damp hair in the towel, Tomasina followed her new friend through a neat kitchen and dining room into a small parlor.

The wrinkled woman with a halo of silver hair beamed when Manuela brought Tomasina into the room. "How pretty you are— lovely—even with that bruised face." Tomasina was surprised that the woman spoke perfect Spanish.

"This is Tomasina, Mrs. Lori, the one I was telling you about. We must look in the paper for a job for Tomasina, and tomorrow I'll take her to Salvation Army Thrift Store; her few bits of clothing are so old fashioned."

"You won't need to go to the thrift store. My closet is full of clothing I won't ever wear again, and Tomasina is about my size."

"You are too kind. I have some money to give you in return," Tomasina spoke for the first time since entering the room.

"Nonsense! You'll be doing me a favor to take the things off my hands. I need the space in my closet."

"You and Manuela—you are both so kind—like saints," said Tomasina clasping her hands to her heart as if she were praying.

"First a glass of wine," said Mrs. Lori. "My children disapprove of my sip of wine before dinner, and insist I eat a low fat diet. I am glad to see them on the weekends, but I also feel deprived of Manuela's good company and good cooking."

The three women relaxed with a glass of sweet red wine, and then, sitting in front of a cheerful electric fireplace, they enjoyed a meal of quesadillas and black bean soup served on TV trays. Mrs. Lori and Manuela talked constantly, often interrupting each other.

For the first time since leaving Agua Dulce, Tomasina felt safe.

"Manuela, please get today's paper from the table in the hallway," said Mrs. Lori, thoroughly enjoying her role as benefactress of Tomasina. "We'll take a look at the help wanted ads, then make our plans."

"Look under domestics wanted," suggested Manuela.

"Here's one in Tamlin, Oregon. Interesting—I wonder—I have a very good feeling about this one." Mrs. Lori's crooked finger shook slightly as she pointed to a small advertisement. She looked up and studied Tomasina's face.

Chapter Five
Tomasina

Mrs. Lori translated the little advertisement into Spanish and read it out loud to Manuela and Tomasina: *Domestic wanted, lonely bachelor seeks single woman for housekeeper/wife. Must know how to cook and clean. Send replies to POB 283, Tamlin, Oregon.*

"Just like in the movies," Manuela said, "and if Tomasina isn't happy there she must return to us." Manuela reached for the string bag that served as her purse and drew out a bus schedule. "Tamlin is very small. Look, the bus from Crescent City along the Oregon coast only makes a loop north through Tamlin once a week—on Monday. Tomasina must be at the bus stop tomorrow early."

The next morning, Manuela, keeping up a steady stream of advice, insisted on walking to the bus stop with Tomasina. "You look very pretty in those black slacks and pink sweater. Remember if you need help go to a church. Churches in small towns are very good to travelers. You can always come back to us, but I think this is the right thing for you. Mrs. Lori has visions; she can look at your face and tell your future. If she thinks this will be a good place for you, then it will be. You must write."

An old-fashioned black suitcase, a gift from Mrs. Lori, held Tomasina's belongings: another pair of polyester slacks, two sweaters, two blouses, a white flannel night gown and two sets of undergarments, all from Mrs. Lori's closet, along with the freshly laundered and mended clothing Tomasina had been wearing at the bus station. Manuela handed the suitcase into the bus, then pressed a twenty dollar bill into Tomasina's hand. "Tuck this away for a return ticket, should you need it," she said.

* * *

"Tamlin Cafe," the sign in the window read, "Home Cooking, open seven days a week from 5 AM until 9 PM."

Pausing to view her distorted image in the chrome coffee urn, Bertha pushed a straw colored curl off her forehead. "I'll need another tint and perm soon," she thought and then returned to wiping the countertop with a damp cloth.

When the bell over the door tinkled she looked up. It was Jake, the mailman. "Have you got anything going out?" he asked.

"There are a few envelopes in the basket next to the register," answered Bertha, smiling coyly at Jake as she sucked in her stomach and pushed her shoulders back causing her ample bosom to stick out even more.

"Old Gus got another batch of letters in his box again today," Jake laughed. "Man, is he ticked off. I wonder who played that joke on him, changing his ad for a housekeeper like that. Well, gotta get going. See you around six. What's today's special?" he called back over his shoulder.

"The usual Monday beef and potato hash," Bertha replied absent— mindedly as Jake went out the door. What had ever possessed her to steam open the envelope Gus left in the mail basket and pencil in the word wife? She supposed she just wanted Gus to realize that he needed a wife. She wanted him to see her as a woman, not just a dinner- dishing-out-machine."

* * *

Gus Schmidt was the son of German immigrant parents. It seemed like he was born old. The only adventure he had ever had in his young life was the time he won a trip to Camp Gold Beach, in Oregon, for selling the most newspapers. After that week in the woods his dream was to own a cabin in an Oregon forest.

Gus was only sixteen when his father died, and he became the man of the house. Dropping out of high school, he went to work as a janitor at Fletcher Bank of San Francisco to support himself and his mother. Eventually he became the lead teller.

Although his mother suffered from severe rheumatoid arthritis, she still managed to keep their home neat as a pin. She was so thrifty that the green grocer once complained she knew how to pinch a quarter until the eagle screamed.

The year Gus turned forty-seven, his mother died. By then he had amassed a portfolio of investments which allowed him to retire quite comfortably. He found the property of his dreams, forty acres in Tamlin, Oregon, and supervised the building of a 3,000 square foot log cabin with an attached workshop.

It was Gus's habit to rise early. After a long walk through the forest, he would go to his workshop and spend the rest of the daylight hours handcrafting furniture for his cabin. Each evening around five o'clock, he drove to the Tamlin Café for the dinner special. He had grown tired of the bland tasting diner fare and the noise of the blaring jukebox. He yearned for a more satisfactory ending to his pleasant days.

He decided to advertise for a cook/housekeeper, hopefully one who knew how to use spices and herbs in her cuisine. What he wanted was someone like his mother, a quiet thoughtful person. Instead he received an avalanche of letters from would-be wives along with glamorous photographs. Looking at the photographs, he could not picture even one of those women in his kitchen cooking, or pushing a broom, or hiking along a forest path with him.

* * *

Gus spent Monday building bookcases across one wall of his living room. At last he would be able to get his books out of their cardboard boxes; they would seem like new treasures after being packed away so long. He looked at his watch, almost six o'clock already. He felt disinclined to stop working and drive to the cafe for a plate of Monday's fried potatoes and beef.

Gus knew he needed to eat something warm. All he'd had all day was cold cereal and cold sandwiches. Reluctantly he went to change his shirt and washed his face and hands.

It was after seven by the time he slid into his usual booth. The regular crowd had eaten earlier and the cafe was empty except for Gus.

Bertha emerged from the kitchen wearing a fresh application of bright red lipstick. "Gus, I almost gave up on you. I would have closed up thirty minutes ago except that somebody on the Monday evening bus might want dinner."

As she spoke the bus pulled up across the street. The doors opened with a hiss and a stylish young lady in black slacks and a pink sweater got out. She was holding a suitcase. The bus pulled away and the young lady stood for a few seconds looking around before crossing the street to the cafe.

The bell tinkled and the young lady entered. Gus and Bertha both turned to stare at the new-comer.

Tomasina, looking back at them, saw a heavyset blonde woman in a grease stained apron standing by a booth. A bearded man sat in the booth. When the man stood up Tomasina could see that he had sandy hair and light eyes. Although the lower half of his face hid behind a bushy beard, she could discern a welcoming expression. It was as if he knew Tomasina from somewhere else, but had not expected to find her here. He seemed delighted to see her.

"Excuse me," she said in her best English, clutching the handle of her suitcase. "My name is Tomasina and I am looking for a lonely bachelor to be his housekeeper. Also I am a good cook. Do you know where I can find this person?"

Bertha felt her face burn with shame. "Oh, I'm so sorry. It was meant to be a joke; I didn't mean for anyone to be hurt."

"I don't understand this joke," stammered Tomasina. "Is there no housekeeper need apply here?"

"Actually," Gus could hear his voice, but did not remember planning to speak. It was as though he were compelled to say these things, "My name is Gus Schmidt and I am in need of a housekeeper and cook. You have had a long journey, come, sit down and have dinner with me. While we eat I will explain the duties to you."

"What would you like?" Bertha asked in a cold voice. For no reason she could figure out, she felt angry at this person to whom Gus was suddenly so attentive.

"A bowl of soup and a piece of bread, please," said Tomasina.

After Bertha had gone back into the kitchen Gus said, "You've hurt your face. "

"It is nothing. My friend Manuela gave me arnica to put on it." Tomasina hesitated. More than anything she wanted to be a good housekeeper for this kindly bear of a man. She wanted to cook such delicious things for him that he would smack his lips and ask for another serving, but she could not go to work for him under false pretenses. "I must tell you how it is with me."

The whole story tumbled out in a mixture of English and Spanish, but he seemed to understand. She told of her family and how they needed the money she had promised to send them from her wages. She told him of her village, of the school and hospital, of the bus ride to the ranch and of the attack by Mr. Seligman. She finished by averting her eyes and said, "And so I am without honor."

Gus broke in angrily. "We will never mention this again and you will never say that about yourself ever!" His face softened. "Tomorrow we'll go to see Father Gallagher and ask his advice. I don't want to lose you, but ...I don't want to take advantage of you." He hesitated, "Do you know that you are beautiful Tomasina? Would you consider being my wife? I'm an ordinary man, an old man...we must talk to Father Gallagher the priest at my church, Saint Anthony's of the Woods."

Gus fell silent, stunned by the commitment he had just made. He looked at the soft curve of Tomasina's bruised face and realized he had just asked this stranger to share his life. For the first time in years, his existence had meaning. "Here comes Bertha with our dinner, " he said, and added "Bon appetite," as he jauntily lifted his water glass in a toast.

Tomasina ate her dinner in a daze. He wanted to marry her. This kind man wanted her for his wife, even after she had told him of her troubles with Mr. Seligman. Well, she would be a good wife and try very hard to make him happy.

* * *

The morning sun danced behind the colored panes of glass, making a rich pattern on the wall of Father Gallagher's study. The priest faced Tomasina and Gus across a big oak desk. When Gus finished explaining, Father Gallagher spoke, "There is no spiritual reason you two should not be married. You are both devout Catholics and you are both of an age to consent to this binding commitment. The only problem you have, as I see it, is a legal one. Tomasina needs certain documents. For this you must contact an attorney."

* * *

Gus and Tomasina were married on a drizzly morning two weeks later. Sheriff Darrell Mc Bride, and the priest's housekeeper, Ruth Casey, were the witnesses. Tomasina wore her own faded black skirt and a white blouse from Mrs. Lori, along with a white lace mantilla, a gift from Ruth Casey. After the ceremony the wedding party had their celebration breakfast at the Tamlin Café.

"If it wasn't for me these two would have never met," Bertha bragged as she refilled the coffee cups.

The two weeks before the wedding Tomasina had stayed at the cabin with Gus. They spoke little, but felt comfortable and relaxed together. Gus was careful to respect Tomasina's natural modesty. "I should tell her that I don't expect anything more than companionship from her, even after we are married," thought Gus.

He tried several times, but could not bring himself to broach the subject. Now they were husband and wife driving home together. He wondered what she was thinking and worried that she might be afraid.

Going directly to his workshop when they returned from town, Gus spent the afternoon putting the finishing touches on the cedar chest he made for Tomasina as a wedding gift. Near dinner time he went to check on his new bride and found her in the kitchen stirring a fragrant stew. She told him it was called, *"ropas viejas,"* and consisted of shredded beef flavored with chilies, cumin and cinnamon. Sauce pans of beans and rice steamed on the stove and freshly made tortillas cooled on paper towels.

Gus exclaimed that he had never eaten a more delicious dinner. "That definitely was a dinner fit for a king. It was beyond a doubt the best meal of my lifetime." He kept it up, and Tomasina's face flushed with pleasure at his appreciation of her cooking.

After dinner when the dishes were washed and put away and the kitchen was restored to order, Tomasina joined Gus in the living room. A brightly burning log in the big stone fireplace kept the room warm. Gus read his newspaper, while Tomasina wrote a letter to Manuela and Mrs. Lori. From time to time he got up to stoke the fire.

"Mr. Schmidt, I'm telling my friends about the rainbow we saw on the drive home after our wedding," Tomasina told him.

"You must call me 'Gus' now that we are married. "

"Goose." Tomasina tried out the name.

"That's perfect," Gus laughed.

At nine o'clock he went around to make sure windows and doors were shut and lights were out before going to bed. Tomasina was not in sight when Gus came back into the living room. Poor little girl, she was probably hiding in her bedroom, hoping he wouldn't bother her. He banked the fire and made sure the fire screen was in place before he went to his room. He didn't remember leaving the light on. He opened the door.

Tomasina sat at his dressing table wearing her soft flannel nightgown. She was in the process of taking the pins out of her hair. To Gus she looked like an angel.

"Hello, Goose," she whispered in a shaky voice.

"Hello, my dear," he managed to answer in spite of the lump in his throat.

He moved behind her, and finished taking out the pins. He had only seen her hair in a tight bun; undone it hung almost to her waist. He began to brush her hair. It was a wonder, thick and smooth in his hands.

After a while he put the brush on the dressing table. He scooped his wife into his arms and carried her to the bed. With his lips he explored her face, kissing her eyes, her cheeks, the tip of her nose and finally her lips. He felt her breath quicken. With a great effort, he sublimated his own desires and concentrated on pleasing his new wife.

Burying his face in her neck, he inhaled the old fashioned lavender fragrance of her nightgown. Her natural scent was clean and sweet. His hands moved over her stomach, her thighs and then rested on her small breasts. He knelt over her. 'I'll try not to hurt you," he said.

In response she put her hands oh his hips and drew him down.

Chapter Six
Tomasina

Her suffering was the work of *el ojo malo*. It had followed her from the place of her disgrace into this haven. Tomasina feared the evil eye, not only for herself, but for the harm it might visit on her beloved Gus. She hugged her worries to herself, not even telling Father Gallagher when she went to confession.

She was alone in this wet dark land with no one to turn to. If only her family in Agua Dulce and her friends at Seligman's ranch were not so far away. If only she could talk to Carmen, or Manuela or to wise Mrs. Lori. One of them would surely know the right thing to do.

The sky was gray, always heavy gray clouds and rain. Tomasina's head ached from finding words in English, so she spoke very little. *El ojo malo* did not stop with infecting Tomasina's spirit; it went on to bury itself in the very center of her body. Every morning she retched into the toilet bowl.

One morning, Gus saw her do this and noticed her white face and dull eyes. He said, "I'm taking you to see Dr. Clark this afternoon."

"Oh no Goose, no please. Always the women in my family go to the *curandera*, a woman healer, for sickness. I can't go to a man."

Gus rarely made demands on Tomasina, but this time he insisted. "I'll go with you. There's nothing to be afraid of. Dr. Clark has taken care of me the five years I've lived here. He's a very good doctor."

* * *

Tomasina, cheeks burning with shame, stood before the bright faced, clean looking man. "Goose, please no." she cried clutching her husband's arm.

"Well," said Dr. Clark. I can see a full physical examination is out of the question, but the symptoms point to a simple diagnosis. Just to be sure I would like to get a urine specimen." He held out a paper cup.

Gus explained Dr. Clark's request, and Tomasina covered her face with one hand to hide her embarrassment as she went into the restroom carrying the cup.

"I'll call you in the morning," Dr. Clark told Gus. "In the mean time make sure she gets plenty of rest. She should eat frequent small snacks and sip weak tea. I'll give you a prescription for vitamins."

When they got back to the cabin, Gus had Tomasina rest on the couch. He tucked a wool blanket around her, threw another log in the fireplace, and then returned to his workshop. Every half hour or so, he looked in to see if she needed anything.

The next morning Tomasina was sick to her stomach again, so Gus insisted she remain in bed. She was taking tiny sips from the cup of tea he brought her, when the phone rang. As Gus listened to the caller a smile replaced his worried frown.

After hanging up he turned to his wife. "My dearest Tomasina, we are going to have a baby." Kneeling at the side of the bed, he kissed her hands, "My sweet little wife," he murmured.

* * *

Tomasina suffered; she grew thin and weak, while in her womb, the baby fought the evil eye. Gus tried to comfort her and Dr. Clark suggested various medicines; nothing helped.

When the doctor said, "We may have to hospitalize her for IV fluid replacement," Gus knew he must do something. The hospital and the procedures would frighten Tomasina to death. In desperation he phoned Manuela. "Don't worry," she told him. "I know of a very wise healer here in Crescent City. I'll send her to you. Tell my friend Tomasina that she's in my prayers."

* * *

Gus was waiting when the bus from Crescent City pulled into Tamlin on Monday evening. A wizened woman shrouded in black, clutched the hand rail and groaned as she descended from the bus. A younger version followed close behind her, Stepping forward Gus reached out his hand for their bundles, but the younger woman refused to let him take them. "I'm Gus Schmidt," he said speaking slowly and hoping one of them understood a little English. "My wife, Tomasina, is pregnant and has been very ill."

These women reminded him of the witches in the fairy tales his mother used to tell. He hoped he had been right in asking Manuela to send them.

"Ah," said the older woman scowling. "I'm Sabina Castañeda and this is my assistant Rosalina. What you speak of is no business of a man. I will care for your poor wife. *El corazón cura corazón.*"

No one spoke during the drive. When they got to the cabin the women looked around, wrung their hands and mumbled to each other as Rosalina helped Sabina struggle up the stairs. Once inside, they went from room to room making a droning sound.

"You must sleep in another room," Sabina said to Gus, motioning him out of the bedroom where Tomasina lay limp and gray-faced. "I will stay with your *esposa*."

The old woman placed candles at Tomasina's head and feet, and then brushed the pregnant women's body with branches of rue while chanting in an unearthly language. When the chant ended the rue and a twisted root were placed under the bed in a pan of liquid. Then Sabina hummed in a high pitched voice as her hands made sweeping motions over Tomasina's body.

"*¡Es imprescindible!* We must drive the evil eye out, but first I must discover what has frightened this poor child? Tell me!" she demanded of Tomasina. But Tomasina drew into herself and refused to answer.

Meanwhile, Rosalina went to work brewing teas of raspberry leaves to relax the uterus and marigold to detoxify the mother. Sabina added other ingredients to the teas; things so secret and magic that not even

Rosalina could be trusted with the recipes. Rosalina made rich soups and broths with cabbage and beef to sustain the fetus as it fought against the evil eye.

Within a week Tomasina was able to be up and about the cabin. She consumed the soups with a good appetite and no longer vomited.

"Your secret will gnaw at your heart as long as you hug it close. You are not ready to give it to me, and so I cannot destroy it, but I've shown you how to be strong enough to carry your burden," Sabina shook her head.

"Now I must return to my other duties," she told Tomasina, "I've arranged for Maya, a local midwife to visit you in two days,"

Before she and Rosalina left, Sabina gave Tomasina many instructions and schedules to follow. She left packets of herbs to be made into tea.

Though Tomasina was physically well, her spirit remained sick. She hid her suffering from Gus. How could a mother hate the baby in her womb? She must be a very bad person.

In the fourth month of her pregnancy the darkness left Tomasina and she rejoiced at the miracle taking place within her body. As she was resting on the couch one afternoon the baby moved under her heart. She thought "I will ask my husband if we can name this child Carlos after my father with Gustave for the second name."

Gus agreed with his wife's choice of names if their child should be a boy, but added, "We will call our little Carlos by his American name of Charlie."

* * *

One morning she noticed a spot of blood on her nightgown and knew her time was near. She and Gus were walking together under the trees when she experienced the first sensations of labor.

"Oh my dear, my dear," Gus said, and put his arms around her.

It was not to be an easy birth. When the midwife checked Tomasina she saw the buttocks presenting first. Using all her skills, Maya performed the painful procedure of turning the baby so that the head was down. "I know this hurts. Take a big breath. Just a little more. There, I'm done. Your baby will enter the world soon."

But still the labor did not progress.

Fifteen excruciating hours passed. The child resisted being born.

Gus leaned against the porch railing, tears running down his cheeks. It was taking too long. Something was terribly wrong. He heard Tomasina moan. The screams which followed were like those of a wounded animal.

"No, no, no…."

It was more than he could bear. He hurried to the bedroom and flung open the door. "I'm calling an ambulance. I don't want my wife to suffer anymore."

Maya stepped to the door and whispered. "That was what I was going to recommend. If this birth does not occur soon, she'll need a medico to deliver the child through a cut in her belly."

The sound of Tomasina's screams again filled the air, and Maya went to comfort her. Gus started for the phone. He was just lifting the receiver, when a strange noise, almost like the crowing of a rooster, rang out. Gus rushed back and looked into the bedroom.

Maya was smiling, "You can enter in just a few minutes. Stay out of my way until I call you. Congratulations you have a son and your wife is tired but otherwise fine."

He paced outside the bedroom door until Maya said, "Okay, you can come in now." She was putting soiled linens into a laundry bag. The room had been restored to order and Tomasina, propped up on pillows, was holding a small blanket wrapped bundle.

He kissed Tomasina's pale face, and bent to admire his new son. One little hand had escaped from the wrapping. It was perfect. The baby's skin was ruddy and his head was covered with a thick mat of black hair.

Gus took the baby in his arms and studied his face. "Charlie looks like you, Ma Tom." The baby opened his eyes and seemed to glare at the man holding him. "But I think he will have the Schmidt blue eyes."

"Let me see Papa." Tomasina tilted the baby toward her. She looked into his eyes. The room began to swirl and her head dropped back onto the pillow. Baby Charlie had Mr. Seligman's small mean eyes.

Maya felt for Tomasina's pulse and found it to be weak and rapid. "She's worn out from all those hours of labor. She needs to rest, and by the way we could all use a cup of tea if you don't mind."

"You're sure she's alright?" Gus said, "You're sure my Ma Tom is okay."

"Yes, yes, of course she is. Having a baby is a lot of work," Maya said taking the baby from him.

A short while later, Gus returned from the kitchen with a tray holding not only tea, but also milk, cookies, crackers, peanut butter, three kinds of cheese and smoked almonds.

"Such a feast," Maya said appreciatively. "I'm starving and I'm sure my patient needs some food after all her work."

"Yes, I'm very hungry. Thank you for this good food, Goose."

Gus bent and kissed Tomasina. At that moment she knew she must keep the secret of Charlie's true father to herself. Gus never mentioned her disgrace after the first night they met. She remembered that he had ordered her not to speak of it again. She would obey her husband.

Later that evening, Maya was massaging Tomasina's abdomen when the baby gave a little cry. "Let's put him to the breast. It's good for your uterus," she carried little Charlie over to his mother.

Tomasina held her infant in stiff arms as memories of the migrant camp and Mr. Seligman flashed into her mind.

"Put him to your breast;" instructed Maya. "See how he roots. This one will be a good feeder."

"Maya, I can't. Take him away please." There was a note of desperation in the new mother's voice.

Maya placed the knuckle of her index finger in the baby's greedy mouth. "I have the bottle and a can of goat's milk, but if he starts on that he won't want the nipple."

"I'm sorry. I think I can give him a bottle, but I can't put him to my breast."

"You act like a spoiled American woman." Maya tried to shame her, but when she noticed the suffering on Tomasina's face she softened.

Maya remembered what the old *curandera* had said to her and made the sign of the cross over Tomasina. "Aiee—the evil eye—poor woman, poor child."

Chapter Seven
Tomasina

"No more *niños*, Mr. Gus. I think another child would kill Ma Tom." Maya was holding a whispered conversation with Gus after the birth of his third child. "Thanks be to God this girl was tiny. Another baby like your big Ernest would have been too much. I'm doing all I can, but still she bleeds."

Three babies in four years, Gus could scarcely take it in. Sometimes he felt like he'd been struck by lightning, but he couldn't imagine a world without his clever little monkey, Charlie, and sweet-tempered Ernest. Now a baby girl, Fern, had joined their family. Underlying his concern for Tomasina was a feeling of elation.

"I'll talk to Father Gallagher," Gus promised.

"Father Gallagher, my foot!" Maya retorted, her face growing red. "Do you want these babies to grow up without a mother? Think about it very seriously, Mr. Gus, because I know another baby will kill your poor little wife."

* * *

Papa Gus sometimes thought of Maya and the births of his children, especially on their birthdays. Even now, he felt a thrill of fear at the thought of losing Ma Tom in child birth. His dear wife and his wonderful children, he was blessed indeed.

At the moment, he was sitting with Charlie and Fern at the big oak table he made in his workshop almost thirty years ago. He and the children were whetting their appetites with a basket of tortilla chips and a dish of hot salsa. Tantalizing scents of dinner cooking wafted to them. Ernest would be there soon, making the family complete.

In the kitchen, Ma Tom hummed to herself as she frosted the cake. Like Papa Gus, she was thinking that tonight the whole family would all be together around the table for Ernest's twenty-seventh birthday party. Nothing made her happier.

She made sure that all birthdays at the Schmidt house were special celebrations. Her three children, now grown into adults, expected their favorite dinner and Ma Tom's delicious *tres leches* cake to mark their special day of the year.

Ma Tom placed both of her hands at the small of her back and stretched. Her back ached more than usual today, but the pain didn't keep her from being pleased as she fried tortillas and stirred the carne asada. She placed lids on pans of rice and beans which she was keeping warm at the back of the range, and tried to catch snatches of conversation from the dining room.

Gesturing with a tortilla chip, Fern said, "You could easily get a job in construction, Charlie. They're going to start pouring the foundations for the new inn any day now." She spoke in a loud voice, so Papa Gus, his beard and hair now completely white, would be able to hear.

Fern knew that Charlie spent most of his time, other than the few hours a week he worked as a handyman, in Papa Gus's workshop fashioning his art-form furniture out of redwood burl and gemstones. So far, all he had to show for his work was six first place ribbons from the state fair, and the few dollars he got from selling two tables and one chair.

"If I can just get a lucky break, I know I could make big money with my furniture," Charlie would say, but the others, especially Fern kept after him to get a regular job.

Papa Gus was opening his mouth to agree with Fern, when Ernest came into the dining room. "I finally made it! Sheriff McBride said I could finish my paperwork tomorrow morning. Why did Bertha and Jake have to have one of their domestic disputes on my birthday?" he asked with a wry smile.

Papa Gus beamed when he saw Ernest in his deputy sheriff's uniform. The tan gabardine shirt tapered from Ernest's broad shoulders to his waist. A shiny silver star was pinned just above his breast pocket.

Charlie laughed and said something. Papa Gus couldn't make out what it was. Fern erupted from her chair and faced Charlie with her hands balled into fists. She was only five feet tall, but Papa Gus thought it was lucky for Charlie that he had the table between himself and his angry sister.

"You're disgusting. What kind of a brother are you? You need a girdle. Who are you to criticize Ernest; look at that pot belly you're developing!"

"I was just kidding, Fern. Get a grip, and I don't have a pot belly," Charlie said, sucking his stomach in.

Papa Gus knew from experience that when Fern went on a rampage it was hard to stop her. He looked at Ma Tom as she hurried from the kitchen to see what the shouting was about. He would like to protect his wife from their children's quarrels, but his hearing had gotten so bad, he didn't even know what they were arguing about most of the time.

Papa Gus had to let Ma Tom figure out why their daughter was angry. Fern seemed to be chronically mad at Charlie. Poor Charlie couldn't do anything right in her eyes. She especially hated it when he picked on Ernest. Charlie was mean to his younger brother, but it seemed to bother Fern more than it bothered Ernest.

Ma Tom placed her hand on Fern's tense arm. "Take a deep breath, and then tell Papa Gus and me what is so important that you have to spoil Ernest's birthday party."

Fern acted like a little girl when she was with her family, but in reality she was a successful and independent woman. She had made a niche for herself in Tamlin with her real estate business.

She stopped yelling and looked ashamed, "I'm sorry *Mamacita* and Papa; I'm sorry Ernest. I really am. I shouldn't let Charlie get under my skin, but he's always putting Ernest down." Fern turned to Ma Tom, "Charlie said Ernest looks like the Michelin tire man. I guess I overreacted."

Ma Tom turned to look at Ernest. He was big like Papa Gus and, Ma Tom thought, very handsome with his golden hair and clear brown eyes, but he did look lumpy. "Well, Ernest you do look a bit— *gordito*—don't you agree, Fern."

Tailored uniform shirts were provided, but the deputy sheriffs had to purchase their own slacks. Doug Simpson, the other deputy sheriff, swaggered about in tight fitting blue jeans. Ernest, however, preferred to be comfortable, and so had ordered several pairs of tan cargo pants with pockets down the legs and elastic in the waistband from the Sears catalogue. Ernest found the pockets handy for carrying notepads, flashlights, his wallet, a bag of jelly beans, a large Swiss army knife, and any number of other things.

In the end Fern had to agree with Ma Tom—and Charlie. "I'm buying you some good khaki slacks, Ernest. And you sure as heck better wear them. I'm not having my big brother going around with lumpy legs."

It had been like this since they were babies. Charlie teased his good natured younger brother, and little spitfire Fern, passionately defended Ernest. Mostly it was harmless enough. Papa told Ma Tom that she worried too much. In the United States brothers and sisters often quarrel.

Now they were all laughing, that is all except Charlie. The smile pasted on Charlie's mouth didn't make it to his eyes. Ma Tom was the only one who noticed. She could see that he felt alone and unhappy. She wanted to go to him, but his cold eyes kept her away.

Her face was calm, even though the old fears about Charlie crept into her mind. She had reason to be uneasy about him, but if anyone had asked why she was worried, she would not have told them. The truth was too shameful.

She remembered the thing with the kitten. Even though it happened many years ago, she still had nightmares about it. Charlie was eight years old. He found a stray kitten and brought it home to show his younger brother and sister. They were enchanted with the pretty little creature. Fern was holding the kitten and singing to it.

"That's my cat, I found it! Give it to me!" Charlie demanded, grabbing the frightened animal. Charlie gave a shriek; the kitten had bitten him. He began to shake the little creature. Ernest and Fern held on to his arms, begging him not to hurt the kitty, but Charlie made his way to the fireplace and threw the kitten in.

The children's cries brought Ma Tom running, but the little animal was dead by the time she pulled it from the flames. The burn scars on her hands were grim reminders of the incident. It was the only time Papa Gus ever struck one of the children in anger.

She was glad when Fern and Ernest grew big enough to protect themselves, but even so she remained alert and watchful. She never forgot the cruelty of Charlie's natural father.

Ma Tom put those unpleasant thoughts out of her mind and went to dish up the supper. "Help me to bring the food to the table," she called to Fern.

* * *

All in all it had been a pleasant evening. As Ma Tom cleaned up the kitchen she wondered where the years had gone. Papa Gus was now an old man, and she felt like an old woman when her crooked back ached as it did tonight.

The babies were grownup and out of the cabin, except for Charlie. Fern had a nice apartment over her real estate office. Ernest shared a little house with the other deputy. He was sure to be elected Sheriff of Tamlin when the current Sheriff retired.

She was thankful they were nearby, but she missed having them at home, like when they were small. How strange that Charlie—the oldest—still lived with them. He was too nervous to work at an everyday job. Poor Charlie, so far he hadn't done anything with his life. What did his business card say? Something like: *Handyman, no job too small, reasonable rates*. Everyone called him "the handyman" even though he thought of himself as an artist. *Aieee, pobrecito.*"

Chapter Eight
Tomasina

Perhaps Charlie didn't mean to take advantage of Widow Weiss. Perhaps he only wanted to help her. Maude Weiss was an elderly woman who lived in a dilapidated Victorian house big enough to be called a mansion. The aging building had originally been surrounded by a large lawn and garden. Before the road was rerouted in1955, the Weiss mansion was considered the showplace of Tamlin.

Her late husband Terrance, a land speculator, ended up selling all of the land around the mansion (except the tiny patch of weeds the house stood on) at dirt cheap prices just to scrape by. The gingerbread of Widow Weiss' house now rubbed elbows with George's Gas Station and Auto Repair on one side, and Barrett's Feed and Fuel on the other.

In some ways it was fortunate that Terrance passed away before he had time to liquidate his forty acres of second-growth timber, or the small cabin on twenty acres high above an ocean inlet. The land rose in value after Terrance's death.

At current real estate prices both of the parcels would bring a tidy sum, but Widow Weiss had no desire to sell her holdings. In fact, she had almost forgotten she owned them. She heard rumors that Oney, the community bootlegger, set up business near her deserted cabin, but it didn't seem worth worrying about. She just went on scrapping by and living at peace with the rest of the world.

When Charlie saw Widow Weiss struggling up the road with her grocery bags one rainy day, he offered her a ride in his old truck, and carried her groceries into the house for her. They chatted together over a cup of tea, and Charlie agreed to return the next day and make some repairs to the house.

One thing led to another—there were an infinite number of things needing fixing—and Charlie moved out of his parents' cabin and into one of Maude's spare bedrooms. It didn't set right with Papa Gus and Ma Tom, but Charlie was almost thirty years old. He hadn't listened to his parents when he was young, why should he now?

* * *

"Mother, how could you?" Joan Graves, the widow's daughter wailed. Wiley Weiss, the widow's son, put his scrawny arm around his sister's muscular shoulders. This was their annual week-before-Christmas visit to their mother. They were shocked to find Charlie living in the house, and referring to their mother as "Maudie."

"This cannot go on," Wiley pronounced. "I am going to take steps—do you hear me—steps." His voice squeaked to a halt as he wiped perspiration from his high domed forehead with his handkerchief.

Charlie, lounging comfortably in one of the faded arm chairs just yawned, but Maude Weiss was upset. With trembling hands she placed the two brightly wrapped Christmas gifts from her children on an end table, and then daubed at her eyes with her hanky.

Wiley and Joan waited expectantly. The silence stretched on for a long five minutes. Their mother seemed to have forgotten the generous Christmas checks she always wrote them.

"Come on Joanie," Wiley finally said.

"How could you, Mother?" Joan's round face was taut with anger as she turned to follow her brother. "What am I supposed to tell your grandchildren?"

"I haven't seen or heard from them in over five years. What would your father think about that," Widow Weiss said in a small voice. At that moment, she couldn't recall the names or faces of her three grandchildren. The thought was impossibly sad; she gave a muffled sob.

* * *

The first step Wiley took was to notify the local sheriff that a young man was taking advantage of his frail parent. "There is an unemployed bum freeloading off our elderly mother. Who knows how he mistreats her when no one is around. He certainly was surly to us. All we care about is our mother's well being."

"Okay Ernest, what are you going to do about this?" Sheriff McBride's face remained hidden behind the newspaper he had been reading when Wiley came in.

Although Ernest's first impulse was to defend his brother by reminding Wiley that Mrs. Weiss needed someone to help her, he merely said, "I don't think there is anything illegal or immoral going on and I'm sure your mother isn't in any danger. I'll speak to both parties and see what we can work out."

Ernest left the Sheriff station and walked the half block to the Weiss house. "Charlie...and Mrs. Weiss...I know you aren't doing anything—a well—a—it just looks—un, wrong." Ernest's face was red with embarrassment.

Charlie looked over at Mrs. Weiss. She had always been a small woman, but since her children's visit she seemed to have shrunk.

"I guess my life is over; I don't want to live if I have to be here in this big house all by myself everyday," she mumbled.

"Ernest, I can't just move back into the cabin with Papa and Ma Tom. What am I supposed to do about all this?" Charlie made a sweeping gesture with his hands.

"Do you know the big barn on my forty acres?" Maude Weiss clapped her hands.

"I know where it is," Charlie said. "So what?"

"Well, you could sleep there at night and come and visit me during the daytime."

"Nobody could live in that barn, Maudie," Charlie said, "but I could use it as a place to work on my furniture. Papa Gus's workshop is too small for my big pieces. Maybe he'll let me borrow some of his tools;

he doesn't do that much in the workshop anymore. Your barn is huge. I could patch the roof and put straw on the floor. I really need to get back to my art."

"What if I get you a trailer and move it into the clearing near the barn?" Ernest offered." It wouldn't be fancy, but you'd have a roof over your head. You can use the barn as a place to work on your furniture and you can do chores for Mrs. Weiss to pay for the use of the barn."

Ernest breathed a sigh of relief. He thought he had worked it out so everyone would be happy.

* * *

Charlie didn't exactly forget. He reminded himself everyday, and for three months he faithfully visited Widow Weiss several times a week. He did a few chores and took her to get groceries. He even escorted her to the Tamlin Café every Friday night for the all-you-can-eat fish and chips special. She delighted in dressing up for their evening out.

But recently, Charlie had gotten so involved in his work; it seemed impossible to find time to visit her. She would have to understand the importance of the pieces he was creating. When he got the rough cutting done, he'd get back into the groove of seeing her at least on Friday evening.

Ernest stopped to check on Mrs. Weiss everyday. "When is Charlie going to come see me?" she always asked.

The little lady looked faded and weak. She spent her days huddled under a quilt on her settee, reading movie magazines. The house was always cold even though Ernest brought in arm loads of logs and built the fire up every morning. He wondered if she got enough to eat. Sometimes he would bring her a hamburger, or turkey sandwich from the cafe, but she only picked at the food.

"I'm worried about Widow Weiss," Ernest told Ma Tom one April morning. She's so lonely and sad. I know Charlie gets in to see her as often as he can; it's just that he's been busy. Every Friday she gets all fancied up and waits for him to take her to the cafe, but I think he has stood her up the last few weeks."

"I'll go and see her this afternoon. I'll take her a bowl of the albondigas soup I'm making for dinner," Tomasina promised. "If she's sick, we'll call her children."

A few hours later, container of soup in hand, Ma Tom tapped with the big brass door knocker, but Mrs. Weiss didn't answer.

Ma Tom wondered where the elder lady could have gone. She gave the door a little push and it swung open with a creak. The house was very cold and had a stale smell about it. Ma Tom went into the kitchen and put the soup in the nearly empty refrigerator. Dirty dishes covered the sink and table. In the adjacent dining room were more dirty dishes.

She looked into the living room, gasped and made the sign of the cross. Poor little Maude Weiss was lying on her settee. The still unopened Christmas presents were on the table next to her; the magazine she must have been reading had slipped from her hand and lay on the floor and she stared at her visitor through wide open eyes.

"Mrs. Weiss," Ma Tom called out, not really expecting an answer. Going to the settee, she put her hand against Maudie's withered cheek. It was icy cold and stiff.

* * *

The doctor said it must have been a sudden heart attack, not surprising in a frail seventy-eight year old woman. "Maude Weiss didn't suffer. She went quick, real quick; would that we could all go so peacefully," Dr. Clark told Ma Tom. His bright face was lined with wrinkles now, and his hair had turned silver.

Wiley came to town and made arrangements for the cremation and to have his mother's ashes scattered at sea. "There won't be a funeral," he told Dr. Clark. "No reason to go to the expense. She didn't have any friends."

The Schmidt's thought that would be the end of their dealings with the Widow Weiss.

Chapter Nine
Tomasina

Do you know Charles Schmidt?" The man in the dark suit sniffed slightly as he looked around the office. He took in the stained walls covered with yellowing wanted posters, the flyspecked calendar advertising John Deere Tractors, and the locked gun cabinet on the back wall, before he looked directly at Sheriff McBride.

Sheriff Darrell McBride was a large man, red faced and big bellied. He was not about to give information to just any yahoo who waltzed into his office, regardless of the fancy suit. "And why might you be wanting, Charlie Schmidt?"

"That's confidential." The man handed Sheriff McBride his card: *Stanley Tillman of Gilbert, Meltzer and Brown, Esquire, Attorneys at Law, San Francisco.*

The Sheriff glanced at the card and then put it into his desk drawer. He spoke into his two way radio, "Ernest, some guy here to see Charlie. Guess you better bring him in to the office. Wearin' a suit—says he's an attorney from Frisco." Sheriff McBride looked up at Mr. Tillman."Might as well sit down. They'll be here in about fifteen minutes."

When Ernest arrived with Charlie, Mr. Tillman said, "This is a private matter and I don't think it should be discussed in front of others."

"That's crap," Charlie snapped. "What do you want? Is it something to do with poor little Maudie's cutthroat children?"

"As a matter of fact, it is to do with the legal heirs of the Weiss estate," Mr. Tillman said, emphasizing "legal". He pulled some papers out of his briefcase, "I just need your signature here and here." He pointed to several lines marked by sticky arrows. "In return for your cooperation, the heirs of Maude Weiss have generously instructed me to present you with a check for one thousand dollars."

"Don't sign anything," Ernest advised Charlie. "I think Fern should look those papers over." Ernest hurried across the street to Fern's office.

He returned almost immediately with Fern at his side. She sat cross-legged in one of the straight wooden chairs and studied the attorney's legal documents for a long time.

Finally she put the papers down and said, "Well Charlie, according to this, Mrs. Weiss left everything to her children, Joan and Wiley, with a codicil stating you and your heirs, should you have any, can live on the forty acres and use any of the resources of that property. If at anytime you wish to purchase the property you may do so for $1,000 per acre. The estate must pay all taxes and the property cannot be sold until you decide to vacate it. If you sign those forms, you relinquish your right to live and work on those forty acres."

Charlie picked up the papers with the sticky arrows indicating where he should sign, but he didn't reach for a pen. Instead he tore the papers into little pieces and dropped them into the wastepaper basket next to Sheriff McBride's desk. "I'm going over to the café for a cup-a-joe. I'll need someone to give me a ride back to *my* forty acres, no hurry though."

* * *

Maudie was a great old girl to look out for Charlie's interests like that. Thanks to having a place to work, he had been able to complete

quite a few pieces. The difficulty now was marketing them, but it looked like those worries would soon be over.

By a stroke of good luck Charlie met Claudine, the owner of a Portland art gallery. They were both attending a New Year's Eve party at an artist's loft in Gold Beach. The room was crowded, smoky and loud. Charlie and Claudine wandered outside onto the balcony. He put his arm around her bare shoulders. She offered him a drink from the champagne bottle she held in her hand.

They talked in a desultory manner between sips of champagne. "I have a little ole art gallery in Portland, darling." Charlie lit Claudine's cigarette and she took a long draw on it, sucking the smoke deep into her lungs. "I discover new artists and help them to get their work in front of the public eye. I'm really quite good at ferreting out new talent." She blew twin streams of smoke out through her nose.

"I wish you could see some of the things I've done lately. They're damned good, if I do say so myself, but I've never had a chance to show them," Charlie told her.

"Well, sweet man, I don't need to be anyplace in particular until Tuesday. Let's go take a look at what you've been up to." Claudine's voice slid over him like a silk glove.

She kept her hand on Charlie's thigh as he drove over twisting roads, through dark evergreens and into the clearing where the trailer and barn showed pale in the misty moonlight. They spent what was left of the night in Charlie's trailer. It was almost noon when, with steaming mugs of coffee in their hands, they wandered out to the barn.

Claudine was wearing one of Charlie's flannel shirts over her lacy black slip. Her stiff burgundy hairdo was flat and her black mascara had made wiggly trails down her cheeks. In the cold sunlight she looked old and shop worn.

She scanned the shapes in the barn. "Some of your work is quite… acceptable," she said with narrowed eyes. "This and this—yes and the large table—yes, I think I could sell those for you. My commission is twenty-five percent and I'll set the prices. We'll have a big show— advertise your work—champagne—the whole nine yards, and then I'll

keep your things in the gallery for one week. I'll need photos of other things you've done for my inventory file."

"You're making my dreams come true." Charlie blew on the back of Claudine's neck, and then half lifted half pushed her into a pile of straw. By the end of the day Charlie had in his possession a signed contract for a show featuring his free form furniture.

* * *

Two weeks later Charlie pulled the big rental truck up to the loading dock at the back of Claudine's art gallery. Checking his watch, he saw that it was eleven o'clock, the time Claudine had specified. A sign stating "PLEASE PRESS FOR ASSISTANCE" hung over a button by the metal roll up door. He pressed it, heard a loud buzz, but no one appeared.

He walked around to the front of the row of buildings which contained two other art galleries, a quaint hotel, a bookstore and three coffee shops. Claudine's, the least prosperous looking storefront in the neighborhood, had a closed sign in the window. He banged on the front door anyway, not really expecting anyone to answer.

After walking up and down the block a few times, Charlie decided to get a cup of coffee. A dapper man with a white beard and rimless glasses followed Charlie into the coffee shop.

"Is that your truck parked behind Claudine's?" the man asked.

"Yes sir, it is," Charlie narrowed his eyes and looked at the man suspiciously.

"My name is Herbert Morris. I manage the art gallery next to Claudine's—*Rose City Fine Art*—maybe you noticed it."

Charlie just nodded and took a sip of his coffee.

"I hope you have an attorney, because if you're going to do business with Claudine you need one. She's the kind of fly-by-night that gives other Portland art dealers a bad name. Most of us really want to help artists get their work noticed."

"I have a contract," Charlie was beginning to feel a little worried. He pulled some folded papers out of his pocket and handed them to Mr. Morris.

After scanning the papers, Mr. Morris said, "It looks like you have a problem here. I never heard of anyone setting up a show with pieces as large as yours for only a week. Usually it's more like several months."

"What shall I do?" Charlie sounded like a frightened child.

"Well son, the best advice I can give you is to try to get Claudine to compromise. According to the contract she's got you sewed up for the next year." Herbert Morris felt sorry for the young man. "I might consider letting you show some of your things in my gallery when the contract with Claudine is finished. I saw your stake-bed truck out back and glanced at your work. Big pieces don't move very fast, but I would be interested in some smaller things, like jewelry boxes. We have a little gift shop where jewelry boxes made of burl and decorated with silver and gems would go very well."

"I only do big pieces," Charlie answered.

'Okay, just a suggestion. Good luck to you," Herbert Morris turned away from Charlie and began to joke with the pretty young barista.

Mr. Morris seemed to have forgotten him, and so Charlie left the coffee shop. Across the street, he saw Claudine unlocking the front door of her gallery. He hurried over to her, "I thought you told me to be here by eleven. It's almost noon. Did you find someone to help me unload my truck?"

"Oh, it's you. I actually forgot all about you. Let me make some calls about the show and get someone to help you set-up."

Later that afternoon, when Charlie, with the help of two college boys, had finished arranging his furniture in the space allotted him, he decided to follow Herbert Morris' advice and try to get Claudine to compromise.

"I've asked around and found out one week isn't long enough to display my work. You've given other artists space for anywhere from a month to six months." Charlie whined, "I've gone to a lot of expense to get my things to Portland. I had to rent a large truck, and they don't come cheap."

Charlie didn't mention his unexpected hotel expense. He'd assumed that he would stay with Claudine. She'd been so friendly in

Tamlin, but in Portland she hadn't even asked him to dinner, let alone to spend the night.

"Your work shows well; this lighting makes the insets sparkle," Claudine, was strolling among the displays of Charlie's furniture. She stroked a table top with her finger tips; her lips formed a slow secret smile, "Perhaps I was thinking of your other talents when I offered you this show," she purred.

Spyder, Claudine's partner in the gallery, gave a giggle and minced over to join them. He was dressed in parrot green leather pants and a sequin studded silk shirt to match. "I adore your stuff, Charlie, I think it's ravishing," he said in a high sweet voice. Charlie backed away.

"Listen Charlie, there's no reason for you to hang around the gallery. " Claudine all but pushed him toward the door. "Be here tomorrow evening by six for the showing. If you know anybody in town, for Gawd sakes get them to make an appearance. It's going to be a pretty dismal crowd."

Charlie drove around town without noticing where he was going. He began to get hungry, and spotted a place large enough to park the big truck. He was in a quiet neighborhood; the only place that looked at all lively was The Wild West Saloon. Charlie parked and went in.

It was awkward being all alone at a table in a place where everyone else was with someone. They were all dancing, and flirting, and talking. Charlie decided to hit on the waitress. She too tall for him, but she was better than no one to talk to. Besides, he could tell that she found him attractive.

After drinking enough coffee to float a boat, Charlie decided he would ask Medora to go out with him after she got off work. He knew her name from her badge, but when she mentioned Big Mike the bouncer Charlie got nervous and decided to ask her to the art show instead. To his surprise Medora and her father showed up at the art gallery the next evening.

* * *

The whole experience was as disappointment. Although two reporters were at the opening, nothing about the show made it into the papers. The only person at the show who really seemed to like or

understand Charlie's work was Medora's father, Ian Whitman, and he didn't buy anything.

Charlie talked Claudine into extending his display for ten more days, and a few of the smaller pieces sold.

On Valentine's Day, he rented the big truck again and went to pick up his furniture.

"What the hell is this," Charlie's hands started to shake when he looked at the amount on the check Claudine had just handed him.

"Darling boy, I had to do some discounting to sell you at all. Then there is the little matter of my commission. Oh, and by the way, according to our contract, I am entitled to a commission on any pieces you sell for one year, and I am able to set the price on any of your work in my photo inventory." Claudine didn't even look up from filing her nails.

"Why don't you just take that file and stab me in the heart with it?" Charlie was pale with anger. "I should have read that contract more carefully. I thought you were my friend. I thought I could trust you!"

"Live and learn," Claudine told Charlie. "Get your junk out of my gallery by noon tomorrow, or I'll have it hauled to the dump."

Charlie knew all about feeling down-hearted and alone, but he had never felt this discouraged before. How could he tell Ernest he didn't have any money to pay back the loan? If Fern found out how much he owed her precious little Ernest she'd have a royal fit. Neither of them cared about him, and he didn't blame them. It would be better if he'd never been born.

He paced up and down by his truck and pounded his fist against his palm. "Selfish bastards! Who do they think they are? They don't know anything about art," he shouted.

He looked at his furniture through the window of the gallery and muttered, "I'll have to get my things loaded into the truck early tomorrow morning. My furniture may not be very good, but it's all I have."

In an effort to throw off his black mood he decided to go out and have a good time. It was Valentine's Day after all.

He drove to the Wild West Saloon, but Gene, the bartender told Charlie that Medora had the evening off. When Charlie asked for Medora's phone number, Gene replied, "I'm not giving it to you, but I'll dial it for you. If she wants to talk to you—okay—if she doesn't, she can hang up."

Charlie spoke to Medora, and then ordered a beer. He had a lot of time to kill before meeting her. A plump blonde woman in blue jeans and a tight western shirt came in alone.

"Hey, pretty, can I buy you a beer?" Charlie called over to her. When she smiled and nodded her head yes, Charlie moved into the seat next to her. "My name's Charlie. Did anyone ever tell you how beautiful you are?"

"I'm Madge. I never saw you in here before."

After a few more beers, Charlie asked Madge to dance. "This evening might not turn out so bad after all," he said as Madge leaned in to him.

"What's going on here?" A large hand lifted Charlie by the belt causing his Levis to cut into his crotch.

"Lay off, Harry," said Madge. "We was just dancin'. I got tired a waitin' for you."

"Who are you," Charlie asked in a confused voice.

"I'm Madge's husband, Harry. Did she forget to mention me?" Harry boomed.

Charlie was glad to see Big Mike headed their way with a baseball bat in his hand. Harry saw Big Mike, too and released his hold on Charlie's belt.

"I'm going to have to ask you to leave, sir," Big Mike said to Charlie.

At first Charlie was going to protest. He wasn't the one who was being obnoxious, but when he saw the murderous look on Harry's face, Charlie headed for the door. "I have to go anyway," he told big Mike. "Could you point me toward the pub? I have to meet someone."

After the trouble at the Wild West Saloon, Charlie was not in the mood for company. The pub was crowded but he found a table in a back corner and ordered one drink after another. Time flowed over him like a muddy river.

Charlie, in an alcoholic haze, was berating himself, "No one likes me; even my own family treats me like a loser. They don't understand my art. No one has ever understood, except maybe poor little Maudie and I left her alone to die." He put his face in his hands and his shoulders shook.

In a few seconds he wiped his eyes with his sleeve and went on talking to himself, "Well, I'm going to turn over a new leaf, or die trying. I'm not smart like Fern, or tall and strong like Ernest, but I'll ask Fern to get me a construction job, and I'll pay Ernest every cent I owe him."

Medora's shy smile of greeting as she moved toward Charlie roused him from his dismal thoughts and tepid resolutions.

Book II
Medora

Chapter Ten
Medora

"You can't expect me to clean this room now. Molly's waiting for me. You always spoil my fun," Medora wailed.

"I've never seen such an ungrateful girl; all your beautiful things are just thrown around like trash." Helen Whitman shook her head.

Medora narrowed her eyes, and glared at her mother. As usual, she felt guilty when she looked at Helen's puckered face and old brown wig. Glancing around her frilly pink bedroom, she could see clothing piled on the bed and spilling over into heaps on the floor. Jewelry, books, a beading project, dirty dishes, an empty potato chip bag and boxes of photos were scattered about.

"I'm sorry, Mom," she gave Helen a gentle hug. At seventeen years old, Medora was 5' 9" tall. She towered over her petite parent. "If you let me go over to Molly's until dinner time, I promise I'll clean up my room before I go to bed. Some piles of clothes are clean, and some are dirty. You don't know which, so don't touch anything. I'll do it. I promise."

Helen sighed, and her scarred face wrinkled in a frown. "You're just like your dad, having fun comes first. Okay, go on, but remember your promise."

Medora went to her dressing table, ran a comb through her unruly copper curls and rubbed a tube of gloss over her lips. The coconut scent reminded her of summer at the beach. She licked her mouth; it tasted sweet. Then, in one fluid movement she scooped up her backpack, placed a kiss on the tough skin of her mother's cheek and was out the door.

The simultaneous sounds of an engine roaring to life and a radio blaring the voice of Bob Dylan, singing a song about going to San Francisco, reached Helen's ears. She sighed again. Her daughter was a gift from heaven, but sometimes even gifts from heaven come with strings.

If anyone had told Helen after the fire that she would marry a man like Ian and have a daughter like Medora, she would have laughed.

Helen closed her eyes and tried to picture what her life had been when she was Medora's age. She tried to conjure up a picture of her parents and little Timmy—nothing came. All she could remember was the day she woke up in the Portland Burn Center, and how that place became her world.

First there were the treatments, surgeries and therapy. Pain—that was what everyone asked her about—pain. To Helen, physical pain was part of living. She couldn't remember ever being without it. Losing her past was worse than the physical pain.

After ten years of procedures and appointments at the Burn Center, Dr. Peters told Helen, "We've done all we can for you. Now it's time for you to resume as normal a life as possible."

That pronouncement devastated Helen. She had no normal life to resume. Thank goodness for Darlene Howard. Darlene ran the vocational rehabilitation program. She gave Helen a reason to keep living. Every morning Helen drove to the Burn Center, where she worked as a volunteer counselor for new patients. Helen knew when she smiled in spite of her scars she gave hope to other burn victims.

"Hello, I'm Helen," she said walking into a private room in the Burn Center. The new patient, Robbie Bryant, was lying on a zoned air surface bed. The smell of singed flesh and hair permeated the air. Like Helen, Robbie had lost his parents in a house fire and had been severely burned. So intent was Helen on assessing the extent of Robbie's fear and pain, that she didn't see a man sitting in the corner.

Robbie was having trouble breathing, so Helen told him not to talk. "I had the same problem just after I was burned," she told him, "It will go away in time." She spoke with Robbie about what to expect in the next few days and finished with, "I will be here to visit you every day. If you like, I can be present during the treatments. You're not alone."

A movement caused Helen to glance across the room. A sandy haired man with a neatly trimmed beard, smiled at her. "You're wonderful, you know," he said and introduced himself as Ian Whitman, Robbie's history professor.

Ian invited Helen to have a cup of tea with him in the cafeteria. On that first afternoon Ian talked about Robbie, and his concerns for the boy's future. Helen suggested things he might say or do to encourage his student.

"I was in much worse condition than he is," Helen confided to Ian. "The people here are wonderful. The thing I needed most was hope for the future, and they helped me find that."

Having afternoon tea together when Ian visited Robbie became a habit. Eventually Ian started talking about himself. "I'm a crusty old bachelor and an absent-minded professor of history at Portland Community College. I've been gallivanting over this planet for half a century. I'm beginning to ask myself, 'did I forget to do something?'"

Helen thought marriage wasn't in the cards. No man would want a woman with scars on her face and body. But then, Ian proposed and a month later they were married.

"At our age, we better not waste any time," he told her when she hesitated.

They had a quiet wedding at the courthouse and she moved from her tiny apartment near the Burn Center into Ian's comfortable townhouse. She went to the Burn Center less often. It was a long drive, but she kept up with her support group and visited new patients one day a week.

Robbie was now living with his aunt and had returned to school. He was as busy as any other teenager and always said his good recovery was due to Ian and Helen's encouragement.

* * *

"What's wrong, Honey," Ian asked. "I bet you haven't eaten all day." He had come home from classes to find her still in bed at two in the afternoon.

"Maybe I have the flu," she answered listlessly.

"Promise me you'll call the doctor today," Ian said.

Helen didn't know who was more surprised, herself, Ian or her doctor. She rarely ever had her periods anymore; she was forty-eight years old and probably going through menopause. But to be pregnant, Helen didn't know if she should weep, or laugh as Sarah in the Bible had done.

* * *

The pregnancy and delivery were surprisingly easy, and little Medora was a delight. She was their miracle. From the beginning it was Ian who carried her about, changed her diapers and warmed her bottle. Helen loved to see them together.

When Medora was a toddler, Ian began taking her on adventures such as looking for polliwogs or visiting an amusement park. Helen didn't really mind being left behind. She told herself they were happy, that was enough. Her pain was a demanding companion. It didn't leave much room for anyone else.

Over the years Helen stood by and watched Ian spoil Medora. He really went overboard on Medora's graduation gift. Especially since the girl barely managed to maintain a B average in high school and her only extracurricular activities, besides the time spent with Ian, were prowling about the mall and giggling over the phone to her friends.

Helen had pressed her lips together in disapproval. "Our family car is an eight year old Toyota Camry, and you still drive the '69 VW square back you had when we met. It doesn't make sense to get that irresponsible child a new car."

"She's a good girl, and she really liked the little red Saturn when we took it for a test drive," he said.

"You think nothing's too good for your little princess. You've all but ruined her character," Helen said. "I'd like to know where the money for all these luxuries is coming from."

That Medora would drive off in her new car to have fun while leaving her room in a mess and expensive clothing like a rat's nest testified to the child's lack of responsibility and appreciation. Helen signed again.

* * *

The room Molly and Bridget shared in the Olson house was even more disorganized than Medora's. Molly, Medora's best friend, sat on a straight backed kitchen chair in the middle of the chaos. Medora stood behind her holding a cup and a flat paint brush. Bridget, Molly's eight year old sister, hovered close by, watching every move the older girls made.

"Knock—knock," Bridget said. Molly groaned.

"Who's there," replied Medora.

"Panther," Molly said already beginning to giggle.

"Panther, who?" Medora played the game.

"Panther falling down," Bridget was so consumed by giggles she could hardly get the words out.

Medora laughed loudly; she loved having Bridget or any of Molly's three younger sisters around. "You are so lucky," Medora told Molly. "I wish I had a sister or a brother."

Medora was using a crochet hook to pull strands of Molly's long blonde hair through tiny holes in a plastic cap. She began to brush purple hair dye onto the exposed locks.

"You can have one of mine," Molly replied, sticking out her tongue at Bridget.

"Do my hair, too," Bridget begged.

"No, you're too young. Get out of here brat," Molly said.

"I'm telling Mom." Bridget thudded down the stairs and headed toward the kitchen where her mother was fixing dinner.

"Why would you want a pest like Bridget? You are the luckiest person in the world," Molly told Medora. "You remind me of Nancy Drew, or someone in a movie or a romance novel."

"Well, Dad isn't Carson Drew and Mom isn't Hannah Gruen, but they are good to me. I just get so lonely sometimes. When I'm married, I'm going to have at least six children," Medora declared.

"Well, you have six years of college ahead before you worry about having children," Molly said. "Personally, I've decided to remain single and childless. I'll have many torrid affairs with rich lovers...." She continued in a dreamy voice.

"Hey," said Medora looking at her watch, "I've got to get going. I promised Mom I'd clean my room. Leave this stuff on for 15 minutes, and then wash it off." Medora hurried toward the door, "Call me and tell me how it looks. See you tomorrow."

Chapter Eleven
Medora

Molly burst into the apartment. "That English Lit mid-term was a killer. What the heck is the difference between classic iambic pentameter and blank verse?" she asked, obviously not expecting an answer. After tossing her book bag on a table littered with books, magazines, and unopened mail, she flopped down next to Medora on the rumpled futon.

Medora, wearing a short denim skirt and a white tee shirt with the words Wild West Saloon printed across the back in red, sat on the edge of the cushion pulling on a pair of cowboy boots.

"Are you off to the library?" asked Molly.

"Yup, got to pay the bills," Medora said with a laugh.

Molly and Medora, now in their senior year at Portland State University, had finally been allowed to get an apartment. Molly had worked at a variety of part time jobs: waitress, mail girl, nanny, tutor, even cage-cleaner in a pet store since beginning her college studies. Medora, until this semester, had relied solely upon her parents for support.

Helen decided it was time Medora learned how to provide for herself. "If you are responsible enough to live independently, you are responsible enough to hold down a job," Helen said. "Dad and I will pay the rent and utilities, but you must pay for your groceries and telephone—and your clothing."

Medora turned to Ian for support. "Dad, how can I work and go to school? Tell Mom," she pleaded in, what she hoped was, a pitiful voice.

Ian just patted her arm and looked pained.

The joke was on Helen and Ian. Medora got a job as a server at Wild West Saloon, a nearby cowboy theme restaurant and bar. In addition to barbeque ribs, beer and wine, there was dancing and a pool table. Once in a while a patron got rowdy, but they had Big Mike the bouncer to keep things under control.

"I got a job at the library," Medora lied to her parents.

"Off to the library," became a code between Molly and Medora. It meant one of them was going somewhere their parents would disapprove of.

* * *

It was a busy night at Wild West. Medora hustled from table to table taking orders and delivering plates of ribs, pitchers of beer and carafes of wine.

In one corner of the room a small stage was occupied by a guitar player, a fiddler, and a vocalist, all wearing tall cowboy hats and rawhide vests. They called themselves *The Texas Long Horns.* Two swaying couples moved around the miniscule dance floor.

Laughter, loud talking, the clatter of plates and the click of pool balls drowned out the music. The air was redolent with the scent of cigarette smoke, beer, barbeque sauce and cheap perfume. A slightly built young man with silky shoulder length hair came in alone and sat at one of the tables assigned to Medora.

"What will you have, sir?" she asked him.

"How about calling me, Charlie?" His melodic voice held the hint of a foreign accent.

Medora backed a short distance away from him; just in case he was one of those "ass patters and butt pinchers" she had been warned against. "Okay, Charlie, what will you have?"

He ordered a pitcher of beer and a platter of ribs. Later, when he had finished the ribs, he ordered coffee. "Don't you ever sit down?" he asked Medora as she poured him his third refill.

"Nope, too busy," she replied.

Medora was starting to be annoyed with Charlie. He had occupied one of her best tables for most of the evening. "That guy over there sure as heck better leave a good tip," she said to the bartender as he placed a pitcher of beer and four mugs on her tray.

Around midnight the patrons began to leave, but Charlie lingered on. He had given up all pretext of drinking coffee and seemed to be waiting to talk to Medora.

"Okay, what do you want?" Medora, hands on hips, confronted him. "Don't make it anything too personal. Big Mike has his eye on you." She gestured with her thumb toward a colossus of a man, his bald head glistening in the overhead lights. The man looked like he took his work seriously. His eyes moved about the room, sometimes quieting a boisterous patron with a hard stare.

Charlie took a brochure from the pocket of his jacket. "I'm showing some of my free-form furniture at an art gallery downtown tomorrow evening. I just wondered if you would like to come to the reception. All my friends and family live in Tamlin; I don't know anybody here."

"I'll think about it," said Medora.

"Good," said Charlie. "I'll look for you there." He tossed a fifty dollar bill on the table, buttoned his jacket and started for the door.

The next day Medora phoned Ian. "Dad, would you like to go to a reception at an art gallery tonight? A guy I just met is showing his free-form furniture."

"Sure Baby, just let me check with Mom and see if she needs me for anything. I'll get back to you."

Medora straightened up the apartment and took out several bags of trash. She lit a stick of sandalwood incense and danced through the rooms with it held high in her hand. The smoke trailed behind her, disguising stale odors. Dad wasn't very fussy, but Medora knew that she and Molly were over-the-top messy.

When Ian arrived at the apartment he settled into one of the beanbag chairs without commenting on the layer of dust on the furniture and floor. "I'm glad you called, Baby. We don't see much of each other these days. Are you managing to juggle the library and your school work?"

Medora felt a twinge of guilt. "Yes, Dad, and I love the apartment. Thank you so much for helping me to live here."

* * *

There weren't many people at the reception, but among those in attendance were several critics. Charlie was busy being interviewed when Ian and Medora walked in, so they looked around on their own.

"Amazing," said Ian, "simply amazing."

The various pieces of furniture, mostly tables but some chairs, were fashioned from slices of redwood burl. The imperfections in the burl had a lacy quality about them. Charlie had imbedded metal and gemstones, mostly silver and turquoise nuggets, into those natural imperfections. The result was unique and beautiful. The legs of the pieces, hand carved geometric designs, appeared to grow naturally out of the burl.

Charlie came up to them. "Hello Medora, I'm so glad to see you."

Ian introduced himself, "I'm Medora's father, Ian Whitman, and I have some questions for you about your art. I find it quite stunning."

Charlie and Ian hit it off right away. They went from discussing Charlie's work to discovering their shared interest in photography.

"I've been saving this as a surprise, but I'm hoping to take Medora to the Dakota badlands for a photo safari during spring break," Ian told Charlie. Turning to Medora, Ian asked, "Would you like that, Princess?"

"Oh, Dad, it will be wonderful. I can't wait."

After the reception, Ian and Medora took a stroll around the neighborhood of the art gallery. They found a small restaurant, Patty's Pie Shop, and went in for a cup of tea. The pies looked too delicious to pass up, so they shared a piece of pecan.

"Charlie seems like a nice young man, and very talented," Ian remarked. "Why don't you invite him to the townhouse for dinner some Sunday?"

"He's not my type: too skinny, too short, and too much hair. Besides I've heard artists are moody," Medora said.

"Suit yourself, Baby. Oh, by the way, I'll send you some information on the Dakota trip. I'm shopping for a good camera for you. Between the two of us we should get some exciting shots. I'm told there is a buffalo herd and wild horses. Spring break will be the last week in March so that gives us about a month to get ready."

* * *

"Can I borrow your black mini skirt?" Molly asked Medora. It was Valentine's Day and the girls were double-dating to a party at one of the fraternity houses on campus.

"Okay, does this outfit make me look fat?" Medora answered as she pulled the sleeves of her peasant blouse down to achieve an off the shoulder effect.

"You look hot," Molly complemented her. "That skirt is swe—eet."

Medora decided the blouse really did look great with the gauzy skirt she had splurged on for the party. The skirt was made of layers of sheer pink and lavender fabric sparkling with hand sewn sequins.

The phone rang and Medora picked it up. "Hello—I didn't expect to hear from you—sorry, I've got a date." She paused and listened. "I don't know. I probably won't be home until late."

Molly was mouthing the words, "Who is it?"

Medora crossed her eyes in comic exasperation. "Okay, but just for one drink," she said and hung up.

"Who was that? Molly asked again.

"It was that artist guy, Charlie. He insists on seeing me tonight. I told him I'd meet him for one drink at the pub after the dance."

"Don't show up. It would serve him right for being so pushy. Do you have time to do my hair in a French braid?" Molly asked, as she slipped into a tight pink shirt that glittered with red rhinestones.

The party at the frat house was wild. Medora's rule was to hold herself to two drinks, but she had gone a bit overboard. As usual Molly had totally overdone it. Medora was starting to worry that Molly was developing a drinking problem.

"I really don't want to see Charlie," she told Molly when their dates dropped them at their apartment. "Come with me," Medora pleaded. In reply, Molly slid to the floor. Her eyes closed and her face went slack. "Come on, let's get you to bed." Medora said.

Medora had a nice little buzz on and didn't feel like sitting around the apartment watching Molly sleep. She threw a shawl over her shoulders and walked the block to the pub. When Charlie saw her, he gave a low whistle, then jumped up and made a courtly bow.

Medora knew she looked good in her new skirt and off the shoulder blouse. It was nice to be appreciated. She was glad she had come to meet Charlie after all.

"I'll have lemonade," Medora told the waitress.

"Okay, if that's how you want to be; make it two lemonades and put a shot of vodka in both of them," said Charlie.

He kept ordering drinks, and she kept saying she had to get home. The last thing Medora remembered was dancing with Charlie to the jukebox.

* * *

It was Molly's cry of outrage that woke Medora. It took a minute to realize where she was, and then Medora began to whimper. She was on the futon and Charlie was on the floor; both of them were naked. Charlie opened his eyes and scrambled to his feet. He tried to pull his pants on and almost fell. He looked like a burlesque comic.

Still screaming, Molly threw a blanket over Medora and yelled at Charlie, "Get out! Get out of our house!"

"I didn't force her. We were both drunk. I didn't rape her," Charlie was saying as he tried to get his boots on. "I don't even like tall girls. It wasn't my fault."

Then Medora noticed her beautiful skirt on the floor. "Molly, he tore my skirt," She pointed to her skirt and burst into tears. "It's ruined." She sobbed

"Ahhhh," screamed Molly. She grabbed her tennis racket and brought it down on Charlie's head. He put up his hands to protect himself and ran for the door.

Chapter Twelve
Medora

"Medora, get up. It's late. Get up! You have a bio test." Molly pushed the blankets off Medora and began pulling her arm. Medora always got herself ready and out the door once she was on her feet.

After "the Charlie thing," as Molly called it, Medora slid into a blue funk. Molly was patient at first, but now Medora's moods were starting to get on her nerves. The incident was in the past—it happened three weeks ago. No one but Molly, Medora, and Charlie knew about it, and they would probably never see him again. Medora should get over it.

Medora was driving Molly crazy with her complaints. She had become—since the Charlie thing—hypersensitive toward the male customers, but she needed to work. She had run her credit cards to the limit.

After waiting on tables for a few hours at Wild West, Medora would come back to the apartment and stand under the shower until the water turned cold. This resulted in no hot water for Molly's shower. Molly was tired of the whole thing.

"I'm too much trouble to everybody," Medora muttered in a monotone. "Everyone would be better off if I was dead."

"Oh, shut up, Medora," Molly snapped. "I've about had it with you. We're going to have a little heart-to-heart, and you are going to come up with a plan for your life. I'm sick of taking care of you."

"I don't blame you. I'm not worth the trouble." Medora had managed to get herself dressed and was stuffing papers into her book-bag.

Molly stopped shuffling through her index card notes. She grabbed Medora by the shoulders. "Boo hoo, poor me," Molly said as she shook Medora roughly, and then kissed her cheek. "We'll talk later; just get yourself to class and do your best on the test." She gave Medora a hug and shoved her out the door.

When Molly got back to the apartment that afternoon she was relieved to see Medora dressed in blue jeans and a yellow sweater rather than the baggy sweats she had worn almost constantly since her encounter with Charlie. The curtains were open and a bunch of wildflowers in a tumbler had been placed in the center of the littered table top, a sign that Medora had taken a walk after class instead moping around the apartment with the shades pulled.

"I made tea," Medora said, as she helped Molly with her backpack and books. "Mol, I'm sorry."

"Oh, honey," said Molly, squeezing Medora's hand.

Medora poured two cups of Chamomile tea before she said, "I decided the only thing I can do is talk to Dad when we go on our trip to the Dakotas. I'll tell him about my credit card bills and my job."

"Are you going to tell him about...the Charlie thing?" asked Molly.

"No, you were right. That's in the past. I'm going to ask Dad to help me with my credit card bills and give me a little money for expenses until I find another job." She added in a quavering voice, "Every time I walk into Wild West and those men look at me, I feel dirty."

"I think you've come up with a very good plan," said Molly, steering Medora away from talking about her job. "No more nonsense about being better off dead—promise."

"I promise," said Medora. "Now let's order a pizza. I'm starved."

Medora nibbled at her pizza. She felt as fragile as an eggshell. Her life was careening out of control. If she didn't have Dad and Molly to depend on, she would just give up. She had contemplated ways of ending her life. Cutting one's wrists was messy. Better to find a high cliff above the ocean; jump and become just one more bit of flotsam. It would be so peaceful.

* * *

Ian was enthusiastic about the trip. He called Medora several times each week. "Layers—we need to dress in layers—it's still very cold there, but sometimes it warms up during the day. I got you a digital camera. Those disposables aren't good enough for this trip."

Medora managed to get through each day, and then it was spring vacation. The shuttle picked her and Ian up from the townhouse. His face was flushed and a vein throbbed in his left temple. He was quieter than usual, and so was Medora. She was preoccupied with the words she would use to tell him about her credit card debt and the job at the saloon.

She paid no attention when he staggered and almost fell as he was hoisting their luggage into the back of the van. "I need my coffee," he panted, steadying himself against the door. He climbed into the van like an old man and plopped down on the first seat he came to. She was too busy with her own problems to see something was wrong.

The first leg of the journey was to be the flight from Portland to Denver. From there they planned to get a connecting plane to Bismarck. Ian kept his eyes shut and seemed to doze while they waited in the Portland International lounge. Usually he was so excited on a vacation he could hardly sit still. Medora welcomed his silence; she didn't have to pretend to be happy.

Ian was breathing hard by the time they boarded the plane, stowed their luggage and got settled in their seats. He pressed his head against the seat rest when they took off. "The pressure in this cabin is fierce today," he moaned. "I've got a headache that won't quit."

Medora noticed her dad's color. He was flushed and damp with perspiration. "Oh, Daddy, do you have a fever," she asked as she pressed her hand to his forehead. He was very warm. "I'll ask the attendant to get you some Tylenol."

Medora waved toward a pretty dark-haired attendant who was giving the emergency instructions, but was unable to catch her eye. However, the attendant must have noticed Medora, because as soon as she was done with the instructions she hurried over.

"I'm sorry we aren't serving anything until we complete the take off," she said.

"My daddy doesn't feel well," Medora said. "Could you please get him some Tylenol?"

"My God," the attendant gasped when she looked toward Ian.

"Daddy!" screamed Medora.

Ian's face was dark purple and he didn't seem to be breathing.

"James! " The dark-haired attendant called to a male attendant, "Tell the captain we have to return to Portland. We have a very sick man here." James hurried toward the door to the cockpit. "Is there a doctor on this flight?" the dark haired attendant called loudly.

* * *

Medora rode in the ambulance with Ian, but once they got to the hospital she wasn't allowed to stay with him. A woman in a pink volunteer's uniform came to sit with her in the waiting room. "I'm Susan," she introduced herself. "I have a daughter about your age." Her soft face was creased with concern. "Is there anyone you would like to call?"

"I'll need to call my Mom as soon as I talk to the doctor," Medora said, thrusting her hands deep into the pockets of her jacket and hunching her shoulders. "I hope it isn't serious—oh, my poor daddy."

Tears slipped out of Medora's brimming eyes and ran down her cheeks. Susan handed her a tissue, then patted her on the shoulder.

Several hours passed before a muscular black man wearing a green surgical suit and paper shoe covers looked into the room. "Is Medora Whitman here?" he asked.

Susan waved him over. "This is Robert Thompson, the RN taking care of y our dad."

"It's hard waiting alone," he said. "I'm glad Susan is with you."

"How is my dad?"

"It looks like a blood clot has lodged in his brain and caused a massive stroke. The doctor is still with him."

"What can I tell my mom?" asked Medora. "This will kill her."

"Here's Dr. Lee. Let's hear what she has to say, and then we'll ask the social worker to help you notify your mother," Robert suggested.

Dr. Lee was a diminutive oriental woman with silver rimmed glasses and a businesslike manner. "Your father's prognosis is very poor. We're doing everything we can to minimize the damage to his brain, but it has already been extensive. As soon as he is stable we can discuss his rehabilitation potential. Frankly, I am not optimistic. I think you should call your mother. Susan will take you to the social worker's office."

Medora had expected Helen to fall apart when she received the news, but Helen just said, "I'll be right there. There's nothing we can't handle together."

It was after midnight when Helen walked into the almost empty waiting room. She spotted Medora and hurried toward her, calling her name.

A flood of relief washed over Medora when she saw her mother. Helen was only a little over five feet tall, but held herself as erect as any army officer on parade. She was wearing a drab polyester pant-suit and carrying her old black purse

"Tell me what happened."

Medora described the whole day, from the time Ian had trouble lifting the suitcases into the van, until Dr. Lee gave the frightening report about his condition.

"I didn't even pay any attention when he had trouble with the luggage," she said as tears filled her eyes.

"I'm going to find out if we can see Ian for a few minutes. I want to be sure he knows we're here." Helen rang the bell by the door which led to the Intensive Care Unit. In a few minutes a nurse came out. Helen spoke to her for a short while.

"Come on, Medora," Helen called. "Loretta says we can go in for ten minutes."

Six open bays made a semi-circle around the nursing station. Three beds were occupied by patients. Each one was connected to tubes and wires. Medora wondered if these sick people had families to care about them.

"I'll be Mr. Whitman's nurse for the next twelve hours," Loretta was saying. "He's doing as well as we can expect. We're having a little trouble stabilizing his blood pressure. He's in a coma. Since he can't breathe on his own, he's on a ventilator. I'm not sure he can hear you, but it has been my experience that people who have been on ventilators often say they remember their loved ones talking to them."

"Oh, Dad," whispered Medora. She hadn't eaten all day, but something sour in her churning stomach was forcing itself into her throat.

Helen took Medora's hand. Ian looked as if he were dead. One side of his face drooped and his eyes stared blankly into space. There was a tube in his nose, and a suction hose by his mouth. Needles in his arms connected tubes to bags of fluid, a blood pressure cuff kept inflating and deflating. Machines, monitors and screens beeped and hissed. A clear plastic bag filled with yellow fluid, probably urine, hung on the rail of the hospital bed. Medora stepped back, but Helen gripped her hand hard and pulled her forward.

"Hello, Ian," Helen said in a low voice. "Medora is here with me. We can only stay for ten minutes. You need to rest so you'll get well. I love you, Ian."

"I love you, Dad," Medora managed to say before she dropped to her knees and retched. Loretta handed her a pan and she vomited.

* * *

Helen spent every day at the hospital, but she insisted Medora continue her classes. "Your dad would want you to graduate," she said.

Medora struggled to keep up with school and work her shifts at Wild West Saloon. Although she was only allowed in to see Ian for ten minutes each hour, she spent most of her weekends at the hospital. "Now I know why they call it a waiting room," she said to Susan.

The stress was taking its toll on her. She was sick to her stomach every morning.

One day Molly asked, "How long has it been since you had your period?"

Medora had to stop and consider. "The beginning of February, I think."

"Well this is the end of April. Could you be pregnant from that night with Charlie?"

Medora's eyes widened at the thought. "Oh, shit," she said and sat down hard on the futon.

They went to the drugstore together and bought the pregnancy test kit. Back home in the bathroom, they watched the strip turn pink. "Oh, Medora," Mollie gasped.

"I can't have a baby now," Medora said.

"We'll go to the clinic. Don't worry. I know a couple of girls who had abortions and they said it was nothing to be afraid of," Molly said.

* * *

Molly went with Medora to the clinic the next day. When they walked in, the receptionist looked up from her paperback novel. "Which one of you is the patient?" Medora shyly raised her hand, as if she knew the answer to a question in school but was afraid to speak out. "Do you have an appointment?" the woman asked in a bored voice.

"No, do I need one?" Medora asked.

"Not really, I can give you the forms." She handed Medora a folder filled with papers. "Fill these out. You have to talk to a counselor. Be back here tomorrow afternoon at two fifteen. There's a twenty four hour waiting period before the procedure—let me see—we can schedule you Saturday morning at nine. Don't eat or drink anything after midnight on Friday."

As they walked back to the car Medora told Molly, "I've got to meet Mom for dinner. We're going to go see Dad this evening."

"Are you okay?" Molly asked Medora.

"I'm messed up, Mol. Everything seems sort of out of focus and unreal."

* * *

Helen had prepared creamed tuna on toast with peas, Medora's childhood favorite, but she only picked at it. When they were done eating, Helen carried their dishes into the kitchen, and then came back to sit beside Medora on the sofa. She rubbed her hands together nervously before she spoke.

"Medora, there is no money. Dad enjoyed life so much, and I'm glad he did, but he just spent and spent, even when he didn't have it. I'm going to sell the townhouse and pay off our debts. I don't mind, because Dad will be going to a nursing home for rehabilitation soon. I want to get a little apartment near him. Of course I'd like you to live with me, if there's room. Unfortunately, you'll have to get a job after graduation instead of going immediately to graduate school."

Medora stared at Helen. She remembered her mother saying, "There is nothing that we cannot handle together."

"Medora, are you alright? I know this is a shock to you," Helen leaned forward and touched Medora's arm.

"Mom, I lied to you. I owe over five thousand dollars on my credit cards. I drank too much. I'm pregnant and I hardly know the father of my baby." Medora took a deep breath, but she couldn't hold back the tears.

Helen straightened her shoulders. She looked like a prize fighter getting ready for a tough round. Medora covered her face with her hands; her shoulders shook. Helen just watched her daughter. When Medora was too exhausted to cry any more, she took her hands from her face.

Helen was looking at her coldly "You must tell the baby's father as soon as possible and hope to God he will marry you. What you did was wrong; now you must face the consequences. Go wash your face and comb your hair. It's time to visit Dad."

Chapter Thirteen
Medora

"Molly, I told Mom about the baby—about everything—my credit cards, lying, drinking, and what a mess I've made of my life." Medora's lips twitched into a half smile. Something about facing her problems and being honest with her mother had made the dark mood lose its hold on her. She now felt strong and in control, able to handle whatever came her way.

Molly was loading books into her backpack. "What did she say?"

"She said I had to tell Charlie and hope he'll marry me. Molly, I don't care what Charlie does; I'm going to keep my baby and nothing will change my mind."

"What about me? What about our plans for graduate school?" Molly sounded angry. "An abortion would be so much easier. You're messing up everything." She turned her back so Medora couldn't see her tears, and kept on shoving things into the backpack.

"I couldn't go to graduate school anyway. There's no money," Medora said.

"I'm sorry," Molly said. "I really am, but what about me?"

Medora handed Molly a folder that had fallen to the floor, and said, "I don't even know Charlie's last name or where he lives. He said he's from Tamlin; I think that's over on the coast. Do you have to do anything after classes today?"

"I have to retype my term paper," Molly sniffed and blew her nose.

"Will you go with me to the art gallery where Charlie had his showing if I proofread your term paper and retype it for you?" Medora used the sleeve of her sweater to wipe away Molly's tears.

"Oh, of course," Molly managed a smile. "I just can't believe you won't be here next semester."

* * *

"May I help you? The burgundy haired woman purred. Ornate silver bracelets jangled as she raised her ring bedecked hand to stroke her hair. "I am Claudine, the owner of this gallery."

Young women like Medora and Molly rarely purchased works of fine art. Girls like these two, with their low cut jeans and pierced navels, were a waste of time. Claudine arched her eyebrows at Spyder, her associate. His expression didn't change. He pulled a white scarf from the pocket of his too tight black leather pants and waved it toward the girls.

"My dad and I came to a show here in January," Medora told her. "We saw furniture by an artist named Charlie. I need to get in touch with Charlie."

"Are you thinking of purchasing something you saw at the show?" Claudine, in a cloud of musky perfume, leaned closer. "Because if you are, it must be done through this gallery. Charlie has a contract with me." She tapped a sharp purple fingernail on the counter top.

Bubbles of giggles were threatening to escape from Molly's mouth. The whole thing was ludicrous. She looked around the gallery. The paintings and sculptures were weird. She glanced at Spyder. Dressed in black turtle neck, black pants and black combat boots, he was currently engaged in the activity of picking his nose. "I'm sorry." Molly, bent over with the effort not to laugh, ran for the door.

Medora and Claudine could hear Molly chortling outside the gallery. "I'll just get you one of Mr. Schmidt's cards," Claudine sneered. "Be sure you let him know if he tries to evade my commission, no gallery in Portland will ever handle his things again."

"Thank you so much," Medora murmured sweetly.

As she left the gallery, Medora heard Claudine say to Spyder, "Groupies!"

Molly grabbed Medora's hand and they ran down the busy sidewalk laughing. When they finally stopped to catch their breath, Molly said, "Groupies," and pretended to pick her nose. That started the laughter all over again.

Medora took a deep breath. "I haven't had a good laugh in months." She looked at Molly, "What do you think my dad would say about the mess I'm in?

"I know exactly what he'd say," Molly replied. He'd tell you that everyone makes mistakes. You're taking responsibility for your problems, and he's proud of the way you are handling things."

* * *

Charlie didn't expect to hear from Medora again, but of course it shouldn't have been a surprise that she called. He studied his handsome face in the chrome toaster which stood on the pull down table in his little trailer.

"This is kind of a bad time," he told Medora. "My truck is at the mechanics." Truthfully, the truck was parked outside. It needed a new axle, but Charlie had not yet been able to talk Ernest into loaning him the money to get it repaired. "Of course, if you really can't wait to see me, you could pick me up at the bus station," he concluded.

* * *

As Medora drove along the rain slick streets of Portland toward the bus station, her thoughts were whirling. "Who is Charlie? Dad liked him and said he was talented. Is he a nice guy when he isn't drinking? I'll never love him like Mom loves Dad. He's not the one I would have picked. Maybe Charlie won't want a baby—or me."

Her thoughts swirled round and round until she spotted Charlie waiting in a sheltered area. Slowing the Saturn, she pulled to the curb and reached over to open the passenger door. "Hello there," she said.

Charlie made no effort to return her cheerful greeting. "Damn, it's one thing after another. That bus trip was the pits and then you were late," he complained. "I think I'm getting a cold," he added.

"I'm sorry," Medora replied. "It started to pour and I had to pull over for about ten minutes." Then she added with a forced smile, "I thought we might go somewhere to talk, then maybe back to my mom's. I have a batch of vegetable soup cooking in the crock pot."

"I don't mean to be a pain," he whined, "but I don't feel like sitting around talking. Let's go to the movies then grab a pizza."

"Charlie, I really need to talk to you. It's important." Medora's eyes pleaded for him to understand.

"We'll have plenty of time to talk over pizza," Charlie said. "The movie I want to see starts at two so we better hustle."

She had to hold it together until she got a chance to tell him. She wanted to blurt it her news out and see what his reaction would be. Maybe he would comfort her and figure out how to make things right as Ian had always done, but he might be upset. It was best to wait until after the movie, she decided—she'd tell him at the pizza parlor.

For Medora the movie was a nightmare. The glare and loud noises, the violence and sex sickened her. She closed her eyes, clenched her fists and prayed for it to be over.

By the end of the movie Charlie was in good spirits. As they huddled under Medora's umbrella and walked toward the pizza parlor he became more animated and spoke in a rapid voice, "I've got an important commission, a huge redwood table for a very rich man in Portland. He saw my stuff and loves it. He might want more pieces and he's willing to pay through the nose." Laughing shrilly, he put his arm around Medora's waist.

Feeling encouraged by Charlie's good humor, Medora smiled and laughed with him. They reached the pizza parlor and Charlie led her to a table in the back near the game machines. Every machine was busy. Kids of all ages were pumping quarters into them. Bells, whistles, merry little tunes and excited shouts pierced the air.

Without consulting Medora, Charlie ordered the super king pizza with anchovies and a pitcher of beer for them to share. Medora didn't want beer or anchovies, but she wanted to please Charlie, so she said nothing. Anyway she was able to scrape most of the fishy smelling anchovies into her napkin with no one noticing.

"I suppose I just condemned myself to a life time of anchovies and beer," she thought. Taking a deep breath, she looked Charlie in the eye and said, "We don't have very long until your bus and I've been trying to tell you something—I'm going to have a baby."

He looked bored. "Who's your boyfriend?" he asked.

"It's your baby Charlie, yours and mine," Medora's mouth quivered.

"Wow! Wow! That's great," Charlie grinned as he thought about Medora being the only child of elderly well-to-do parents. Out loud he said, "We'll get married right away. You can move into the trailer with me. Wow! I'm going to have a baby. Wait 'till I tell my folks and Ernest and Fern that I'm getting married."

"I wish we had longer to talk, but I'm so relieved you're happy." Medora's emotions were mixed. Charlie wanted her and the baby. He would marry her, but she didn't like him.

"We've got to get you back to the bus station," she stood up and moved toward the door.

As she drove through the rain, Medora said, "I told my Mom. She wants me to finish school. I graduate in June. Just one more month and I'll have my degree."

"You aren't going to keep going to school. We're going to be married as soon as possible and you are coming back to Tamlin with me."

"No, Charlie, I'm not going to disappoint my parents and it doesn't make sense for me not to finish. The baby won't be born until around Thanksgiving."

"Drive me back to Tamlin. We need to talk about this," Charlie ordered.

"I can't do that Charlie. I have mid-terms tomorrow."

"I'm telling you—drive me to Tamlin—I came here to see you, and you drop this bombshell on me then don't give me a chance to even think about it. I bet you planned the whole thing. 'Just wait until ole' Charlie has to leave then drop it on him,' you probably said to yourself."

Medora was too amazed to be angry, "Charlie, what are you talking about? I've wanted to tell you ever since you got here. I haven't even told anyone else except Mom and Molly. I wanted you to know first." She pulled to the curb at the bus station.

"You fucking bitch," Charlie's face had a greenish hue and there were little specks of spittle at the corners of his mouth. He got out of the Saturn and slammed the door so hard the windows rattled and the side-view mirror fell off. Before he walked away, he gave the side of the car a vicious kick with his booted foot.

Medora got out in the rain and picked the mirror out of a puddle. The thing that just happened wasn't real. It was some sort of a joke. Raising her hand she waved in Charlie's direction as he strode toward the area for departing buses.

He didn't look back.

Chapter Fourteen
Medora

Medora didn't know what to do. Charlie was hateful; she couldn't imagine spending the rest of her life with him. The thought was frightening—but so was the idea of raising her child alone. "I'll work it out somehow," she vowed. "No matter what happens I'm going to have my baby."

Both Helen and Molly questioned her about the meeting with Charlie. They asked how he looked, what he said, and when she would see him again.

"It was a pretty big shock for him," Medora replied. "I'm sure I'll hear from him after he has a chance to mull it over." Shame kept her from telling them of the cruel way Charlie had treated her. No one had ever been so disrespectful.

A week went by with no word from him. She didn't know what to do. She couldn't depend on Charlie, but she couldn't live with Mom in a little apartment either. She would try to raise her baby by herself. She would get a job, and pay someone to take care of her baby. Medora's thoughts twisted round and round as she drove to work.

Her shift at Wild West Saloon went surprisingly well. A group of visiting ornithologists occupied all Medora's tables that evening. For the most part they were shy and polite, asking her about various birds she might have seen in the area. Medora had always been fond of hummingbirds, so she told her customers of how the jewel-like little creatures came in droves to the feeders she and her dad hung from the balcony of the townhouse. The best thing about this group was that they left an extremely generous tip—fifty dollars.

After work, she was tired, but more hopeful than she had been for a long time. As she walked from the parking lot to the apartment she was aware of a flutter in her abdomen. It must be the first movements of her baby. Feeling, at that moment, able to handle anything she made a promise, "I'm going to make a good life for my child."

When she drew closer to the apartment, she noticed something on the porch. The light was dim and it was hard to make out what it was. Two luminous spheres floated in the air above a chunky white base.

"Oh, my goodness! Who could have sent this? It's precious!"

Balloons, one green and one yellow, were anchored to a black and white panda bear. Medora hugged the bear to her chest as she carried it into the apartment and turned on a light. The card, bearing the logo of a neighborhood florist, read: "I'm a fool. If you can find it in your heart to forgive me, please call. Charlie."

Medora reached for the phone, her heart pounding. She dialed Charlie's number and let the phone ring five times. She was just about to hang up when he answered.

"Hello," he said.

"Hello Charlie," her voice quavered. "I just got home from work and found the panda and balloons. Thank you so much."

"Medora, I'm sorry I was such a jerk," he paused and cleared his throat. His voice shook with emotion. "I hardly know you, but I can tell that you're a nice person. You and the baby are the best thing that has ever happened to me, and I don't want to screw it up. Can I come see you next weekend? I'd like to meet your mother."

* * *

"Sit down Medora, you're making me nervous," Helen called from the kitchen.

"He was supposed to be here half an hour ago," said Medora. Maybe Charlie was drinking again, or had changed his mind about coming to meet Mom, or he might have decided to…there was a knock, and Medora went to open the door.

"Hi," Charlie said as he handed Medora a bouquet of yellow and white daisies. "These are for you and your mom."

"Thank you. You look nice," said Medora. His shoulder length hair was pulled back into a pony tail, and he was wearing black tailored jeans, a soft plaid flannel shirt, and high heeled cowboy boots. The boots made him almost as tall as Medora. "Come in and meet Mom."

Since the bear and balloons, Charlie and Medora had talked on the phone every evening. He knew about Helen's burn scars and Ian's stroke. Medora found it easy to talk to him about her life.

Charlie had spoken of his family, going on at length about some of their disagreements. "My brother, Ernest, and sister, Fern, are very close; it's always been them against me." He told her how he felt left out. Ma Tom, his mother, disapproved of him and was always finding fault. "My dad, Papa Gus, is great though. He's the one who taught me to do fine woodwork."

Charlie described his studio and the trailer where they would live until his work began to sell. "It's rather rough, but beautiful here. I wish I had a fancier place for you and our baby. Someday you can design a house, and I'll build with my own hands."

Now, Charlie, the stranger who was the father of her child, was in the townhouse where Medora had grown up, and waiting to be introduced to Mom.

Helen came into the room still wearing her apron. She held out her hand, "Hello, I'm Medora's mother, Helen. "

"I'm glad to meet you, ma'am. Did Medora tell you, I met your husband a few months ago? I'm sorry he's sick," Charlie said.

Helen swallowed, took a deep breath and said, "Lunch is ready. Medora, show Charlie where to wash up; then come help me get the things on the table."

Charlie and Helen seemed to hit it off. They chatted about selling the townhouse, and what needed to be done to get it ready. After lunch

Charlie went out to his truck and came back with a tool box. He fixed a leaky faucet and tacked down a loose carpet.

When Charlie had finished the repairs, Helen made a fresh pot of coffee and Medora carried it into the living room. They sat together, sipping the rich brew. Rain streamed down the window panes and a log crackled in the fireplace. Turning to Charlie, Helen asked, "What are your thoughts about the baby?"

To Charlie's credit, he didn't look away from her direct stare. "I think I'm a lucky man, and I'll do my best to be a good husband and father."

"Medora has three more weeks of classes before she graduates. She must finish and get her degree," Helen's voice was uncompromising.

"If that's what you want," Charlie looked down at his boots, "I really think we should get married as soon as possible. It's not right to wait until she looks really pregnant...you know," he added lamely.

Helen pressed her lips together and nodded in agreement.

* * *

Medora's final exam was the afternoon of Friday, June 15th. Helen decided the wedding should take place on Sunday, June 17th, at seven in the morning, before the first church service, in Pastor Alderson's study.

To Medora, Helen said, "It's a shameful business; let's get it over with early before there's a bunch of people around." She told the pastor a different story when she made the arrangements for the unusually early wedding ceremony. "The newlyweds will have a long drive ahead of them," she said.

"It seems like just yesterday that I baptized your little girl," Pastor Alderson spoke directly to Helen. Reaching for his calendar, he said, "I can see Medora and her young man for premarital counseling on Saturday afternoon at two. Will that be convenient?"

"That will be fine," Helen answered.

* * *

Medora couldn't see how any of it pertained to her. She felt disoriented when they met with Pastor Alderson for the counseling. They had arrived together but, as if by common consent, chose separate chairs instead of sitting together on the loveseat. The pastor's voice droned on.

What was he saying, something about obeying and bodies belonging to each other? Oh my God, she couldn't imagine 'obeying' Charlie, let alone having sex with him. It was all a mistake. She would tell Helen that she could work and care for the baby on her own. But while her entire being silently screamed "no", she sat in the chair and nodded her head in agreement.

The whole thing was a runaway train speeding down a track toward disaster. Medora didn't sleep at all Saturday night. On her wedding morning she felt frowsy and tired. Her short coppery hair, usually so bouncy, was flat and dull against her scalp.

As a mild form of rebellion, she wore blue jeans and the top Molly gave her for Christmas. Molly had stitched a red velvet heart onto the front of the long sleeved purple tee shirt. The casual outfit made Medora feel a bit more cheerful.

The one bright spot in that morning, for Medora, was Charlie's brother Ernest. He was to be the best man. Of course Medora had chosen Molly as her maid of honor.

"You didn't tell me how pretty the girls in Portland are," Ernest said when Charlie introduced him to Helen, Medora and Mollie. Medora didn't know why she found Ernest so comforting. He looked rumpled and loveable in an ill fitting, slightly out of fashion gray suit. Later, she realized he reminded her of Ian.

* * *

"I'm ugly," Medora complained to Molly and Helen as they waited together in a little room off the pastor's study. "And you both look darling," she added patting Molly's blue velvet blazer.

It was Molly who spoke, "No you aren't, Honey. I love your wedding outfit, especially the shirt—very unique. You look beautiful, but too pale," she said. "You need a bit of blush on your cheeks and a smile on your lips."

Helen remained silent and didn't make her usual remarks about outward beauty not being important. Dressed in her best navy blue pants suit, she looked more like she was going to a funeral than to a wedding. Her lips were set in a thin line.

Medora forced a smile while Molly brushed a trace of pink across her cheekbones, then handed her the bouquet of white roses, a gift from Ernest. When they heard the sound of recorded organ music, the women opened the door and went into the pastor's study where Charlie, in his high-heeled cowboy boots, waited with Ernest and Pastor Alderson. Sweat gleamed on Charlie's face, and his hands were shaking.

"He's as unsure about all this as I am," Medora realized. For some unknown reason, that thought made her feel better.

The ceremony was short. Pastor Alderson made a few remarks about the duties of a husband and wife to each other, and then read the vows. Charlie placed a thin silver band on Medora's finger. He kissed her on the cheek and the wedding party exited the study.

* * *

Medora and Charlie planned to travel to Tamlin in Medora's Saturn. Ernest would follow in his van. "That stuff won't fit in my trailer," Charlie whispered in a peevish voice when he saw the boxes and suitcases Medora had packed into the cargo area of the Saturn.

"Goodbye for now Medora. We'll keep in touch. God bless both of you." Helen's voice shook.

Molly went to put her arm around Helen. "Your mom and I will take care of each other. Write, call, email, yell, shout, whatever—but let us know how you are doing," Reaching into her purse, Molly drew out a baggie filled with rice and proceeded to throw handfuls of the stuff toward the Saturn and the newlywed couple.

"Hey, Mol—catch." Medora tossed the white roses into Molly's arms and then slid into the passenger side of the car.

"Get me out of here quick" she said to Charlie. She smiled and waved at Helen and Molly, but as soon as the car was out of sight of the well-wishers her smile vanished, and she broke into racking sobs.

Chapter Fifteen
Medora

The red Saturn station wagon, her high school graduation gift from Ian, was carrying Medora away from her old life and everyone she loved. The sound of her sobs and nose blowing punctuated the silence.

"I can't take much more of this," Charlie told her. "God knows, I didn't want this either. We have to try to make the best of it. You're acting like a baby."

"We don't love each other. We don't even know each other," Medora, sounded sad and hopeless. She stopped crying but continued to blow her nose and sniffle.

Charlie kept his eyes on the highway. Gripping the steering wheel so hard his knuckles turned white, he drove on in silence.

Exhausted from lack of sleep, and the emotions of the day, Medora rested her head against the back of the seat; in a few minutes her breathing was deep and regular. Charlie glanced at her. With her tousled hair and pale face she looked very young. "I'm sorry. I didn't mean to make you unhappy," he whispered.

Southbound Highway 5 was a ribbon of gray in the morning rain. There was practically no traffic; Charlie was making good time. Hours went by, and the only sounds were Medora's breathing and the drone of wheels against pavement. His mind filled with plans for the future. Most of his thoughts were of the furniture he wanted to create, but once in a while he reflected on Medora and the baby, "I'm going to take good care of my family," he vowed.

He imagined himself at a show in a fancy art gallery. People were raving over his furniture and vying to pay huge prices for it. Medora was there looking as beautiful as she had on Valentine's Day. He would point to her and say, "That's my wife." The words sounded good to him. She was a fine looking woman. He was proud of her.

Glancing at the gasoline gauge, Charlie saw they had less than a quarter of a tank. "I might as well fuel up at the Stop & Gas." He eased into the right lane and turned off on the freeway exit. After pulling into the pump area he killed the engine.

Medora, her eyes red and swollen, looked about in confusion. When she saw Charlie, she remembered where she was. "Why are we stopping," she asked as she reached into her purse for a hairbrush and lip gloss.

"I thought I'd fill it up and stretch my legs. Do you want anything to eat?"

"I have to use the restroom, and then I'll see what they have to offer. Milk and cookies will do for me, how about you?"

"Go ahead; I'll get the gas. I'm not very hungry."

* * *

Holding a small carton of milk and a bag of vanilla wafers in her hands, Medora approached the check-out stand. Charlie, his back toward her, was making a purchase. When she saw the bottle of whiskey and six pack of beer, Medora drew back and waited behind a pyramid of bottled water while he finished his transaction and left the store.

After paying for the milk and cookies, she went back out to the Saturn. "Why don't you let me drive for a while? I feel refreshed after my nap," she told Charlie.

"Great," he answered, "If you're sure you feel up to it. Just stay on Highway 5 until we get to Grant's Pass. Then we take the two lane dirt road over Klamath Mountain. It's a little hairy, especially in the rain, so

I'll drive from there. He climbed into the passenger seat and fastened the seatbelt.

The clerk had wrapped the whiskey in a brown paper bag and placed it into a plastic shopping bag along with the beer. Charlie took out a beer. He popped the tab, took a long swig, sighed and made a little burping noise. Next he placed both hands into the plastic bag, and surreptitiously poured a slug of whiskey into the open can.

How could he think she wouldn't know what he was doing? She stared at the road and said nothing to him, but her face was stony.

Charlie wasn't bothered by her silence. After consuming three whiskey laced beers, he began to talk in a rambling fashion.

"You're one fine looking woman. Yes sir, one fine looking woman. Fern and Ernest will be laughing out of the other sides of their mouths. They think they're such big shots, but I've gone and got me a fine looking woman."

He drank two more beers then started to snore. Medora drove on. She slipped a Jolie Holland CD into the player and adjusted the volume. The cookies were stale, but she ate a few and drank all the milk. The bluesy music matched her mood, and the milk and cookies gave her a spurt of energy.

"I'll just watch for the turn off sign for Tamlin," thought Medora. "My new husband is a lot better company asleep than awake."

She began to notice signs announcing off-ramps to Grants Pass, but nothing pointing the way to Tamlin. After seeing a "You are leaving Grants Pass," marker she pulled off the side of the road.

"Charlie, wake up and tell me which way to go," she shook him but he didn't respond. "Maybe this will wake you up," Medora rolled down the side window next to Charlie's face and let the cold rain blow in on him. He snored even louder.

"I'll call Mollie and ask her to get on the Internet and find the directions to Tamlin," decided Medora, but when she attempted to use her cell phone she found they were in a no service area.

An official looking gray van pulled up behind Medora's car. "Oh great, all I need is a ticket for pulling off in a no-stop zone," she thought. "And how am I going to explain an unconscious man to the police?"

She felt hysterical laughter rising to her lips and took several deep breaths in an effort to keep it from erupting.

In the rear view mirror she could see a tall figure walking toward the Saturn. The man was wearing a loose fitting sweat suit under a gray plastic rain coat. He walked over to the open window on Charlie's side of the car, bent down and peered in.

"Are you okay, honey?" he asked. It took a minute for Medora to realize the man was her new brother-in-law.

"Ernest, I was never so glad to see anyone in my life. I'm lost and Charlie is well …" her voice trailed off.

Ernest saw the beer cans and empty whiskey bottle on the floor. He scowled. "Don't worry little sister-in-law, we're going to get you safely to Tamlin. Ma Tom and Fern will probably skin Charlie alive for the stunt he played today."

Ernest opened the door, hoisted Charlie over his shoulder and returned to the van. He dumped the unconscious man into the back seat, placed a rolled up blanket under his head and shut the door.

When Ernest came back to the Saturn he had a pad of paper in his hand. "I want you to follow me, but I'm drawing you a map in case we get separated. I'm also giving you Ma Tom's phone number. You can't use your cell phone in these mountains, so you'd have to find a payphone. I'll keep a watch in my rear view mirror. If don't see your car, I'll come back and look for you."

"I'm an only child, but now I feel like I have a big brother. Thank you so much."

"Don't worry little sis; everything will be alright," Ernest gave her a reassuring grin. "Old Charlie's really a pretty good guy; don't judge him by today."

Chapter Sixteen
Medora

She was glad Ernest drove slowly. The road was a narrow affair made up of hairpin curves. One edge of the pavement snuggled close to the mountain base, but the other side was a steep drop. Signs spaced sporadically along the way warned "DANGER—FALLING ROCK" and "DANGER—MUD SLIDES" and "CAUTION—DANGEROUS ROAD. "

The wheels of the Saturn slipped and spun. Rocks and gravel tumbled down off the mountain as the wheels caught and the car surged forward. "This would be a good time to use the four-wheel drive," thought Medora, "but how the heck do you activate it?" She glanced at the controls for a brief second. Looking back at the road, she gave a little scream and slammed on her brakes. The station wagon fishtailed, slid sideways and came to rest just inches from Ernest's van.

Heart pounding she relaxed her grip on the steering wheel and took several deep breaths. A few minutes later Ernest appeared from behind the van and walked over to the Saturn.

"A broken branch was blocking the road. I moved it," he told her. "How are you doing? Are you getting tired? We're almost over the mountain."

"I'm doing okay," Medora answered, but her voice came out in a ragged whisper.

The sky was growing dark and the rain fell in sheets when Ernest turned the van onto a four lane paved highway. A few more miles and they passed through the village of Tamlin. A decrepit looking Victorian house, Saint Anthony's of the Woods Catholic Church, a small grocery store, the Tamlin Cafe and various other small business buildings clustered around a park which served as the town square. Tiny lights, strung on four large trees, twinkled though the rain and a beam of light shone on the cross atop Saint Anthony's steeple.

"What a charming place," Medora thought dreamily. "It looks like a picture post card."

The van drove straight through the town and then veered left on another two lane road. It twisted and turned through tall trees. "Oh no, here we go again," Medora moaned as she followed the van. "At least this one isn't on the side of a mountain."

Ten minutes later she spied lights shining through the trees, and soon the two vehicles pulled into a clearing in front of a huge cabin. Bright windows glowed with a warm welcome. It looked as if every lamp in the house had been lit in greeting.

Ernest hurried over to open the door of the Saturn for Medora. "I'll bet you're stiff from all that driving," he said.

A little figure dressed in jeans and a blue sweater came out onto the covered porch of the cabin. Long black hair gleamed in the porch light and a woman's voice called, "Ernest, don't keep her out there in the rain. Bring her in. I want to meet her. Ma Tom and Papa Gus have been waiting and waiting for her to get here."

"It's muddy. I hope you don't mind," Ernest scooped Medora into his arms and carried her to the porch.

Medora was reminded of the times Ian had carried her to the house from the car when she was a child. She felt comforted, but at the same time a wave of homesickness rolled over her.

"I'm Fern," the person on the porch was saying. She was tiny, only coming to Medora's shoulder, "and you must be Medora. Come in where it's warm. Ma Tom and Papa Gus will be so glad you are finally here." She grasped Medora's hand in her firm grip. Then, as if the thought has just come to her, she added, "Where's Charlie?"

"He's in Ernest's van," replied Medora. She didn't have time to say anything else because a tall man who looked like an older version of Ernest, and a fragile little lady with a bent back and huge dark eyes were hugging her and saying over and over again, "Welcome, welcome, we are so glad you are here."

Ma Tom, wearing a long black silk skirt and a lacy white blouse, led Medora into one of the most beautiful rooms she had ever seen. Flames in the stone fireplace cast dancing shadows on the ceiling and highlighted log walls which had aged to a soft sienna hue. The polished wood floors were covered with colorful braided rugs. Cozy groups of carved rocking chairs and tables were scattered around the room, and a pair of plump sofas faced each other on either side of the fireplace.

Ernest half dragged, half carried Charlie onto the porch and into the house. He hoped to pass the living room without being seen, but Fern's eyes were too sharp for that.

"Oh, Charlie," she called out and started to say more, but Ernest shook his head in warning,

"I'm going to put him to bed in our old room. I'll be right back."

Ma Tom and Papa Gus had also seen Charlie. The pleased smiles melted from their faces. Ma Tom looked sad and ashamed, and Papa Gus's shoulders slumped as he seemed to age right before Medora's eyes.

Medora wanted to get the happy moment back. Charlie should not be allowed to hurt these kind people. She said the first thing that came to her mind. "I have to go to the bathroom and I'm hungry."

"Of course, forgive me. I feel shame for my son, but still I'm so happy to have you here. This is your new home." Ma Tom put her hand on Medora's arm. I made for you my special chicken soup. It's the recipe of my friend, Manuela. The name in English is 'friendship soup'.

Newlywed or not, Ma Tom was determined not to let her oldest son's very young bride go out to the trailer with him in his drunken condition. She looked over at Fern and nodded slightly. Fern nodded back; she understood her mother's signal.

"Fern show Medora the things we fixed up for her."

"Finally I have a sister to share my bedroom," Fern said putting her arm around Medora and leading her up the stairs. Fern's bedroom was larger than Medora's room in the townhouse. It held twin beds and a double dresser. The walls were lined with bookshelves.

"What beautiful quilts," Medora exclaimed. She was grateful for the invitation to spend the night in Fern's cozy room. "What do you call that pattern?"

"Ma Tom makes up her own patterns as she goes along," Fern replied. "My name for this one is ocean waves. See how the light blue gradually changes into darker and darker blue until it becomes almost black. The quilt on the other bed—your bed—I call 'starburst'. It starts with yellow gold at the center and kind of explodes into orange, red and purple at the edges. Don't let on I told you, but wait until you see the quilt Ma Tom is making for your wedding present."

"Oh, Fern, everything has happened so fast. My head is spinning. Your parents are kind, kinder than I deserve," Medora's legs felt wobbly and she sat on the edge of the bed.

"I think you're hungry," Fern said. "Our bathroom is across the hall. Ma Tom stocked it with special lavender soaps and lotions, and the best towels for you. Go freshen up. Do you need anything from the car?"

"I'm okay for now. Just give me a minute."

* * *

"You were right," Medora told Fern "I feel better after that good dinner. I must get the soup recipe so I can send it to Mom."

When they finished eating, Medora offered to help with the dishes, but Ma Tom wouldn't hear of it. "We'll just put them into the kitchen and forget about them until tomorrow," she insisted.

They returned to the living room. Ernest poked at the coals, and then put another log on the fire. "I wish you could have been with me today," Ernest indicated Ma Tom, Papa Gus and Fern. "Medora's mom is a very nice woman and Molly, the maid of honor, is a real knock out."

"Well, I'll have to let Alice know tomorrow when I have my coffee at the Tamlin Cafe," Fern teased.

"I told you, Fernie, Alice is just a friend. I'm still one of American's most available bachelors." Ernest was used to Fern kidding him about Alice. He and Alice had been dating off and on since high school; it didn't mean anything to him. Alice was free to see other men, he had told her so more than once.

He glanced over at Medora. The poor kid was having trouble keeping her eyes open. "Medora, you can't go out to the trailer tonight. Charlie and I will bunk in our old room. He should be feeling more like himself in the morning. It will be better for you to see the trailer then."

"It's all planned, Ernest. We're going to have a slumber party. Medora will sleep in my room. It's the first time all three of us have spent the night here at the cabin in years and now we have Medora ..." Fern was saying when Charlie stumbled into the room.

Standing there in his stocking feet, he looked small, sad and miserable. "I took the petty cash out of your office, Fern. I'm sorry. I thought Medora's mother would give us money for a wedding present, and then I could put your money back before you found out," he slurred.

"Charlie, you know Mom paid off my debts. She told us both her gift to us is a fresh start," Medora blushed.

Fern hit the arm of the sofa with her fist. "That money was to pay my temporary office help," she yelled. "I have to get someone in soon. I can't handle it all by myself anymore. What am I supposed to do now?"

"It's my fault," said Medora. "He probably used it for the trip to Portland and my ring."

"That's right, that's exactly what I needed the money for," Charlie's eyes darted around the room as if looking for an escape route.

"If it's okay with you, Fern, I can work in your office. I don't know much about real estate, but I learn fast. I'm pretty good with the computer; I should be after all the term papers I churned out in the last four years," Medora leaned toward Fern. The idea of working in a real estate office was appealing. She had to do something with her time and here was a wonderful opportunity.

Fern took a deep breath, "Medora, this is not your fault and you know it, so stop taking the blame for my loser brother. I'd love to have you help me in the office, but won't you be looking for a teaching job or something to do with your degree?"

"Oh no, I mean not right now. Maybe when the baby is old enough to leave with someone ..." Medora didn't know what she had said. They were looking at her as if she had just sprouted two heads. After a second of silence, everyone—except Medora—stood up.

"Woops, the cat is out of the bag," Charlie giggled as he staggered out of the room.

"Oh, no," Medora pressed herself back into the chair as if trying to disappear. "Didn't he tell you we had to get married?"

Papa Gus' eyebrows came together in a straight line. "Did she say 'baby'?" he asked loudly. No one answered, but he could tell he had heard right when he saw the guilty look on Charlie's face. Gus didn't even glance at Medora as he passed by her on his way to the door. "Tomasina, come with me," he ordered.

"I'll be there in a little while, Goose" she replied. "I want to talk to my new daughter about our first grandchild."

"Both Fern and Ma Tom reached Medora at the same time. Fern went down on her knees next to Medora and took her hand, while Ma Tom kissed Medora on the forehead and stroked her hair, "I'm so happy," Ma Tom said.

"If I'd known, I would never have let her drive that Klamath Mountain road," Ernest was saying over and over again in the background. "Are you sure you're okay, Medora? You don't think the drive hurt the baby or anything? I guess I'll make you a cup of tea—or something," he said awkwardly and left the room.

"Let's move to the couch where we can be comfortable," suggested Fern.

Ma Tom tucked a knitted afghan over Medora's legs. Fern, still holding Medora's hand, said, "Tell us about it. Where did you and Charlie meet?"

Medora told them about Wild West Saloon, the art gallery, and dancing together after the Valentine's party. "The rest is kind of embarrassing," she said. "We really don't know each other very well."

"Tell me *niña*, did my son—force himself on you?" Ma Tom clasped her hands to her chest.

"No, we both had too much to drink. I don't remember anything about that night, and I don't think Charlie does either.

"It's been a sort of hard time in my life. My dad had a stroke recently. He's still in the hospital. My mom isn't well either, but spiritually she's the strongest person I know. Hopefully you'll get to meet her sometime soon."

"Your poor papa," Ma Tom patted the afghan, "Will he be able to go home to your mother?"

"I don't think so. Mom's looking for a long term nursing home. When she finds one she plans to sell the townhouse and get an apartment near the nursing home. I'm so glad Dad met Charlie before the stroke. He said he liked Charlie, and I know Mom likes him, too."

Ernest came into the room with four cups of tea on a tray. "Oh darn," said Fern, giving Ernest an affectionate glance, "no more girl talk."

Chapter Seventeen
Medora

When Medora opened her eyes the next morning the sun was streaming into the room. "Finally," Fern called from the other bed where she sat cross legged with her laptop across her knees. She punched a few keys and then closed it.

Medora noticed that Fern was already dressed. "What time did you get up?" she asked, pushing the tousled hair out of her eyes. "I didn't hear you. What time is it now?"

"You slept almost twelve hours. It's after ten and I thought you would never wake up. I wanted to see you before I go into the office. Toss on a robe and let's go downstairs. We'll ask Ma Tom to make us some toast and tea."

After yawning Medora sat up and stretched "Did you hear me get up to use the bathroom about twenty times? I'm constantly up and down during the night; the baby presses on my bladder."

"I heard you once or twice, but it didn't bother me," Fern replied. "Medora, I'm so excited about the baby. I hope the little guy or gal has red hair like yours."

Medora was having such a pleasant time with Fern, she had almost forgotten about Charlie. Talking about her baby brought the baby's father to her mind. "Is Charlie up yet?"

"No, Ernest said Charlie was still snoring like a buzz saw when he left for work this morning."

"Is Ernest a policeman?" Medora asked.

"We have a sheriff in Tamlin, and Ernest is one of his deputies. I'm pretty sure when Sheriff McBride retires in a couple of years he'll be elected sheriff."

"Ernest is a kind man. He reminds me of my father. I think he'll be a good sheriff."

"So do I," said Fern, "I'm very proud of him, but I don't let him know it."

Medora, splashed some water on her face, brushed her teeth and ran a comb through her hair; then she and Fern went downstairs. "Good morning, my daughters," Ma Tom called from the kitchen. "I will fix for you huevos rancheros with fresh flour tortillas."

"Just tea and toast for me, thanks anyway Ma Tom," said Fern as she sat down at the kitchen table. She whispered to Medora, "I'd be as big as a house if Ma Tom had her way."

"And for Medora, the mother of my grandchild?" asked Ma Tom rolling the "r" in Medora.

"A glass of milk, one of your delicious tortillas and some fruit, or juice if you have any, please," Medora replied. Pulling up a chair, she watched Ma Tom moving about efficiently. A long black cotton skirt and plain white blouse showed under her flowered apron.

The door opened and Papa Gus ambled into the kitchen. Not knowing what to expect, but remembering his stern look last night, Medora kept her eyes on her plate and said nothing.

He pulled out a chair and sat down next to Medora. "You certainly took us by surprise last night," he said.

"I'm sorry, I thought you knew," Medora felt like a naughty child caught with her hand in the cookie jar.

"No, it is I who must beg your pardon. I was rude. My only excuse is that I am old, and old people get cranky," he said. "Will you forgive me?"

"Of course," said Medora. "But there is really nothing to forgive. You've been wonderful to me."

"I've been searching in my workshop, the attic and the basement; I finally found the little cradle I made before Charlie was born." Medora noticed Papa Gus's large calloused hands. They were capable hands with the long tapered fingers of an artist. "Ernest and Fern used it too," he went on. "I'd like to refurbish it for my grandchild, if you don't mind, but perhaps you'd like new things for the little one."

"There's nothing I would like more than the cradle you made for Charlie," Medora's voice was husky. She had just met these people, and she already felt like part of the family, but she didn't feel married to Charlie. It was very confusing.

Papa Gus returned to his workshop and Fern went off to her office. Feeling lazy and relaxed for the first time in months, Medora, still wearing her bathrobe, remained in the kitchen. She and Ma Tom chatted together as Ma Tom rolled out and browned enough tortillas to last several days. After finishing the tortillas, she started cutting up vegetables for the dinner stew.

"I have to get dressed," Medora said. "It's almost noon."

"What are you doing? What have you been saying about me?" Charlie burst into the room. His sharp voice cut into the relaxed atmosphere like a knife.

"Good morning, Charlie," Ma Tom's tone was flat. Medora remained silent.

"I asked you a question," he said to Medora, ignoring his mother.

Ma Tom opened her mouth to speak, but instead turned toward Medora and nodded her head. At first Medora was puzzled. Why didn't Ma Tom stick up for her; then she understood. She was Charlie's wife. This was up to her.

She got up from the chair. "I'm going up to get dressed; that's what I'm doing. I hope you're in a better mood when I get back, because I can tell you right now I'm not your doormat." Her voice was shaking and she felt as if she was going to drown in Charlie's moods, but she stood her ground.

She started out the door; then turned back," Thank you, Ma Tom, the breakfast was delicious." She returned to the kitchen twenty minutes later dressed in jeans and an oversized tee-shirt. Charlie was gone—presumably back to bed.

Ma Tom, having put her pot of stew on the backburner to simmer, was at the table with a cup of tea. After pouring a cup for Medora, she said, "Papa Gus and Ernest put the things from your car into the spare room. You must decide what you will take to your new home in the trailer and what you will leave here at your second home. The trailer closet is this big," Ma Tom measured off about thirty inches with her hands.

* * *

Because Charlie seemed to have a touch of the flu, Medora didn't get to see the trailer until two days later. She packed four pairs of blue jeans, a sweat shirt, three sweaters, several tee shirts and assorted underwear and socks into one suit case, the rest she left at the cabin in the room she now shared with Fern.

Ma Tom insisted that Medora take sheets, towels and a down comforter with her. "I am making a quilt, which I promise to finish by the time my grandchild is born," she said, "but you must wait until it is done to see it."

* * *

The day was fair. Rays of sunlight made rainbows in the small pools of standing rainwater. Medora kissed Ma Tom and Papa Gus goodbye. Leaving the big cabin was almost as heart-rending as saying goodbye to Mom and Mollie.

She had to keep reminding herself that Charlie was her husband. If only Fern was her friend instead of her sister-in-law. She didn't like being married, but she loved Ma Tom, Papa Gus, Fern and Ernest.

Charlie, driving the Saturn, was in a good mood and seemed to enjoy pointing things out to her. "Look at the redheaded woodpecker; watch in the underbrush, you'll probably see a deer."

Medora only half heard him. "Will we go through the town?" she asked. It had left a magical impression in her mind, and she wanted to see it again.

"No, my property is in the other direction, but I'll take you into town and introduce you around real soon. We'll have the famous Tamlin

Cafe special."

Charlie smiled to himself. His thoughts were of his beautiful wife. She belonged to him and the pastor said she had to obey him.

It was rugged country, but lovely. Huge trees with beards of gray and green moss crowded against the narrow road. Medora was thinking it was as if she and Charlie were the only people in the world, when she saw a man and a large brown dog at the side of the road. The man leaned heavily on a stick as he limped along. "Who's that?" she asked.

Charlie pulled to the side of the road, "Hey, Carl, come meet my wife," he yelled.

The man looked ready to dive into the undergrowth, but he paused when Charlie called to him. He looked at Charlie, back at the brush covered path and then back at Charlie before he made up his mind and started toward the Saturn. "Lobo, heel," the man commanded the big dog when it started to push past him. The dog obeyed, but the hair stood up on his back as he bared his teeth and growled.

When she saw the dog, Medora decided to remain in the car. Charlie hopped out, "Hi Carl, this is my wife. I'm taking her to see the trailer for the first time."

Carl bent down and looked through the window at Medora. She quickly rolled it down. "I'm Medora. Excuse me for not getting out and shaking your hand, Carl," she said, "That dog looks like he would like to take a bite out of me."

To Medora, Carl seemed like a lumberjack, except he was dressed in camouflage clothing instead of the typical Paul Bunyan wool plaid she had always imagined lumberjacks wearing. He had long shaggy hair, and a bushy beard. She glimpsed intelligent eyes behind wire rimmed glasses.

"Don't mind Lobo. He's all bluster and not much fight. Here boy, come meet the lady." Carl snapped his fingers and Lobo lumbered up to the car. "Sit up pretty. Now say your prayers. Wave to the lady." Carl put Lobo through about a dozen tricks. "Here," he slipped Medora a dog biscuit. "Give him this and he'll be your friend for life."

Medora closed her eyes and extended her flat hand with the dog biscuit on it. Lobo reached over and daintily picked his treat off her palm. She opened her eyes and laughed at the dog's comical expression. "Good boy," no longer afraid, she scratched his ears and he wriggled with pleasure.

"Well, we gotta get going," Charlie said importantly. "I just wanted you to know, if you see some strange woman at my trailer, it's only my wife."

"Gee thanks," Medora screwed her face into a grimace.

"I gotta split, too," Carl said. His cautious eyes scanned the trees. He spoke to Medora without looking at her, "If you need anything—and I mean anything—just let me know." Then he and the dog melted into the forest.

Charlie turned the car back onto the narrow road which had become little more than a dirt track. "He's a crazy old coot," he commented as he learned forward to watch for deep ruts, "a Viet Nam Vet. I guess he was a medic or a doctor or something before he got shot up. I'm surprised he didn't run away instead of coming to talk to us. I don't trust him or his dog."

Charlie was odd. Why did he call the man and dog over to the car if he didn't trust them? Medora wondered, but she just said, "I bet we'll be glad for the Saturn's four wheel drive when the road gets muddy."

Medora clutched her abdomen as the road became increasingly bumpy. Finally they pulled into a clearing. A dented silver trailer rested on bricks at one side of the cleared area; about twenty paces away an ancient barn leaned gently toward the dense forest.

"That's my studio," Charlie pointed to the barn.

"Aren't you worried about the way it leans? It looks like it could blow over in a good wind."

"It's been there for seventy years; it'll probably still be there seventy years from now."

Medora eyed the trailer. It was small, and unlovely. "Well, I might as well take my things into the trailer," she said.

"I'll get your suitcase," Charlie reached into the Saturn.

"This isn't so bad," Medora said, once she had looked around the interior of her new home. "It's kind of like a play house." She hung her clothing in the closet, and then looked through the cupboards in the miniature kitchen. The dishes, pots and pans, and utensils were an eclectic assortment, but there seemed to be everything she would need. The cupboards were stocked with canned milk, honey, vegetables, soups, tuna, flour, sugar, coffee and tea. When she opened the little refrigerator, she found a tube of biscuits, a carton of cottage cheese, and two slices of dried up salami and a jar of jalapenos.

She turned to ask Charlie if he would like a cup of tea, but before she could get the words out he grabbed her and pressed his body roughly against hers. She felt the pulsing bulge in his jeans and concern for her baby gave her extraordinary strength. Without thinking, Medora made a fist of her free hand and swung at him. She hit him squarely on the nose.

"You're my wife," he said with surprise in his voice. When he took his hand away from his face; it was covered with blood. "I'm bleeding," Charlie scurried into the bathroom.

"Oh, my goodness, what a start we've gotten off to," Medora, weak with relief, sat down heavily on the plastic covered bench by the table and giggled. Hitting Charlie had been very satisfying. She could hear him running water. "I hope I didn't hurt him, but he sure has been asking for it. I'm glad he's little like Ma Tom and Fern. If he was as big as Papa Gus or Ernest I would be in real trouble."

When Charlie came out of the bathroom he was holding a damp cloth to his nose. He looked sullen.

"Give me my car keys. I'm going back to the cabin." Medora said.

"You're my wife …" he began, and then stopped and thought of what people would say if she walked out on him.

"Wife or not, I won't sleep with you Charlie. "

Okay, okay—I usually sleep in the barn. I have a sleeping bag and cot out there. Please don't leave, and don't tell anyone what just happened."

With Charlie sitting at the table holding a damp cloth to his nose and staring at her, Medora prepared a simple dinner of canned chili and refrigerator biscuits. Dessert was canned peaches and cottage cheese. Afterward Charlie went to the barn, and she spent the evening looking around the trailer and putting the linens Ma Tom had given her on the bed.

The sheets and comforter smelled of lavender and cleanliness. Medora slept surprisingly well that night. She was pretty sure Charlie wouldn't try to force himself on her again.

The next morning around eleven Charlie came into the trailer and fixed a cup of instant coffee. "Did you sleep okay?" he asked.

"It's so quiet here. I slept like a log," she answered. "Charlie, Fern told me that your family goes to mass on Saturday evening. I'm not Catholic, but I'll go to church with you if you want me to." She was going to add something about the baby and baptism when she noticed Charlie's clenched fists and flared nostrils.

"I think religion is all a damn bunch of fairy tales and lies," he snarled and threw his coffee cup into the sink where it slivered into a thousand iridescent pieces. Coffee dripped down the cupboards. He stomped out of the trailer, slamming the little aluminum door as if it were to blame for his unhappiness.

Medora's insides churned and she felt hot tears close to the surface. Why was he nice sometimes and other times hateful? She had intended to marry someone like her dad, not the petty, angry little man she ended up with.

A flood of memories washed over her. She was sitting on Ian's lap and he was reading her the story of Noah and the ark. "Dad, what happened to all the other people?"

"Well, princess, I'm not sure. Each person must build an ark of beauty and compassion for themselves and their loved ones, or drown in a sea of despair."

She hadn't understood what he meant then, but now she did. It was up to her to make a good life for herself and her child. She hoped it would include Charlie—but he would have to figure that out for himself.

Chapter Eighteen
Medora

Medora stretched her arms and looked around the tiny bedroom. She wanted to stay in bed, but felt an urgent need to use the bathroom. Once she was up, she decided to get dressed, make the bed and start the day.

In the bathroom, she stripped off the oversized tee shirt she slept in and looked at her changing body in the mirror over the sink. Her breasts, normally rather small, were large and firm with a map of blue veins showing under white skin. The pink nipples had darkened and become more prominent. Sliding her hands down the mound of her abdomen, she poked at her protruding belly button.

"I wonder if I'll ever look like myself again?" she thought as she pulled on a baggy sweat shirt and drawstring sweat pants. Even her face had gotten fatter; the only thing that remained the same was her hair.

The quilt, Ma Tom's wedding gift was folded on the back of a chair. After smoothing the sheets and feather comforter, Medora spread it over her bed. As usual she spent a few minutes admiring it. Ma Tom, using blue, green and brown shades of cotton cloth, had fashioned a design which looked very much like the view Medora saw when she stepped out of the trailer. Random bits of blue, red, gold and black fabric made her think of the birds in the trees and the shy creatures on the forest floor.

Medora's life had fallen into a routine. Saturday and Sunday she spent at the trailer. When she did the cleaning and cooking, she felt like a little girl playing house. After her bit of work was done she would sit at the kitchen table and gaze out toward the edge of the forest or go for a walk.

At first she called Molly often. "Hi Mol, what's going on up there?"

Molly would go on and on about parties, cute new outfits, interesting boys, registering for graduate school and petty complaints against various friends. "Eva isn't as much fun as you were, but she's a pretty good roommate. You can't believe what she does! She cleans the kitchen and takes out the trash everyday. I think she's a little anal—but what the heck—the apartment looks nice, and less work for me.

"I'm going to a battle of the bands with a cute guy from the bakery this afternoon. What are you going to do today?" Molly would ask.

"Clean house and watch the birds from my kitchen window; maybe go for a walk if the weather's nice."

"Oh," Molly would reply, sounding at a loss for words, "Well, I gotta go. I'm meeting someone for lunch. Take care." Gradually the calls to Molly grew farther and farther apart. They just didn't have anything to talk about.

Medora telephoned her mother every Sunday afternoon. Talking to Helen was like wading through quicksand. They said the same things to each over and over.

"I wish I could see more progress in your dad's condition," Helen always said. "I hope and pray that eventually I can bring him home, but he's not even strong enough to move to a nursing home yet."

"You know Dad, he's a real fighter. I bet this time next year he'll be in the apartment with you." She encouraged her mother with the same words every week, but lately Medora was beginning to wonder about something Ian told her a few months before the stroke: "If I ever get to where I can't take care of myself I won't want to live. I've had an exciting life and I don't want to end up as a babbling fool who needs someone to wipe his butt."

"Mom, did Dad ever talk to you about …" Medora began, but Helen broke in, "Your Dad will be fine and I don't need to hear anything negative from you.

"I got a hospital bed for the apartment. I'm not sure what other equipment Ian will need when he comes home." Helen had abruptly changed the subject and was now talking in a shrill rapid voice.

"I miss you Mom—and Dad. I plan to come up for a short visit before the baby is born," Medora broke in,

"That will be nice dear," Helen said without enthusiasm.

"If the baby's a boy I want to name him 'Ian' after Dad."

"I don't think that would be appropriate considering the circumstances," Helen sounded as if she had just smelled something unpleasant.

* * *

At Ma Tom's suggestion, Medora fastened birdfeeders filled with grain, and humming bird feeders with sugar water in tree branches. She also scattered corn and seeds for the deer, squirrels, and ground birds. She told Ma Tom about some of the unusual creatures visiting the feeders, and Ma Tom loaned her a bird book with pictures and names.

Medora kept a list of the birds she saw: magpies, jays, and darling quail so plump and proper with their red heads and one fancy black feather sticking up. She was almost positive the owls nesting high in a tall tree were Saw Whets, but she had yet to identify the white birds that roosted occasionally in treetops. Could they be egrets?

At first the forest had just seemed like a bunch of trees to Medora, but she had come to consider some of them old friends. She watched three baby squirrels playing in the branches of, what she named, "the Squirrel Tree". She sometimes saw the mother squirrel carrying corn up to the hollow. Then there was the Man and Lady Tree with its double trunk, the larger—the Man—leaned out into the clearing and seemed to be held in place only by a crooked branch which grew from the Lady Tree trunk to form a circle, something like an arm, around her leaning partner.

When the weather was nice, Medora went for long leisurely rambles along the dirt track that led toward the highway. The first time she ventured out, she told Charlie, "I'm going to walk down the road. I'll be back in about an hour."

That was on one of her first days at the trailer. Charlie's nose was still red and swollen and he sounded a little peevish. "If you have to go for a walk be careful. There's a family of bears living in the forest. I'd go with you, but I'm applying stain to a couple of my pieces, and I can't stop right in the middle of it."

With Charlie's warning ringing in her ears, she started out. The pine scent of the forest reminded her of a Christmas tree lot. Birds twittered in the branches; once or twice she saw a big gray squirrel run along a limb and disappear. She was having a wonderful time—what Ian would have called "a peak experience"—except for imagining a bear behind every bush.

Just as she reached a side trail which led into the forest, she heard a crashing in the underbrush. "Oh, no, a bear!" She froze, too afraid to run. Her shriek turned into a sob of relief when a doe and her twin fawns charged out of the woods only a few feet from where Medora stood. The pretty animals had twitching tails and wild brown eyes.

"Are you alright?" a man's voice called, and Carl, carrying a rifle, emerged from the trees. Lobo, tail between his legs, was at Carl's heels. "Lobo has a habit of chasing anything that will run. Bad dog!" he scolded. "I've been trying to break him of it. I'm afraid someday he'll come up against something that won't run away."

"Charlie told me about the family of bears. Is that why you have a gun and that big knife?"

"Everyone talks about the bears. They get blamed for a lot of things, like ravaged trash cans, but nobody has actually seen a bear around here for years. Tell you what …." he reached up and broke off a dead branch about six feet long and two inches in diameter. Unsheathing his knife, he used it to remove stubs of twigs and rough bark. He handed the smooth branch to her and said, "This is about the right size for you to carry. If you see a bear just wave it around. He'll be more scared than you."

Medora noticed that Carl kept his eyes on the ground and didn't look directly at her as he spoke. She decided that, being a recluse, he must be shy around women.

"Why do you carry a gun and knife?" she asked again. Lobo sidled over to her and she scratched his ear.

"It's just a bad habit I got into in Nam," his mouth tightened. "Gotta go, come on Lobo." He turned once, "If you need anything give a good loud yell. Lobo will hear you. That dog can hear a leaf fall a mile away," and then he disappeared into the forest with the dog at his heels. Medora didn't see Carl again until the night Timmy was born.

* * *

Sometimes she took a cup of tea to Charlie in his studio barn and admired the pieces he was working on. She liked the roomy interior of the old building and the scent of wood, sawdust, and musty straw. It was nice to be there as long as Charlie was in a good mood and not drinking. The more she saw of the furniture he was making, the more she admired it.

Charlie, for his part was usually careful not to intrude on her privacy. He showed more affection to her in public than when they were alone.

In the beginning she was disturbed by his habit of disappearing for hours, often in the middle of the night. The first time it happened she ran out when she heard the sound of his truck returning and asked, "Where did you go? I was worried."

"When you share your bed with me you can ask me where I go at night. Until then it's none of your damn business," he started for the barn, then looked back, "Just give me some space. Leave me the hell alone."

Strangely Charlie's actions didn't bother Medora. He had done so many unpredictable things since she had known him. "I guess that's just Charlie," she shrugged and went into the trailer to heat up a can of soup for her lunch.

She supposed it was his artist's imagination, but some of his drawings and plans were a bit over-the-top. For instance, a couple of weeks ago, he hadn't slept at all Friday or Saturday, but had worked day and night on plans for the house he said he wanted to build her. Early Sunday morning Charlie had been at the trailer door, with reams of paper in his hands. At first she thought he was joking, but then she saw he was serious. The designs included a multilevel house, indoor pool, billiard room, wine cellar and a network of secret rooms and passage ways. He went on and on telling her about the virtues of the house. He sounded drunk.

Finally she interrupted, "Don't you think it's rather large for us?"

"Forget it then," he had said and stomped out of the trailer. His truck sped out of the clearing and she didn't see him again until the next Friday at the Cafe. Neither of them mentioned the house plans again, but Medora kept them tucked away in the bottom of her sock and underwear drawer.

Sometimes Medora thought Charlie was nice except for his drinking problem and unpredictable temper. She was beginning to feel fond of him, the way a mother will for a backward child. When she smelled liquor, she kept out of his way.

Sunday nights through Thursday nights, she stayed at the cabin with Ma Tom and Papa Gus. Monday though Friday, she was the secretary, errand runner, multiple listing filer and what ever else Fern needed her to be at the real estate office. Fern kept telling Medora how glad she was to have her help.

* * *

One evening when Medora was curled on a couch in front of the fireplace, Fern approached her with a stack of books. "I don't know how I got along without you, but your talents are wasted as a Girl Friday. What would you think about studying for an associate's license? You could work under my broker's license for a while and then if you like it, you could become a broker, too. After the baby comes you can make appointments and show property part-time. I hope it's okay, because I already signed you up for an online course."

"I'd love to be a real estate lady, Medora replied. " What's more important than helping someone find a home? Oh thank you Fern." Medora fit her study time into her other activities. When she found time to think about it, she realized that she was busier and happier than she had ever been in her life.

More often than not, Fern spent nights at the cabin with Medora during the week. It was like being on vacation. Ma Tom brought the girls cups of tea in bed and fussed over them. Even if Charlie was sometimes difficult, Medora thought it was wonderful to be a part of his family.

Every Friday Medora got her paycheck, bought groceries, and met Charlie at the Tamlin Cafe. It was usually noisy and crowded. Medora would have preferred to get take out food and go right to the trailer, but Charlie enjoyed seeing people and catching up on the goings-on. She thought Charlie probably craved an evening in town after being alone all week. Friday night at the Tamlin Cafe became a tradition with them

Chapter Nineteen
Medora

"Don't go back to that old trailer. Stay at the cabin this weekend. The office is closed for Labor Day on Monday so it will be a nice long lazy weekend. We'll go to the movies tomorrow. I know you want to see *Beautiful Mind*. That Russell Crowe—what a hunk! And besides, Ma Tom and Papa Gus love to have you at the cabin—so do I—Ernest does, too."

Fern was helping Medora load groceries into the Saturn. She enjoyed Medora's companionship, both as a colleague in the real estate office, and as a friend outside of work hours. It was, however, more than selfishness which prompted Fern's request. She had an idea, though Medora never complained, that being alone with Charlie on the weekend was unpleasant.

"I can't. I promised Charlie, and he's meeting me at the cafe. He's been alone all week; he deserves some company on the weekend. Besides, I know you have a date with the guy you met in Gold's Beach at the brokers' conference. "

Fern stuck out her tongue. "Oh him, I'd whether be with you."

Medora yearned to stay at the comfortable cabin. She felt guilty about not wanting to be with her husband, but Charlie was so unpredictable and he could be obnoxious.

Medora turned to Fern, and blurted out, "I appreciate you," which she followed with a hug.

Fern returned the hug, "You look so cute with your little belly." Medora was wearing one of Ernest's flannel shirts over her blue jeans. Under the shirt, her unzipped jeans were held in place by the wide elastic band which Ma Tom had sewn across the opening. "Is my niece or nephew kicking?" asked Fern.

Medora took Fern's hand and pressed it to the side of her abdomen. A rounded shape, probably the baby's bottom could be easily felt. The warmth of Fern's hand must have activated the little fellow, because he—or—she gave several fluttery kicks against his—or—her aunt's palm.

"Look," Medora pulled away; her voice was tense. "Charlie's truck is already parked in front of the cafe. I better get over there."

She didn't want to say anything to Fern, but he had been disappearing for hours at a time almost every weekend. His moods were getting out of control; it was best not to give him a reason to be angry.

Charlie was sitting at the counter when Medora walked into the cafe. His head was thrown back and he appeared to be laughing at something Alice was saying. Alice, like her mother Bertha, was blonde and buxom. She wore a soiled white apron over a tight neon pink sweater and bottom hugging knit slacks which accentuated more of her anatomy than was pleasant to view or proper to display. One melon sized breast rested casually against Charlie's arm and she also was laughing.

When Charlie saw Medora in the mirror over the cake and pie display, he jumped up and went to greet her. He handed her a long stemmed red rose with a flourish, and she felt ashamed that she cared so little for him.

"An American Beauty rose for my American beauty," he said loudly, and then made a little bow before kissing her on the lips. The strong scent of liquor perfumed his breath.

Many of the diners had stopped eating and were watching the drama. Medora felt big and awkward. She was only two or three inches taller than Charlie, but it seemed like she loomed over him. She was heavy, too. In her sixth month of pregnancy she already outweighed him by at least fifteen pounds.

Charlie was delighted to be the center of attention. He made a show of putting his hand on Medora's arm and escorting her to a booth in the back. "That Alice is a real doll," he said slurring his words. "My brother better propose to her pretty soon or someone's liable to steal her away."

Once they were settled in the booth, Medora attempted to make conversation.

"How is your work going?"

"It's going, it's going," Charlie replied vaguely. "Did Fernie pay you? We need bread, lunch meat, butter, instant coffee—a bunch of stuff—and the phone bill came. Those calls to your mom every week cost a bundle. You have to give me some spending money. You can't expect me to scrape along with no cash in my pocket." His voice was increasingly rapid like a runaway truck rolling downhill.

"Charlie," Medora began patiently. "I got the groceries—as usual—they're in the Saturn and…She was going to tell him—again—that she was trying to save money for when the baby came, and how she needed to pay Naomi, her midwife and the other bills. She also wanted to tell him she planned to take the bus to Portland and visit her parents before her baby was born. She had talked to Fern and Naomi about it, but hadn't as yet worked up the courage to tell her husband.

Before she could begin her explanation, an undersized man wearing dirty overalls walked up to the table. His jaws worked on a chaw of tobacco, the juice dribbling from one corner of his mouth. He plunked himself down right next to Medora. The goatish smell of him almost caused her to vomit. She swallowed hard, pressed her nose into the red rose and breathed its sweet scent.

"Does she have my bread?" the man asked Charlie.

"Medora, this is Oney," Charlie sounded embarrassed. "I owe him some money. I told him to come by and get at least part of it from you."

"Listen Lady, you gotta pay up or ...." The bell over the entrance tinkled and Oney's eyes narrowed and shifted back and forth. Quickly getting to his feet, he slipped through the kitchen and out the back door.

"Why was Oney sitting next to Medora?" Ernest, in his deputy's uniform, moved through the Tamlin Cafe and sat down next to Charlie. "Are you okay, honey?" he asked Medora, noticing her pale face. "That Oney smells worse than ten skunks."

Medora didn't want to be alone with Charlie. "Have dinner with us Ernest," she pleaded.

"I'm starved," he said, "but I have something to do first. Order the fish and fries for me. I'll be right back."

As soon as Ernest was gone, Charlie turned toward her and said, "Medora, I'm really in trouble. You have to help me out here. After all, you're my wife. I need money—a lot of money...."

He stopped talking when Alice came over to fill their water glasses and take their order. Watching Alice gave Medora an idea. "Alice, did you know I used to be a waitress? I was a pretty good one, if I do say so. I was wondering if you could ever use an extra waitress in the evenings."

"I'll have to ask Mom, but it sure would be nice for me to be able to get out of here once in a while."

Ernest returned to the booth and slid in next to Charlie. "Hi Allie," he said. "Did Charlie tell you to fix me up with some of those greasy beer battered fish fillets and a big pile of fries?"

"Ernie, I got some good news. Maybe Medora's going to work some of my evening shifts. That means me and you can see a lot more of each other, go to the movies and stuff, you know ...."

Frowning, Ernest turned toward Medora. "What's going on," he asked. "You can't be lifting those heavy trays. That's just crazy." He looked at Charlie "Tell her Charlie."

Alice and Medora both looked at Ernest in amazement. Alice had thought he would be delighted to spend more time with her. So what if his sister-in-law was pregnant, big deal.

Medora was as confused as Alice. She wasn't sure rather to feel gratitude or anger at Ernest for meddling in her affairs. Of course he was right; she hadn't thought about how heavy the trays would be, and there was no bus boy at the Tamlin Cafe.

"Hey, Alice, can I have some catsup?" a voice called.

"I better give the cook your order and see if anyone else needs anything," she said giving Medora a nasty look.

Ernest waited until Alice was out of ear shot, "I caught up with Oney," he said. "He won't bother you again, Medora. If you know what's good for you Charlie …." Ernest noticed Charlie's clenched fists and twitching lips. He knew his older brother was on the verge of losing control, so he turned the conversation to other matters. He'd find out later, in private, if Charlie had gotten in trouble by gambling and drinking at Oney's place. No need to drag Medora into it.

Chapter Twenty
Medora

Medora sat up straight and rubbed the side of her belly, trying to get comfortable on the hard seat. Her suitcase was stowed under the bus, but the bag containing the jewelry box Charlie had given her last night rested on top of her protruding abdomen. Closing her eyes, she replayed the events of the past week.

She had made up her mind to tell Charlie about her trip when they met for dinner on Friday. That was just a week ago, but so much had happened. Charlie, as usual, had been watching for her. He jumped to his feet when she entered the cafe. Putting an arm around her shoulders, he kissed her on the cheek. Medora's nose detected the odor of alcohol.

They gave Alice their order. The waitress didn't look at Medora and spoke only to Charlie, "Anything else, handsome?" Bending low to take the menu from Charlie, she gave him a good look at her cleavage. This left Medora with an unfortunate view of Alice's rather large derriere.

When Alice was out of hearing, Medora took a deep breath and said, "Charlie, I'm taking the bus to Portland next Friday morning."

His small blue eyes widened in surprise. "No, Medora please give me another chance. I know I can do better. I wasn't flirting with Alice; she does that to everybody. I don't know why Ernest likes her."

She had expected him to be angry or indifferent. His pale face, quivering lips and pleading tone confused her. She leaned toward him.

"Charlie, it's not like I'm going to the end of the earth. I'll be back on Saturday evening. I just want to see Mom and Dad before the baby's born."

"God, I'm such a fool. I thought you were leaving me." His shoulders slumped and his breath came out in a sigh. He lifted the glass of water to his lips with a trembling hand.

Medora tried to think of a way to smooth over the misunderstanding. "Everything okay back at the studio?"

"As well as can be expected."

"I didn't know what kind of lunch meat you wanted, so I got salami."

"It doesn't matter."

Finally Medora gave up and they finished their dinner in silence.

"I'll see you back at the barn," Charlie mumbled.

He left while Medora was paying the bill. She walked back to the table to leave a tip for Alice, and used the restroom before she started the drive to the trailer.

Charlie's truck was already in the clearing when she pulled in. There was a light in the barn, but she went directly into the trailer.

The next morning when she looked out the window, the truck was where it had been the night before. For the first time in over a month Charlie hadn't taken off on one of his nighttime excursions. When Medora took a cup of tea out to the barn she found him lying on his cot huddled under his sleeping bag.

"I have the flu or something," he groaned.

He looked as small and fragile as a child. His body was seized by a fit of shaking. When that passed, he sat up and reached under the cot for a pail. After retching convulsively, but not throwing up anything, he sank back onto his pillow. His face was red like Ian's had been on the day of the stroke.

"Charlie, I'm going to call Ma Tom. You need a doctor. What doctor do you see? I'll call and tell them I'm bringing you in."

"Just leave me alone. I've been sick like this before. It will pass," he closed his eyes.

Medora pulled the sleeping bag over him and tucked it around his shoulders. It was chilly and so she lit the kerosene heater before returning to the trailer. Her concern for Charlie was strongly colored by the fear that his sickness would somehow interfere with her trip to Portland. Charlie could come and go as he pleased, but she knew she would feel obliged to put her own interests aside and care for him if he was still sick next weekend. It seemed unfair.

She telephoned the cabin. Ernest answered. "Ernest, this is Medora. Is Ma Tom there? Charlie's sick and I want to ask her what to do."

"What do you mean sick?" Ernest asked.

"He's shivering and he's been throwing up. Now he has the dry heaves and he looks terrible."

'I think I know what it is," Ernest said. "I'll ask Ma Tom for some of her teas and potions, and bring them out to him. It sounds like he's coming off alcohol, and God only knows what else. We've been through this before. I better stay with him for a couple of days."

Ernest arrived half an hour later and set Medora to work boiling water and making a strong tea from a combination of milk thistle, dandelion root, valerian and kava. He told her to add lots of honey. Ma Tom also sent a bottle of capsules containing ground sea-weed, which she instructed Ernest to give Charlie three times a day as soon as he could keep it down.

"This pill will pull his mind back from the land of dreams, "she said.

Ernest held Charlie while Medora spooned tea into his mouth. They worked together to change his soiled clothing. Charlie seemed to be asleep and so Medora went back to the trailer to make Ernest a bite to eat.

Carrying a tray of sandwiches, cookies and mugs of cocoa, she entered the barn just in time to see Charlie leap from the cot, eyes wide with fear.

"Demons, demons!" he screamed, knocking over the work table. He dropped to his knees and picked up a hammer from among the tools, nails, screws, and shards of broken glass. With strength born of terror, he charged at the kerosene heater.

Medora, unable to think of a way to help, stood holding the tray as Ernest grabbed at Charlie. She screamed when Charlie broke away and aimed the hammer at Ernest's head. Ernest ducked, taking the blow on his raised forearm. With the other hand he twisted the hammer out of Charlie's grip and tossed it to the side of the room. Ernest pinned Charlie's arms to his side and held him. In less than a minute, Charlie stopped struggling and allowed Ernest to lead him back to the cot.

"Oh Ernest, are you okay? What about your arm?" She was trembling. "He could have killed you with that hammer." Medora's voice was shrill and she couldn't seem to stop talking. "He might have burnt the barn down and himself with it."

"I'm fine, honey," His arm throbbed, but it didn't feel like anything was broken. "Everything's going to be fine. Don't worry."

He set the work table back on its legs, took the tray from her and placed it on the table. He picked up the two plastic yard chairs which had been knocked down in the scuffle and said, "These sandwiches look delicious. Let's eat."

After that episode, Charlie slept for almost twelve hours. Ernest remained with him when Medora, as usual, left for Ma Tom's cabin on Sunday afternoon. He called several times during the next few days to report on Charlie's condition. On Wednesday he said, "Charlie's doing fine now. He's up working on a project, and I'm getting ready to go into the office. Doug Simpson has been covering my shifts; I owe him big time."

When Fern and Medora got to Ma Tom's cabin on Thursday evening after work, Charlie was there. He was pale and his hands moved as if they had a life of their own. He put them in his pockets to keep them still. His loud voice and theatrical gestures had been replaced by a subdued, rather shy manner.

"I have something for your mother," he said getting up from the couch and holding out a brown grocery bag in trembling hands, then sitting immediately back down as if standing was too much of an effort.

Medora took the bag and settled herself next to him. "I'm glad you're feeling better," she said as she reached into the bag and drew out a small box made of polished redwood. The top was inlaid with chips of turquoise and silver in a starburst design. "Oh Charlie, it's beautiful," Medora whispered. "Mom will love it. I'm so glad you made this for her. Thank you."

Ma Tom came into the room just then. Medora showed her the box, but Ma Tom didn't look at it closely, or say anything about it. She avoided touching or looking at her oldest son. Medora couldn't remember ever seeing Ma Tom rest her hand on Charlie's shoulder, or brush his hair out of his eyes, although she frequently showed these little affections to her younger children and Medora.

"Surely Charlie must notice the way she leans away from him or takes a step backward when he talks to her. Come to think of it, she doesn't even look into his eyes when she speaks to him. It's very odd," Medora thought to herself.

Charlie left soon after giving Medora the box, even though she urged him to stay for dinner. When she walked with him out onto the porch he said, "Have a good trip. I'll miss you, and when you get back things will be different—you'll see."

* * *

Medora wrapped Charlie's little box in tissue paper, and placed a towel around it for extra protection before she put it back into the bag which she now held.

She thought of how he must have struggled to make it when he was sick and shaky. The little redwood box would be the first really pretty thing she'd ever given Mom. They'd always ended up buying dishtowels and kitchen utensils when Ian and she shopped for Helen's gifts.

"I would hate to get practical gifts all the time," she said aloud.

"Sorry?"

Medora turned to look at the woman sliding into the seat next to her. She was about Medora's age, but seemed worn and tired. Her long greasy hair was pulled back in a ponytail and she wore a poncho, faded jeans and scuffed cowboy boots.

"I guess I've taken to talking to myself," Medora laughed. "My name's Medora; I'm headed for Portland and then Rosamunde."

"I'm Bobbe." She smiled, revealing missing front teeth. "I'll be getting off in Eugene. My boyfriend's there and he got me a job in a bar. I'm a country and western singer."

"Well, good luck," said Medora.

"Look, does it bother you—being pregnant and all—me sitting here I mean—I've been homeless for the last couple of weeks, and you know…"

"Of course not," answered Medora, noticing the stale sweat and cigarette smoke smell of Bobbe for the first time. "Does your boyfriend have a place for you to stay?"

"Yeah, in his car, but he says I can go to the YMCA to shower and clean up before I start work."

They rode along in silence until the bus driver called out, "We'll be in Eugene in a few minutes."

"You sure are brave," Medora said.

"Listen, you do what you gotta do. Are you scared about the baby and all?"

"Sometimes, but I guess all of us got born or we wouldn't be here and so if that many people got born it can't be all that hard." The words Medora had been telling herself for the past months sounded odd when they finally tumbled out of her mouth.

Bobbe looked confused, "Yeah, well what ever floats your boat. This is my stop.

Nice meetin' ya."

Chapter Twenty-one
Medora

"Over here," Helen called when Medora got off the bus in Portland. At first Medora didn't recognize her mother. Helen had shrunk during the last four months, and she moved like an old woman. She had stopped using her special make-up. Her face was a patchwork of puckered scars against tight pink facial skin. The only familiar thing about her was the brown wig, and it needed a trip to the hairdressers.

"Mom, it's so good to see you," Medora tried to cover her dismay at the change. "Here, hold this very carefully," she handed Helen the bag. "I have to get my suitcase."

Medora couldn't wait; as soon as they were in the car she gave Helen the redwood box.

"Oh, Medora, this is the most beautiful thing I have ever owned," Helen said, brushing the bright top of the box with her fingers.

Medora wished with all her heart she and Ian had shown more imagination in the gifts they choose for Helen. This pretty little box obviously meant a lot to her.

"We're to stop by Molly's house. She wants to see you," Helen said.

"I hope she gives us something to eat; I'm starving," Medora said.

"We don't have time to stop for anything, but I'm sure they'll offer us some sort of refreshment…don't bother me with that," Helen muttered.

"Do we have to be there at a specific time or something?" Medora asked.

"No, no, it's just that they might be …." Helen's voice drifted to a halt.

Medora was no longer paying attention to the conversation. She was busy looking at scenes from her childhood. She saw the library, and the park where she had played when she was a little girl. The movie theater, flanked on both sides by video stores, had closed down several years earlier. "Look Mom, there's the townhouse. Doesn't it seem odd that we don't live there anymore?"

"The move has been harder than I thought it would be. The apartment doesn't seem like home, although I'm sure it will eventually, especially when your dad is able to be there with me."

"Will Dad be coming home to the apartment soon?"

"He's not doing well. Perhaps when he gets into the nursing home…intensive rehabilitation …. Don't ask me about it," Helen said.

They parked in front of Molly's house. "Well, here we are. I hope they're home. It looks all closed up," Medora said, knocking on the door.

No one answered.

"Go on in," Helen said, "They said they'd leave the door open."

Medora turned the knob and pushed. "Hello is anyone home?" she called.

"Surprise!" people jumped from behind the chairs and emerged from other rooms.

At first Medora was confused. Looking around, she saw crepe paper streamers and balloons in pink and blue; then she got it—a surprise baby shower. "Oh, my goodness, oh my goodness," she said.

Molly, with Eva, her new roommate right behind her, hurried over to hug Medora. "I've missed you so much. Wait until you see your cake. Edgar made it special for you."

"You're going to love it Medora," Eva put in.

Medora remembered Eva from high school days; she had always been into everybody else's business and a gossip to boot.

"Who is Edgar?" Medora asked, ignoring Eva, "and why does talking about him make you look so happy?"

"His folks own the bakery. You remember Edgar Gelfiner, the tall blonde guy two years ahead of us in high school. We both had a crush on him." Molly was waving her left hand around as she talked.

The diamond on her finger sparkled. "Molly, what's this? Tell me about it."

"They're engaged. Isn't that the most romantic thing you ever heard of?" Eva made the announcement.

"Oh, Medora I'm so happy. Edgar is wonderful, and brilliantly artistic. He's won all sorts of prizes for his cake designs. Come see what he made for you,"

It was a huge sheet cake with a blue and pink parasol painted in frosting on the top. The most unique feature was the hundreds of tiny raindrops which splashed all around the parasol. "It's beautiful. I've never seen anything like those raindrops. I didn't know there was such a thing as transparent frosting," Medora said.

Molly seemed pleased at the compliment. Medora smiled and hugged her friend again, but when she glimpsed herself and Molly together in a large mirror on the wall, she felt dowdy. Molly was so fashionable in her mini-skirt and fluffy sweater; while Medora, wearing her usual flannel shirt and jeans, looked like a hick.

Her wedding ring probably cost less than the tax on Molly's engagement ring. She felt ashamed of the way she had botched her chance for the good things in life.

"I was sorry to hear about all your problems," Eva was saying in a sugary voice, "but it sure worked out for me. I love Molly's and my apartment. Of course I had to give it a good cleaning after you moved out." She placed a neatly manicured hand on Medora's sleeve and the corners of her glossy pink mouth turned up in a tight lipped smile.

"Medora, Medora, come on—we planned the games." Two of Molly's sisters danced around her and pulled her by the hand into the living room.

"Can I hold the baby after it's born? I took a special babysitting class so I can take care of your baby when you visit." Fourteen year old Shannon, the youngest sister, was jumping up and down.

"I'll be totally glad to have your help," Medora told her. "In fact I'm officially naming Molly and all of her sisters, honorary aunts."

"Come on Medora, let's play the games. What do you want first—baby bingo or baby trivia?"

After the games, as Medora was opening her gifts; she told her friends about how it felt to carry a baby. "Since I got over the morning sickness, I think it's the happiest feeling in the world," she said patting her stomach.

Then she told them about her job at the real estate office. "My sister-in-law, Fern—she's a broker—drove me to Salem to take the real estate exam. Now I'm waiting for the results, so be sending good thoughts my way."

"It's too bad you have to work, being pregnant and all. I guess your boyfriend, or husband, or whatever he is must be pretty messed up," Eva said.

Medora expected Molly or her mom to say something in her defense, but no one seemed to notice Eva's unkind remark.

"Oh, I love my job," Medora answered after a pause. "And my husband is very talented. I'll get the jewelry box he made for Mom from the car so you will have some idea of his work. Most of his pieces are much larger, but the box was created especially for Mom. Charlie's in the process of designing the home he plans to build for us on our forty acres of forest. I wouldn't live anywhere else, or have my life any different."

When she stopped for a breath, she realized that most of the things she had said were true. She wouldn't trade places with anyone. It was nice seeing Molly and her family again, but fancy clothing and diamond rings no longer seemed important. Although she dearly loved her old friends, her real home was in Tamlin.

* * *

"I put a futon in your dad's room and that's where you'll sleep tonight," Helen explained on the drive to the new apartment in

Rosamunde. "It all feels rather temporary right now, but I want to wait until Ian is able to help me make some of the decisions. The apartment is small, so I put most of our things in storage. I couldn't bear to hold a yard-sale or call in a secondhand dealer. After all, our whole lives are tied up in those things."

When they got to Helen's apartment building, Medora looked around doubtfully. It was certainly nothing like their gracious townhouse with its enclosed garden entrance. This ugly gray stucco edifice was studded with rows of brown doors and separated from the street by tiny cement porches. Graffiti on the walls was still visible, through the rainbow of paint colors that attempted to cover it. Helen put the key in the lock of Number 189 and pushed the door open.

"It's no wonder Mom doesn't feel at home here," Medora grimaced at the blank walls. The apartment was musty and dark. A big leather couch and chair, furniture from Ian's study, took up the whole of the front-room. The adjoining dining area was overpowered by a massive mahogany table which had been pushed against a wall leaving room for only two chairs. Framed pictures leaned against the side of the couch.

"I put so much into storage," Helen was saying, "but this apartment still looks terribly crowded. I don't know what your dad will say when he comes home. He loves these pieces," she patted Ian's sagging armchair affectionately as if it was a pet dog, "but they looked so much smaller in the townhouse."

The master bedroom was filled wall to wall with a king size bed and double dresser. In the second bedroom the furniture: a hospital bed, a single dresser, and a futon, was more to scale.

"I hope you sleep well on the futon. I got it because I thought perhaps a nurse would have to stay overnight when Ian first gets home," Helen explained, putting a tray with a pot of tea and two cups on the dining room table. "I'm sure I can learn how to provide his care myself, but at first I might need some help."

After placing Charlie's box in the exact center of the table, Helen pulled out a chair and sat down. Medora was exhausted but she made an effort. "Would you like me to help you hang the pictures? Having our old pictures on the wall will make you feel more at home here."

Helen stiffened, "Absolutely not. Where the pictures go is up to Ian and me to decide. Remember, you won't be living here."

"Good-night," Medora, close to tears, carried her teacup into the kitchen and rinsed it out then headed for the bathroom. She had one more day to get through, before she could go home to Tamlin.

"We have to get up early in the morning. We have a lot to do tomorrow. First we'll look at a nursing home near here; then we'll visit your dad," Helen called out.

"Okay Mom," Medora muttered through the toothpaste in her mouth. Helen hadn't even wished her a good night or inquired about her pregnancy and the baby. Come to think of it, there had been no baby gift from Helen at the shower.

Chapter Twenty-two
Medora

It was an autumn day, clear and crisp. Sunshine slanted through the car window providing a warm caress. Helen, however, was too wrapped in her worries to pay attention to her surroundings.

"I've looked at four nursing homes so far and haven't found one I would put your father in even for a short while," she said. "They all smell like a diaper pail and the patients look dirty and unhappy."

Medora concentrated on her driving. Rosamunde was a small, but busy town. After glancing at the map and written directions on the back of the Mount Saint Elfreda Nursing Home brochure, she turned right at Elm Street.

"There's Sunny Hills Nursing Home," Helen sneered and pointed to a shabby two story building. "Worst one I looked at. Just filthy, and all the old people tied into their chairs, moaning and crying."

They continued down Elm for several blocks. When Medora spotted the Savoy Drug Store on a corner she turned left. Another right onto Pinecone Drive, and they were headed out of town on a wide highway edged by forests and meadows.

"We should be at Mount Saint Elfreda in about ten minutes. It must be less than a thirty-minute drive from your apartment." Medora loosened her grip on the steering wheel and relaxed, glad to be out of the traffic.

"I hope so," Helen muttered. "I wouldn't keep a dog in some of those places."

"I think this is it," Medora said.

An enormous redwood stump, about fifteen feet high and twice as big around, supported a billboard which proclaimed *MOUNT SAINT ELFREDA NURSING HOME PRIVATE ROAD* in foot high Gothic Script.

Medora pointed to the stump. "What a magnificent tree that must have been."

"Well, it's nothing but a convenient place to stick an advertisement now," Helen said in her dry flat voice.

Medora steered the car into the tree-lined avenue. In some places shadowy branches met high over the pavement, blocking the sky from sight and giving a tunnel effect to the approach. "I feel like I'm traveling back in time." Medora made an attempt at being pleasant.

Helen pressed her lips into a thin line and muttered "humph."

"Here's the gate," Medora slowed the car. "It looks like the entrance to a mansion."

The guard pressed a button and the gate swung open. He leaned out of his booth and waved them in.

"Or a prison," Helen sighed. Then in a hopeful tone, she said, "The grounds are well kept. I could take Ian out for a walk when I visit. I'm sure he would like that. The poor dear has been in that hospital for seven months." She made a choking sound and reached into her purse for a tissue.

Medora parked Helen's old car in the circular driveway. Walking around to the passenger side, she helped her mother out, and kept her hand on the older woman's arm as they climbed three steps to a wide porch. Medora pushed an ornately carved door open, and they entered a marble floored lobby.

The woman at the receptionist's desk looked up from her computer and smiled, "Oh, good morning. Mrs. Whitman? And this must be your daughter. I hope you didn't have any trouble finding us. We're very private here. Please have a seat." She pointed to a blue velvet sofa. "I'll call Ms. Kelly. She's the person in charge and will be the one to take you on a tour of our facility. If you have any questions, I'm sure she'll be able to answer them for you."

As they waited, Helen looked around the lobby. "This is the nicest place I've visited by far," she whispered.

Caroline Kelly greeted them with a smile. "Hello, I'm Caroline, the head-nurse. You'll be talking to me if you decide Mount Saint Elfreda is the right place for your loved one." Reaching into the pocket of her uniform, she drew out a business card. "This is my phone number. If you think of any questions later on, feel free to call. I'm here from eight-thirty in the morning until nine every evening."

Caroline was so heavy that she wobbled when she walked. Her breath came out in little puffs as if she was running a race, but her round freckled face beamed with kindness. "I'll show you the dining-room first," she told them. "Please come with me."

* * *

Ruby heard voices coming from the dining room. Caroline must be showing a prospective patient's family around. That should take at least half an hour. She let herself into the nurses' station, opened the medicine cart and slipped a bottle of Haldol into her pocket. The narcotics, locked in their own drawer tempted her, so she helped herself to four morphine tablets and four Valiums. It was getting harder and harder to procure the sedating medicines she needed to keep David under control, and she liked a touch of morphine once in the while. What the hell was she going to do after retirement?

The voices were coming closer. Ruby locked the medicine cabinet.

"I thought you had already left," Caroline called to her, "I'm glad you're still here. This is Mrs. Whitman and her daughter, Medora. Mrs. Whitman is looking for a nursing home for her husband." Turning toward Helen, Caroline said, "This is Ruby. She's in charge at night."

Her wig looked like a dead cat and her face was a mess, but the old woman in the dowdy pants suit seemed vaguely familiar. Ruby said, "Hello, nice to meet ya." There was an awkward pause during which

Ruby racked her brain to think of something else to say. She hated interacting with families.

The old woman spoke, "This is a lovely facility."

Ruby leaned on the med cart. She felt as if she would explode. One hand reached up to press the ring which hung between her breasts.

That voice belonged to Helen Trent. This battered old battle-axe was Helen Trent. She hadn't been killed in the fire after all. She was married and had a daughter. From the looks of things she would soon have a grandchild.

How could Helen have escaped? Ruby waited half an hour after the lights went out in the Trent house. They must surely have all been asleep when she put the wadded newspapers and gasoline soaked rags against the foundation. Besides touching the barbeque lighter to the papers and rags, she squirted lighter fluid against the wooden siding.

She watched the flames climb up the outside wall and reach into the bedroom windows to lick the curtains before she ran away. When, two blocks later, she stopped to look back, the house was a pillar of fire.

The next day's headlines read, *THREE DEAD AND ONE IN CRITICAL CONDITION NOT EXPECTED TO LIVE.* It seemed impossible that anyone lived through that inferno. Ruby could see the patchwork of skin grafts on Helen's face and the fused fingers.

Helen may have managed to survive the fire, but Ruby vowed that she and her husband and their spawn would pay dearly for the misery they had caused.

"Excuse me," Ruby said abruptly. Her rubber soled shoes squeaked on the tiles as she rushed out of the room.

The night nurse gave Medora the creeps, but otherwise, the facility seemed exceptionally clean and cheerful. "It's nice here, Mom," Medora said.

Helen nodded in agreement.

They followed Caroline into an office and Helen signed the papers which would allow Ian to be transferred to Mount Saint Elfreda when his condition stabilized.

"My only regret is that I can't afford a private room for him," Helen said, "but of course he'll be coming home with me in a short time."

* * *

After leaving Mount Saint Elfreda, Medora and Helen stopped at The Burger Shack in Rosamunde for a quick lunch before heading to the hospital in Portland.

Helen was embarrassed when she saw the hospital volunteer, Susan, crossing the waiting room to greet them. Susan was an understanding listener and Helen had poured out her complaints about Medora on many occasions. "We gave her everything, and now that we need her she takes off with a man she hardly knows. I stood on the sideline while she monopolized her father's life. He wanted to give her the world. Well, this is how it ends. Ian needs her and she doesn't care enough to be here."

Susan didn't mention Helen's complaints, but took Medora's hand and gave it a little squeeze before she turned to Helen. "Would you like coffee or tea? I know this hospital is quite a drive from Rosamunde."

"No, no nothing. I can't relax until Ian knows I'm here," Helen went to ring the bell by the door into the step-down unit.

"It seems like a lifetime ago since I first met you," Medora said to Susan. "I was such a kid when my dad first got sick."

Susan's smile was sympathetic. "How are you doing? I didn't know about the baby. Your mom never said anything."

"I'm actually doing great. I almost feel guilty for being content when my folks are going through such a hard time."

"That's silly," Susan said. "Your folks need to know you're doing well. That gives them one less thing to worry about—it gives them a corner of happiness in their lives."

"Well, I hope my baby makes Mom happier than my pregnancy has," Medora said. "How is my dad?" she asked, changing the subject.

"Dr. Lee wants to talk to you," Susan replied. Just then Helen came back to say they could go in to see Ian.

"Go ahead," the nurse, a young lady not much older than Medora, said to Helen. "I want to talk to your daughter for a minute."

Helen went to stand by Ian's bed while the nurse led Medora into a vacant cubicle. "First of all," she began, "you are going to notice a tremendous change in your dad. He's not doing well at all. "

"Oh, my poor parents, I wish I could be here with them."

"Medora, do you know if your dad ever made out a document saying what level of care he would want if he became irreversibly ill?" asked the nurse.

"He always said he wouldn't want to live if he couldn't take care of himself," Medora replied, "but I don't think he had anything written down."

"Dr. Lee wants to talk to you and your mom; I'll page her. Remember, your dad has deteriorated. You may find his appearance upsetting."

The sides of the bed were covered with thick pads. Helen was looking down into the bed and whispering, "Medora found time to come see you. I told you she would."

"Me—Me—Medora," a weak voice moaned from within the valley of the bed.

Medora dreaded to see what her strong handsome father had become. She forced herself to go over and stand by Helen. Giving an involuntary gasp, she looked for a place to sit down, but there wasn't a chair or stool in sight. Holding onto the rail, she forced herself to speak. "Dad, I'm here. Oh, Dad, I love you so much," her words came out in sobs.

Ian was nothing but skin and bones. He was curled into a C with his knees drawn up to his chest. A thick plastic tube ran from a hole in his stomach up to a bag of milky looking fluid. Worst of all, he was naked except for a flimsy hospital gown, open at the back, and a blue diaper.

"Why are his wrists and ankles tied to the bed?" Medora asked, pointing at the white bands around Ian's extremities which were fastened loosely to the rails by ribbons of white twill tape.

"He pulls the tubes out. Isn't that obvious." Helen snapped.

Medora wondered what she had done to upset Helen. Couldn't her mother see how heartbreakingly pitiful Ian's condition was?

"Medora," Ian gasped.

"Yes, Dad, I'm here," she leaned down and kissed his cheek.

"Me—Medora. Die me, please."

"Dad, I don't understand." Medora wiped tears from Ian's cheeks with her sleeve and then realized her own cheeks were also wet with tears.

Helen shook Medora's shoulder to get her attention. Dr. Lee was motioning to them from the doorway.

"I'll be right back, Dad," Medora said.

"Did you discuss the matter with your daughter?" Dr. Lee asked Helen when they joined her in the hall.

"This has nothing to do with my daughter," Helen's tone was cold.

Dr. Lee turned toward Medora. "Your father has verbally requested, and physically shown us by pulling out tubes and lines, that he wants to discontinue treatment. That would mean taking out the feeding tube. We are in an ethical dilemma because your mother insists that we continue to aggressively manage his medical condition. Has your father ever made his wishes known to you and what is your opinion?"

Helen was glaring at Medora.

"Oh Mom, I'm sorry, but he told me he wants to die."

Helen turned toward Dr. Lee, "My daughter will be returning to her own life in a few hours. She deserves absolutely no say in this. My husband will recover and I refuse to let you stop treatment. If necessary I will contact an attorney." She turned and walked back toward Ian's bed.

Giving the doctor a helpless look, Medora joined Helen. They stayed with Ian twenty minutes, and then the nurse said they would have to leave because the patient was agitated. He kept shouting, "Die—me—please Medora."

On the drive to the bus station Medora tried to talk to Helen about Ian's condition. "Dad is suffering Mom, and he's begging for us to let him go."

"I won't hear that kind of talk," Helen said. "You and that so-called doctor would let your father starve to death. Well I won't stand for it. I'll have him in that nursing home we saw today before another month goes by."

The sound of Ian's voice pleading for her to let him die echoed in Medora's mind, but she didn't know how to help him. On the other hand, Medora wanted to believe her mom was right. Perhaps Ian would get better and go back home to sit in his leather easy chair again.

"Isn't God supposed to decide when someone gets born or dies?" Medora whispered.

"That's what I used to believe," Helen replied through clenched teeth.

Chapter Twenty-three
Medora

The bus was nearly empty on the trip back to Tamlin. Medora was able to have a seat to herself. She slipped her feet from the too-tight tennis shoes, stretched out and let her thoughts drift.

It was nice to be going home to Tamlin. She had certainly grown up during the last four months. She remembered crying like a baby after the wedding. What a little kid she had been—poor Charlie.

Gradually her thoughts gave way to uneasy dreams filled with the laughing faces of her old friends, Helen's harsh words, and her dad tied to the hospital bed, pleading to die.

The hiss of brakes as the bus came to a stop across from the Tamlin Café jarred her awake. Medora forced her puffy feet into her shoes, but didn't bother to tie the laces. She held onto the back of the seat and hauled herself up. Her mouth had a nasty taste and her clothing felt wrinkled and stale.

She saw Charlie waiting for her by the bus stop. He was resplendent in high heeled cowboy boots, pressed slacks, and a tailored western jacket. His thumbs were hooked in his silver studded belt, and he had a bouquet of orange and yellow chrysanthemums tucked under one arm. With a theatrical bow, he handed Medora the flowers. She noticed his hands still shook, causing the fringes on his leather jacket to dance.

"For me, thank you so much Charlie. They're beautiful. I didn't expect anyone to meet me." She took the flowers, put them to her face and inhaled deeply. Their fresh scent was wonderful after the long ride in the old-smoke interior of the bus.

"I missed you. Are you coming back to the trailer tonight? It's only Saturday," he said.

Medora longed to go straight to Ma Tom's cabin, take a hot bath and go to bed, but poor Charlie had waited for the bus. She thought of the jewelry box he made for Helen and now the flowers. "I wasn't planning to, but I can," she told him.

When her suitcase was unloaded from underneath the bus Charlie carried it over to the Saturn. His truck was parked next to her car. "Do you want to get something to eat at the cafe?"

"I really just want to buy a couple of cans of clam chowder and a box of soda crackers to have at home. Do we need milk or anything else at the grocery store?"

As he loaded her suitcase into the Saturn he replied, "Let's see. I need Cheerios, instant oatmeal, half and half, peanut butter, lunchmeat and bread. Don't get that wholegrain stuff again; I like plain old white bread."

"I better write that down, Charlie." Medora searched in her purse for a pen and scrap of paper. "I'm too tired to remember everything."

"Or what I need isn't important enough for you to remember," she heard him mutter.

Medora, feeling a twinge of guilt, wrote the list, and then read it back to him to make sure she hadn't missed anything.

"I'm gonna get going," Charlie said climbing into his truck. "I'll see you back at the trailer. Get me some hotdogs and canned beans—and potato chips."

* * *

Medora was thankful when Charlie came out of the trailer to help with the groceries and her suitcase. Inside the trailer was pleasantly warm. It was considerate of him to light the propane heater. It showed he was trying.

The first thing Medora did was place the flowers in a water-filled mason jar. She set it on the table and stepped back to admire the bright fresh blossoms. Then she busied herself putting groceries away and preparing dinner.

By the time she sat down to eat, she was exhausted. The image of her dad in the hospital bed haunted her thoughts. "Die," he had said. She tried to picture her smiling parents together in the gardens surrounding Mount Saint Elfreda Nursing Home. She had let them down; the guilt was a knife in her heart.

Charlie fidgeted as they ate their dinner in silence. "What are you thinking about?" He finally asked.

"I'm just enjoying being here. The trip was a little tiring, but it was nice to see everyone. Now I'm glad to be home."

She longed to talk to about her parents and what they were going through, but couldn't confide in Charlie. She would wait and talk to Fern and Ma Tom, maybe Ernest, about it.

Medora watched as Charlie drank his soup from the bowl. She realized the tremor in his hands made it impossible for him to eat with a spoon. "How are you feeling," she asked him.

"Better every day. Thank you for sticking by me."

"I didn't do anything. It's Ernest you should thank."

"Those people.... My supposed family.... Medora you don't understand." He waved his hand. "They live in their own little world. While you were gone I thought about it. You and the baby and me, we belong together. It was preordained." His words came out in staccato bursts. "I love you Medora. I'd die for you. I'll kill anyone who tries to hurt you."

"Charlie …" she tried to break in.

"No, I mean it. I love you more than I love my life. I don't care if you ever sleep with me. I don't care about anything but being near you forever."

"Charlie—stop! You're scaring me. That's crazy talk."

"Okay, I don't want to scare you, but that's how I feel. I'm going to do everything in my power to make you happy. You'll see."

Medora got up awkwardly and began to clear the dinner dishes from the table. She carried them over to the sink and turned on the hot water.

"I'd like a cup of tea," Charlie said.

She filled the tea kettle and lifted it onto a burner. When the kettle boiled, she poured the hot water over a teabag, and set the cup in front of Charlie.

"Here you go," she said.

"Do you have any honey?" he asked.

Her shoestrings flopped along the floor as she wearily walked the few steps to the pantry cupboard and rummaged around for the honey. Placing the plastic honey bear container by Charlie's tea cup, she said, "I'm going to get ready for bed. Enjoy your tea. I'll come back out and lock up when you leave."

"Don't forget what I said. I'd do anything for you." He took a sip of tea. "I need a spoon."

In the bathroom, Medora brushed her teeth and washed her face. She slipped out of her travel clothes and into the baggy sweatpants and sweatshirt she slept in. When she went back to the kitchen to lock up, Charlie was gone. He had barely touched his tea. The plastic bottle containing the honey was on its side in a sticky pool.

Medora decided to wait until morning to clean it up. She felt drained, but when she lay down she couldn't sleep. Images made up of her mother's frail figure and cruel words, Molly's hand waving about with the diamond ring, the big stump in front of the nursing home, and her dad's pleading voice, swirled in her brain.

It was after midnight. She hadn't slept at all. It wasn't just the thoughts. Her bulky midriff made it impossible to get comfortable and she had been up to the bathroom three times. Turning on the light by her bed, she found a pencil and pad of paper in the drawer of the nightstand.

She began to diagram her dream house. It would be a small cabin, just the right size to fit into the clearing without cutting down any of the trees. It would have two bedrooms; one for her and one for the baby, but wait—there should be a third bedroom for Charlie. The living-room and dining area would have a picture window and …. Her eyes closed and she slept.

* * *

She didn't wake until late the next morning. She cleaned up the sticky honey mess. Then, seated at the table with a cup of tea in her hand, she studied the house plans of the night before. This was the beginning of a new day, filled with hope. She could make this home a reality.

The real estate test had seemed easy enough. She must have passed it. Once she had her license and made a few sales she could buy at least a piece of the forty acres from the Weiss family. Perhaps the house should be a bit larger, that way Dad and Mom could live with her when he was well enough to leave the nursing home. Anything seemed possible on this sunny morning.

She finished her tea and went to bundle her laundry into a plastic bag. Every Sunday afternoon she took her laundry to the cabin and told Ma Tom, "Just leave it for me to do tomorrow after work," and every Monday evening she came home to find her things washed and folded.

"Ma Tom, I didn't mean for you to do my laundry," Medora would say.

"It is my great pleasure to do a little something for the mother of my first grandchild," Ma Tom always answered.

Ma Tom enjoyed spoiling her children. Medora smiled thinking of the welcome she would get when she arrived at the big cabin.

She was loading the laundry and her overnight bag into the Saturn when Charlie emerged from the barn. "I don't want you to leave," he told Medora.

"Don't be silly. I have to be at work early tomorrow morning. I'll see you on Friday, as usual." Medora struggled to keep the impatience out of her voice.

"What do I have to do?" Charlie spread his arms wide. "I want you here with me. I told you, I'll do anything for you. I'd even take a construction job if you asked me to. Of course it would mean giving up my art and the important money I can eventually make.

I don't want you to take a job unless you really want to, Charlie. I don't mind working; I like my job. I have something to show you." Medora went into the trailer and came back out with the rough floor plans. "When I start making real estate sales we can buy some of this land. We can build a cabin here. I love this place, Charlie."

Charlie took the plans and studied them. "I really had something bigger in mind, but we'll have to cut down some trees."

"I don't want to do that, Charlie."

"Okay," he took a pencil from his pocket, and leaning Medora's plans against the side of the trailer he made a few marks. "We need a beam here to support the roof if we are to have an open floor plan. We'll leave the high ceiling over the living room and dining area. Lowering it in the bedrooms will make those rooms easier to heat and allow us to have a loft. You can use the loft as your office."

"Charlie, that's wonderful." Medora took the plans from him and studied them. When she glanced at him she saw he was smiling. It was the first time she had ever seen him look truly happy.

Chapter Twenty-four
Medora

The Saturn wheels crunched on the gravel in front of the big cabin. Medora felt the steering wheel press into her belly when she leaned forward to set the emergency brake. In the two months since her trip to Portland she had gained twelve pounds. With a sign of relief, she released the tight seat belt and squirmed from the driver's seat.

She was getting her overnight case and laundry from the back of the car when Fern came out onto the porch.

"Hey, Mama, don't be lifting those things." Fern, waving an official-looking envelope over her head, hurried down steps. "I'm so glad to see you. I called the trailer. Charlie said you were on your way here—what a grump he is."

She hugged Medora and took the laundry bag from her. "I thought you'd never arrive. This notification came from the Realty Board, and I'm dying to see how you did on your test."

"What if I didn't pass," Medora said. Ma Tom and Papa Gus had come out on the porch. "I'm afraid to look," she told them. "Fern, you open it." Medora returned the envelope to her sister-in-law.

Fern tore it open and drew a document out. She glanced at the slip of paper and gave a whoop of delight. "You aced it! Wow! You really aced it!"

Medora burst into tears.

"What is it sweetie?" Fern asked.

Ma Tom took Medora's hand and led her inside to a comfortable couch. "Now tell us what is troubling you."

Medora took a deep breath. "I'm so happy that I passed the test, and I'm so lucky to have you all, and Charlie said he will build a nice cabin for us… You know how he can be…. And I'm afraid about having the baby, but I miss my dad so much…."

Ma Tom nodded. "Yes," she murmured. "Like you, I was far from my family when my first child was born." She placed her hand on Medora's abdomen. "Waiting for the birth of a baby brings both joy and fear, like the two sides of a coin."

"Yes," Medora said. "That's the way it is. Sometimes I am so happy, but other times I feel alone and afraid."

"You aren't alone; you have us," Fern broke in. "I'm going to make us a nice pot of tea to celebrate your new career."

Medora sensed that listening to her worries about the baby made Fern uncomfortable and decided to wait until she was alone with Ma Tom to talk about it.

* * *

The real estate office had red and white checked curtains and a braided rug on the floor. A little wood-pellet stove stood in one corner on a brick hearth. The atmosphere was informal and friendly. Usually Medora liked being there but the last few days had been miserable. Her ability to concentrate seemed to have disappeared. It was taking her much to long to balance the office checkbook this morning.

She felt fat and ugly. The only clothing she could still get into was a pair of old blue jeans and a couple of Ernest's extra large flannel shirts. Fern must have thought Medora looked awful, because just that morning she remarked, "I'm going to take you shopping for some decent work outfits after the baby arrives."

Medora's thoughts were interrupted when Fern sat on the edge of her desk. "I've been working on an idea," Fern told her in a thinking-out-loud sort of voice. "The Weiss' listed their cabin on twenty acres, and the Victorian house, with a big out-of-the-area real estate firm. Nothing came of it and the properties recently fell off the market. I think that was partially due to Oney blocking the roads with tree branches and throwing rocks at the realtors who tried to show the cabin." She gave a rueful laugh. "They weren't able to unload that big old Victorian house either."

Medora gazed out the office window at the Victorian house across the street.

"It's a white elephant, but I may have a prospective buyer. I heard through the grapevine of a group who might be interested in developing it as a sort of a combination art gallery/ bed and breakfast." Fern began to pace as she spoke.

"I was thinking, if you could get the listing and maybe even sell the cabin and twenty acres, and/or the Victorian, you could use your commission as a down payment on your forty acres."

Fern paused to write some figures and a few words on a stenographer's pad. "The Weiss's should jump at the opportunity to get something from those properties. They have to pay taxes, and the vacant buildings are falling into disrepair." She gestured toward the old Victorian house. Several of the windows were broken and pieces of gingerbread were hanging loose.

"Maybe Charlie would like to pick up a little money for doing the cosmetic fix-up stuff on the house. He's good at that sort of thing and we can get the Weiss' to foot the bill." Fern wrote more figures on the pad.

"Ernest will have to do something about Oney—he should have done something about that situation months ago, but he has a soft spot for Oney." She continued, I'm sure you could get an interest only loan on your forty acres, and refinance it when you get ready to build the cabin."

Medora wasn't paying attention to what Fern was saying. She was looking at the main street of Tamlin. She noticed Jake the mailman trudging along with his bag and wondered if he was ever going to retire. Perhaps work was more appealing than being stuck at home with

Bertha and Alice. That family seemed to enjoy their perpetual domestic disputes. Oh well, quarreling was probably their only recreation.

A young woman holding the hand of a little girl, and carrying a baby was going into Dr. Clark's office. Medora had never seen them before, but that didn't surprise her. The population of the area was growing like wildfire. Dr. Clark had taken on a partner and the town council was planning to build another grammar school and a high school.

Fern thrust the stenographer's pad into Medora's hand. Medora sighed and tried to study Fern's calculations. They made no sense to her. "Oh Fern, I feel overwhelmed. Do you think I could work on it after the baby is born?"

"I think you should call Weiss' son right now, and follow it up with a letter to both the son and daughter. A San Francisco attorney is managing the properties, but he isn't invested in getting them sold and losing his nice fat fee. You'll need to send him a copy of the letter you send to the family."

"Okay, I'll finish with the check book this morning and make the calls this afternoon. Then I need to get busy filing those multiple listings." Medora sounded exhausted.

"Take off your girl Friday hat and put on your salesperson hat," Fern said obviously thinking only of the project at hand. "The multiple listings will wait another day." She picked up the phone, punched in a number and handed it to Medora.

"Wiley Weiss here," the voice on the other end said.

"Hello, Mr. Weiss? This is Medora Schmidt with Fern Schmidt Reality in Tamlin." Her voice quavered.

"Is everybody in Tamlin named Schmidt?" Wiley Weiss snarled.

"No sir, not everybody. I have a proposition for you which could prove to be to your benefit."

"I always like to be propositioned by a pretty young lady. Are you pretty and young?" His laugh was nasty.

A surge of anger toward the rude Wiley Weiss gave Medora energy. "How would you like to liquidate your mother's estate in Tamlin? The three properties should bring a pretty penny."

"I can't sell the forty acre parcel as long as that damn asshole is camped on it, and I listed the damn cabin and that fucking wreck of a Victorian for three months without a single interested buyer for either."

Medora gripped the phone tighter and took a deep breath. "Well, Mr. Weiss, I believe my office will be able do a better job for you than an out-of-the-area realtor. I have an idea which may allow you to sell the forty acres. I know you are paying property taxes and the buildings on your holdings are deteriorating. Those three properties are a liability to you. I'll send you, your sister, and your attorney copies of a tentative proposal."

"What about that maniac hillbilly who blocks the road to the cabin and throws rocks?"

"I'll work with the local law officials to remedy that problem." Medora hoped she sounded professional. "By the way, the Victorian needs a little work. I know of a man who does excellent home repairs for reasonable rates."

In the end Wiley agreed to consider the proposal. "How soon would you be able have the cabin and the Victorian ready to put on the market?" he asked.

"Look at the proposal. If it's agreeable to you, sign it and return it. My office will get to work as soon as we receive the signed proposal."

Medora hung up the phone. She pushed herself out of her chair and did a clumsy victory dance around the office.

"Way to go sister." Fern grabbed Medora's hand and twirled her faster.

"Whoa," Medora groaned. She hobbled to her chair and dropped into it.

"Are you okay?" Fern asked.

"Yes, but we have to get this deal going in a hurry."

Medora struggled through the rest of the work week. Her heavy body kept her from sleeping, and her mind felt like a damp sponge. The baby moved constantly. It was hard to think, hard to get around, hard not to be irritable.

Charlie came to town on Friday as usual. "Are you ready to go eat?" he asked Medora.

"Can we get something to take out and eat at the trailer?" Medora begged.

"I want to eat in town. It's fine for you, but I'm stuck out in the boonies all week. I'm sick of you going off and leaving me to rot."

"Okay Charlie, okay, forget I mentioned it." Medora, supporting her stomach with both hands, plodded toward the cafe.

"Gawd, I've never seen anyone as big as your wife in my whole life." Alice, as usual, addressed her comments to Charlie. "She looks like a prize sow all fattened up for the county fair.

Charlie laughed and said. "Yeah, maybe I've got me some twins. Wouldn't that be something?" He winked at Alice.

Ignoring Charlie and Alice, Medora tottered to a booth and found she could barely slide in. She pushed the table forward a few inches.

"Hey, leave me a little room." Charlie, still laughing, had followed her.

After Alice took their order, Medora tried to tell Charlie about the deal she was working on. "Just think, we might own our forty acres in the near future and be able to start on our home. You can pick up a bit of money sprucing up the Victorian house, and maybe there'll be some work for you on the old cabin."

"Wait a minute, wait a minute; I already have a big project in the works. It's fine for you to make your own commitments, but don't be trying to plan my life."

What happened to his promise to do anything for me? Medora wondered. Oh well, she and Fern could find somebody else to do the work. It was easier to hire a handyman than to deal with Charlie's moods. She would probably end up having to get someone else to build their cabin, too.

"Tell me about your big project," Medora tried to keep her disgust with him from showing.

"It's a surprise," he said. "That's all you need to know tonight,"

He was so irritating. She longed to throw the ice water in her glass into his face. She controlled her impulse by imagining him as a pencil drawing and herself as a big eraser.

Alice set their dinners on the table. Charlie opened his hamburger bun and liberally applied salt and pepper, and catsup. He took a big bite. With his mouth full of hamburger and catsup dripping down his chin, he said, "Maybe I'll show you my project tomorrow."

Chapter Twenty-five
Medora

Medora frowned at her pale face in the bathroom mirror. What a terrible night it had been. It had been impossible to get to sleep. She was so angry at Charlie for insisting they eat out, and for not wanting to do the work on the Weiss property, and for talking with food in his mouth, and for a thousand other annoyances, major and minor.

This morning she felt guilty for being angry. The jewelry box Charlie made for Helen popped into her mind. "I'm all screwed up," she complained to the empty room.

To assuage her guilt, she decided to take him some chamomile tea, and to try to be enthusiastic about his new project. Holding the mug of tea carefully, she stepped out of the battered trailer into a gray drizzle. With her feet far apart and leaning backward to balance her heavy middle, she trudged toward the weathered silver of the old barn.. She thought it was a beautiful structure. Although it sagged a little on its crumbling stone foundation, it looked sturdy and comforting.

Rain was pelting down by the time she made her way to the shelter of the barn. She took a deep breath and thought the medicinal aroma of the tea blended pleasantly with the fusty scent of the straw strewn about the floor and the fresh tang of wood shavings.

Like miniature suns, three spot lights illuminated the massive redwood burl standing in the center of the room. The thing glistened in the pools of light. Charlie paced around it, studying each inch with infinite care.

This must be the new project. Big deal. Why couldn't he just get a job? She handed him his tea and forced herself to say, "It's beautiful."

He took the tea, but didn't bother to thank her.

"This piece will be the finest thing I've ever done," he said with a wide sweep of his arm. "If it turns out as I hope I'm going to dedicate it to you, my love. I'm going to call it 'Birth'."

His work table held hammers, bottles and tubes of glue, a can of linseed oil, chisels, saws, drills, a jar of turquoise nuggets and a jar of silver nuggets. Charlie placed his mug among these things, then leaned over and kissed Medora on the mouth. The touch of his moist lips filled her with disgust and she turned away.

With a rough gesture, he grabbed her shoulders and pulled her back against his chest. Her curls gleamed copper in the lamplight. He twisted his fingers in them, and pushing her head forward, pressed his lips against the back of her neck. His other hand brushed across her heavy breasts and swollen belly.

Folding her arms over her abdomen, she fought the impulse to push him away and run from the barn.

"I'm memorizing every inch of you, every move you make, everything you do from now until our baby is born. I want to capture it all in this burl," he said.

It was too much. He had no right. She pulled away. "Drink your tea while it's still warm. I'm going back."

The rain pounded down, and the wind blew coldly from the north. She left the barn and hurried across the muddy clearing. With a gasp of relief, she stepped inside the trailer and pulled the door shut against the storm.

She massaged the lower section of her back with both hands. Dropping her wet shirt and jeans on the bathroom floor; she slipped into her old sweat pants and a baggy sweater. For two days she had been bothered by small cramps. They seemed to be getting worse. It was probably nothing, but she decided to call the midwife. Easing herself onto a chair, she reached for the phone.

Naomi picked up on the first ring.

"Hi, Naomi, I hate to bother you. It's probably a false alarm, but my stomach muscles have been tightening up—sort of cramping—for a couple of days now."

"Hey kiddo, this could be it," Naomi Goldstein-Gonzalez's voice came over the line. "Get your gear out and line it up on the bench in your bedroom. Where's your husband?"

"He's out in his studio, I haven't told him about...."

"Listen girl, tell him right away," Naomi interrupted. "And if there's any change or those cramps start to come more often than five minutes apart, let me know. I can be there in less than fifteen minutes."

Naomi's voice was comforting. Medora could picture her sitting at her big round table surrounded by little girls with crayons and picture books. The midwife was a buxom woman with lively blue eyes and an abundant mass of curly hair the color of lemon pie. She and her handsome husband had three children, all girls, each one a rosy image of her mother, and were expecting the fourth.

"I promised my Memo a dark haired *hijo* this time," she often joked.

Naomi taught Medora what to expect during the last part of pregnancy and labor. She provided Medora with a list of items which would be needed during the birthing process, and Medora had gathered these things in a laundry basket.

Now, after folding her wedding quilt and putting it away on the closet shelf, she pulled the basket from under the bed and began placing its contents on the bench Naomi had directed Charlie to put along one wall.

What is this brown paper bag for? Medora tried to remember Naomi's instructions as she placed the empty bag and a jar of hard candy—cinnamon—her favorite on the bench. The lavender scented oil Charlie would use to massage her back and the rags made of torn up old sheets were arranged next to each other.

Then there were the surgical-pads, scissors, pink suction bulb, antiseptic soap, warm quilt, and diapers. Medora buried her face in a mint green flannel wrapping blanket, savoring the clean scent. Ma Tom had hemmed it using a fancy feather stitch. Finally Medora set out a basin for bathing the baby, and a CD of specially chosen Indian flute music, now she was ready.

*　*　*

When they had first discussed it five months ago, Medora was against a home birth, but Charlie argued that Ma Tom had birthed both himself and his younger siblings, Ernest and Fern, in her remote cabin without any problem. Of course, thought Medora, MaTom came from a village with no hospital or doctor, but plenty of loving family members. Ma Tom knew about having babies, Medora did not.

"I want to be a part of everything. If you are miles away in a hospital, I'll be completely left out of the birth of my own child," Charlie said in a shaky voice, his fists clenching and unclenching.

Medora felt the muscles along the back of her neck tighten. She recognized the signs which indicated Charlie was near an out-of-control angry outburst and knew she must placate him or suffer the consequences.

"Of course I'll have our baby at home." She tried to sound confident, but she was frightened.

Charlie had listened to Naomi's prenatal instructions. "When the labor starts I'll be right there with you," he promised Medora. "I'll rub your back and play our Indian flute music; it will be beautiful."

"Remember Charlie, your first job is to call me when Medora's contractions are five minutes apart," Naomi reminded him with a serious note in her voice.

"Of course, of course," Charlie replied through clenched teeth. He didn't like any woman bossing him around.

*　*　*

When everything was ready in the bedroom, Medora returned to the kitchenette. The cramps were almost continuous but not painful, nothing to really worry about.

Her hands were in sudsy water, scrubbing the sticky oatmeal pan from breakfast, when a giant claw clutched her so hard around the middle that she had to hold to the sink to keep from falling.

"Oh Gawd," she grunted.

This was not the mild cramping Naomi had described as the beginning of labor. Medora concentrated on breathing in little puffs.

With a cold blast of wind and rain, Charlie entered the trailer.

"Damn, we're really catching it," he said, turning the radio on and twisting the knobs to his favorite country and western station.

"I've been so blue since you walked out on me," the music blared into the room.

"Charlie," Medora panted, but he continued to twist the radio knobs for a few seconds before turning to look at her.

"What's up?" he asked.

When he saw Medora's contorted face, Charlie's jaw went slack and his small blue eyes widened in panic. Without saying a word, he backed out the door. She heard the roar of his old truck and the spraying of mud behind the tires as the vehicle sped down the track leading to the main highway, leaving her alone. Her body softened and relaxed as the contraction subsided.

The rain on the tin roof was a drum roll as a nasal voice announced through the radio speakers, "and now a classic country and western blues tune, goin' out to all you broken hearted lovers on this rainy day."

She felt abandoned; it wasn't supposed to be like this. What was wrong with Charlie?

No energy to waste worrying; must get these dishes done before calling Naomi. Her mind was a bog. Getting the trailer in order for Naomi's visit seemed monumentally important.

Medora had washed the dishes and was on her knees scrubbing the postage stamp size floor when she was overtaken by the most vicious contraction so far. The thing was a vortex drawing her down—down—down before it slowly released its clutch.

When at last it let go, Medora checked her watch and noted with concern that the two big contractions had been only eight minutes apart. She dialed Naomi's number and let the phone ring for a long time before the answering machine picked up.

"You have reached the Gonzales' residence. We can't come to the phone right now. Please leave a message."

"Naomi, I need you," Medora sobbed into the phone.

She had never felt so isolated in her whole life. There was nothing to do but ride out the contractions and pray for help to arrive before the baby came.

The labor pains followed one after the other in rapid succession. Sweat dripped from Medora's face, stinging her eyes; her body was soaked with it. She began to shiver; her teeth chattered. Teetering like an old woman, she made her way to the bedroom and curled onto the bed with her knees to her chest. She pulled the blanket over her head.

She must have dozed. It seemed like she was back in her pink and white bedroom in the townhouse. Dad was in the other room with Mom. Soon he would come in to hear her prayers and make sure she was tucked in.

Another contraction grabbed her and drove her to her feet. She vaguely noticed that the trailer was dark now, and very cold. Her fingers turned white as she gripped the bedpost. The urge to squat and push was becoming too strong to resist.

"Where are you Charlie," She screamed wildly. "This is your fault. Damn you Charlie Schmidt!"

The baby was coming and she was all by herself in a rusty old trailer with rain and hail crashing on the roof above her head and the hateful twang of cowboy music assaulting her ears. She squatted by the bed grunting. The cords on her neck stood out like a tangled cluster of ropes.

"Someone help me. I can't do this. Oh God."

Chapter Twenty-six
Medora

The image of Charlie backing out the door came to her mind and her fear was replaced by rage. He had wanted to see the baby born. He was the reason she wasn't in a hospital getting the care she needed. The hell with Charlie, she would have her baby without his help.

The pains were coming one after another, huge bone crushing contractions. Holding the bedpost for balance, she squatted and pushed. Although the trailer had grown icy cold; sweat streamed down Medora's face.

Frantically shoving her sweatpants and underwear down, she managed to get one leg out. When she ran her hand over her perineum she felt her baby's fuzzy hair.

"That's good...that's good," she gasped, remembering the things Naomi told her about the last stages of birth. The baby was presenting head first. She felt calm and in control; she knew what to do.

The rain beat down and music twanged, but that was all far away—in another world. The little bedroom was a safe place, a womb enclosing and protecting Medora and her baby.

She sensed something was missing. At first she wasn't sure what, but something unpleasant had been removed leaving an oddly hollow sensation. The rain still pounded on the roof and the wind still rattled the windows.

The loud music—that awful cowboy stuff had stopped.

"Medora, I'm here."

"Naomi?"

"Yes sweetie, Charlie stopped by my house. He said you needed me and I came right away. Everything is going to be okay. You're doing a good job. Just a few more pushes." Naomi squatted next to Medora. She slid her hand between Medora's legs and felt the top of the baby's head.

"Oh thank God, you're here. Thank you Naomi."

"It's okay, you're doing fine." Naomi pressed one hand against Medora's back. The midwife's touch felt wonderful.

Another contraction grabbed Medora. She screamed and strained. Her face was red and the veins pulsed. Naomi wrapped a towel around the bed post and gave it to Medora to pull on; then she knelt and placed both hands between Medora's legs.

"I can feel the head; here it comes—good—I've got it. Now I have to turn a little bit for the shoulder don't push yet—pant—pant—good …. Now one more big push …."

"I can't…I can't…I can't," Medora grunted as she pushed.

"Good. I've got the little guy," Naomi held the baby up by his feet and suctioned the mucous from his mouth and nose with the pink rubber bulb. He began to wail.

"He's a big husky boy; must be close to nine pounds. He's beautiful. Take a fast peek. I have to get him wrapped up quick. It's cold in here."

Medora watched as Naomi fastened a tiny diaper around the baby before wrapping him tightly in one of Ma Tom's lavender scented receiving blankets. His crying changed to a whimper. He put his fist in his mouth, gave a few sucks, and was quiet.

"I can't believe how beautiful he is. He's so beautiful," Medora whispered.

"Yes, he is." Naomi agreed. "Now I'm going to get you into bed and lay him on you chest—skin to skin. I want this blanket over both of you. Once the placenta's delivered we'll get everything cleaned up.

"Oh Naomi, thank you, thank you so much."

"You did all the work, kiddo. You would have gotten along fine even if I wasn't here to help at the very end. You're really something special."

Medora raised herself on an elbow and studied her baby's red face. It was covered with a white film that she cleaned off with the edge of the blanket. He had a little button of a nose, perfect ears. She couldn't see his eyes; they were tightly closed.

"What color are his eyes? Did you get a chance to see?" Medora asked.

"They looked dark like Ma Tom's, but babies' eyes can change. Tomorrow we'll get the trailer nice and warm and give him a bath. We'll have a better look at him then. Do you want me to call your mom, or Ma Tom and Papa Gus?"

"What time is it?" Medora asked.

"Just after midnight."

"I think I'll wait until tomorrow—it's late—I feel too tired to talk to them right now."

"Okay, you try to rest. I think you should go to Ma Tom's for a few days to recuperate."

"Okay. Will you take me there tomorrow?"

"Sure honey," Naomi answered, thinking how odd it was that Medora hadn't mentioned Charlie, and where was he anyway?

The trailer door slammed.

"Charlie?" Naomi called out.

"Naomi, how's Medora?"

"I don't want to see him." Medora was trembling.

"She's half frozen, and so am I. Get that propane heater going. I'll be out to talk to you in a little while." Naomi said.

The trailer began to warm up. Naomi set the bedroom to rights. She sponged Medora's face and brushed her hair. "Looks like Mr. Man is going to sleep until tomorrow. What are you going to call the little guy?"

"He's going to be Timothy after my mom's dad and Gustave after Papa Gus."

"I thought you were considering your dad's name, Ian, for the baby."

"I was, but Mom didn't like the idea," Medora sighed. "I guess for her there'll never be another Ian. I didn't tell her I had decided to name my baby Timothy." Smiling into the baby's tiny face she said, "Timmy, my sweet Timmy," loving the sound of the name.

"I'm going to ask Charlie to come in now. Is that okay?"

"Naomi, he left me all alone."

"I know Sweetie, he panicked. He has a right to see his child."

"I'm not so sure about that, Naomi, but I'll try to be nice to him. It won't be easy. I'm so mad at him right now."

"It'll work out, Sweetie. Maybe you should ask Charlie to take you to Ma Tom's tomorrow morning."

"No, I want you to do it, if you don't mind. Naomi, I don't trust Charlie to drive the car with the baby in it. Am I being awful?"

"You aren't being awful. New mothers are often over-cautious, and it's not unusual to be angry at the husband around birthing time. I'll be glad to help you get settled at Ma Tom's."

"Thank you Naomi. I'm hungry and tired. There's some tomato soup in the kitchen cupboard. Will you please fix me some? After I eat Charlie can come in."

Charlie was sitting at the table and adjusting the flame of the propane heater when Naomi entered the room. His eyes were red and swollen as if he had been crying and his clothing was sodden.

"God, Charlie, you look like you've been through worse than the mother of your baby. For heaven's sake get into some dry clothes."

"Naomi, is Medora okay?"

"Yes, and you have a fine big son; in case you forgot what this is all about."

Charlie began to sob. "You should have seen her face Naomi. I thought she was going to die and it would be all my fault. I got so scared I didn't know what to do. I drove around for an hour before I thought to get you."

"Pull yourself together, Charlie. I'm going to fix something for Medora to eat; then you can go in and see your new son."

"Do I have to? I thought I'd just stay out here and make sure the heater doesn't go out. I'll keep the trailer warm. If Medora needs anything she can call me and I'll help her; otherwise I'll just wait out here. I'll see the baby tomorrow. I feel weird—I need time to get used to all of this."

Medora drank two mugs of tomato soup and ate a few saltines. "I'm so tired Naomi. I just want to sleep now."

"Okay honey. Timmy's tired too, but if he wakes up, do your best to get him to take the nipple like I showed you. I'm going home and catch a few hours sleep, but I'll be back early tomorrow morning. If you need anything, Charlie is right outside the door, all you have to do is call him."

Naomi looked over at Medora, she was already asleep.

* * *

Medora slept soundly for a few hours, but was awakened by the cold. The fury of the wind and rain continued. She pulled the blankets up to Timmy's chin and got unsteadily to her feet. A trickle of blood ran down her leg and she reached for another of the surgical pads on the bench. She removed the old pad and put it in the plastic bag Naomi had left by the side of the bed. By the time she had fastened the new pad in place and pulled up her sweat pants she was breathing hard. Each thing she did seemed to require great effort.

Charlie must have fallen asleep and let the heater run out of fuel. She decided to go out and wake him up. Calling to him might disturb Timmy.

Medora pushed open the door into the kitchen area and saw she had been right. Charlie sat at the table with his head thrown back, snoring. The heater was off.

Wrinkling her nose, Medora looked around to discover the source of an unusual odor. Two mason jars, filled with clear liquid, sat on the sink. Letting go of the door, she wobbled across the room using a chair, and then the sink for support. She unscrewed one of the jars and sniffed.

"This must be Oney's moonshine," she whispered. A bolt of pure hatred for Charlie and his weaknesses zigzagged through her body.

That's where he went when he left. He knew she was all alone. It's a miracle he even remembered to get Naomi.

She unscrewed the tops of the jars and emptied their contents into the sink. Propelled by anger, she walked the two steps to the table without needing to hold anything for support. An almost empty jar containing an ounce or so was on the table near Charlie's hand. As she was reaching for it, Charlie's eyes opened and he sat up.

"Oh, no you don't," he said. He playfully pushed her away and tilted the jar to drain the remaining liquid.

It took him three tries to get to his feet. He staggered toward the sink. He saw the two empty jars and stiffened. "What the hell happened here?" His face was white and bubbles of spittle formed at the corners of his mouth,

Medora was frightened. She remembered Charlie charging at the heater and hitting Ernest. She must protect her baby. Blocking the bedroom door with her body, she looked around for a weapon. Her walking stick was by the back door. Taking a quick step, she grabbed it and then went back to guard the bedroom door. She steadied herself by leaning on the stick and stared hard at her intoxicated husband. He wouldn't dare try to get into the bedroom.

"What the hell did you do that for?" he asked Medora adding a whine to his bellow. "You don't understand. I can't get through this without a little help. You don't know how it is. You didn't see the expression on your face. I thought you were going to die, then what would happen to me? Now I have to go out in the storm to get some more hooch and it's your fault. I don't deserve all this grief."

Charlie grabbed his truck keys from the table and pushed the back door open. He didn't bother to close it. The door swung back and forth—open, shut—open, shut. Each time it opened a torrent of rain blew into the trailer.

Medora was trying to close it, when she heard the engine of Charlie's truck, and saw the lights as it backed up and turned it toward the track. There was a crack, loud enough to be audible above the storm. A large branch broke from a swaying tree and landed on the hood of Charlie's truck.

As Medora watched, he got out of his truck and tugged at the branch. When he couldn't budge it, he ran back to the Saturn. Opening the driver's door, he got in.

Medora wondered where she had put her keys. She usually dropped them into the pocket of her coat, or into her backpack. What would she do if he demanded the keys?

He was out of the Saturn and running toward the trailer when Medora heard another crack, much louder than the first. This time it was the whole tree that crashed to the ground, landing on Charlie.

"Charlie," Medora screamed and ran down the steps to the place she had last seen him. Frantic, she pulled and pushed at the fallen tree. The warmth provided by a gush of blood felt good on her leg, until she realized what it must be. "The baby," she moaned and turned to go back to the trailer. Blackness washed over her and she fell.

Chapter Twenty-seven
Medora

Lobo's legs moved in his sleep. His ears twitched and he gave a low moan. Seconds later he was on his feet, alert and ready for action. Some remnant of his primordial nature sensed danger. A rumbling growl came from his throat and the hair on his back bristled. Amber eyes blazing, he raised his head and unleashed a long howl, chillingly expressive of fear and urgency. Then he was running back and forth between Carl and the outside door.

"Shut-up Lobo damn you!"

The dog, usually so well behaved, didn't shut-up. His barking and howling became louder as he scratched desperately at the door.

"What the hell is wrong with you?" Carl screamed reaching for the pistol that lay on a nearby table. Thunderstorms stretched him to the limit. It took all of his concentration to hang on to reality. Please Lord, he didn't want to go through another flashback. God those were terrible. The smells, the sounds, the shape of objects—it was the same as being back in Nam.

Unspeakable images were seared into his brain, inscribed indelibly on his reality. They were always there, lurking on the edge of his consciousness.

When he first arrived back in the states he thought he'd be okay once he got past the chanting crowds which lined up to welcome the returning warriors with curses and spit. He soon discovered he would never be okay again. Loud noises, or being touched, or someone coming up on him quietly, could catapult him back into the midst of the horror.

For a while he escaped by sleeping, but then his dreams turned into nightmares and, asleep or awake, he was doomed to live the same hell over and over.

About seven months ago he'd had the worst flashback yet. When he came back to reality he found himself with the cocked semi-automatic in his hand pressed against his temple. Shit, the safety was off. He always carried it with the magazine full and a chambered round. A little pressure on the trigger and it would have been all over.

By some sort of minor miracle he hadn't had a bad flashback since Medora came to Tamlin. She was spunky and hopeful, like Janet had been. Having her around made the world better. He watched her from the woods when she went walking, just to make sure she was safe. It wasn't good for a young lady, especially one that pregnant, to be wandering around on her own.

Sometimes he and Lobo hiked the narrow trail through the woods to a place above the clearing where the trailer and barn sat. They went there to stand guard duty whenever they heard Charlie's truck leave in the middle of the night. Carl didn't know what it was, but he had a premonition the girl was in some sort of peril.

He sure as hell didn't want anything to happen to her. She had set him to seeing things in a new light. If it wasn't for Nam, he probably would have finished med school and settled down with Janet. They might have had a daughter like Medora.

Medora's old man should never have let her marry someone like that weak-ass Charlie Schmidt. Pregnant or not, he should have kept his sweet little girl from marrying that loser.

Thunder shook the sturdy little one room cabin. A bolt of lightening exploded into a tree nearby, and a branch crashed to the ground. Carl put a couch cushion over his head in an attempt to block out the sounds of the storm.

Lobo barked incessantly. For a moment Carl was afraid the dog's noise would give their position away. "Shut up," he screamed and pointed the forty-five at Lobo. His hand began to shake and he let the gun drop onto the couch. "God what am I doing. This isn't Nam, it's just an Oregon storm."

He looked at his dog and was frightened at how close he had come to pulling the trigger. "Come Lobo." The frenzied dog ran to Carl, nudged him and then took Carl's pant leg in his teeth and began to pull.

"What's wrong with you? Why do you want to go out in the storm? Let go, damn it." Lobo gave one final tug before charging across the room. He jumped to the table, knocking books and dishes onto the floor, and leapt through the window with a crash of glass. The big animal ran through the trees, his howling harmonizing with the fury of the storm.

Forcing his arms into his canvas jacket, Carl grabbed a flashlight and hobbled out the door yelling, "Lobo, Lobo—LOBO!"

The dog's barking seemed to come from the trail. Carl, wishing he had a walking-stick, jogged in that direction. Branches, twigs and slippery pine needles littered the ground. He fell, but quickly scrambled to his feet. Sliding, pushing and crawling, he kept going, driven by a sense of urgency. The feral howl of his dog was still distinguishable above the noise of the storm.

Putting three fingers into his mouth, Carl produced an earsplitting whistle, but the dog didn't return to him. Lobo sounded farther away now; like he was heading north toward Charlie's place. Carl quickened his pace. His damaged leg and hip throbbed. His knee kept giving out and three more times he pitched forward, but each time he got up and continued his unsteady trot through the pouring rain.

A massive tree trunk with branches protruding every which way completely blocked the lane leading to the clearing. Carl held the flashlight in his mouth and clawed through the tangle. He saw some sort of blue metal under the debris. Holy crap, it was Charlie's truck.

Carl shined the flashlight into the truck, but didn't see anyone in the cab. He continued to work his way over the mass of tree trunks and broken branches. Lobo was somewhere close by; his howls had turned to snuffling.

Carl saw a booted foot sticking out from under a giant tree trunk. "Charlie—oh shit, don't do this now you stupid bastard." Carl's thoughts went to Medora and the baby she carried, then to Ma Tom and the rest of the family. He twisted and turned until he was able to reach the body.

The tree trunk was too heavy to move. It covered the shoulders and head, Carl couldn't see the face, but through the leaves and twigs he glimpsed a piece of branch lodged deep in someone's chest. Carl put his hand on the deathly still torso. When he pulled it away it was slick with blood. In the beam of the flashlight he could see a large pool of rain diluted blood around the corpse.

It must have gone right through the aorta. It was probably Charlie under there—whoever it was—they died quickly.

He closed his eyes, "too much death," he whispered. Lobo was whining, over near the trailer. Carl started to stand, but changed his mind. His hip and knee hurt too damn bad.

With the flashlight in his mouth he crawled through the mud toward the sound of the dog. He saw Lobo standing guard over a dark shape. Oh God, it was the girl.

"Medora," Carl yelled and pushed himself to his feet. Ignoring the pain, he ran to where she lay.

"Good dog, good boy." Pushing Lobo aside, he hoisted Medora over his shoulder. It was the same rescue carry he had he used to transport a wounded buddy in Nam when the stretcher bearers were too chicken-shit scared to help out.

His training as a medic kicked in and he automatically noted Medora's shallow breathing and icy cold extremities. He had to get her to a warm place and into some dry clothing.

The door to the trailer was blowing back and forth in the wind. Carl winced with pain as he climbed the three steps. "Come Lobo," he called. The dog clambered up after him; crawled under the table and settled down with his head on his paws.

Carl carried Medora into the bedroom and laid her on the bed. When he reached for pillows to place under her feet, he saw the sleeping baby. Except for the face it was covered by a down comforter. Its head was wrapped in a flannel blanket, thank God it looked okay.

"I gotta elevate her feet and get some heat in here before I call for help. Please Lord, let that phone be working."

Carl pulled the trailer door shut and fastened it securely. "Good boy, Lobo," he said again to the dog. First he replaced the empty propane bottle with a full one; then he lit the heater and the oven. He let the door of the oven hang open and placed a folded blanket on it to warm. When that was done, he reached for the phone and dialed 911.

"911, please state your emergency," a man's voice said.

"This is Carl McGee. There's been an accident. A man is dead and I have a woman here who just gave birth."

"What is the woman's status?" the voice broke in.

"Her pulse is weak and rapid; her respirations are shallow. It looks like she's hemorrhaging, and she was out in the storm for—I'm not sure how long—at least half an hour. She's probably in shock. The baby seems to be fine."

"Please state the location?" the voice said.

"Notify Tamlin Deputy Sheriff Ernest Schmidt, he knows the location. It's his brother's family. Send an ambulance. It won't be able to get through, but we'll bring the mother and the baby up to the main road. I don't know the phone number here. I'm going to hang up and see what I can do for the new mother."

Carl grabbed the now warm blanket from the stove door and put several folded towels in its place. After removing Medora's wet sweat pants and tee shirt, he wrapped her in the warm blanket. He saw that her pants were soaked with bright red blood. He removed the surgical pads and fastened a double layer of fresh pads, from the bench next to the bed, into the belt around her waist.

Her eyelids fluttered. "Where's Timmy?" she asked weakly.

"Stimulant, we need a stimulant," Carl muttered

The coffee pot on the stove caught his eye. It contained a few ounces of bitter black liquid. Carl lit the burner. When he judged the coffee was hot enough, he poured it into a mug, added three heaping spoonfuls of sugar and stirred.

Supporting the Medora's head, he spooned the warm liquid into her mouth. A bit of color crept back into her face.

"Where's my baby?" she again asked.

"He's asleep. Just hang on, young lady. Everything's going to be fine. Help will be here soon," Carl said.

"I killed my husband. I killed Charlie. If I hadn't poured the liquor out, he would still be alive. Oh my God, oh my God. He's out there in the rain and I killed him. Oh my poor baby."

Carl didn't speak again. Instead he gathered Medora into his arms and held her against his chest rocking her back and forth, as if she were a child.

"You see, he only wanted to celebrate Timmy's birth. There's nothing wrong with that. He wasn't doing …."

"You didn't kill anybody," Carl whispered. "The tree fell on Charlie; it could have just as well fallen into the clearing, or on the trailer. It was an act of nature. Stop blaming yourself. Think about your baby. You have to think about your baby. Think about your baby." His voice was a lullaby.

Her eyes closed again. She was too pale. He laid her back on the bed, adjusted the pillows under her feet, and went to retrieve the warm towels from the oven door. As he wrapped one towel around her feet and one around her wet hair, he thought about getting Medora and her baby to the road.

"This damn leg!" he thought. "There's the stick I made for her by the door. I can lean on that and carry the baby under my coat. The little guy will be warm enough, at least for the time it takes us to hike the trail through the forest. Ernest is a big strong fellow, he can carry the girl. There should be some sort of a slicker in the closet to wrap around her."

* * *

Doug Simpson was on duty when the call came through. He was sitting in the Sheriff's chair with his feet on the desk. The log book was in his hand, but his eyes were closed. When the two-way radio started crackling it took him a moment to get awake enough to respond.

"Emergency out your way," the dispatcher said, "man dead, injured woman and baby. Caller said to get a hold of Ernest Schmidt. Said, it's his family. I'm sending an ambulance. Caller said it wouldn't be able to get through. You'll have to get the injured parties up to the main road."

As soon as the dispatcher stopped speaking Doug said, "Copy that." He looked at the clock. It was four a.m. He reached for the phone.

Ernest sounded sleepy when he answered. "Deputy Schmidt here."

"Listen, Ernie something's gone wrong at your brother's place. The dispatcher called for an ambulance. I'll meet you there. "

"I'm on my way," Ernest was wide awake.

As Doug pulled on his jacket he was thinking of how Charlie never gave anybody anything but grief—Charlie was too mean to be dead—the dispatcher must have been wrong. It must be the girl, Medora. She was probably having the baby, and what a night she picked. Grabbing the first aid kit and his flashlight, he headed out to his jeep

Chapter Twenty-eight
Medora

Carl heard the door open, and then Ernest's frantic voice calling out, "Medora!"

"It's okay. She's in here," Carl called back, "bleeding pretty bad; we got to get her and the baby out to the main road to the ambulance."

"She had the baby! Is it all right? Oh my God, Medora. What happened?" Ernest, usually so calm, sounded hysterical.

"Far as I can tell the baby is fine. It was cold in here, but the little guy is all bundled up under a down comforter," Carl said.

Ernest entered the bedroom. When he saw the baby's rosy face and Medora lying pale and still, he began to tremble.

Carl went on, "It's the girl I'm worried about. She was outside the trailer when Lobo found her. She must have tried to move that tree off Charlie." Carl's voice was steady and matter-of-fact.

He took note of Ernest's pinched lips and wide eyes. The poor guy was close to losing it. Seeing his brother's feet sticking out from under the tree must have been a shock. Carl had to help him hold it together

Glancing sideways at Ernest, Carl said, "Did you see the body? I'm pretty sure it's Charlie. He didn't suffer; it was fast."

"Good," Ernest replied shortly, waving his hand as if to shoo away a fly, and immediately changing the subject. "How are we going to get Medora and the baby up to the main road?" His voice was shrill and rapid. "There's no way an ambulance could get over the track to the clearing. I was only a few yards off the main road when I bogged down, and that's with my four wheel drive. I ran the rest of the way and had to climb over trees and branches. No way can a vehicle make it."

Carl gave him a look. Could Ernest be that indifferent to his brother's death? He must be in denial, unable to take it all in. Carl decided not to say anymore about Charlie until Ernest was calmer.

"I got it all planned out," Carl said, speaking slowly and in short sentences, a technique he knew was effective when dealing with panic stricken people. "I'll take the baby inside my jacket. We'll wrap the girl in a slicker. Can you carry her to the road? It's a mile by the trail through the woods."

Now that he knew there was something he could do to help, Ernest seemed to settle down. "I can carry her as many miles as I need to," he replied.

"Ernest," Carl said, deciding he should know of the situation surrounding Charlie's death, "She thinks it was her fault. She poured his booze down the drain and he was going out for more when the tree fell on him."

Ernest started to speak, but the door opened.

Doug stepped in and pulled the door shut against the cold and rain. "I had to hike in from the main road. Ernest, I think it's Charlie under that tree trunk and I'm pretty sure he's dead. I'm so sorry."

"Listen Doug," Ernest was once more in control. "We have to get Medora and the baby to the hospital." He nodded toward Carl, "Carl has it figured out. We're going to carry them up to the main road; the ambulance will meet us there."

He looked at the toes of his boots and took a deep breath before resuming. "We'll need to have a couple of guys with chainsaws out here before we can remove the body—Charlie's body—but all I can think about right now is my sister-in-law and her baby."

His voice trembled as he said, "I'd sure appreciate it if you'd file the report and clean up things on this end. I'll call my folks and Fern from the hospital as soon as I know how Medora and the baby are doing."

"Don't worry Ernest. I'll take care of things here," Doug said.

Using one of the small flannel blankets, Carl made a sling for the baby, which he slipped over his shoulder. When he was satisfied with the baby's position, he put his coat on and buttoned it over the little bundle, making sure there was a breathing space.

Then Carl helped Ernest wrap Medora's unconscious body in the slicker. When that was done Ernest lifted her, leaning slightly back to adjust her weight in his arms.

The rain was a gentle, but persistent, downpour when they left the trailer. It looked like the storm had spent its fury.

"Come Lobo," Carl called. The dog bounded ahead of them. Because Carl knew the trail he went first. Leaning heavily on the walking-stick, he hobbled along, favoring his left knee, but keeping up a steady pace.

The sky began to lighten in the east. Ernest twisted his hand so he could see his watch; it was a little after six. The rain had changed to a light drizzle, but the ground was sodden. His feet sank several inches into the mud with each step. It was like walking in cement shoes. He kept the slicker over Medora's face to protect her from the dampness and trudged along behind Carl.

Images whirred through his mind as he automatically put one foot in front of the other: Charlie making him a whistle for his birthday when he was seven; Charlie taking it back and crushing it under his foot the next day; Charlie crying on Christmas Eve—not wanting to open his presents—for some reason no one in the family could understand; Charlie pushing, pinching and shoving and then crying when Fern and Ernest wouldn't play with him. Ernest's mind was reviewing a movie from the past and he couldn't find the button to turn it off.

They had walked for what seemed like hours, but was probably more like thirty minutes, when Carl called, "We cut up this draw for about fifty yards and we'll be at the main highway."

The baby was starting to move around under his coat. The poor little guy was hungry. "Just hang on for a few more minutes," Carl whispered.

They climbed up out of the draw and felt pavement under their feet.

"How's she doing?" Carl asked Ernest.

"She's white as a sheet and hasn't opened her eyes. God, Carl, she's got to be okay. She's just a kid. How's the baby?"

"The little guy is fine. He's been making gurgling noises like he's getting hungry and he might need a dry diaper." Carl's forced laugh came out in a harsh croak.

The two men leaned against a moss covered boulder. Lobo, tail between his legs, came to stand by them. No ambulance was in sight yet.

"Where is it?" Ernest asked impatiently.

"They'll be here. Remember they have to come all the way from Gold Beach," Carl said.

They waited without speaking until Carl broke the silence, "I'm sorry as hell about your brother, Ernest.

"I'm not," Ernest replied. "You probably think that's harsh. It's not that I didn't care about Charlie—I cared a lot—but there was something wrong with him.

"I was worried all the time that he would hurt Medora. When we were little kids he was always after Fern or me. Once he pushed Fern off the porch, then stood there laughing at her when she cried. It turned out she had a broken arm. Fern and I stuck together when we were little. It was us against our big brother."

He rolled his shoulders, trying to ease his aching muscles, and then went on, "Ma Tom kept a close eye on things. I don't think she trusted Charlie. He was always watching for a chance to hurt someone, or something smaller than himself. "

Ernest's lips twisted into a humorless smile, "When we got older and I got bigger than him, he was usually decent, but he could lose it at the drop of a hat—especially when he was drinking. He was my brother, but it was all I could do to stand by and watch the way he treated Medora. She's a real sweet girl. She sure as heck deserves better than someone like Charlie."

He looked at Medora's white face, "The worst thing is, I knew he wouldn't be safe around a baby—say it got to crying or something and he lost his temper.... "

"I hear the siren," Carl said, not commenting on what Ernest told him. He had suspected something wasn't quite right with Charlie.

The ambulance crested the hill and slowed. Ernest, carrying Medora, walked to the edge of the road.

"I'm going with the ambulance," Ernest called to Carl. "Will you be okay? You're limping pretty bad."

"I'm fine," Carl told him. "You just take care of your sister-in-law and your nephew." The baby whimpered, and then began a lusty wail which was lost in the sound of the approaching siren. Carl unbuttoned his coat, put his arms around the baby, and rocked him side to side.

The ambulance had pulled up near where they were standing. Two men jumped out, ran around to the back, and lifted out a stretcher.

Carl watched as Ernest placed Medora on the stretcher. Bending his neck, Carl kissed baby's forehead.

Ernest came back to where Carl was standing and held out his arms.

At that moment Carl almost hated Ernest. For the first time since Viet Nam he felt connected to the human race. Now Ernest was casually assuming responsibility for, what Carl had been thinking of as, his family.

He lifted the crying baby from the improvised sling and handed him to Ernest. The place where the baby had been, next to his heart, felt empty.

"Come, Lobo," Carl said. He started back down the trail, leaning heavily on Medora's walking stick.

"Carl—thanks—I don't know why you were there or how you knew what to do, but you saved their lives. I'll stop by and let you know how they are doing," Ernest called. Holding the baby in his arms, he climbed into the passenger seat of the ambulance and it roared away, sirens shrieking.

Chapter Twenty-nine
Medora

Ernest tried to concentrate on one of the outdated waiting-room magazines, but even Popular Mechanics and National Geographic, two of his favorites, failed to hold his attention. He got up, stretched, and went to pace in the hallway. He should call Fern, but he wanted to talk to the doctor first. It was after nine AM; what was taking so long for the love of Pete?

A silver-haired woman dressed in pink approached him, "Is there anything I can do for you, sir? Would you like to make a phone call, or I could get you a cup of coffee?"

Ernest was uncharacteristically annoyed. "No, the only thing I want is for someone to tell me how my sister-in-law and nephew are. It's been over two hours since they went into the ER." Then he realized how brusque he sounded and apologized, 'I'm sorry. I don't mean to be rude. Perhaps a cup of coffee would be just the thing to calm my nerves."

"You don't need to apologize, sir. I understand how difficult waiting can be. My husband died in this hospital two years ago—heart attack—it took four hours for them to come out and tell me." After imparting that cheerful bit of information, she went in search of a cup of coffee.

Another hour passed before a doctor, wearing a white lab coat, called, "Mr. Schmidt?"

"Yes." Ernest hurried over to him.

"I'm Dr. Stern. I'm taking care of your brother's family. I've got good news and bad news. The baby boy is doing fine," the doctor paused and searched for words Ernest would understand, "but the mother—your sister-in-law—is hemorrhaging. We don't know why. She's lost a lot of blood and we can't get the bleeding to stop. The human uterus is a delicate organ, especially immediately after birth. We're going to have to perform an emergency hysterectomy."

"What does that mean?" Ernest asked.

"It means we are going to remove her uterus. We'll do it vaginally so there won't be a scar, and I'm quite sure we can leave both ovaries. She'll be normal in every way, except she won't have any more children.'

"The poor kid. She's a sweet girl. She doesn't deserve this." Ernest's voice quavered.

"How close are you to your sister-in-law?"

"We're a very close family, and I care deeply for Medora," Ernest said without hesitation. "Why?"

"I have to go in there and tell that young woman that I'm going to remove her uterus. Do you feel comfortable being with her when she gets the news?"

* * *

Medora's face was as white as the pillowcase. Tubes ran from her arm, through a black box, to a bag of liquid hanging from a metal pole. Her eyes were closed.

Going over to her, Ernest bent down and brushed his lips against her cold cheek. Her eyelids fluttered, and then opened.

"Ernest. Where's my baby? Is he okay?" she whispered.

"The little guy is the picture of health. They're taking care of him in a nursery on the second floor. You can see him pretty soon. The doctor is waiting to talk to you."

Ernest stepped back and the doctor took his place. He spoke to Medora for a few minutes.

"Ernest!" She sounded terrified.

He went to stand next to the doctor and took her hand. "I'm right here, Honey."

"I have to have an operation. I'm afraid. I might die; my baby needs me."

'You're going to be fine and I promise I'll keep and eye on the little guy for you. You'll be feeling almost like your old self by tonight," he said with false heartiness. "The doctor says you won't even have a scar.

"Ernest,"

"What Honey?"

"Thank you."

Ernest kissed her cheek again. He winked and gave her a confident smile. Then he turned quickly before she could see the tears spilling from his eyes. "Take good care of her, Doc," he said in a gruff voice.

* * *

Ernest tried to call Fern's apartment, but no one answered. It was Sunday morning; where would Fern be on Sunday morning? At the big cabin or catching up on work in her office, he decided to try the office. She answered on the second ring.

"Fern Schmidt Realty, Fern speaking."

"Fernie, it's me."

"Ernest, where are you? I'm so glad you called." He opened his mouth to speak, but Fern went on without a pause. "Wasn't that a terrible storm? I hope you weren't out in it. I just this minute tried to call the trailer to make sure Medora is okay and Doug Simpson answered."

"Fern…" Ernest tried to break in, but she went on.

"He wouldn't tell me anything. What the heck is going on? Why was Doug at the trailer? Where are Medora and Charlie? Did she go to the hospital to have the baby? Is everything okay?" Fern paused to take a breath.

"No, nothing is okay. It's all upside down. Charlie's dead and Medora is in surgery." Ernest managed to get the message out, ending with a muffled sob.

"That can't be right, Ernie."

He blew his nose, and then tried to speak, but couldn't. After a long moment, he was able to say, "Fern, a tree fell on Charlie and killed him. Medora had the baby, a little boy. I don't know if Naomi was with her or not, but the baby is fine."

His cheeks were wet with tears. "Charlie was drinking and Medora poured his booze down the drain. He was going to get more when the tree fell on him."

He paused. Fern said nothing, so he cleared his throat and went on. "That's what Medora told Carl—he's the one who found her. It looks like she tried to lift the tree off Charlie and messed herself up. She started bleeding. Now she's in surgery."

There was silence on the other end of the line.

"Fern," Ernest's voice became hard, "She told Carl it was her fault Charlie was killed. She thinks that if she hadn't poured the moonshine out he would still be alive. Fern," his words were like ice. "I hate Charlie for doing this to Medora."

She finally spoke, "Ernest, I'm having a hard time believing what you're telling me. It seems like a nightmare. Are you at the hospital in Gold Beach?"

"Yes."

"I'm going to go over and tell Papa Gus and Ma Tom. Then I'm coming to the hospital. They'll probably want to come with me. Ernest—don't say anything bad about Charlie to them. They don't have to know he was drinking. It will just hurt them."

"Okay, I won't. Ma Tom will probably find out anyway; nothing gets by her. Hurry Fern. I think it will do Medora good if you and Ma Tom are here when she wakes up from surgery."

Ernest hung up the phone, and looked at his watch. It was almost noon.

* * *

Ma Tom was standing by Medora's bed when she opened her eyes. This was Ma Tom's first sight of the inside of a hospital, and it seemed all wrong to her. The cold bright rooms, hissing machines, alarm bells and harsh odors—how could a person recover wellness in such a place?

Nonetheless she sat patiently on the hard chair next to Medora's bed, her hands busy with her rosary.

The band around Medora's arm began to tighten, and she moved restlessly. Ma Tom stood up and tried to figure out how to unfasten it.

"What are you doing?" a large woman completely dressed in green gave her a sharp look.

"This tightness is disturbing my daughter. I must remove it," Ma Tom said.

"That is to monitor her blood pressure. You must leave it in place. But look, I think your daughter is waking up," the woman said, all the time wondering how a tiny dark Hispanic woman such as the visitor, could have this Viking of a girl for her daughter.

Medora saw Ma Tom. "It must be a dream," were her first words.

"It is not a dream, but a great blessing that you have given me a grandson," said Ma Tom.

"Charlie, where's Charlie?"

"I will pray for his soul. God be praised that you and the child have lived."

"Oh Ma Tom," it was beginning to come back to Medora. "I was so afraid when he ran away. Then Naomi came and Timmy was born. I didn't want Charlie in the bedroom. Ma Tom, he never saw the baby."

The words tumbled out, weak but urgent. "After Naomi left, I got cold and went to the kitchen. He was asleep and I poured the liquor out. I was angry, but I didn't want him to die. I tried to push the tree off of him."

Her last words came out in a sob, "He really wanted the baby; he wanted us to be a family."

"My dear daughter," Ma Tom's dark eyes were intense, "My son struggled. Even in my womb good and evil fought to control him. We must believe that in the end goodness won out. I do not wish to hear evil about him. I do not want to know about 'liquor'."

"Yes Ma Tom."

Medora's eyes closed. She could hear the sounds of the hospital all around her, and the comforting click of Ma Tom's rosary beads. She was so tired, too tired to live. But she must stay alive for her baby.

The next time she opened her eyes she was being wheeled on a gurney down the hallway. "Hello Red," the orderly said. "I'm taking you to the maternity ward. You're doing well enough to be transferred out of the recovery room, congratulations.

"Your sister said to tell you she had to go to the gift shop, and then she'll be right up to sit with you. Boy, you and your sister sure don't look anything alike."

"I look like my dad," Medora whispered, and felt secretly satisfied with her little deception.

She couldn't feel her legs. "The numbness is from the anesthesia," the nurse said. "It'll wear off in a few hours. Use the call button if you need anything. Most important of all, don't try to get up until I'm here to help you."

A few minutes after the nurse left the room, Fern appeared in the doorway with a vase of yellow carnations in one hand and a book in the other.

"Hello, Mamacita, these are for you" she said, putting the flowers on a side table.

"Fern, Charlie..." Medora began.

"Let's not talk about that," Fern said in an unnaturally cheerful voice. "I don't want to know about it. Let's talk about happy things. Ma Tom wants you to come home as soon as possible. She doesn't trust hospitals, and she thinks you should be nursing baby Timmy. What do you think?"

"My mind is in a whirl, Fern. I don't know—can I nurse him after that surgery? When can I see him?"

"I called Naomi, and she says you can and should start nursing as soon as you're up to it. By the way, she feels terrible for leaving you last night."

"It wasn't her..." Medora started to say.

Fern cut her off. "Let's agree not to talk about Charlie. It's pretty obvious what he did, so why keep rehashing it?" She wiped her eyes with her sleeve and then went on in her strange, new cheerful way. "I talked to the lady at the desk. A lactation consultant will be coming by in about an hour. They'll bring the baby to you and the consultant will work with you to get started—if that's what you want."

"Oh, yes. I don't even feel like a real mom yet. I want to hold my baby and if I can nurse him after everything that's happened, I'll be so thankful."

So much had happened, but no one wanted to talk about it. They all seemed to want to pretend everything was fine. She felt like an actress in a play.

Where are Ma Tom and Papa Gus and Ernest?"

"Ernest drove the folks home in my car. I'm to stay here and guard you. As I said, Ma Tom doesn't trust hospitals. They'll put a lounge chair in here for me. And look what I got for us to read," she held up the book: *The First Six Months, Everything You Need to Know.*

"You're really great Fern, you know that?" Medora said, acting out her part in the deception.

Later, she held her baby in her arms and watched his greedy little mouth latch onto her nipple. It wasn't until after she and Fern had marveled at the beauty of baby Timmy, and Fern was dosing in the lounge-chair, that Medora found time to consider the events of the past twenty-four hours.

She looked at Fern, sleeping peacefully, and remembered how easy it had been for all of them to forget about Charlie the night after the wedding. Now, on the day of his death the same thing was happening.

Was it because of her? She believed Carl when he told her Charlie hadn't died because she poured the moonshine out. Did her wish to be part of his family without being his wife have anything to do with his death? No, she had never wished him dead, but now he was gone. Why hadn't she shown him more affection and respect?

Chapter Thirty
Medora

Ernest had paperwork to do, but he couldn't put his mind to it. He hadn't had a good night's sleep since Charlie died. Energy, generated by anger, had been replaced by remorse for not having been more patient and kind. He ruminated about sharp words he had uttered, and things he should have done to help Charlie.

He rearranged the papers on the desk, and was reaching for his pencil when the phone rang. "Tamlin Sheriff's Office, this is Deputy Ernest Schmidt speaking."

"Hey Ernest, its Carl. I'm over at your brother's trailer. You promised to let me know how things were going."

Ernest felt more guilt being piled onto the load he already carried. Medora and Timmy would have died if it weren't for Carl, yet he had forgotten all about his promise.

"I'm sorry. I meant to get by and let you know, but...."

"No sweat. I've been keeping an eye on things here. I hope it's okay—I used the phone to call you."

"Sure Carl, use it anytime. Medora and the baby are doing pretty well under the circumstances. The doctors couldn't get the bleeding stopped so they had to do an operation. She seems fine now. Listen, I need to take a run out there anyway. Are you going to be at the trailer for a while?"

"Yeah, see you later."

Carl, with Lobo at his heels, went back out to where his old truck stood in the clearing. An axe and a chainsaw rested in the rusty bed.

The crew Doug Simpson hired to get Charlie's body out and to remove the big branch blocking the road did a minimal job. It had looked pretty sloppy when they finished.

Carl cleaned up their mess, and trimmed the trees at the edge of the clearing. Every branch with even the remotest chance of falling on the trailer had been cut back. The clearing looked spacious with the overhanging greenery gone.

He was in the process of sawing the larger limbs into firewood, having already pulled the small branches into the forest. While waiting for Ernest, Carl stacked the firewood into neat piles. When the van pulled into the clearing, he limped over to meet it.

"When did you get the old truck going?" Ernest asked. "The last time I saw it, it was up on blocks." He looked around. "Did you cut back all of those branches? This place never looked so good."

Ernest's appreciation pleased him, but Carl didn't let it show. He just said, "I figure I been out in the woods too long. All the truck needed was a tune-up and oil change. I had the battery and tires in my woodshed. Now I got wheels there's no holding me back. I might even decide to come into Tamlin and have coffee with you at the cafe."

"When you do I'm buying," Ernest said, "but I owe you more than a cup of coffee. Without you and Lobo, I can't even think of what might have happened to Medora and her baby."

Carl waved his hand in a dismissive way and looked uncomfortable, so Ernest changed the subject. He filled Carl in on the details of Medora's trip to the hospital and her stay there, finishing up with, "She's in fairly good spirits and the baby is cute as a button. Ma Tom and Fern are bearing up well. They spend a lot of time at the hospital with Medora and Timmy.

"It's Papa Gus we're worried about. He doesn't say much, mostly stays in his workshop, hardly comes out to eat. He was probably closer to Charlie than anyone; they spent a lot of time together in that workshop."

"What about Charlie? Will there be a funeral?" Carl asked.

"That's the hard part. Charlie was baptized in the church and took communion, but then became a very vocal atheist. Ma Tom talked to Father Gallagher and they decided Charlie should be buried in the church cemetery at Saint Anthony's of the Woods and have Mass said for his soul, but there won't be a big funeral. I guess Ma Tom thinks a public funeral would be hypocritical."

"I want to tell you something Ernie," Carl leaned toward him. "You'll think I'm crazy, but every once in a while when I'm working here I think I see Charlie, all tricked out in his fancy western garb and high heeled boots. It must be my imagination. I spend too much time alone." Carl laughed, a little embarrassed about what he had just said.

Ernest's radio crackled and Sheriff McBride's voice boomed, "Ernest. Call Detective Sergeant Sullivan, Rosamunde police department; it's about Medora's folks." The sheriff gave the phone number which Ernest wrote on the back of an old envelope.

"Copy that," Ernest said as he got out of his van. "Gotta make a call," he said. "I don't know if Medora plans to come back here, but I think I'll leave the phone in for a while. It's coming in real handy." He went into the trailer. Carl stood just outside, eavesdropping.

"This is Deputy Ernest Schmidt from Tamlin. I need to talk to Detective Sergeant Sullivan."

"Hello, Deputy Schmidt," the voice on the other end of the wire said. "Sullivan here, thanks for returning my call. The person I'm inquiring about must be a relative of yours—Medora Schmidt?"

"She's my sister-in-law," Ernest replied. "She's in the hospital and shouldn't be bothered right now. What is this about? Is there something I can do for you?"

"Unfortunately, I have distressing news. Both her parents are deceased. Her father died—in all probability—of a stroke. I'm waiting for the results of the autopsy. The evidence points toward the mother's death being the result of suicide. I have to notify Mrs. Schmidt and get her permission to open a letter, addressed to her, from her mother. I thought I'd take a ride out there this afternoon. Is there someone who can be with her when she gets the news?"

"My mother's with her right now," said Ernest. "But, can't this wait. Her husband, my brother, was killed the same night her baby was born and Medora had to have major surgery after the birth. That was just three days ago."

"Believe me, I don't look forward to breaking the news to her, but she has the right to know. I'm going to head out your way as soon as we finish talking. Which hospital is she in?"

Ernest gave the requested information, then hung up the phone and went out to tell Carl what the detective said.

Carl said, "Shit! Son of a bitch!" and went back to stacking wood.

"See you later," Ernest called to Carl's back. "I'll stop by and let you know how things are going. You're part of the family now, Carl."

He drove back to town, and went directly to Fern's office. "It's horrible," he told her, "Medora's dad had a fatal stoke and her mom was killed in an automobile wreck—probably suicide."

Fern stared at him; she wasn't used to seeing him angry.

"That big-shot detective from Rosamunde insists on seeing Medora and telling her about her parents' deaths." Ernest paced the floor as he spoke. "I told him how much she's been through and asked him to wait. He says she has a right to know. Doesn't that guy have any compassion?"

"He has a point," Fern said. "Medora does have a right to know. She tried to call her mother to tell her about the baby all day yesterday. Do you want me to go to the hospital with you?"

"You better stay here and keep an eye on Papa Gus."

"Okay," Fern took her purse from a filing cabinet. "I was just going to go up there to fix him some lunch." She put her face in her hands. "Oh God Ernest, I miss Charlie so much. He was always getting on my nerves. Now that he's gone it feels like there's a huge hole in my world."

Ernest sighed, "I know what you mean. He had a real sweet side, but all I ever saw were his faults. I didn't mean it when I said I hated him."

"I hope the doctor lets Medora come home pretty soon. Maybe then we can get back to normal, whatever that's going to be for us without Charlie," Fern said.

"I've got to head out for Gold's Beach, Fern. I don't want that detective to get there before me. Are you going to be okay?" Ernest put his arm around her shoulder.

"Yeah, I'll be okay. It's a rough time for all of us." Fern forced a smile. "Go on. I'll see you tonight."

* * *

Ma Tom and Medora undressed the baby, and marveled at his rosy body, tiny fingers and toes, and fuzz of golden hair. All their fussing reminded him that he was hungry. He opened his big brown eyes, screwed up his little face and started to wail. Medora quickly fastened a diaper on him and wrapped him in a blanket before putting him to her breast.

Her nipples were sore, but still she felt a pleasant pressing in her shoulder when he started to suckle. "I'm so glad you said I should breast feed," she told Ma Tom.

Little Timmy finished nursing and Ma Tom was patting him on the back; trying to get him to burp, when Ernest knocked on the door.

He felt a surge of love when he saw them. They made a beautiful picture, and he would have given anything not to have to disturb this moment.

"Uncle Ernest, what a nice surprise," Medora called out.

A nurse bustled into the room and took the baby from Ma Tom, who frowned as she handed her grandchild to the uniformed stranger.

"What is it my son?" Ma Tom asked, noticing Ernest's serious face.

"More terrible news," he answered. "It's your parents Medora."

"Did my dad pass away? It was what he wanted, but I hoped he would live to see his grandson." Tears trickled down her cheeks.

"It's your dad, but more than just him, Honey." Ernest looked down at the floor. He heard Ma Tom's sharp intake of breath. "A detective from Rosamunde will be here soon to talk to you. I'm so sorry. Your mother is dead too. They think it was suicide."

""But..." Medora began.

"May I come in?" a man's voice called from the door.

Ernest went to meet him. "I'm Deputy Schmidt and this is my mother, Tomasina Schmidt and my sister-in-law, Medora Schmidt."

"I'm Detective Sergeant Sullivan." He shook hands with Ernest and then looked at Medora. "Has Deputy Schmidt told you why I need to see you?"

"Yes, about my parents." Her voice was barely audible.

"Your mother left a letter addressed to you. Do I have your permission to open and read it?" he asked.

"No," she replied. "I want to open it and read it, and then you can look at it."

He took a long white envelope from the clipboard he was holding and handed it to her. He stepped back to give her some privacy.

She tore one of the ends off and shook a sheet of paper onto her bedside table. "Ma Tom…" Medora sounded like a frightened child.

"You don't have to read it now," Ma Tom told her. "Perhaps it would be better to wait until you are stronger."

"I don't want to look at it, but I have to know what it says. I'm glad you're here with me—that's all," Medora unfolded the single page and read:

My Dearest Medora,

I haven't been much of a mother to you. I guess I just didn't know how. I don't remember my own mother or father you know. When you gave me the beautiful jewelry box, I was both happy and ashamed. I put it on the dining room table where I could see it every day. For some reason it gave me hope, but now all hope is gone. Please forgive me for the thing I am about to do. Your father is dead and without him there is no reason for me to go on living. You have your new life and will soon have a child of your own. I know you will be a better mother to that child than I have been to you.

Pray that God will forgive me, and that Ian and I will be together. Goodbye my beloved daughter.

She read it twice and then handed it to Sullivan. "Thank you," he said. "I'll get it back to you,"

"That won't be necessary. I don't want it back," Medora answered.

She was no longer crying. Behind her stony face emotions were roiling like the white waters of the Rogue River.

Her mother promised that whatever happened they could handle it together. Medora trusted her. She believed her mother was a spiritually strong person. How could she leave her grandchild this terrible legacy? Didn't she care about Timmy—or Medora—at all?

Medora remembered the last time she saw Helen. She asked her mother if God decided who would die. Helen replied, "That's what I used to believe."

Medora shook her head to clear it of the bad thoughts. She couldn't think about it now. She had to keep going, at least until Timmy was weaned. The family would take care of him. He'd have a better life without her—when Timmy was weaned she could think about it again.

Sullivan was speaking. "What?" Medora said.

"Did your mother ever talk about a nurse named Ruby?"

"No, why should she?" asked Medora.

"No special reason, I guess that's all. I'm sorry for your loss." Sullivan put the envelope back on his clipboard.

Chapter Thirty-one
Medora

It was a drizzly day—no real rain—just heavy gray overcast. As Ma Tom rolled fresh tortillas around cooked chicken and slices of avocado, she was thinking that a sunny day would make them all feel more cheerful. There were many winter days ahead, but she vowed to do her best to brighten her family's spirits.

She used a long fork to pull a basket down from the top of a cupboard. She lined it with a clean white napkin, and then placed the plastic wrapped taquitos, two Comice pears and a container of milk in it.

Going to the door of the workshop she called loudly, "Goose, I am taking food to the children, and when I return I'll prepare your lunch."

Gus sat, with his head bowed, on a stool next to his workbench. Rows of tools hung on the wall above the empty bench. He closed his eyes when his wife called to him, and did not speak.

"Did you hear what I said Goose? Perhaps you would drive me to town?"

He finally looked at her. "I have to stay here."

This was more heaviness in Ma Tom's heart. Since Charlie died— and that was more than two months ago—Papa Gus spent most of his time in the workshop. She often heard him talking to the emptiness.

* * *

The door to Fern's office opened and Ma Tom, wearing a pink jacket over her black cotton dress and a smile on her face, held up the basket for them to see. "Lunch for my daughters," she announced.

Putting the basket on a desk, she went to the cradle and leaned down to smooth the blankets over the sleeping baby.

"Ma Tom, did you drive here?" Fern asked crossly.

Ma Tom answered without looking up, "It was necessary to bring your lunch."

"Where's Papa Gus? In his workshop I suppose." Fern answered her own question then continued in the same irritable tone. "Well, Ernest is going to have a fit if he sees the pickup out in front. You know you're only supposed to drive on the property, not on public roads. You don't have a driver's license."

"The mother of my grandchild is hungry," Ma Tom replied.

"Yes I am," Medora said.

Fern groaned.

"Are you going to eat lunch with us?" Medora asked Ma Tom.

"I must get back to Goose," Ma Tom said, "but my daughters, do you not think Timmy needs another blanket? It's chilly in here." She took a blanket from the diaper bag and tucked it into the cradle. "Fern, you will be at the big cabin for dinner? Ernest says he will join us."

"I'll try to make it," Fern replied without enthusiasm.

* * *

To have a baby without a husband is a lonely thing, and so Ma Tom was glad Fern was there to help when Medora brought Timmy to the big cabin from the hospital. Fern slept in the bedroom with them. Medora was still weak, and it was Fern who got up at night to change Timmy's diaper.

Ma Tom knew this special time of closeness could not last forever. During the second week it became obvious that trying to keep her business going while being available for Medora and the baby every night was taking a toll on Fern. Medora noticed it, too.

"Ma Tom, I love having Fern help me with the baby, but she's not getting enough sleep, and she has a life of her own," Medora said one morning after Fern left for her office. "She has dark circles under her eyes and hardly ever smiles, but I guess none of us smile much anymore since…"

"Nothing is more important than family," Ma Tom interrupted, "Fern is needed here."

When Timmy was two weeks old, Medora said, "Fern, I plan to go back to work in two weeks. I'll take you up on the offer to bring Timmy to the office with me so you'll see him everyday."

Fern started to say something, but Medora went on: "I'm fine now. You need to start sleeping in your own apartment and getting back to your own life. I heard you telling someone on the phone that you are too busy to have a social life—that's a load of bull feathers!"

"It wasn't anyone important," Fern answered, but Medora wasn't through.

"I think you were talking to Dr. Lopez. I'm glad old Dr. Clark got a partner in to help him, and I'm glad that new partner is as handsome as a movie star. I saw you two talking when he came by to do Timmy's well baby check-up.

"Don't be ridiculous," Fern said, but she followed Medora's advice and moved back into her apartment.

* * *

Even though Ma Tom tried to bring back the happiness of other years, the holidays were all wrong. She cooked the special foods: turkey, cranberries, candied yams and tamales, and then watched Papa Gus, Ernest, Fern and Medora silently push the food around their plates, their faces set in sad lines.

After the holidays, Ma Tom continued to insist Fern and Ernest have dinner at the big cabin two or three times a week. Papa Gus could usually be persuaded to join them for a short while. When they sat around the table it was like the old days; except Charlie's chair was empty and they no longer joked and argued.

The evil eye lives on after the death of its dwelling place, thought Ma Tom as she studied the unsmiling faces of her husband and children. It was her secret plan to remove Charlie's chair and put a highchair for Timmy in its place. Perhaps when the chair was gone her poor son would cease walking the earth. As long as his spirit remained, she was afraid.

She battled the pall that settled over her family with food and words. Most of her conversation centered on Timmy. "Such a big boy, like his grandpapa and uncle...." Her words were followed by silence as they all thought of, but didn't speak of, Charlie's small stature.

Ernest tried to help, "That Doug Simpson always acts like pets are a nuisance. Well, yesterday he brought home a kitten. Apparently someone had dumped a litter of three in the trash bin behind the Sheriff's office and this was the only one that survived. Cute little thing—and feisty—you should hear it hiss. Anyway, Old Doug is feeding that kitten with a doll-baby bottle."

Once again silence as everyone but Medora thought of the kitten Charlie had thrown into the fire that long ago day. Charlie seemed to be more with them since he died than he ever was when he was alive.

Medora was the only one with an appetite, and that was probably because of nursing Timmy. Her baby was getting plenty to eat. He had rolls of fat on his little legs.

Sometimes he fussed while they were having dinner. Medora would bring him to the table, unbutton her shirt and nurse him while she ate. At first Ma Tom was embarrassed by Medora's lack of modesty, but now having Timmy join them for dinner seemed like the most natural thing in the world.

Often Ma Tom and Medora were the only ones at the big table for dinner. The meals, and long evenings they shared might have been lonely, but for the stories. It started the first evening Fern stayed at her own apartment in town.

After doing the dinner dishes, the two women went to sit in the living room. A fire of small logs kept the area warm. In one of the rocking chairs, Ma Tom was knitting a blue sweater for Timmy.

Medora held Timmy on her knees. As he stared up at the shadows the flames made on the ceiling, his eyelids kept drooping and then popping open. Medora studied his features, searching for likeness to Ian.

"I plan to write down the stories my dad told me of his childhood on the farm in Kansas for Timmy when he is older," she told Ma Tom. "I don't know much about my mother's family. They lived in Rosamunde and my grandfather was a preacher at a small neighborhood church. The whole family: her father, mother, and younger brother, were killed when their house burned down. Only my mother survived, and she was terribly scarred." Medora kissed the top of Timmy's head and then asked, "Where did you grow up, Ma Tom?"

Ma Tom told Medora of her childhood in Agua Dulce. "My family was considered well off to have a three room adobe house: one room for storing the maize, frioles, and garbanzos, one room for the children to sleep, and one for the papa and mama." She put down her knitting and gazed into space—remembering.

"When I was still very small it became my job to carry the water from the well in the town square to our home. Even though I was only seven, I was the oldest girl. That is why my back is crooked.

"My family was fortunate because my papa and brothers were hard workers. We rarely went hungry. Mama cooked in the open kitchen lean-to Papa built for her on the side of the house." She went on to tell Medora the story of her childhood and about her job at the government school.

This was the beginning of a new tradition of sitting together and sharing stories. It brought great pleasure to Ma Tom. She had known this sort of storytelling when she was growing up. In her village laws and customs came from long ago times and were kept fresh in the minds of the people, not by writing down on paper, but by the spoken word.

"I hear of your life and I feel ashamed," Medora told her. "I was pampered. When I think back, it was my dad who took care of me. Mom was always in the background, and I feel bad about that. I guess

I'm kind of like my dad—a tendency not to think before I act—but I did enjoy life before all the sadness."

Ma Tom counted the stitches on her knitting needles and then answered, "Sadness does not last forever my daughter. You will again know great joy."

"How do you know that?" Medora's voice was low.

"In the many years I have lived, I have seen dreadful suffering and loss replaced by hope and new beginnings. You are strong. You will survive this dark time; praise be to God."

But Ma Tom didn't know the demons Medora wrestled with everyday.

* * *

"Medora, you're spending too much time keeping this office organized. I have a couple of perspective buyers coming this afternoon. Why don't you show them some properties?"

Medora looked up from the fliers she was getting ready to mail. "I'm not quite ready yet, and I don't want to leave Timmy. Maybe in a few weeks I'll start making contacts and showing property," she replied.

She couldn't tell anyone her thoughts. Once, when she saw the butcher knife lying on the sink in Ma Tom's kitchen, Helen's words *"all hope is gone"* flashed through her thoughts and for an instant she had an urge to plunge the knife into her own heart. Another time, if it weren't for Timmy in the car seat, she might have run the Saturn into a tree when Helen's voice: *"all hope is gone…no reason to go on living,"* came into her mind.

Medora was frightened. Things were tilted—out of focus. She wasn't used to her dad not being there for her. Her mom was gone. She didn't have Charlie. She was sure that Charlie loved her, despite all the odd turns their relationship had taken. They made plans for a life together. They were going to build a home, but that was gone now…*"all hope is gone."*

To die would be easy, but the time wasn't right. Timmy needed her. She couldn't leave him yet.

Medora turned her pale face to Fern. "I'm just scared, Fern. It's like the world is shifting under my feet and I can't find a firm place to stand."

Fern paused for a moment before she answered. "I don't know what you're going through, exactly. It's hard for me, too."

Medora began to cry and Fern's anger bubbled up. She kicked the wastepaper basket and it spun across the floor. "You're disgusting. You say you love Timmy so much—well prove it—start taking clients out."

Medora stopped crying. "You're right. I have to get a grip. I have to think of Timmy/. Okay, okay. I'm going to follow up on the Weiss property the first thing tomorrow morning."

"I'll believe it when I see it," Fern said.

* * *

Papa Gus put his coffee cup on the table. He didn't want coffee; he wanted to be back in his workshop. Ernest and Medora had insisted he sit in the living room with them for a while. Why couldn't they leave him alone?

The door slammed and Fern tromped in looking like she was mad enough to spit bullets. She didn't even glance his way.

Medora said something and Fern answered, "Don't bother," in such a loud voice even he could hear her. He closed his eyes, trying to shut the world out.

Ernest noticed Papa Gus' reaction to Fern's loud voice, and told her, "Don't take your anger out on the people around you."

Trying to change the subject, Medora said the first thing that came into her mind. "I'm thinking of spending weekends at the trailer, like I did before Timmy was born."

"I don't think that's a good idea," Ernest said. "What if the baby got sick or something?"

"Don't worry Ernest. She's only 'thinking about it'." Fern imitated Medora's voice.

Medora went on as if she hadn't heard them. She had spoken impulsively, but she really did want to go to the trailer. She hadn't been there since the night of Timmy's birth. "There's a telephone. Carl's just down the road, and I'm only ten miles from town. I want Timmy to have that property. It's his legacy, and if we don't live on it at least on weekends, we could lose it," she was saying.

Papa Gus, opened his eyes, cleared his throat shouted, "My son tells me I should check the barn roof. Medora may want some of the pieces in there for the cabin she is going to build."

They looked at him in surprise. "I didn't say that, Papa, but it's a good idea. I should have thought of it myself. I'll do it tomorrow." Ernest said.

"I know you didn't tell me, Ernest. Charlie did, it's his barn you know."

Chapter Thirty-two
Medora

Even though she was uneasy about being alone, Medora went ahead with her plan to spend the weekend at the trailer. It was the first time she had gone grocery shopping since Timmy was born. She adjusted the sling so that the baby was on her back, making it easier to push the cart and reach items on the shelf. At least she no longer had to worry about pleasing Charlie or the gruesome Friday evening meals at the cafe with Alice, but her new freedom brought no joy.

She strapped Timmy in his car seat before loading her groceries into the Saturn. Rain had fallen off and on all day, not hard, just enough to make the world seem gray and dismal. Her tires squished in the mud, and she drove out of town feeling as dull and leaden as the sky.

It didn't happen until she was almost to her destination. *"All hope is gone."* Her mother's voice echoed through her mind. She grasped the wheel hard and made the turn off the main road onto the track leading to the trailer. *"No reason to go on living."* Her hands loosened on the wheel and her foot pushed the pedal to the floor. The car fishtailed and slid sideways. Timmy began to whimper.

"My God, what am I doing?" She brought the car to a stop and sat trembling. The baby's noises stopped. He must have gone back to sleep. As soon as she started the car the voice—her mother's voice—was in her head again. '*No reason to go on living.*"

Medora bit her lip and tasted metallic blood. When she focused on the pain the voice faded. Releasing her lip, she ran her tongue over the tiny cuts left by her teeth.

"*No reason to go on living,*" Helen's voice was loud.

"Shut-up Mom! I won't listen to you. Go away!"

Medora forced herself to concentrate on a mental list of the things she wanted to do: check cupboards for signs of mice and put out traps if necessary; fill bird feeders; clean refrigerator; take Timmy for a long walk if the weather allowed. Helen's voice was still there, but when Medora kept her mind busy, the frightening words were pushed into the background.

The cold sunlight was fading when she parked the Saturn next to the trailer. Gentle rain began to ping lightly on the roof of the car. Things looked different. The clearing seemed spacious and bright. Perhaps it was because the big tree was now nothing but a clover shaped stump.

Someone had given the steps and porch a coat of white paint. Medora was glad to be back; it felt like she was coming home.

Timmy woke up and started to cry. Medora went around and opened the door. She slipped the diaper bag over her arm, undid the buckles of the car seat and lifted her red faced baby out. "Okay Mr. Man. We'll get the groceries and Mama's suitcase later. Let's get you fed."

It must have been Ernest who painted the porch and steps. The small improvement lifted her spirits. She expected the inside to be in need of a good cleaning, but someone had been there with a dust cloth and mop. Whoever it was had placed three red apples in the center of the table. "It looks like somebody has been busy making our trailer nice." She jiggled the crying baby up and down. "Let's go in the bedroom and change your pants then you can have your dinner."

The bedroom, like the kitchen was neat and inviting. Medora pulled her wedding quilt to the foot of the bed. She put a rubber pad under Timmy; changed his diaper and then lay beside him.

"Your head smells so sweet." She kissed his silky fuzz and closed her eyes. As she dozed, half awake—half asleep, a dreamlike memory of the night Timmy was born floated though her mind. In those desperate moments the trailer had seemed like a womb, protecting and nurturing. Once again the feeling of being at peace, sheltered from harm, enfolded her and she slept.

She woke an hour later feeling refreshed and hopeful for the first time in ages. After placing pillows next to the edge of the bed in case Timmy moved around in his sleep, she made several trips to the Saturn to get the groceries, her suitcase and a folder containing information on the Weiss property. The rain had stopped and bright stars lit up the night sky.

In the refrigerator she found a container of Ma Tom's vegetable soup and a plastic wrapped package of ten tortillas. She heated a bowl of soup and two tortillas for her dinner. As she ate, she studied the contents of the Weiss folder. On a notepad, she estimated her commission should she be able to sell the cabin and the Victorian. It was more than enough for a down payment on Charlie's forty acres.

Medora knew she had the upper hand, because the property couldn't be sold if she was living on it. Nevertheless, she promised herself that she would offer a fair price—didn't Fern say something about $1,000 an acre? She would find out.

When she tiptoed into the bedroom to get the two sets of rough house plans she kept in the bottom of her sock drawer, Timmy opened his eyes and gave her a sleepy smile. "Well, little man, I need some company," she told him. "Let's look at the house plans your daddy drew for us while you eat."

At that moment Charlie seemed alive. It was as though he were close by, perhaps out in the barn. She had been going to look at the grandiose plans first. She wanted to understand how his mind had worked. Instead she slipped them back into the drawer, and kept the simple drawing she and Charlie had both contributed to. She didn't want to embarrass or shame his memory by bringing up past mistakes.

She leaned on a pillow and studied the sketch of their dream home while Timmy nursed. They would have a porch across the front made in such a way that it would serve as a very large play pen for Timmy. He could watch the birds and trees while playing.

The placement of a washer and dryer was puzzling. Did they belong in the kitchen, or in the bathroom? Maybe there should be a small utility porch by the kitchen door… Medora drifted off to sleep. She woke half an hour later and went to the bathroom to wash her face, brush her teeth and change into her pajamas. Then, with Timmy in the crook of her arm, she fell back to sleep.

Sunshine was coming in the window, and Timmy was just waking up when she opened her eyes. He had slept through the night for the first time. After changing his diaper, Medora held him close, and they both dozed again.

It was almost ten before she got out of bed, shuffled into the kitchen and turned on the fire under the tea kettle. By the time she came out of the bathroom, the kettle was singing. She made a cup of instant decaf, put her jacket on and went to sit on the top step of the porch with her coffee.

Ernest mentioned that Carl had done some work in the clearing. The brush and overhanging branches had been trimmed away. Medora knew, from Ernest, that it was Carl and Lobo who found her and called for help on the night Timmy was born.

Carl and Lobo were their guardian angels. She smiled at the idea, and then realized that she hadn't been bothered by her mother's voice since she arrived at the trailer. "This is a good place," she said out loud.

Medora lit the propane heater so the trailer was nice and warm the next time Timmy woke up. After he nursed, she gave him a sponge bath; dressed him in a blanket sleeper and put him into the sling, "We're going exploring, little man." She carried the walking stick Carl made for her even though she was no longer afraid of bears.

* * *

Carl spent so much time at the trailer it almost seemed like a second home to him. He worked hard to make things nice for Medora and her baby, but when he saw the Saturn drive down the track he felt shy and out of place. He couldn't bring himself to walk down to the trailer to say a neighborly "hello". Suppose she was afraid of him, or wanted to be left alone.

Carl was removing brush and debris from his own clearing when Lobo perked his ears and began to whine. "Okay, come on; let's see what's going on—heel." The dog dropped back to walk behind his master.

Medora was just coming into view when they stepped from the path onto the track. She saw them right away and increased her pace. "Carl and Lobo," she called.

Lobo twitched like he was aching to run to her. "Stay!" Carl told him, "You might scare the baby."

By the time Medora got to them she was out of breath. She reached down to scratch Lobo behind the ears and he wriggled with pleasure. Looking up at Carl while still petting Lobo, she said, "I was hoping I would see you two. I don't know how I can ever thank you enough. Ernest told me you saved me. I vaguely remember. I was so cold and Lobo was there. Then I felt warmer and you were helping me drink something hot."

"It's Lobo you need to thank. How in God's name he knew you needed help is beyond me. And I was so stupid I didn't pay attention. He went right through the window."

Medora straightened up and twisted the sling around so that Timmy rested on her stomach. He was sound asleep, but she whispered to him, "Look Timmy. It's Carl and Lobo, our guardian angels."

"Some pretty rough angels." Carl laughed as he peered at the sleeping baby.

"You cleaned up the clearing. It looks so nice," Medora said. "Who painted the porch and steps? Was that you or Ernest?"

"Ernie brought the paint over and I did the painting,"

"How would you and Lobo like to come back to the trailer for some lunch? I have Ma Tom's soup left over from dinner and I'll make us some sandwiches to go with it."

"I'd like that," Carl told her.

While they were still seated at the table after lunch, Medora showed Carl the house plans. "I have to make a few sales before I can actually think of building. I'm nervous about taking clients out to look at property, but I'm going to do it."

She knew she was babbling, but Carl was a good listener. Although he didn't say much, she could tell he cared.

When Timmy began to fuss, Carl excused himself, "Lobo and I better get back to work on our clearing. Take good care of that big boy." He held out a calloused finger. Timmy fastened his chubby fist around it and tried to bring it to his mouth. "Strong grip," Carl said.

After her visitors left Medora cuddled Timmy on the bed, and thought of how natural sharing her hopes and plans with Carl had been. Her friends in Portland were a lifetime away. She belonged in this place with her son and her new family.

The afternoon light began to fade. In the bedroom, Medora held her baby and pondered their future. A shadow darkened the window for an instant, as if someone had walked across the porch. "Who's there?" Medora called, and carrying Timmy, got up and opened the door to look out. She thought she glimpsed the figure of a man, but when she blinked it was gone and there was no one in sight.

"It must have been a trick of the light," she whispered to Timmy as she repositioned him over her shoulder and patted his back.

The old barn, listing to one side, was spotlighted in a beam of sunshine which shone through the clouds like a beacon. To Medora, it seemed as if Charlie must be inside, perhaps working on the redwood burl sculpture he had been going to call "Birth."

She knew if she went to the barn and opened the door the illusion would fade. "Oh, Charlie, I wish you could hold Timmy and kiss the top of his sweet little head."

Timmy gave a loud burp; Medora laughed and the spell was broken.

Chapter Thirty-three
Medora

"How was your weekend?" Fern asked as soon as Medora finished hanging her coat on the rack.

"It was wonderful. I wasn't sure how I'd handle seeing the barn and trailer again, but it was easy—I feel at home there. Timmy must like it too. He slept the whole night. I got a good rest, and on Saturday I had lunch with Carl and Lobo."

Medora sorted the mail on her desk as she spoke. When she finished she looked up at Fern. "Can I show property to our next walk-in?"

"Yes," Fern said. "I was hoping you'd say that."

"Seriously Fern, I want to get Charlie's forty acres into my name and start building a cabin on it before Timmy is much older. I'm going to call Mr. Weiss again and if I can get the listing I'm going to advertise it right away. The property can be sold as-is or we can get the repairs done while it's on the market."

"You go girl."

"There's something else." Medora went to stand by Fern's desk. "I don't want to seem like I'm criticizing—it's just that I think this weekend was hard for your folks."

Fern put her hands over her face. "I didn't stop by or even call. God, I'm such a jerk," she said through her fingers. "It's not their fault everything is screwed up, but I sure have been taking it out on them—and you." She took her hands away and asked, "What happened?"

"Papa Gus didn't come out of his workshop. Ma Tom took food to him, but he wouldn't eat." Medora put her hand on Fern's shoulder. "When I got back to the cabin, she coaxed him out to see Timmy, and he ate dinner with us."

"From now on I'm going to stay at the big cabin when you aren't there," Fern promised.

"I plan on spending every weekend at the trailer, like I did when Charlie was alive," Medora said.

Fern tensed at the sound of Charlie's name. "Did you go in the barn?"

"No, this probably sounds odd, but if I don't look in the barn I can pretend Charlie is in there working, like he was the day before he died. I know Papa wants Ernest to make sure the roof is okay and check that Charlie's work is properly wrapped. When he gets ready to do that—you, Ernest and I will go in there together—maybe Ma Tom and Papa Gus, too."

Fern's eyes filled with tears. She impatiently wiped them away with her sleeve. "Do we have anything scheduled for today?" She asked.

After reminding Fern of several appointments, Medora made her phone call. "Mr. Weiss, this is Medora Schmidt."

"I'd almost forgotten about you. Are you calling to tell me you're vacating my property?"

"I haven't received the signed contract for listing your property. Real estate is really jumping in Tamlin. This would be a good time to put your properties on the market, unless you like paying taxes and property management fees," Medora said, ignoring his taunts.

"I sent the contract to my attorney a couple of months ago; didn't he get back to you?"

"No." she replied. Timmy stirred and Medora knew it would be just moments before he began to wail. "I have a client waiting for me, Mr. Weiss. Think about the listing and I'll call you tomorrow." She hung up and went to take care of her baby.

* * *

The family was again gathered for dinner at the big cabin. This meal was different from the silent meals of the past few months. Medora had been talking almost nonstop.

"This has been the most fruitful day of my life, except the day Timmy was born."

Papa Gus, Ma Tom, Ernest and Fern, responded to her enthusiasm and it was beginning to seem almost like old times.

"If I were a few years younger I'd fix that Victorian up pretty as a picture," Papa Gus said.

Fern turned toward him, wanting to hold onto the spark. "What color would you paint it?" she asked.

"What?" he couldn't hear Fern's question and the light in his eyes faded.

"What color would you paint it?" Fern yelled.

"It doesn't matter," he said dully, but he continued to eat with an unusually good appetite.

"We're going to list the properties 'as-is'," said Medora. They would bring a great deal more after renovation, but even as they are, they're worth a small fortune. She mentioned a figure and Ernest whistled. "The commission will be a nice down payment on the forty acres." she told him and then added, "Charlie's forty acres."

"How are things at the trailer?" he asked.

"Wonderful. The porch and steps are newly painted. Someone had cleaned inside and put food in the refrigerator—and three apples on the table. I wonder who it could be." She looked around the room. "Hmm you all look suspicious," she said, laughing.

"Ah, my children, more tamales?" Ma Tom said a silent prayer of thanks as she passed the platter. The tangled threads of her family were weaving a beautiful new pattern.

* * *

When Medora walked in the door of the real estate office the next morning, she found Fern's digital camera pointing at her

"We'll take pictures of each other, and then you and Timmy can get pictures of the Victorian and the cabin. I already have photos for the other listings."

"Why? Wait, let me get Timmy settled. I need to comb my hair and put on some lipstick. What happened?"

Fern said, "I just got off the phone with your boyfriend, Wiley Weiss." She was dancing with excitement. "He's faxing the contracts over and wants you to get busy selling his property. I explained to him that real estate prices have gone up since November. I told him our suggested asking prices. He's going to make the corrections and initial them." She took Timmy from Medora's arms, whirled him around and held him up over her head.

"He just ate. You're liable to get a face full of spit up," Medora warned.

"My little nephew is going to have his cabin in the woods and Auntie Fern is going to buy him a rocking horse for his porch." She handed Timmy back to Medora. "I'm glad we got the playpen. There was no room for him to stretch and roll around in the cradle now that he's gotten so big and frisky," she said, smoothing a blanket in the bottom of the mesh-sided playpen.

"It takes up a lot of room." Medora said. She put Timmy on the blanket, and wound up a musical mobile.

"Don't worry about that," Fern said. "He's such a good little guy; this office would seem bleak without him."

The two women spent the morning working on the layout for the advertisement. It was Fern's plan to create an insert for newspapers in nearby towns like Gold Beach and Brooking, and also as far away as Portland. "Thousands of older people are out there looking for a place to retire, and tons of young families looking for a good place to raise kids," she speculated.

Timmy napped; when he woke Medora changed and fed him, then set out to take pictures for the advertisement. With Timmy in the sling, she walked to the Victorian. Wiley Weiss was mailing her the keys; until she received them she could only take photos of the exterior. The cupolas, bay windows and gingerbread trim looked imposing through the camera's lens, despite their run-down condition.

Next she fastened Timmy into his car seat and drove the winding road to the Weiss cabin, following the map Fern drew for her. It was certainly remote; she hadn't seen a mailbox or fence or car for almost fifteen minutes. Whoever bought that property would have to really value privacy.

Medora was beginning to wonder if she would ever find the turn off. "When you get to the twisted dead tree on the right, drive half a mile, and then look on the left for the road to the cabin," Fern instructed her. "Turn left when you see a beat up old mailbox cemented onto a pile of rocks."

Medora saw the twisted tree, but drove past the mailbox marker, and had a hard time finding a place wide enough to turn around. She finally negotiated the turn off the main road and bumped along a dirt track few yards until she came to a place where the road was blocked with branches. She slammed on the brakes.

"Darn it!" she muttered. "Now I have to put Timmy into the sling and hike in. I'd like to get my hands on that Oney; I'd make a citizen's arrest and force Ernest to throw him into jail."

The trees and underbrush were dense, but she found a path that seemed to head in the right direction. Twenty minutes later she emerged from the forest into a small flat area. Tree stumps studded a rocky surface that was not much bigger than the porch at Ma Tom's. On three sides a dense stand of pine trees pushed against a split rail fence and a precariously perched cabin.

There was no place to turn a vehicle around. Oney did her a favor with his shenanigans. If it weren't for him she would have driven all the way in and perhaps gotten stuck.

Medora threaded her way through the tree stumps to inspect the fourth side of the clearing. It was a bluff, high above a churning ocean inlet. The trapped waves crashed against the boulders as if desperate to escape. She looked down and stepped closer to the edge.

"*No reason to go on living.*" Her mother's voice roared inside her head as loud as the pounding ocean. Medora felt dizzy. "No, not with Timmy," she whispered.

As she backed away she noticed a ragged rope ladder hanging down the steep face of the cliff. The ladder had originally been in three sections, but only the top two sections remained intact and they were badly in need of repair. The third section dangled by a thread fifty feet above the rocky beach. Each time the wind blew, the ladder slammed against the rocks.

Raising her eyes, she looked across to the bank on the other side of the inlet. In stark contrast to the roughness of the terrain and the wildness of the fomenting brine at the foot of the cliff; brown cows were grazing placidly in a golden meadow on the far shore.

"*No hope left.*" She moved away from the precipice, but she knew, in a flash of certainty, her life would end here—not today—when Timmy was older—when she had purchased life insurance, and secured the forty acres for him—then a step over the edge of the cliff. It would look like an accident. Timmy wouldn't have to know. He would be better off without her.

Turning her back on the seductive surf she walked toward the weathered A-line cabin. Its shiny red tin roof gleamed like a warning-sign in the dull gray landscape. The crumbling rear foundation rested on solid ground; the prow-like glass front and widow's walk jutted over the cliff, supported by weathered timbers anchored onto the sheer rock face with concrete boots.

Medora took several pictures of the front, and then, camera in hand, she walked to the back of the cabin. A heavy wooden door, held closed by a deadbolt, caught her eye. To the side of the building, a rusty axe leaned against a few sticks of firewood. She thought, as she snapped pictures, it must be some sort of basement storage area, perhaps a wood shed or a tool shed.

She slid the deadbolt aside and pushed the door open. "Oh my God! This must have been where Charlie was on the night Timmy was born. He was headed back here when the tree fell on him," she gasped.

The shelving on the walls held fruit jars of every size and description; each jar was filled with clear liquid. The tangy odor of alcohol permeated the room. Medora left the door open and ran along the path toward the Saturn. She had to get Timmy away from this place.

Chapter Thirty-four
Medora

Fern added hard-wood pellets to the little stove in her office and then looked out the window. The afternoon had grown cold and the sky was clouding over, might be getting ready for another big storm. She hoped Medora and Timmy would get back soon.

Telling herself it wouldn't do any good to worry, she went back to work on her biggest, to date, advertising campaign. She studied the display on her monitor. At the top of the screen she had placed the name of her company, "Fern Schmidt Realty" in large block print, but now she was thinking of changing it to gothic and adding something like "We will guide you to the home of your dreams."

She inserted a picture of herself on the left and a picture of Medora on the right with their names and titles:" Fern Schmidt, Broker," and "Medora Schmidt, Associate," under each picture. On a whim she placed a picture of her nephew, with his name "Timmy," in the middle.

Fern smiled as she looked as she worked on the brochure. She had never dreamed of such success. She had twelve listings, an even dozen—pretty good for a little outfit that had started out on a shoestring. She owned property in town and several parcels of acreage, stocks and bonds, and had a nice balance in her bank account. Even so, she continued to live frugally. ~~She must have inherited Papa Gus's~~ preference for saving, rather than spending money.

There was the sound of feet on the mat outside of the door, and then the door banged open and Medora stomped inside.

"Fern I'm so mad I could scream."

"Where's Timmy?"

"Asleep in the car; I can see him from here." Medora pointed out the window and went on, "Fern that damn Oney has the road to the cabin blocked. I had to hike in. When I looked in the storage room, I saw shelves and shelves of moonshine."

A vein pulsed in Medora's forehead. "He's the reason Charlie's dead."

Taking a deep breath Fern replied, "No he's not. If Oney wasn't there Charlie would have found liquor somewhere else. What Oney does is illegal and it's a nuisance having him hanging out at that deserted cabin, but Charlie's death wasn't Oney's fault."

" I thought Ernest was going to run him off."

"He did. A few days after you got home from the hospital Ernest and Doug went up and warned Oney the next time they caught him around there he was going to jail, and most probably prison," Fern said.

"They shouldn't have warned him; they should have locked him up in jail and thrown away the key."

"It's hard for Ernest and Doug, and me. We went to school with Oney. He was a decent kid—smart too—but he had to leave school when his dad got sick. He took over the family business. He wanted to be a computer technician, but he ended up just like his daddy and his granddaddy before him."

Fern yawned. "Tomorrow I'll tell Ernest he's moved back in." She looked at her monitor. "Bring Timmy in, and once you get him settled, we'll paste the photos you took into the ad. It's going to be in the Sunday paper and then things should start popping."

* * *

The pleasant-looking, silver haired couple sat at Medora's desk and signed the documents.

"When will we know they accepted our offer?" the woman asked.

"It will be two days at the most, Mrs. Brown. I'll call you right away,"

Medora said as she walked them to the door.

"Your first sale—I'm so proud of you," Fern said as soon as the door closed.

"Well, it's not final yet, but I'm pretty sure the sellers will accept the Brown's offer. I won't make much, being it's on the multiple listing and given the selling price. But still, it's a start and I owe it all to you."

"Where are the Browns from?"

"They're retired teachers from Palm Springs. They have a town house in the desert—their winter home. They want to spend summers on the Oregon coast. They said they love the property I showed them— said it's exactly what they want, even though the modular home on the lot is small and needs fixing up.

"Fern, the Browns are nice people, and I love helping them, but I'm a bit envious." Medora paused and picked at her nail. "When I'm their age, I'll be all alone."

"Where did that come from? You have a little boy. Think how lucky you are, we all are, to have Timmy." Fern looked tired. She massaged the back of her neck and said, "Poor baby, he hasn't seen much of his Auntie, or his Mama the last few days. How's the little guy doing with the bottle?"

"I'm a regular dairy cow." Medora sighed. "I've got probably ten bottles of breast milk in the freezer at the big cabin, and three or four more at the trailer." Her voice quavered; Ma Tom says he's doing fine. My only worry is that the bottle will be easy for him and he'll forget about me."

"Take a couple of days off," Fern said. "You and Timmy go out to the trailer. We've worked our butts off since the ad came out."

"I will," Medora said. "I feel like I need to spend some good one on one time with Timmy, and the birdfeeders probably need filling. Sorry for whining. When I get tired, I get gloomy."

Fern slipped into her raincoat and grabbed her umbrella. The sun was trying to peek through the dark clouds, but every few minutes there was a burst of rain.

"Hank…I mean Dr. Lopez, and I are going to the Inn for dinner. I'm so glad we finally have a decent place to eat here in Tamlin."

"Drive safe," Medora told her. "This weather is unpredictable. I'll just finish up here, pick up Timmy from Ma Tom, and head out to the trailer. Tell Hank, I mean Dr. Lopez, 'hello' from me," she teased.

"See you in a couple of days," Fern said and looked at her watch. "Here comes the bus from Portland, right on time.

As soon as Fern closed the door, Medora gathered the folders from both desks, carried them over to the file cabinets, and placed them in alphabetical-chronological order according to Fern's system. She locked the cabinets and was making sure the fire in the little stove was out when the door opened.

"I'll be with you in a minute," Medora called as she closed the damper at the back of the stove. "Ah—oh," she gasped when she saw the woman. She tried not to stare at the emaciated body, bald head and grotesque face. The poor thing looked like she had some horrible disease. Forcing a smile Medora asked, "May I help you?"

The woman held up the advertisement insert, "I want to see this property." She stabbed her finger at the pictures of the Weiss's cabin and twenty acres."

"I don't think that would be the best property for you," Medora said. "It's very remote and needs some repairs." She didn't add that it also needed someone to get rid of the dirty little moonshiner who sold his bootleg alcohol from that location,

"This is exactly what I am looking for and I am prepared to pay cash. The thing is, I'm short on time and I want to see it this afternoon."

"We don't have much daylight left, only about an hour," Medora told her. "It's been raining off and on, and the road to the cabin isn't accessible. We'd have to walk almost half a mile."

Medora was excited about the prospect of selling the cabin, but this woman didn't look like she could walk a city block—let alone half a mile in the rain through rough terrain. Then there was the worry about Oney and his pranks.

"Fine," the woman said. "Let's go."

"I have another appointment scheduled," Medora told her. "I'll have to see if I can change it." She decided to use the phone on Fern's desk to call Ma Tom. If she talked in a low voice it would be harder for this woman to overhear.

"Hello, Ma Tom, this is Medora. Is every thing okay there?"

"Timmy just took the bottle and now he is sleeping. I'll prepare some dinner for you. What time will you arrive?"

"A client came in. She wants to see the Weiss cabin, so I'll be a while. Ma Tom…" Medora tried to think of a way to communicate her client's disturbing physical condition. "*Esta un mujer de delor.*"

"You will tell me later, my daughter," Ma Tom said. Medora had called the client "a woman of pain." That couldn't be right.

"I should be at the big cabin in a couple of hours. Thanks Ma Tom."

"You must hurry to show the property before the light is gone. Perhaps you'll sell the Weiss cabin this evening."

After placing the phone back on the base, Medora pulled her old wool cardigan over her flannel shirt, got her backpack and an umbrella. "Do you have an umbrella?" she asked the woman.

"No, I don't need one," the woman answered sharply.

There was something familiar about the voice. Medora was sure she had heard it before, but couldn't remember where. The woman was staring out the window and tapping her fingers on the desk.

"My car is out in front—the red Saturn," Medora told her.

The woman snorted, banged out the door and strode over to lean on Medora's car.

Grabbing her keys, Medora locked the office door and hurried to open the car door for the woman. "I didn't introduce myself, I'm Medora Schmidt."

The woman's trembling hand flew to narrow silver chain around her neck. Clutching the ring which hung from it, she snarled," I'm Ruby—Ruby Kruger."

Book III
Ruby

Chapter Thirty-five
Ruby

Mommy was reading an article about managing difficult children. Noticing the time, she called out, "Ruby Jones, you get down here right now." Sighing, she put her magazine, the October, 1945, issue of *The Parent's Companion Journal*, on the table and started toward the stairs.

When Ruby heard Mommy call her, she turned the faucet off with her elbow, and considered using the towel on the rack to dry her hands. No, the towel might have germs on it. Instead she held her hands out and, letting the water drip, she thudded down the stairs.

"Ruby Jones, you are a naughty dirty little girl," Mommy said when she saw the splashes of water on her polished floor.

"She's only nine years old; give the kid a break," Daddy yelled down from the landing. He was getting ready to go to his job at the gas station near their house in Rosamunde.

"You just shut up, Earl," Mommy said putting on her jacket and fishing a set of keys out of her purse. "I have to get to work. Someone has to hold down a decent job in this house. Get into the car Ruby. You took too long, now no time for breakfast. I warned you."

Mommy was the cosmetic counter girl at the Savoy Drug Emporium on Main Street. Ruby stared at Mommy's profile as they drove toward

Rosamunde Elementary school. Mommy was beautiful. She was little and round with dark curly hair and long eyelashes.

Ruby wished she looked like Mommy, but she had inherited Daddy's long face and wide spaced eyes. She was a head taller than anyone else in her class and her hands dangled on the ends of her too long arms, like a gorilla. One of the names the kids called Ruby was Gorilla Girl; they also called her Horse Face, and Bird Legs.

"Get out, hurry, we're late." Mommy slowed the car and pulled over to the curb.

As soon as Ruby closed the door the car sped away. She was left standing alone on the sidewalk. Something was odd about the school. It was too quiet. There were no cars and no kids. When she tried the front door she found it locked. Then she remembered; school was closed for Christopher Columbus' Day.

Ruby knew the way home. She often walked when Mommy worked late. Skipping up Quince Street, Ruby enjoyed the trees and sunshine, but then she began to worry about germs in the air. The worry grew into a fear so big that she could go neither forward nor backward. Her heart began to pound. Taking a deep breath, she pinched a piece of her skirt material with the thumb and forefinger of each hand; she rolled the material over her arms to form a barrier against the germs in the air.

Now Ruby was able to proceed toward home as long as she stepped over each crack in the sidewalk. When she turned on Elm Street she could see Daddy's truck in the driveway. That meant he hadn't gone to work and was probably drinking again. Mommy was going to be mad.

Ruby went through the kitchen door into the living room. Daddy was on the couch in his pajamas. He sat up when he saw Ruby.

"Come over here, Honey," Daddy said in a slurry voice. As he lifted Ruby onto his lap, the winey smell of his breath tickled her nose and made her sneeze. "Ha, ha, ha," Daddy laughed and then he kissed her on the lips and put his hand under her skirt to pat her fanny.

Ruby hungered for touching and cuddling. She snuggled up to Daddy. The door creaked open and Ruby watched Mommy tiptoe in. Ruby had heard Mommy telling Gram that Daddy was up to some sort of hanky-panky. Mommy must have left her job and came back to spy on Daddy and his hanky-panky—what ever that was.

Both Daddy and Ruby jumped when Mommy screamed. "Earl, you leave her alone. Get out of this house; get out pervert!"

"You're the pervert—that's what you are—a pervert," Daddy snarled.

Mommy picked up the antique wooden rocking chair she got at a yard sale, and smashed it over Daddy's back. A splintery piece of wood stabbed Ruby in the arm. Blood ran down and dripped on the rug. Neither Mommy nor Daddy seemed to notice.

Daddy towered over Mommy. Red blotches stood out on his white face. "Leave me the hell alone, Arletta. Just stay the hell away from me." He stomped over to the refrigerator and took out a big jug of wine. Then he stuffed his feet into his boots and pulled his baseball cap onto his head. Still in his pajamas, he took the truck keys off the table, and carrying the jug in one hand, slammed the door behind him so hard the knick-knacks fell off the shelf over the table.

Turning on Ruby, Mommy screamed, "This is your fault. You were always a nasty little girl." Mommy ran to the door, "Earl, come back, I'm sorry, don't leave." The truck sped down the street.

"Call Gram to come over here right now," Mommy sobbed and then ran up the stairs. Ruby heard the bedroom door slam.

In less than fifteen minutes Gram rushed into the kitchen. Her pink scalp showed through her untidy white fluff of dandelion hair, and she was still wearing her furry purple bedroom slippers. "What happened to your arm, Ruby?" she asked and reached down to pull the splinter out. She handed Ruby a bunch of paper towels. "Press these against it while I find some gauze and tape."

Upstairs Mommy began to howl when she heard Gram talking to Ruby. There was the sound of glass breaking and the howls grew louder. Gram scuffled up the stairs as fast as her purple slippers would go. She came back almost immediately and dialed the phone, "My daughter is bleeding badly, please send an ambulance." Then, without saying a word to Ruby, Gram went back to Mommy.

All alone in the downstairs, Ruby pressed the paper towels on her arm like Gram had told her to do. An ambulance wailed up in front of the house and two men ran through the front door carrying a stretcher. Ruby pointed toward upstairs.

When the men came down they had Mommy on the stretcher. Her wrists were wrapped in fat white bandages and she was crying. Gram shuffled along behind them in her slippers saying, "Arletta I can't go to the hospital. There's no one to stay with Ruby."

"Fine then, take care of your ugly little granddaughter and let your own daughter suffer alone," screeched Mommy. The stretcher men were headed out the door toward the ambulance when Mommy yelled, "Call Earl. Tell him I need him. Tell him to come to the hospital."

As the door was closing, Mommy glimpsed Ruby sitting on the couch and cried out, "Ruby, Ruby, Mommy needs you!!" The door clicked shut and Ruby heard the siren wailing down the street.

"Your arm is going to be fine, Honey." Gram put iodine on the hurt and blew to make the stinging stop; then she taped gauze over the iodine. When she was done fixing Ruby's arm she said, "Let's go over to my apartment and play Crazy Eights or Go Fish."

"Aren't you going to call Daddy like Mommy said?" asked Ruby.

"Maybe later…we'll see," Gram replied.

* * *

After one week Mommy came home from the hospital. The pills the doctor gave her made her a little drowsy and much calmer.

Mommy tried to find Daddy, but couldn't. He had been to the house and taken all of his things. Daddy's friend Jake told Mommy that Daddy went to the big city of Portland fifty miles away, to work in a garage during the day and attend Bartending School at night. Ruby kept hoping Daddy would come walking in the backdoor some evening.

At first Mommy was mad at Ruby. "It's your fault he left, "she said.

As the weeks passed, Mommy depended more and more on Ruby to keep her company. "What would I ever do with out you?" she began asking Ruby. Sometimes when Ruby was out in the yard playing, or up in her bedroom reading she would hear Mommy calling her, "Fix me a cup of tea, honey," or "Bring me my cigarettes," or, "Twist the rabbit ears, the TV is all snowy."

Every month Daddy sent a check. No letters or phone calls, just a check. Mommy was much nicer to Ruby now. She turned check days into a holiday. They would go to the bank and cash the check; then they would choose some sort of special treat like going to the movies or buying a new toy. They usually ended their holiday at the Stone Oven Italian Kitchen. Mommy loved spaghetti with mushroom sauce and Ruby loved sausage pizza.

Ruby was happy when she was home with Mommy, but school was different. The kids were mean and they made fun of her because she had to wash her hands so often. She tried hard at school, but she had to erase and start over so many times that she couldn't get her papers in on time. That upset the teachers.

Helen Trent was only in second grade. Ruby was a fourth grader, but Helen was nice. Helen never called Ruby names, and would say "hello" to Ruby and wave. Helen invited Ruby to play at her house after school, Ruby was thrilled to have a friend; she smiled to herself all day no matter what mean things the other kids did or how mad the teacher got.

Mrs. Trent picked the girls up after school. Two year old Timmy sat in the front seat beside her. He was clutching a grubby toy car and making putt—putt—putt sounds. His nose was running and he slobbered onto the front of his Mickey Mouse shirt. Helen and Ruby got into the backseat.

"My Mommy's car is nicer than your Mommy's car." Ruby twisted her skirt around to protect her hands and arms.

"My Daddy is a minister and he said God wants us to be nice to each other," Helen replied.

"My Daddy is a movie star and he has a horse that I can ride whenever I want," Ruby retorted.

Helen didn't say anything.

Inside the Trent house it smelled like vanilla and cinnamon. "I hope you like fresh baked cookies," Mrs. Trent said to Ruby. "Now you girls run in and wash your hands."

After splashing a little water on her hands and wiping them on her skirt Helen was ready to return to the kitchen for cookies. "Come on, Ruby," she said.

"Go ahead, I'll be there in a little bit," Ruby replied.

Ruby kept washing her hands over and over. After Helen left, Ruby looked around in the bathroom. On the counter was a little crystal dish with some rings in it. One ring had three small diamonds in a sort of a band. Ruby held it up to the light; it sparkled. On the gold inside of the band was some tiny writing: "TT to CT with love." Ruby put the ring in her pocket.

When Mrs. Trent came into the bathroom to get Ruby she had Timmy balanced on one hip. He stared at Ruby with round eyes. Mrs. Trent said, "Dear, I must insist you stop washing your hands and come have some cookies and milk. It's almost time for your mother to pick you up."

"I'm not hungry, thank you," Ruby replied.

While Mommy was making dinner that evening, Ruby took the nail scissors and made a small hole in her pillow then pushed the ring inside. Later she would fish it out and wear it on a string around her neck under her clothing.

At school the next day Ruby smiled and waved at Helen, but Helen looked away. During reading class, the principal, Mr. Newsome, called Ruby to his office. "Did you see a diamond ring at Helen Trent's house when you visited yesterday?" he asked her in a hard voice.

"No, sir." Ruby looked him right in the eye when she replied.

"People who take things which don't belong to them end up in jail," Mr. Newsome said. " The police know how to figure these things out. You may return to your class, Ruby."

Instead of going back to class Ruby walked home. "I'm never going to school again," she told Mommy that evening.

The next day Mommy went to see Mr. Newsome. "It is obvious to me that you are not diligent in monitoring normalcy in this school," she said, quoting from *The Parent's Companion Journal*.

"We would prefer that Ruby not return to Rosamunde Elementary," Mr. Newsome replied. "She is a misfit, too smart for the retarded class and too odd for our regular classes. We would prefer that she study at home. The home teacher, Mrs. Benson, will spend several hours with her every week."

Ruby loved staying at home, and Mommy loved having her there because Ruby kept the house in perfect order. When Mommy came home from work she could just rest and let Ruby wait on her. Ruby was so busy taking care of Mommy that she often forgot about washing her hands.

School work was a breeze for Ruby now. Mrs. Benson wrote "good work," and drew stars and happy faces on Ruby's papers.

Mommy started calling Ruby, "my good girl."

Chapter Thirty-six
Ruby

Dr. Lockland owned the drugstore where Mommy worked. The tragedy was his fault. Ruby and Mommy were so happy before he started coming around. Dr. Lockland wanted to go everywhere with them: to the movies, to the zoo, and to the children's museum. Nothing was special anymore. The check holidays were a thing of the past.

The door bell rang three times on the night of the tragedy. Mommy was in the kitchen getting dinner ready. The dining room table had been set with the best dishes and candles.

"Ruby, for Pete's sake, answer the door," Mommy called.

Ruby was upstairs in her bedroom; she ignored Mommy. Pretty soon Ruby heard the click, click of Mommy's high-heeled shoes across the linoleum floor in the foyer, and the sound of the front door opening.

After a few minutes of quiet talking Mommy called, "Come on down here Ruby, honey," in a high sweet voice. Ruby knew Mommy meant business when she used that voice, so Ruby slowly made her way down the stairs.

Mommy was standing in the hallway with a big smile on her face. In one hand she held a bouquet of roses, in the other a bottle of wine with a little basket on its bottom. "Just look what Emile brought for you,"

Mommy said as Dr. Lockland held out a box containing a 1000 piece jigsaw puzzle of Venice.

"Thank you, Dr. Lockland," Ruby's voice was flat. Dr. Lockland awkwardly patted her on the shoulder. Ruby stretched her mouth into a fake grin.

"Emile has ordered a sausage pizza for your dinner. Emile and I are going to sit on the front porch with a glass of wine and watch for the delivery boy. You play in your room or in the backyard," Mommy said to Ruby without looking at her. Mommy was busy looking at Dr. Lockland.

"Yes, Mommy," replied Ruby.

Ruby went into the backyard. She put the puzzle in a trash can, and sat in her tire swing. Toadstools grew under the pine tree in the corner of the yard. Ruby made up a little song to sing to her self as she swung back and forth: *"Aunt Mandy doesn't know, the old grey goose is dead. Who'll tell Aunt Mandy, her old gray goose is dead?"*

After a while Ruby went into the kitchen. Little spurts of red juice were jumping from the bubbling spaghetti sauce onto the stove top. She used the big wooden spoon to stir the sauce; then she turned the burner to low and wiped off the stove top before returning to her swing.

When Ruby heard the voice of the delivery boy, she went out to the front porch. Dr. Lockland was telling a joke. She didn't think the joke was funny, but she laughed anyway. After Dr. Lockland had showed off by giving the boy a five-dollar tip, they went in to have dinner.

Ruby thought her sausage pizza was very good. The grownups ate the spaghetti with mushroom sauce. They talked to each other, and smiled at each other and didn't even seem to notice Ruby was at the table.

After dinner Dr. Lockland said, "If there is anything I enjoy, it's a home cooked meal. Your mushroom sauce and spaghetti is the best I have ever tasted, Arletta."

Ruby said, "I'll do the dishes so you can sit on the porch with your coffee."

"I have the best little girl in the world," Mommy said.

"I consider myself a very lucky man," said Dr. Lockland.

Ruby slept very well that night, but towards morning she had a bad dream. Daddy had come home and he was pushing her higher and higher in the tire swing. Ruby wanted him to stop, but he kept pushing. She screamed for Mommy to make him stop. The sound of her own cries woke Ruby up.

The hands on the clock next to her bed pointed to 8:30. She didn't hear any noise in the house. Mommy must have overslept. First Ruby went down to the kitchen, but Mommy wasn't there. Then she went back up to Mommy's bedroom. Mommy was there but she was very still and quiet. Her pretty face was contorted into an ugly mask and her room smelled bad.

Ruby started to scream. She couldn't stop screaming. She was afraid of Mommy. Ruby ran screaming down the stairs and out the front door, and almost collided with the milkman.

"Ruby, what's wrong?" the milkman asked her.

Ruby couldn't talk, she could only scream and point toward the upstairs.

An ambulance came for Mommy, and the policemen took Ruby to the police station. The police lady who stayed with her was very nice. She asked Ruby lots of questions about Mommy and Dr. Lockland, and the pleasant dinner they had shared just last evening.

Eventually Gram came to get Ruby. "Arletta's in the hospital. She's very sick, so you'll stay with me for now, Honey," Gram said. Her eyes were red and puffy. When she tried to smile at Ruby her lips quivered.

Dr. Lockland was dead when the police went to his apartment over the pharmacy to check on him. Mommy died three days later.

Ruby cried for a week. Inside her head the idea whirled around that if she had been a better girl Daddy wouldn't have left, and Mommy would still be alive. All the fun times Ruby and Mommy had shared tumbled through her mind, and now Mommy was dead. Ruby would never see Mommy again.

Ruby spent most of her days in Gram's bathroom, washing her hands. Everything felt so out of control. After a while, her sadness was replaced by burning anger and hatred toward Dr. Lockland. Mommy's death was his fault.

The coroner said Mommy and Dr. Lockland died from eating Death Cap mushrooms in their spaghetti sauce. Gram called a lawyer and asked who she should sue for the poison mushrooms. The lawyer said maybe the mushroom growers, but they couldn't really prove where the poison mushrooms came from. Death Cap mushrooms grew wild around their area.

The police investigator found a patch of Death Cap mushrooms growing in the back yard by the tire swing and in the leftover spaghetti sauce. He said Mommy or Dr. Lockland might have picked some thinking they were safe to eat.

Daddy arrived two weeks later to take Ruby back to the house where she and Mommy had lived. Daddy had graduated from Bartending School so he was able to get a job at his friend Tony's place, just about a mile from the house.

Gram looked sternly at Daddy, "My daughter told me all about you, Earl Jones. I'll have the authorities on you if you don't watch your step. You keep your hands off that child!"

Living with Daddy was lonely. He was gone a lot. Ruby had to fix her own meals and eat alone. When Daddy was home he was tired and nervous; he never asked about her school like Mommy did. If Ruby tried to sit in his lap or give him a hug he would push her away.

"You're getting to be a big girl now. You're fifteen years old. Teenage girls don't sit in their Daddies' laps," he would say in a cross voice.

In August, Daddy went to the principal of Rosamunde High School, Mr. Lord, and talked to him about Ruby.

Mr. Lord said, "We'll try her out in a traditional program, if that doesn't work she can go to special education. Either way, she won't be left to her own devices. I agree with you that is not a good thing."

Ruby was furious when she heard what Daddy had done. How dare he treat her like this? Daddy would be sorry.

Ruby no longer washed her hands over and over. She stepped on all the cracks in the sidewalk. She wasn't afraid of anything anymore. Daddy had better watch out.

The next bad thing Daddy did was to bring Carol to live at their house. "This is my very dear friend, Carol Merritt," Daddy had said, "I better not catch you giving her any trouble."

Carol had a big chest, yellow hair and peacock blue painted on her eyes. She wore tight slinky clothes and laughed a lot. Carol liked Ruby because Ruby stayed out of her way and kept the house neat.

"You sure have a funny little girl Earl, "Carol told Daddy a couple of days later. "She's quiet as a mouse, such a nice little thing, very polite and neat."

Carol was one of the cocktail waitresses at Tony's Lounge. Sometimes after the bar closed Daddy and Carol invited their friends back to the house to smoke something they called "weed'. They laughed and talked in loud voices. They danced and did other things with each other. Ruby watched them from the top of the stairway.

If Daddy thought Ruby would refuse to go to school he was wrong. "You are going to school, if I have to hog tie you and carry you there," he said on the day before school was to start.

"Don't worry Daddy, I want to go to school. "

Daddy drove her to school the next morning. He escorted her to the office and got her schedule before he left. The first class was pre-algebra which was easy since Ruby had covered most of the material with Mrs. Benson long ago.

At lunchtime Ruby went out into the schoolyard. Six tough looking boys wearing black leather jackets bearing the word, "REBEL" on the back, sat together on a low wall in front of the cafeteria. They called out insults and jeered at passersby. Most of the kids stayed far away from the Rebels and their foul talk.

Imitating Carol's hip swinging walk, Ruby strolled over to the group of toughs. "Hello, there." Ruby said mimicking Carol's throaty voice.

"Oh, babeee!! Let's get it on after school," a boy with a greasy blonde ducktail and splotches of acne on his forehead and cheeks, yelled to her.

"Sure," answered Ruby.

"Meet me by the flag pole, then," the pimply boy, who went by the name of Spike, told her.

"Okay." As Ruby walked away she heard the boys' excited laughter.

For a long time, Ruby had craved for someone, anyone, to touch her. Now she was able to satisfy that craving. The sex was exciting, but she had no fondness for the Rebels. She considered them immature and stupid.

Although Ruby never got invited to a football game or school dance, she was popular with the Rebels. She often stayed out until dawn, partying with them. She didn't think Daddy would notice the late hours she kept, or the clinging sweaters she wore, but Daddy did.

"You little slut, who do you think you are coming in at all hours? Look at you; you look like a bitch in heat with all that make up! Where did you get that piece of white trash sweater?"

"Carol loaned it to me," Ruby's flat stare drilled through Daddy's angry eyes. It was Daddy who looked away first. Without a word, Ruby turned and walked out of the room. "Daddy will be sorry now," she said to herself.

Chapter Thirty-seven
Ruby

Even though Ruby got good grades, B's and C's except for an A in Chemistry, Earl kept up his harping. Nothing Ruby did suited him. "I never thought a daughter of mine would turn out to be the town tramp," he said.

"Give the kid a break, Earl. She's not the prettiest girl in the world, so she's a little wild. At least she's popular," Carol was always defending Ruby. She had taken Ruby under her wing, and knew all about the Rebels. She advised Ruby on birth control, loaned her clothes, and showed her how to tweeze her eyebrows and apply eye shadow.

In return for Carol's kindness, Ruby watched Earl and reported everything he did to Carol. "I think Rita called. Anyway I heard Earl on the phone telling a woman that he'd meet her at the motel. I heard him laugh and say, 'Carol is the kind of fat cow that only gives sour milk.'"

"Thanks for lettin' me know, kid," Carol said. "He's a bastard. We gals gotta stick together."

January was very cold. Despite the gas floor furnace in the living room, the bedrooms and bathroom upstairs were frigid. One evening Ruby went out to the garage. She turned on the overhead fluorescent light. It had been a long time since there had been enough room for a car or truck to park in the garage. Boxes and cartons, their contents marked in black on sides and tops; old toys; odds and ends of broken furniture and appliances filled the interior.

Ruby searched through the piles. Memories of Mommy flooded her mind when she found a battered cardboard box containing some of Mommy's dresses and shoes. She put her nose into the moth eaten assortment of clothing and thought she could still smell Mommy's Shalimar perfume.

Mommy would have never died if Earl hadn't walked out on them. "Earl will be sorry for what he did to us," Ruby muttered.

She found the things she had been looking for: an electric heater, a big outdoor thermometer and an old barometer. The heater had a fan behind the coils to push the warmth out. After turning off the light and shutting the garage door, Ruby carried the heater, the barometer and the thermometer into the house and upstairs. She went into Mommy's room—the room now occupied by Earl and Carol.

Wearing the rubber dishwashing gloves, Ruby arranged the fan so it would blow the heat toward the bed. She broke the thermometer and the barometer tubes, and smeared the pretty silver liquid from their insides onto the coils of the heater.

She watched the mercury slither down the heater coils and form little balls on the bottom of the heater case. How glad Earl and Carol would be for the heater on these cold nights.

Ruby made sure the windows and door to the room were shut tight. She carried the gloves and the broken thermometer and barometer outside to the garbage can. She tucked them under the coffee grounds, whiskey bottles and newspapers. Tomorrow was Wednesday—trash pickup day.

Going back into the house, Ruby scrambled a couple of eggs for her dinner. After eating she tackled her homework. At nine o'clock, Ruby made sure the house was neat and tidy, and then went up to her room and closed the door behind her.

Around three o'clock in the morning, she heard Earl and Carol come in. They were yelling at each other. Earl was mad because Carol had been dancing with a man in the bar.

"You two-bit, two-faced loser Earl, you have a lot of nerve yelling at me. I know about you and your floozy. You've been putting the make on Rita and you know it. I've had it with you! I feel sorry for that poor kid of yours—stuck with a screw-up like you for an old man."

Ruby heard sounds of dresser drawers and closets opening and banging shut. Carol must be packing her things. She was glad Carol was leaving Earl; she liked Carol.

Earl shouted, "Stupid cow, I'm glad you're leaving."

"Loser!" Carol screamed.

The front door slammed. The cabinet in the dining room where Earl kept his booze creaked open, then shut. There were footsteps on the stairs.

Opening her door a crack to peek out, Ruby saw Earl on the landing with a bottle of whiskey in his hand. He opened his bedroom door and went in, but didn't close it behind him.

Ruby waited a long time; then quiet as a mouse she tiptoed over to Earl's bedroom door and looked in. The lights were on and Earl was still dressed, but he looked sound asleep. The heater coils glowed brightly.

The whiskey bottle on the floor next to the bed was half empty. Ruby crept in and picked up the bottle. She went into the bathroom and looked in the cabinet. The container of Tylenol elixir—a brand new medicine Dr. Lockland had given Mommy to try—caught her eye. It was almost full. She dumped it into the whiskey bottle.

Ruby put the bottle near Earl's hand in case he got thirsty in the night. She closed the door and pushed the hallway rug against the gap at the bottom of the door. Now Earl would be nice and warm.

When Ruby got home from school the next day Earl's truck was still in the driveway. The downstairs was still neat and clean. Earl usually scattered the newspaper, left dirty dishes standing on the polished furniture, and dropped his soiled socks and underwear in the living room. To find the house so tidy was a pleasant surprise for Ruby.

"Earl must be asleep," she thought. "I better check on him; he'll be mad if I let him be late for work."

The bedroom door was still shut. She slid the rug away from it and knocked.

"Ruby..." Earl's voice was weak.

"What Earl?" called Ruby from behind the door.

"I'm so sick, help me," came Earl's faint voice.

Ruby opened the door slowly. It was hot in the room; the air smelled of whiskey, cigarettes and sickness. Ruby gagged, then swallowed and went in to help Earl.

The empty whiskey bottle lay on the floor. Ruby turned off the heater and placed it and the whiskey bottle out side the door.

"It's hot in here," Ruby said and she opened a window.

"I'm so cold," Earl moaned, "Ruby—call the doctor."

"Earl, you look yellow," she replied in the tone of a casual observer.

After she carried the heater to the garage and hid it in the box with Mommy's clothing, Ruby tossed the whiskey bottle into the trash and went in to call Dr. Kelly.

First the nurse talked to her; then Dr. Kelly came on the line, "I'm sending an ambulance for your dad. He needs to go to the hospital, but don't worry honey, I'm sure he will be alright."

The next afternoon when school was out Ruby went to the hospital to visit Earl. He was looking a little better, but he was grumpy.

"It's my liver. The doctor says I have to quit drinking. That's pretty hard to do when I'm a bartender." Earl smiled at Ruby. "You couldn't bring me a bottle from the liquor cabinet, could you Sweetheart?"

Before she left Ruby asked a nurse, "Can I bring my dad some orange juice tomorrow? He loves orange juice."

"That would be a nice treat for him," the pretty young nurse patted Ruby's arm.

Ruby took the bus downtown. She went to Perkins Grocery Store and bought a bottle of orange juice and a box of children's orange flavored Aspirin. Then Ruby went to the Savoy Drug Store and bought another box of children's orange flavored Aspirin. Her errands done, she returned home.

The house was nice and tidy downstairs, but upstairs Earl's room was a mess. Ruby got a big cardboard carton from the garage. She carried it upstairs and put all of Earl's stinky bedding into it. Then she went to the closet and started pulling Earl's clothing off hangers and stuffing it into the box. When the box was full she carried it down and placed it by the trash cans. Back and forth from the garage to the house, to the trash cans, she went. It took five big boxes full before all of Earl's things had been removed from the house.

Ruby was tired. She opened a can of chicken noodle soup for her dinner. After eating she went right to bed.

The next day was Saturday, so she slept late. When she awoke, Ruby thought how nice it was to have the house to her self. It was fun to lie around in her pajamas and to watch cartoons with the TV turned up as loud as she wanted. Earl would never yell at her again for being noisy while he was sleeping.

In the afternoon Ruby went to the hospital. Earl was looking less yellow now, but his disposition hadn't improved.

"What have you got there?" the nurse asked Ruby, taking the lid off the bottle and sniffing it. "Just orange juice—sorry I had to check no booze allowed."

"Where's my booze?" was the first thing Earl said to Ruby.

Did he ask about her school work? No! Did he ask if she was alright in the house all alone? No! Earl didn't care about anyone but his own stupid self. If it wasn't for him, Mommy would still be alive!

"I brought you some orange juice, Earl," Ruby said in her flat voice.

Earl gulped the whole bottle down. "That was extra sweet. Most things just don't taste right. I have a metallic flavor in my mouth. Listen up Ruby; next time bring something from the cabinet!" he snarled.

"Good bye Earl," said Ruby and she left the room.

* * *

Dr. Kelly himself came to the house the next morning to tell Ruby about Earl. "He started hemorrhaging in the night," Dr. Kelly said. "We don't know what caused it, but it probably had something to do with his alcohol intake."

Dr. Kelly was so nice. He stayed with Ruby until Gram came to get her. Ruby held a handkerchief to her eyes and made little sobbing noises. She just couldn't help crying; she was an orphan after all. It was so sad.

Chapter Thirty-eight
Ruby

Smoke swirled around the old elm tree and floated into the air. Dense gray clouds obscured the sun, and moisture dripped like tears from the bare tree branches.

Ruby's heart was a cold, hard stone in her chest. First she lost Mommy, now Earl was gone. One by one she poked her brightly colored sweaters and skimpy skirts into Gram's incinerator. She promised herself she would never smile, or laugh, or care about anyone again.

The clothing she wore, a baggy black skirt of Gram's and Earl's oversized black sweatshirt covered by a belted black trench coat from the thrift store, suited her mood and she vowed never to wear anything but black.

When Ruby returned to school a few days after the funeral, the boys on the wall eyed her warily; she was beginning to make them a little nervous.

She waited several weeks before approaching them. Then one day she marched up to them with an authoritative step that was much different from her usual hip swinging stride.

The Rebels stared at this new Ruby, with her metallic blue black hair and shaved eyebrows. "You—Butch—meet me behind the school auditorium tonight," she commanded a tall boy with an elaborately oiled ducktail.

Butch hunched his shoulders and pulled his neck, turtle-like, into the up-turned collar of his leather jacket. "I have something already …" he began in a squeak.

Giving a backwards jerk of her thumb toward the auditorium she marched off.

Ruby didn't crave sex very often after Earl died, but when the urge was upon her—he wanted it—and the rougher the better. The Rebels became alarmed by the way Ruby intimidated them, used them, and then ridiculed them. Behind her back they called her, "The Black Widow".

They came to dread Ruby so much that they gave up their seat on the wall. Butch and Killer joined the army. Spike and Leroy were too young. They exchanged their black leather jackets and greasy ducktails for plaid shirts and flat top hair cuts; they hid in the crowd of similarly dressed students.

If Gram was sad to see Ruby wearing black like an old widow lady she didn't say anything. No matter what Ruby wore, Gram loved having her share the cozy little antique filled apartment. Ruby was a real pleasure to have around, always quiet, neat and polite.

Ruby liked being with Gram, "I don't know how you ever managed without me," she told Gram. Although she was only sixteen when she moved in, she immediately took over the shopping, cooking and cleaning.

This arrangement left Gram plenty of time to read her romantic novels. Gram didn't mind Ruby changing furniture about or rearranging closets and dresser drawers, as long as she didn't interrupt when Gram was engrossed in a juicy love story.

Ruby eventually took to choosing Gram's clothing and hairstyle. The teenager was bossy and opinionated, but the only bit of mutiny Gram showed was to annoy Ruby by leaving her teeth in the jar on the sink.

"I have the best granddaughter in the world," Gram said to Ruby and whoever else would listen. Ruby kept their little home neat, cooked tasty meals, and got all A's and B's in her high school classes.

By the time Ruby turned eighteen, she knew exactly what she wanted to do after she graduated high school. She stripped the black tint from her drab blond hair and traded her black wardrobe for a white nurse's uniform. She got a job at the Sunny Hills Skilled Nursing Home just three blocks from Gram's apartment.

The Nursing Assistant training classes provided by Sunny Hills for newly hired employees lasted six weeks. Ruby excelled; she was a natural born nurturer. After completing her classes, she spent her abundant energy caring for the elderly patients at Sunny Hills, and taking care of Gram. She felt needed and appreciated.

* * *

Two years later on a day in June, as she sat in the dayroom reading the local newspaper to old Mr. Elliot, Ruby received a shock. She saw a familiar face staring back at her from the society section. According to the article, Helen Trent was to be valedictorian of her graduating class, and Reverend Trent, Helen's father, was to make the keynote speech.

"I can see it now." Ruby's heart began to pound. "Helen's mother and her little brother, Timmy, will be there clapping and acting so proud. Helen probably has a beautiful new dress for the after graduation dance. It's so unfair." Pulling the ring from under her uniform, she shoved it roughly up and down the silver chain.

"Go ahead, keep reading," Mr. Elliot whined.

"Shut up you old fool," Ruby hissed.

"What, speak up," the old man said leaning toward her and cupping his ear.

Ignoring Mr. Elliot, Ruby continued to dwell on the injustice. Helen Trent and her goody-goody mother were the reason she left school. Ruby didn't have a mother or father or brother, and here was Helen Trent in the society pages, big as life, just rubbing it in. Helen probably planned this whole thing in order to belittle Ruby. Did Helen spend her days cleaning up after old people? No not Miss High and Mighty Helen.

"Ruby," Mr. Elliot's voice broke into her consciousness. "Tell me what the weather is going to be and read me my horoscope. What's wrong with you; this is my time to read the paper; it's on my schedule, RUBY!"

Ruby scowled at Mr. Elliot. He leaned back in his wheel chair, as far away from her as he could get.

Sour anger growing in the pit of her stomach flowed into her throat and filled her mouth with the taste of bile. She hated the Trent family with a passion so fierce it was almost sexual in nature—and like sexual tension—it called for release.

Closing her eyes, Ruby amused herself by imagining all of the Trent family—goody-goody Reverend Trent, saccharine sweet Mrs. Trent, their angelic little Timmy, and most of all, two-faced Helen—dead. A thin smile played over her lips; she opened her eyes and looked at Mr. Elliot.

"Sorry, Mr. Elliot, I have a little headache," she said as, humming to herself, she picked up the paper and looked for the horoscope section.

Chapter Thirty-nine
Ruby

Ruby was a fixture at Sunny Hills Skilled Nursing Home. She had been there longer than any other employee. Four silver stars, each signifying five years of service, adorned her name badge. The families of the patients, the administrators, and the doctors all agreed, Ruby had a natural aptitude for caring for elderly people.

It was a comfortable life. She made enough money to buy herself a new car every two years, and to repaint walls, and put new carpet and linoleum in Gram's apartment. Of course, living with Gram kept Ruby's expenses to a minimum.

Ruby rarely ventured beyond the few shabby blocks that made up Gram's neighborhood. There was no reason to buy fancy clothes when she always wore a uniform. She didn't have any friends, and never went on vacation. Sunny Hills and Gram were her whole world.

Sometimes Ruby felt disappointed in the way her life turned out. She was on a hamster wheel. She got up every morning and took care of Gram. She went to work and took care of patients, and then she went home and took care of Gram again. There had to be something more to living.

* * *

Mrs. Meyers, a seventy-year old spinster, was admitted to Sunny Hills for rehabilitation after suffering a mild stroke. She had worked as a registered nurse right up to the time she got sick. She often talked to Ruby, encouraging her to consider working part time at Sunny Hills while attending nursing school. "There are a lot more opportunities in nursing when you have a license," Mrs. Meyers advised.

* * *

Although she was on time for her appointment with the nursing school counselor, Ms. Carson, at Rosamunde Community College, Ruby had to wait almost half an hour before the she was called into the cubical.

Ms. Carson had short, spiky blond hair and was wearing an electric blue silk blouse. She reviewed Ruby's qualifications, and then said, "You don't have the necessary prerequisites for the RN program. The LVN program is less stringent. It only takes eighteen months. You might consider that. Your experience as a nursing assistant will be helpful."

As she drove toward Gram's apartment that afternoon, Ruby mulled it over. She was almost forty. If her life was going to change, it had better be soon. She just didn't think she could handle Gram, her job, and school. There had to be an easier way. She remembered something Gram often said, "God helps those who help themselves."

* * *

Poor Mrs. Myers passed away suddenly one evening. Ruby was the one who found her. There was no need for an autopsy; Doctor Bridges had been by to see her that morning. He decided she must have had another stroke. "I kept increasing her medication, but when I saw her this morning her blood pressure was sky high and her kidneys were starting to deteriorate."

Ruby put her hand into her pocket. Her fingers touched the little pills.

Mrs. Meyers had been interesting to talk to. Ruby felt a pang the first time she saw poor bewildered Mrs. Epstein, the new patient, in the bed where Mrs. Meyers had died. Like Mrs. Meyers, Mrs. Epstein was a stroke victim. Ruby chatted cheerfully as she went about providing care, but the frightened lady only nodded her head while tears streamed down her cheeks.

"It's funny how things happen for a good reason," Ruby said. "Mrs. Meyers had a stroke, just like you, but she could still talk. She did me a favor by dying—of course I gave her a little nudge. Thanks to her I won't be changing diapers for old dollies like you much longer. I'm going to be the boss, the one in charge. As soon as I get the money Mrs. Meyers left me, I'll be off to nursing school. I'll be gone, but you'll still be lying here like a slab of meat."

* * *

She knew she looked nice. It was the night of nursing school graduation. Nurse graduates traditionally wore uniforms to the ceremony; Ruby was at her best in a white uniform. And she had a little secret, Helen's mother's diamond ring, hanging from a silver chain, nestled between her breasts.

She had been to the beauty parlor. "This suits you, my dear." The beautician held the color swatch for the tint named "Dark Desire," next to Ruby's sallow face. Ruby was very pleased with the results. Her mousey grey streaked hair was now a rich, shining brown and the new mannish cut gave her confidence.

"Sweet Mrs. Meyers, I'll never forget her," Ruby said to Gram on the ride home.

Gram, looking stylish in the pink polyester pant suit Ruby had chosen for her, was beaming with pride. Her granddaughter was an LVN.

Now that graduation was over, Ruby was nervous about applying for a position as an LVN. She decided to give Gram's apartment a good cleaning before she looked for a job.

"There's an advertisement in the paper for Elite Cleaners. They specialize in the gentle treatment of old items. I'm going to take your Sunbonnet Sue quilt to them. It's just filthy." Ruby was sorting out the closets and dresser drawers.

"I wish you'd leave my things alone. My grandma made that quilt; I don't want to risk anything happening to it," Gram said.

"The thing reeks. It's either going to the dumpster or to Elite—you decide." Ruby poked the faded quilt into a black trash bag and headed out to her car.

Elite Cleaners was in a new strip mall about five miles away. It was much nicer than the run-down shopping center near Gram's apartment.

"That quilt is very old, and probably valuable. It will fall apart if we use our chemicals on it," the cleaner said. "You'll have to sign this form saying you've been warned and won't hold us to blame."

She signed the form and left the quilt to be cleaned. When Ruby went to pick it up three days later, she was told it had disintegrated. Gram moped around, and Ruby felt terrible, until she made it up to Gram by buying a polyester, crazy quilt patterned, comforter to take the place of the dirty old rag.

As she walked toward her car after leaving the quilt at the cleaner's, she noticed a sign on one of the store fronts: *Grosham Physical Therapy Clinic, opening in three weeks, specializing in sports injuries.*

When Ruby peered through the window, she saw a stout man, wearing a Bob Marley "One Love" tee shirt, directing the carpet layers. She brought her knuckles up to the glass door and rapped several times. The man looked toward the sound, nodded at Ruby and came to open the door. "Can I help you with something, Miss?" His smooth pink face was boyish, but his head was completely bald.

"Where can I get a job application? I just received my LVN license, and I've had years of experience as a nursing assistant," Ruby explained in, what she hoped, was a businesslike voice. She was glad she had combed her hair and put on lipstick before her trip to the cleaners.

The man smiled. "I'm Dr. Grosham. I planned to advertise for a nurse next week. Let's go over to Flo's Coffee Shop and discuss your employment over a cup of tea."

Ruby and Dr. Grosham hit it off right away. They spent two hours talking that first day. He hired her on the spot. He even paid for her to go to special classes where she learned about sports therapy. She studied hard and worked hard.

Dr. Grosham was never sorry he hired her; Ruby was sure of that. If Dr. Grosham wasn't pleased with her work, he wouldn't have been so eager to write her a good recommendation when he asked her to leave.

* * *

It was love at first sight. Ruby had never seen anyone as virile as David Kruger. He was twenty-two years old and looked gorgeous spread out on the examination table wearing just paper gown and bikini underwear.

"What brought you in to the clinic today?" Ruby asked even though she held David's records in her hand.

"I hurt my knee last year. The doctor says it's a torn ligament. You should have seen me, I played varsity defensive tackle. Everyone said I was awesome. Two colleges offered me scholarships, and then I had to go and get hurt. Now look at me; I work part time for my Uncle, moving furniture. Nobody else would give me a job. Nobody cares that I'd have gone to the pros if it wasn't for my knee."

Ruby nodded her head in sympathy, "I'm sure Dr. Grosham will be able to help you. Before he comes in, I'm going to massage your leg, and put the infra red light on your knee." Her voice came out in gasps, as if she had been running.

Swirls of golden hairs covered David's muscular calf and thigh. They disappeared under his skimpy underpants. His skin was firm and smooth, so unlike the bodies of the elderly patients at Sunny Hills Nursing Home. David's scent was a combination of musky aftershave and sweat.

"Ruby, is Mr. Kruger ready for his treatment?" Dr. Grosham's voice broke into Ruby's reverie.

"Give us a couple of minutes. I'm just starting the infrared," Ruby managed to answer.

* * *

When David arrived two days later for his next appointment, Ruby had a plan.

While she massaged his leg, David once again told her, "It's so unfair. I would have been in the pros if it wasn't for this knee. Do you know how much money guys just like me make in the pros? I would have been making six figures, maybe seven, but instead I move furniture part time and my uncle pays me minimum wage."

"You must have been wonderful," she told him. "I'd love to hear more about it, and perhaps see some pictures if you have any." Ruby acted as if the idea had just occurred to her, "I know—why don't you meet me at The Half Time Sports Bar around eight this evening. I'll buy you dinner, and you can tell me all about football."

That evening they met for dinner and then, at Ruby's suggestion, went for a drive into the country. She parked her car in a dirt side road, and they looked at the stars. "I don't think I've ever seen so many stars," Ruby's voice was husky. "It's beautiful out here in the country."

"I better get home," David told her nervously.

"Don't be silly," Turning toward David, Ruby put her right index finger on the tip of his nose and then slowly traced a line across his lips, down his chest and belly to his groin.

David moaned.

* * *

"When can I see you again?" Ruby was reluctant to say goodbye to David. They were back in the deserted Half Time Sports Bar parking lot. It was almost three in the morning.

"Well, I have to work tomorrow, and I'm going to be tired afterward. It's not all that easy. I shouldn't be lifting with my knee like it is, but the doctor won't sign my disability claims form." David knew he was babbling, but Ruby made him edgy. She was too old and she came on too strong. Having rough sex in a car with someone the age of your mom was weird, and now he just wanted to get away from her. The worst of it was that he'd have to change doctors.

"How much do you get paid?" Ruby asked.

"Oh, well, it comes out to about six dollars an hour, and I'll work probably eight or ten hours."

"I'll tell you what," Ruby reached into her purse, "don't go to work tomorrow. Sleep in and call me when you wake up. I'll meet you here tomorrow night at eight. If you aren't here, I'll come to your house to pick you up. Which ever you want." She handed David a hundred dollar bill.

Chapter Forty
Ruby

It wasn't that the car was in bad shape mechanically, or that the body was dented or rusty. No, that was all perfect. The upholstery had been perfect until Ruby started going with David.

After each date she felt compelled to give the back seat a thorough cleaning. Thanks to frequent soap, disinfectant, deodorizer and hot water treatments, the cushions in the back seat were permanently damp. Bits of black fuzz grew along the seams and the whole car smelled like moldy sweat with an overlay of musk. She needed a new car.

That evening at the Sports Bar she said, "David, do you always have to order the most expensive things on the menu? I'm trying to save for a new car."

Ignoring Ruby, David ordered three appetizers, a large steak, a side of shrimp, and a second pitcher of beer. As soon as the waiter walked away, David looked at her. "Uh, Ruby," he stammered. "You know the sweatshirt you got me?"

"I certainly do. Eighty dollars for a high school sweatshirt, I never heard of such a thing and I don't know why you need it."

"Well," he continued. "Some of my friends have these cool old-school skateboard shoes and I really need a pair."

"How much?" Ruby asked. At this rate she was never going to get another car.

The after dinner romantic interlude was a disappointment. David wasn't feeling well. As she was driving back to the Sports Bar, Ruby decided it was time to do something about the situation.

"I'm going to meet your parents," she told David. "We've been going together for over a year. Surely they know you have a fiancé."

David was shaken when he heard the word fiancé. He felt trapped. It was like a net tightening around him. The harder he struggled to get free, the more entangled he became. At first it had been great getting presents and making good money for just a few hours of companionship, but for a long time he had wanted to be rid of Ruby. She was a creep and she was disrupting his life.

He lived in fear that his parents would somehow find out he no longer worked for Uncle Bob at the Van and Storage. He had to pretend to go to work. The hours he spent away from home were lonely. There was no one to hang out with, his friends were either working, or had gone away to school.

The best he could do was to hide out in the library and spend his time worrying that one of his mother's nosey friends might see him. He was miserable.

Even worse than the empty days, were the twice a week dates with Ruby. He hated the rides into the country. He wanted his life back; he wanted to be rid of Ruby—but how? Now she was talking like they were going to get engaged or something—holy shit! Maybe he could stall her.

He said, "It's just that Mom and Dad are older, and Dad has a heart condition. I'm their only child; it makes it difficult for me to tell them. Anyway, there's no big hurry is there? If you're short of money, maybe we shouldn't see each other for a while."

"Not see each other! You're kidding. We'll always be together—always!"

* * *

As soon as Ruby dropped David in the parking lot of the Sport's Bar, he put her out of his mind. He went right home, made a little snack, and climbed into bed. He slept late the next morning and spent the day skateboarding up and down the driveway and around the patio. He enjoyed a good dinner and was looking forward to a relaxing evening. He stretched, pulled up his shirt and patted his belly, then started stacking the dinner plates.

"That was good, Mom. You make the best meatloaf in the world. Don't worry about the dishes; I'll help you cleanup later." David carried the plates to the kitchen.

Meanwhile, Mary Kruger eased her plump body down onto the couch. As she arranged pillows around her hips and back, a warm flush spread over her neck and face. She pushed a strand of faded blonde hair out of her eyes, and began to fan herself with the TV guide.

"Stop messing around in the kitchen," David's father, George Kruger, called from the big leather recliner. "You can do that later. It's time for our show, Davie."

The family made a ritual of watching Jeopardy together every night. They'd done it for years. When the questions were asked, they would try to outdo the contestants and each other in yelling out the answers.

David settled himself on the couch. He put his feet in Mom's lap, and she began to massage them. The contestants were being introduced when the doorbell rang.

"Don't answer it," said George.

"Don't be silly dear. I've got to see who is out there," Mary replied.

David lifted his feet out of her lap. In a few seconds the men heard her confused voice, "Oh, well Davie never mentioned it to his father or me. Fiancé—you must be teasing—oh I see."

David held his breath.

Mary, with her plump arms folded across her middle as though she had a stomachache, came back into the living room. Her usually smooth round face was puckered in a worried frown. Ruby, showing all of her crooked yellow teeth in a wide grin, followed close behind.

"Don't let me disturb you. Go ahead and watch your program," Ruby said.

"Who the heck are you?" asked George.

"As I told your wife, I'm David's fiancé. My name is Ruby Jones. I don't know your names, so I'll just call you Mom and Dad."

"Davie, who is this person?" A distended vein in George's left temple pulsed like a little heart.

"Ruby's the nurse at my doctor's office, Dad. That's all, I don't know why she came here," David's voice shook. "My parents' names are George and Mary," David told Ruby in his quavering voice.

"I won't disturb your evening, so don't bother to ask me to sit down. I'll run along. I'm very glad to have finally met you—George and Mary."

Mary automatically said, "Oh yes, a pleasure, come again, dear."

George interrupted, "Just show her out; it was not a pleasure at all." He pointed the remote control at the TV and the volume increased,

Ruby started toward the door. She raised her voice so it could be heard over the TV. "I'll be dropping in again soon. You'll have to get used to the idea that David is a man now, and he has a man's needs." She stared critically at Mary. "Next time I'll bring my tweezers so I can pluck the hairs from that ugly mole on your chin."

"Oh my goodness," Mary said.

"That crazy woman looks old enough to be your grandmother," George shouted.

* * *

David was a nervous wreck when he met Ruby at the Half Time Sports Bar two evenings later. "Don't ever come to my house again," he pleaded. "I'll do anything you want; just don't upset Mom and Dad."

"What did your parents say about me?" Ruby demanded.

"Nothing, absolutely nothing, they acted like nothing unusual had happened. We watched Jeopardy like always, and they never mentioned you."

"Your parents probably want you to marry some young twit and keep her pregnant. They want someone to supply them with grandchildren. Selfish, selfish people, that's what they are. Just because you live in their fusty little house they think they have the right to direct your life," she told him.

David felt like a traitor. He wanted to defend his parents, but Ruby's voice was getting loud, and people were turning to look at them. He decided to keep quiet.

"I'm taking you to meet my Gram tonight. Our families have to get used to the idea that you and I are in love," Ruby yelled.

David couldn't remember ever telling Ruby that he loved her. It was a stupid idea and she was yelling it and everyone was turning to look. His voice came out in whisper. "I'm not dressed right to meet your Gram."

"It doesn't matter. You look fine," she snapped.

* * *

Half an hour later they were standing in Gram's apartment. "I'd like you to meet my fiancé, David Krueger," Ruby said to the old lady.

Gram, always set in her ways, was becoming difficult. She put down the romance magazine she was reading, and scrutinized David. "He's a child. How could you take up with a child?"

"He is not a child. He's going to be my husband!" Ruby's face was a mask of rage.

David didn't know which way to look. The two women spoke as though he were some sort of a big dumb animal who couldn't understand what was being said.

"Then he's nothing but a two-bit hustler. He's not living in my house," Gram said in the lisping voice which indicated that her false teeth were in a jar on the sink instead of in her mouth.

Ruby had told Gram a hundred times to keep her teeth in her mouth. Now here she was, meeting David without her teeth. It was embarrassing. Gram's cheeks sunk in and she made chewing motions, like an old cow. "You're too stupid to live," Ruby snarled. "Come on David, let's go."

In the car Ruby told David, "It's a shame you and Gram didn't hit it off better. The two of you are the most important people in my life."

* * *

Ruby was never cross or unkind to Gram—thank goodness. She would have felt terrible if she and Gram had been arguing or holding a grudge against each other when Gram died suddenly.

It happened two days later, on Ruby's day off. She had fixed a little surprise, a breakfast tray with fresh squeezed orange juice and a rose in a bud vase. When she pushed Gram's door open and said, "Good Morning, Sunshine," she thought the old lady was sleeping.

Gram was propped on her pillows and covered with her cheerful crazy quilt comforter. Even though Ruby was a trained nurse, it took her several seconds to realize, Gram was not just asleep.

"She snored terribly and sometimes she would stop breathing," Ruby told the medical examiner. "I tried to get her to go to her doctor about it, but she refused. I think she was embarrassed about the snoring; she thought it was unladylike." Ruby wiped the tears which were flowing down her cheeks with a tissue and then blew her nose. "I'm sorry. It was all so sudden, and Gram was my only family. I don't know what will happen to me now."

* * *

That evening, in the car, under the stars, Ruby turned to David. "We're going to be married next week."

"I'm not ready for marriage," David said.

"I'll bet George and Mary would love to know you don't have a job. They would love a detailed description of what goes on in the back seat of my car, and they'd love to know about the money I give you. One of them might even have a stroke."

"Don't tell them, please don't tell," David begged. "I'll do whatever you want."

They were married at the courthouse one week later.

Ruby looked for a house out in the country where she and David could see the stars at night. She found the ideal place, twenty miles outside of Rosamunde. It was a little run down, but they could fix it up. Agricultural chemicals had been stored on the property at one time, rendering the soil sterile. It was perfect.

David suggested calling a used furniture dealer. "We can sell all this old stuff and get enough money to buy a big screen TV," he told Ruby. They carted a lot of Gram's old junk—the windup Victrola, the collection of faded postcards, and a big box of family photos and old letters—out to the dumpster. The used furniture dealer gave them a surprisingly large sum for the rest of Gram's furniture and bric-a-brac.

* * *

"I want to get my skateboard and stuff from my house," David demanded.

At first Ruby refused, but later relented, and so when George and Mary Kruger were at church the next Sunday morning, Ruby and David removed his belongings from the room he had occupied since birth.

When David wanted to keep his truck, Ruby put her foot down, "I let you get your junk from your parents, but you aren't going to keep that truck. There is no reason for you to go anywhere without me."

That afternoon Ruby and David traded his truck and her old car for a new car—an elegant 1979 Crown Victoria, white with white leather upholstery—Ruby vowed to keep this car in perfect condition, which meant covering the seats with black plastic

Then she turned her attention to their new house. She scrubbed it from top to bottom. When everything was clean, the newlyweds went shopping for a king size mattress, a freezer and a microwave. David got his big screen TV and faux leather lounge chair.

When they had everything unpacked and arranged, Ruby hugged David. "It's wonderful having everything shiny and fresh," she told him, "and we have enough money left to put an eight foot chain link fence with a row of barbed wire on the top around our property."

"That's stupid," David said. "I'd rather have my truck."

Ruby's fingernails dug into his arms and his eyes watered. "David," she said. "I value my privacy."

* * *

Dr. Grosham was beginning to worry. He knew Ruby had recently lost her Grandmother, had married, and had moved to the country. He hoped she would settle down and get used to the changes in her life. Just then a patient approached him and yelled, "That nurse is crazy!"

"She certainly is," shouted a man just entering the clinic. "My name is George Kruger, and I want to know what kind of a place you're running? That nurse of yours seduced my son at your so-called clinic, and he's less than half her age!" George pounded the receptionist's desk with his fists. "I've just about made up my mind to get the vice squad to investigate what goes on in this brothel."

Dr. Grosham calmed the two men the best he could. As soon as they left, he called Ruby into his office to tell her he was letting her go. "We won't say I'm firing you, but you need to look for another situation. I'm going to give you a letter of recommendation and two weeks pay. Clean out your locker and leave immediately."

Chapter Forty-one
Ruby

"David, come here and get your shot; I have to leave in a few minutes." Ruby smoothed the skirt of her dazzling white uniform and bent to flick a bit of dust off her freshly polished white shoes. After patting her hair into place, she pinned her nurse's cap on it with two long black bobby pins.

The last time she colored her hair she made the mistake of leaving the Dark Desire tint on a tad too long. Her hair now had a three toned appearance: white at the roots, brassy in the middle, and frizzy burnt black on the ends. Thank goodness her cap covered most of it.

"Don't make me come in there, David Krueger"

"I don't want that stuff. Go away." He whined, and pressed himself into the cushions of his chair.

"Here I come, David; and you are going to be sorry you didn't obey me."

Trembling, he pulled himself to his feet and shuffled into the bedroom. His chin and the front of his shirt were wet with drool. He looked at his wife and cringed.

Ruby was a mass of muscle and sinew—a very strong woman. She grabbed him and plunged the hypodermic into his biceps. Before releasing his arm, she twisted it up behind his back.

He screamed.

Ruby smiled as she helped him back to his chair, and like a good wife, made sure he was comfortable. "In the twenty years we've been married, dear," she said lovingly. "I haven't changed much at all, but you—well I don't think your own mother would recognize you. Relax, watch your TV and take a little nap." She took his left arm and moved it up and down. "You're stiff; I'll give you a massage when I get home."

"No," David whined.

"Shut up," she snapped, and took a good look at him. He had doubled his weight from one hundred and eighty to almost four hundred pounds. His eyes, face and even the skin on his bald pate were the color of saffron. Between the fat and the stiff muscles he looked like an obese zombie.

"You're an old man while I'm still young and attractive," she told him.

Head back, mouth open, he answered with a snore.

She kicked his leg and he groaned but didn't wake up. "How the hell am I going to get the drugs I need to control you in six months when I retire?" she asked her unconscious husband. "You little bastard, I know you'll try to run away if I don't keep you medicated. Maybe alcohol injected intravenously will work as well as Haldol. We'll find out."

As she drove toward the nursing home that night, she remembered the time, early in their marriage, when she was working at the sport's clinic in town. David scaled the chain link fence, and even though he was badly cut by the barbed wire, tried to hitch hike into town. Luckily she spotted him on her way home from work.

That was a long time ago. She had worked the night-shift at Saint Elfreda, just a mile from their house, for most of the years of their marriage. From there it was easy for her to sneak home to check on David, and she had access to the medication cart.

Ruby looked at her watch. "Goodbye, David. I'm off to work." She unlocked the freezer and choose eight TV dinners which she stacked on the on the counter. Your food's in the kitchen she called as she went out the door and locked it behind her.

* * *

The next morning, Ruby, having worked all night, settled herself in bed for a nap. She was nodding off when the honking of a horn followed by the wail of a siren jarred her awake. She pushed the black plastic curtain aside, and peeked out the window. A tall man in a suit was standing by a police car down at the gate. Pulling a jacket over the rumpled old sweat suit she slept in, she hurried to see what he wanted.

"Sorry to disturb you," Detective Jim Bayley's eyes took in the strange looking woman approaching on the other side of the locked gate. She had to be over six feet tall—a real weird looking broad. He showed his identification and introduced himself. "Does David Krueger live here?" he asked.

"Yes, he's my husband, but he's not well enough to talk to you," Ruby answered.

"Sorry, ma'am, I need to have a look around your place and talk to your husband," Bayley said. "Please unlock the gate for me." He hoped she would comply voluntarily; there were no grounds for a search warrant, but he had a hunch ….

She reluctantly opened the gate and the detective drove his jeep up to the driveway, parked next to the Crown Victoria, and followed Ruby into the house.

David was in his chair, remote control in one hand and a cherry frosted donut in the other.

"Sir, did you write this letter?" Bayley showed David a sheet of paper with childish writing: *Dear Dad and Mom, Help! She is trying to kill me. Your loving son, Davie.*

David glanced sideways at Ruby and giggled. He didn't answer the question.

"Sir, is anyone trying to harm you?" Bayley asked.

More giggles from David.

It was one of the strangest setups Bayley had ever come across. The guy was a four hundred pound fruitcake. The broad wasn't quite right either. Something was going on, but he couldn't identify any illegal activities.

"I'm sorry to have to tell you, sir, that your father is dead. He died almost ten years ago of a heart attack. Did you know that?

"Your mother is concerned about you. This letter has upset her. I have to look around. If you have anything to tell me, now is the time."

David said nothing.

Bayley waited. The scent of disinfectant was strong and the detective's eyes began to water. Holding his handkerchief over his nose and mouth, he gazed around. The floors were bare white linoleum. The only furniture was David's plastic covered lounge chair, and a widescreen TV. Black plastic covered the windows; the sole source of light was the glow of the TV screen.

When David began to snore, Bayley gave up on getting a statement from him and continued the tour of the house. It turned out to be three rooms and a bathroom. All of the interior doors had been removed. When he went into the combined kitchen and dining room, he saw a microwave on the counter top, but no regular stove. The space that should have held a refrigerator and stove was occupied by a large chest type freezer, the lid secured by a heavy chain and padlock.

"Please open this," Detective Bayley said to Ruby. She searched in the dilapidated tote bag which served as her purse, found a key and unfastened the lock. The inside of the chest was filled with every imaginable kind of microwave meal. There was also a wide variety of microwave desserts. "Thank you," he said and turned his attention to the room,

The walls, where cupboards must have once been attached, were scarred by nail holes. There were no doors on the cupboards under the sink and counter. Empty spaces showed where drawers for utensils must have been. As in the living room, the kitchen window was covered with black plastic. An array of purple, brown and gray disinfectant bottles lined up like soldiers on the counter. The room was barren of anything else except a box of white plastic spoons on the edge if the counter.

Bayley looked into the bedroom.

"I didn't have time to make the bed. You woke me up," Ruby was verging on hysteria. She clutched her purse and prayed the policeman would not ask to look in it. The hypodermic needles and vials of Haldol would be difficult to explain.

There was nothing in the bedroom except a plastic wrapped king sized mattress covered by a cheap crazy quilt patterned comforter. Aside from the disinfectant bottles, it was the only spot of color in the house. Three white uniforms hung in a row in the doorless closet. Two white plastic laundry baskets held, what looked like, white undergarments and socks.

The bathroom was more of the same. No mirrors, no wall cabinets, no drawers, no shower curtain, no bath towels, just a roll of paper towels and a roll of toilet paper. Everything in the house was scrupulously clean and smelled of disinfectant.

"I'm done here. I'll show myself out," Bayley called to Ruby. He could hear high pitched giggling. It sounded like David was enjoying the cartoons. He stepped into the living room and handed David one of his business cards, which David slid under the cushion of his chair.

* * *

After the detective's visit, Ruby was as jumpy as a cat on an electric fence. There was no telling what David would do; he was completely out of control. He must have rummaged through her purse, found a postage stamp and managed to mail a letter to his parents. He probably waited down by the fence until the mailman came by. The little sneak did it while she was asleep. Even thinking about it made her angry.

She nailed the front door shut and installed three stout hasps on the back door which she secured with heavy padlocks. It was risky, he looked so yellow, but she increased David's dose of Haldol and fastened all the locks before she went to work that evening. He wasn't going to be getting into any more trouble if she could help it.

Chapter Forty-two
Ruby

Thank goodness her shift was over. Ruby ran through the rain to her car. Gripping the steering wheel, she threw back her head and screamed. She felt as if she would explode. Helen Trent, married, and with a pregnant daughter, had come to Saint Elfreda's to taunt her. Well, when Ruby was done, Helen would wish she had died in the fire.

The Crown Vic sped down the bumpy road. Ruby opened the gate with shaking hands. She needed to hurt someone; that was the only thing that helped when she felt like this.

David heard the backdoor slam and knew Ruby was home. He didn't dare get out of his chair. Maybe if he was real good she'd give him something to eat. Ever since the policeman's visit six months ago, she'd been punishing him. "I'll teach you to send letters to your bitch of a mother," she'd say when he begged for something to eat. Sometimes he had nothing for two or three days in a row.

From the kitchen came the sounds of screaming and cursing. Ruby was so noisy; he couldn't even hear his program. He reached for the remote control and increased the volume.

"*Stand thar and don't move a muscle,*" the cartoon sheriff yelled into the room. He raised a huge gun, aimed, and pulled the trigger. A flag popped out with the word "BANG" written on it. The sound of the laugh track was followed by a drum roll.

Ruby burst into the room. "Helen's alive and she has a husband, and pregnant daughter. All these years I've thought she was dead, but she's been alive and happy." Ruby swung her purse and hit David on the side of the head. He started to whimper.

"I'm gonna get rid of them all and you're going to help me!" she raged.

"*With Patty Purse you will never be lonely*," the TV was even louder during the commercial. On the screen three little girls, each with a Patty Purse doll, were having a tea party while a carousel tune chimed merrily in the background.

"I'm hungry," David whined. "You didn't leave me anything to eat again."

"Shut up, shut up," Ruby screamed. She threw first one rubber-soled shoe, then the other at him.

He wrapped his arms around his head and shut his eyes.

"And keep this damned TV off while I sleep!" She yanked the cord from the wall and the room went silent.

"I'm starving. Can I have something to eat?" David pleaded, but Ruby went into the bedroom and banged the door shut.

"Where the hell did I put them?" She lifted one corner of the mattress, then another. Under the third corner she found her stash of opiate pain killers. Tossing a handful into her mouth, she chewed them like candy, as she paced around the room shouting, "All these years she's been alive and happy while my life has been crap—CRAP—CRAP—CRAP." Her voice rose to a scream and she pounded the wall with her fists.

Fifteen minutes later, exhaustion and the opiates caught up with her. She curled in a ball on top of the old polyester crazy quilt comforter, and slept.

When everything was quiet, David got out of his chair and, holding his baggy sweatpants to keep them from falling off, tiptoed toward the bedroom door. He looked like a size small skeleton wearing size extra-large skin. Putting his ear against the door he listened for several minutes before returning to the chair.

The bedroom seemed quiet, but better to be cautious. He sat back down and waited. She had really gone insane this time, leaving the doors unlocked and her purse where he could get at it. He stared at the bedroom door. When an hour had passed without Ruby coming out, he went over and picked up the purse. This could be one of her tricks, but he would risk it. He fished the keys out and shuffled into the kitchen.

Unlocking the freezer, he took out an armload of frozen meals. He thrust two dinners, one a: spaghetti with mushroom sauce and, one a beef stroganoff, into the microwave. He punched a button; the light came on and the little table whirled his food around. When the icy hardness began to show signs of melting, he took them out. Like a feral dog with a fresh kill, he tore frosty chunks from the dinners with his teeth and swallowed them without chewing. All the while he remained alert for the sound of the bedroom door.

He placed two more meals: chicken portabella and fettuccini Alfredo, into the microwave, and then two more. He repeated the action over and over. He threw up on the floor twice, but kept shoving frozen food into his mouth as fast as he could.

When his appetite was finally sated, he began to think of some of the things Ruby had said. She was going to "get rid" of a man and a lady, and a pregnant girl. That meant she was going to kill them; it was terrible. His mother would want him to stop her.

Even though they didn't have a mailbox, David knew if he waved his arms, the mailman would see him and stop. That was how David had been able to mail a letter to his mom the time she sent the policeman to check on him.

He reached his hand under the cushion of his chair, and pulled out Detective Bayley's card. It was a little wrinkled, but the detective's name, address and telephone numbers were still readable.

Using a pen from Ruby's purse, he turned the card over and wrote in his best handwriting:

Danger—Ruby wants to kill the man, the lady and the pregnant girl. David Kruger. P.S. She is starving me.

The backdoor was ajar; more proof of Ruby's lapse. David pushed it open, and in his backless bedroom slippers, he shuffled along the dirt driveway toward the front fence. It was such a long way and he didn't feel at all well, but this was the right thing to do. He kept looking back at the house. If Ruby saw him, she would be very angry.

The mailman was coming. He was stopping at each mailbox along the highway. David ran the last the last few yards. The blood pounded in his head and he thought he was going to faint. He leaned against the fence and waved one arm.

"Oh jeeze, it's that crazy guy again," the mail carrier muttered. "Poor guy, he looks terrible." He slowed his jeep and pulled over. "How can I help you, sir?"

"Very important, very important," David's voice squeaked. "This must get to the policeman—here see—Detective Bayley." He handed the carrier the tattered card.

"Yes sir. Right away." The mail carrier took the card and dropped it into the ashtray which already contained an array of gum wrappers and paper clips.

It was a long trip back to the house. David vomited on the way. His heart thumped as if it was trying to escape from his chest and his legs felt like they didn't belong to him. The third time he fell he couldn't get up. He crawled the rest of the way. It took forever, but he made it to the house and pulled himself into his recliner. The room wouldn't stop spinning. He closed his eyes and began to snore.

Ruby had a way of walking very quietly. Even though the TV was off, David didn't hear her come up behind him with the hypodermic needle.

"I saw that mess in the kitchen," she whispered. "I'm going to make you so sorry you'll wish you were dead." She planned to give the shot in his upper arm as usual, but when she saw the thick carotid artery pulsing in his scrawny neck, she couldn't stop herself from stabbing the needle in and pushing the plunger all the way down.

He never knew what hit him. His right arm flew up reflexively. It hit Ruby on the nose. Tears streamed down her cheeks. "Stop it," she screeched. Thinking David was fighting back, she grabbed his hair and banged his head into the side of the chair.

It took Ruby a few seconds to realize something was wrong. He was not whimpering or begging her to stop. When she let go of his hair, his head lolled forward. She placed her hand on the side of his neck and felt for a pulse.

"No! David, I didn't mean to!"

His death left her all alone. She had never in her life been by herself. There had been Mommy and Daddy and Gram, and then David. They were all gone and she was on her own.

What if her mother-in-law found out about David's accident? What if the policeman came back to look around the house again. She would have to get things cleaned up right away.

Ruby was no stranger to death, but she had never before had to dispose of a body. She looked at David slumped in his chair. He was thin and she was strong, but what should she do with him? It would take hours to dig a hole big enough to hold him, and how would she get him into it? What could she do with him?

She winced when she surveyed the mess he made in the kitchen, but it had to be dealt with. The open freezer door gave her an idea. The first thing was to get things back in order. She cleaned up the vomit with paper towels and put them, along with the empty boxes and half eaten trays of food into a black plastic trash bag. She carried the bag out to the front gate and left it for the garbage man to pick up the next day. Then she removed the rest of the TV dinners and desserts from the freezer and stacked them alphabetically along one wall in the kitchen.

She rolled her massage table over to David's chair. She pushed a button, leaned her weight on the table, and it slowly sank to the floor. Then she stood in front of David's body, placed her hands under his arms and leaned backward. She got him out of the recliner, but when she attempted to pivot and lower him onto the table, she lost her balance and fell backward with his body on top of her.

"Get him off me! Get him off me!" she howled to the empty room. Although he was emaciated, his weight pressed heavily against her, making it hard to get a breath. She kicked and pushed to no avail.

Worn out by her efforts, she closed her eyes and experienced her husband's strange final embrace. She remembered their first meeting and had a moment of regret for those lost times. "David," she said.

His left leg kicked out and his left arm jerked. Ruby opened her eyes and gazed directly into his blank stare. She screamed, and terror gave her the strength to roll out from under his dead weight.

For a few minutes she lay panting on the floor. It took a huge effort, but she forced herself to get back to the job at hand. She got onto her knees and pushed at David's body. Now that he was on the floor, rolling him onto the massage table should have been simple, but his arms and legs kept sliding off.

She decided to roll him into a sheet, and to use safety pins to hold the wrapping in place. It was a job, but the sheet made keeping him on the table much easier.

Getting the table to its full height proved to be another difficult chore. It would have been less complicated with two people, one at each end. Running from head to foot she raised it one or two inches at a time. By the time she was done, she was dripping with perspiration and very tired.

She rolled the massage table, with David on it, into the kitchen. Now luck was with her. The height of the table was a few inches above the height of the open freezer. She easily rolled him into the freezer and was delighted he fit with no alterations necessary.

If David hadn't been such a glutton there would have been enough TV dinners to completely cover him. Ruby did the best she could, but she would have to go into Rosamunde and buy some more boxes of frozen food at Perkins Grocery tomorrow morning after work. Loaves of bread might work well, too. She replaced the lock on the freezer and dropped the keys back into her purse.

Ruby's nerves were as taut as fiddle strings. She began cleaning house, paying particular attention to David's recliner, remote control and TV. She scrubbed everything with disinfectant. When the house was as sanitary as she could get it, she took the disinfectant into the shower and massaged every inch of her body with it. She paid especial attention to her hands, washing them over and over until they bled.

Three more hours until time to leave for work, Ruby tried to nap, but she tossed and turned. After an hour, she wrapped herself in Gram's polyester quilt, and lay on top of the freezer. She drifted off to sleep.

* * *

That night Ruby was late to work for the first time in all her years at Mount Saint Elfreda, and she didn't care.

Caroline gave her a tongue lashing, "When you are late it means I have to stay, and I have already worked at least twelve hours."

How petty the head-nurse was. Ruby had never noticed before, but she was too busy to let it bother her. It turned out to be a hectic night at Saint Elfreda. After Caroline left four of the elderly patients died in their sleep.

Chapter Forty-three
Ruby

A white uniform hung on a hook by the back door. Ruby clad in bra and panties was perched on the edge of the open freezer. A diamond ring hung from the silver chain she wore around her neck. David, eyes wide open, seemed to stare up at her from the interior compartment. It was as though he was watching her eating the piece of pizza.

"Just a few hours and I'll be home with you all of the time, but first I have something important to accomplish. After that, I'll kiss good old Saint Elfreda goodbye."

Ruby slipped from the freezer and began to pace, eating and talking at the same time. "Remember how I told you Helen's husband was admitted two days ago? Well, David, she arrives at the crack of dawn and fusses over him until we make her leave."

Her words came on like machine gun bursts. "It's disgusting; I want to batter them with my fists every time I see them. I don't know who I hate more, him or her."

She waved her partially eaten piece of pizza in the air. "Don't worry, after tonight we won't be bothered with them any longer. I'll make them suffer, just like I've suffered all these years." She sat on the freezer again and finished the last bite of pizza.

It was nice to have David to talk to. Reaching down to pull a loaf of bread away from his chin, Ruby thought how much easier he was to manage now. He'd only been in the freezer a little over a month, but she wished she'd put him there sooner. She didn't have to worry about him running away, or mailing letters to his mother. The house stayed neat. She didn't have to steal medicine and force him to take it. Yet, here he was, as handsome as ever, listening to her every word.

"I don't know where the daughter lives. She hasn't come to visit the old man yet. That is a problem for me. If I'm not working there, how can I find the daughter? It has to be done; both she and her baby have to pay for Helen's cruelty."

Ruby tugged at the silver chain she wore around her neck and slid the diamond ring hanging from it back and forth. "I won't have a minute's rest until the whole damn bunch of them is burning in hell."

David's expression didn't change. Ruby began to wonder what was going through his mind. He might be docile, but still she couldn't trust him. Even now, when he was seemingly so agreeable, she couldn't know what he might be up to when she was gone.

"You don't really care, do you?" she shrilled as she slid off the hard edge and leaned into the freezer. After everything she had done for him, he should be more supportive. Well, the hell with him. "Fine!" she screamed her face just inches from his.

"If that's the way you're going to be."

She slammed the lid of the freezer. Pulling the heavy chain around it, she snapped the big padlock shut, and gave it a tug to make sure it was securely fastened.

Ruby went into the bedroom; crawled onto the bed, and covered herself with Gram's old crazy quilt. The rain beat against the roof and the wind whistled through broken windowpanes. She tried to sleep, but couldn't stop thinking of David's smug face. Taking the quilt, she padded out to the kitchen in her bare feet. "Okay, David, you win. You know I can't stay away from you for long."

She wrapped herself in the ragged quilt, curled up on top of the freezer and immediately fell into a deep sleep.

According to her watch, it was five minutes after nine o'clock when she woke. "Oh, shit, Caroline will have a fit." Ruby slipped into her uniform and tried to run a comb through her hair, but it was too matted and snarled. She settled for pinning her white nurse's cap on the top of her head.

The rain and wind had not let up, if anything the storm had worsened. Taking a rumpled yellow plastic poncho out of her purse, she flung it around her shoulders, fastened the snaps and pulled the hood over her head.

"You wait here for me," she called to David. "I'll have lots to tell you when I get back tomorrow morning."

It took all of her strength to push the door open against the wind. She slipped out and let it slam shut. There was no need to lock it. No intruder would be out on a night like this, but then you never knew what David might be up to. For her own peace of mind she snapped each of the four big padlocks shut.

When she stepped away from the shelter of the house, the force of the wind almost knocked her over. Nevertheless, she fought her way to her car and then back to the house three times to recheck the locks on the door before she was satisfied. Head down, she struggled, for the fourth time, toward the big powerful 1984 Crown Victoria which gleamed white each time the lightening flashed.

After fastening her seat belt, she inserted and twisted the key. It was as if the forces of nature were conspiring to keep her from completing her mission. The starter ground and ground, but the engine wouldn't catch. This was her last chance to deal with Helen's husband. She had to get to Mount Saint Elfreda. Cursing, she twisted again. The starter grunted weakly, but this time the engine sputtered to life.

Ruby negotiated the driveway which was like a river of mud. Leaving the car running she got out and opened the gate, drove through, and then got out again to close and lock it, before turning on to the main highway.

The wind howled and the rain fell in torrents. Ruby hunched over the steering wheel. The jarring unevenness of the pavement and the blinding rain made any sort of speed impossible. Lightning sliced the sky; followed by the boom of thunder. "That one was close," she muttered. Sheets of water splashed around her windshield wipers.

After creeping along for twenty minutes, she slowed even more before turning into a side road which was marked by a billboard sized sign fixed on top of the huge redwood stump. Foot high Gothic script, barely visible in the downpour, spelled out: *MOUNT SAINT ELFREDA NURSING HOME PRIVATE ROAD.*

This narrow lane was lined by ancient fir trees and ended at tall gates set in a towering wrought iron fence. The gates were monitored by a uniformed guard who dozed in his mist shrouded glass and cement booth. Ruby honked. He opened his eyes, nodded, and the gates creaked open.

The world around Ruby's car danced to the wail of banshee winds. A gray-stone edifice crouching at the end of the drive looked like a large animal in search of prey. The rumble of the thunder could have been the enraged roar of the hungry beast.

On this vile night it seemed impossible, but in pleasant weather these grounds were green and inviting. Visitors and their "loved ones", for that is how the staff was trained to refer to the patients, enjoyed the delightful gardens.

Ruby had always been proud of Mount Saint Elfreda. The grounds were well kept and the foyer and dining room, tastefully decorated in burgundy and blue, could easily have graced the finest country club. Everything was clean and neat, bright and hygienic.

Unfortunately the well-organized milieu of the main facility didn't continue into the nurses' lounge where magazines and newspapers were scattered casually about, and a pot of strong black coffee on a spattered utility cart kept the room permeated with its burnt fragrance. The lounge was the head-nurse's territory. Ruby had been told more than once not to clean or organize things in there.

* * *

"Oh my aching back," groaned Caroline Kelly, the head-nurse, as she pushed up smudged bifocals to rub her weary eyes, and then poured herself a cup of muddy coffee. She had started at eight in the morning, more than thirteen hours earlier. Ruby, the night-shift nurse was to have arrived at eight—thirty, but this was Ruby's last night before retirement. No wonder she didn't care about being on time.

Caroline's bulk spilled over the narrow seat of her chair. The table she leaned her freckled elbows on was piled with a stack of notebooks, each bearing the name of a patient. Opening one of the books, she scribbled a note about the patient's condition.

Mr. Hoffman ate more than fifty percent of his dinner. He watched TV until he received evening hygiene and was assisted to bed. He is oriented to his name only, but does not appear to be in distress.

Sometimes she made changes on the blackboard which hung on the wall next to the table. Patients' names, ages, diagnoses, dates of admission, last shower and last bowel movement were chalked upon its surface.

All of the patients, except one, had the words *no code, comfort care,* by his or her name. The exception was the newest admission, Ian Whitman. The words *full codes, full care,* were printed in bright blue next to his name.

Caroline disagreed with keeping patients alive against their wishes, but the wife, Helen, insisted. She needed time to get used to the idea that Mr. Whitman would never be well enough to go home again.

Pushing the books aside, Caroline looked at her watch. It was after ten. It seemed like she had been on duty forever. She was exhausted.

The door opened and Ruby, trudged into the room on rubber soled shoes. "Good heavens, what is that hullabaloo?" she said irritably. She jerked the poncho off and shook it, as if it was responsible for the offensive noise.

A steady stream of fretful babble came from one of the rooms, "Helen, Helen, come back ba, ba, ba. I'm sorry Medora, come back Helen, come back Medora, I'm sorry, I'm so sorry sorry sorry."

"It's Mr. Whitman in Room 15, Ruby," replied Caroline. "Come in so I can give you today's report. I need to go home. I'm really beat."

"Why haven't you medicated him?" Ruby demanded. "I'm not going to listen to that all night!"

This was an ongoing argument between the two women; Caroline accused Ruby of over-medicating the patients and not spending enough time with them. Even though Caroline was in charge, Ruby called Caroline's interactions with the patients, "too much stimulation," and advocated for heavy medication, saying it was in the best interest of everyone.

Caroline worried that something was terribly wrong with Ruby. The night nurse had always been a bit odd, but recently she had become downright bizarre.

"Has the wife been here again?" Ruby sneered.

"Yes, she was here most of the day and through the evening until about an hour ago. He was fine then. It's when she leaves that he gets anxious."

"She shouldn't be allowed to visit. She upsets the patients," Ruby spit the words out. "Her husband's as good as dead and the family needs to be told that! He's a corpse taking up space and time."

Caroline's stomach churned. She was thankful this was Ruby's last night. Despite being a bit odd, Ruby used to be a good nurse, but she had changed. It would have been better if she'd retired before she became so angry and hateful.

After filling Ruby in on the condition of each patient, Caroline returned to the ward and drew up the small dose of Ativan, a sedative, ordered for Mr. Whitman by his doctor.

Two night-shift nursing assistants, Selina and Topaz, were in the main station. Topaz's forehead puckered with the effort of concentration as she punched the computer keys one at a time. It was her job, using the new computer system, to input each patient's vital signs. Every time she moved her head little silver bells at the end of her many braids jingled.

Selina strummed a guitar and sang in a low voice, "*The Lord is my rock*," as she watched monitors displaying views of the hallways and day room. Her clean white shoes sat side-by-side under her chair and she had propped her swollen feet on a stool.

"Ladies, do me a favor and keep a close eye on Room 15," Caroline said.

"Don't you worry Miss Caroline," Topaz replied, "me and Selina know what's goin' on around here and we plan to be watchin' real close. I don't like to speak evil of nobody, but that Ruby Kruger has turned meaner than a junkyard dog—and that's mighty mean."

"Thanks ladies, I'm glad you're here to look after things," Caroline said, but she was still uneasy. In the past week there had been four deaths on Ruby's shift. The patients were old and sick, but four deaths in one week…Caroline was worried.

"No, no, I want to die. Die, die, die, please die," Mr. Whitman pleaded when Caroline entered his room. In the other bed his roommate Mr. Duncan snored.

"Poor Mr. Whitman, I know you want to cross-over, but your wife isn't ready to let you go. We have to do everything we can to keep you alive. She wants a little more time with you."

"Die, die, please," begged Mr. Whitman

"Shh, I have a sedative for you, and then I'll stay with you for a bit. Close your eyes and try to rest." As Caroline slid the needle into Mr. Whitman's arm she glanced at the photo of a young lady with red-gold curls on the bedside table. "Your pretty daughter keeps calling to see how you are doing. Too bad she lives far away. She loves you very much."

Caroline sat in the easy chair next to the bed and held Ian Whitman's hand. Except for two dim night-lights, the room was dark. The muted sound of rain on the roof was comforting. She stroked his arm and murmured, "Go to sleep now; everything is going to be okay; go to sleep." Mr. Whitman's tense body relaxed and his breathing became regular and deep.

Caroline must have dosed. She was startled awake when the door swung open and Ruby entered the room holding a large syringe. Caroline's eyes were accustomed to the dark; she could see more than double the amount of sedative ordered in the barrel of the syringe.

Chapter Forty-four
Ruby

Ruby gasped when she realized Caroline was sitting in the easy chair. She dropped the syringe into her pocket and said, "I thought you went home."

"I wanted to make sure Mr. Whitman was settled for the night before I left," said Caroline. "As you can see, he's already received his sedative." Ruby didn't reply, so Caroline added, "Be sure that narcotic in your pocket is wasted according to protocol."

Ruby snorted. Her rubber-soled shoes squeaked as she marched out of the room.

Caroline sat for a few moments wondering what she should do. Tiredness clung to her like a lead weight. She was letting her imagination run wild, Ruby couldn't have …. Without finishing the thought, she got to her feet and went to her locker for her purse and umbrella.

As soon as Ruby saw Caroline let herself out the back door, she returned to Mr. Whitman's room. She glanced at the snapshot on the bedside table. The girl in the photo had messy orange hair and a self-satisfied smirk. She resembled Helen Trent before the fire. Ruby slipped the photo into her pocket. It would make a nice addition to her scrapbook.

She turned toward the bed. At the sight of the open mouthed old man sleeping so peacefully the acid taste of bile filled her mouth. Her heart pounded against her chest and she felt as if her head would burst.

Mr. Ian Whitman was so ugly. The left side of his face drooped like a melted wax mask and a dribble of spit dampened his chin stubble. Ruby's hands shook and her fury crowded out all other emotions. It swept away reason and left paranoid rage in its wake.

She was sure he was involved in it. Maybe he knew about the diamond ring she wore on a chain around her neck. His precious wife Helen was responsible for the death of Ruby's parents. Well they were all going to pay—Helen, this man, the daughter and the unborn baby—they were all going to suffer for what they had done to her.

"You damned old freak!" Ruby picked up a pillow and held it over Mr. Whitman's face.

He kicked his right leg, and flung himself about in the narrow bed. For a hemiplegic he was amazingly strong. His right arm flailed out and the ragged nail of his index finger drew a crimson line from the lobe of Ruby's left ear to the corner of her mouth. She let out a screech.

Footsteps hurried down the hall toward the room, probably one of the nursing assistants. Ruby dropped the pillow just as the door opened.

"Help, murder, me, me, me, me," Mr. Whitman screamed.

"Is there a problem in here?" Selina asked. Her shining green eyes took in the bloody line on Ruby's smooth face. "Serves you right," Selina muttered.

Ruby suspected that Selina and Topaz loathed her, but their fear of her was even stronger than their contempt. After all she was in charge at night when there was no one else around. She could do as she liked.

"You fool!" Ruby yelled, "You left the side rail down and he attacked me when I was putting it up. I could have been killed." Mr. Duncan began to cry and Mr. Whitman continued to scream for help.

"Stay here while I get sedatives for them." Ruby hurried out of the room.

Selina closed the door. Her face gleamed with sweat. "Now fellows, I know she's somethin' terrible evil, but we got to put up with her for one more night." She smoothed each patient's blankets. "Selina ain't gonna let nobody hurt her buddies," she promised, and then began to hum a childhood lullaby, while the rain on the roof thum thumed an accompaniment to her soft voice.

The invalids stopped their noises and drifted back to sleep. The room became quiet except for the soothing sound of rain overhead, the swish of warm air through the heater vents, and the gentle snoring of the two frail men.

The door was thrust open and Ruby slithered in. "Hold them for me while I give the injections," she hissed and her pale hand reached toward the light switch.

Blood pounded in Selina's temples. She wanted nothing so much as to get away from this devil woman, but she could not leave Ruby alone with these two helpless old men. She took a deep breath and stood her ground.

"Don't turn on that light," Selina growled. "We don't need no light, or no medicine here, Miss Ruby."

She approached Ruby, transfixing her with cold unblinking eyes. Although Ruby was nearly six feet tall, at this moment Selina seemed to tower over her.

"You fool. I won't stand for this, I'll make sure you lose your job," Ruby quavered.

Selina saw the pillow on the floor. She bent down and picked it up. Holding it out in front of her, she stepped closer to Ruby. "Some of us has accidents, some makes mistakes, and some is just plain mean. There's lots of bad things been happenin' round here in the night. Whatcha' know 'bout them other deaths Miz Ruby? Maybe the policemens need to hear how you an' death goes in a room together. "

Ruby turned and ran down the hall to the nurses' lounge. She banged the door shut. Selina heard the seldom-used lock slide into place with a click.

With her hands pressed against her throbbing temples, she stumbled toward the main station. Her neat white uniform was marred by dark circles of sweat under her arms.

"Hey, Topaz, check my blood pressure will ya. I'm really shook—thought I was gonna pass out—but I stopped that she-devil, by gawd."

Topaz unfolded from her chair with cat-like grace, and reached for the blood pressure machine. "Sistah, you better take an extra blood pressure pill. Your eyes is all red." She wrapped the cuff around Selina's arm, and then said, "You done real good tonight, but don't it give you the willies to think she's gonna be out there in the world—like a landmine—waiting for some unsuspecting brutha to stumble on her—then—kaboom!"

* * *

After locking herself in the nurse's lounge, Ruby relaxed. All she had to do was bide her time. She wasn't tense. She could sit back and wait until the coast was clear. Selina and Topaz would relax their vigil after a while.

An hour went by before she quietly opened the door and stepped out into the hall. Immediately Selina came out of the nurse's station and went to stand in front of Ian Whitman's room. Ruby attempted to sneak out of the lounge three more times at hourly intervals, and each time either Selina or Topaz hurried out of the nurse's station and went to stand in front of Mr. Whitman's room. They seemed determined to maintain control of his room.

She would have to wait until change of shift. The day-shift nursing staff, except for Caroline, began at six each morning. Selina and Topaz would leave and the day nurses would be busy passing out medicine and getting patients ready for breakfast.

Ruby had wanted to watch Ian Whitman slowly suffocate, but thanks to Selina and Topaz she'd have to be quick. Oh well, she could spend more time on Helen and her daughter—and her daughter's child.

A nice big bubble of air in his vein would look just like another stroke. She took the large bore syringe out of her pocket, squirted the medication into the sink. She dropped the empty syringe back into her pocket and glanced at her watch; it was six thirty. Selina and Topaz probably left thirty minutes ago. She unlocked the door, turned the knob, quietly opened the door and gave a shrill scream when she came face to face with a young, newly hired nurse. Ruby couldn't remember her name and had to look at her badge—Annie, yes that was it, Annie.

"Good heavens, Ruby, you almost scared me ta ta to death," Annie squeaked.

Selina had, just minutes before, said to Annie, "That Ruby Kruger is getting' crazier than a bedbug—mean, too—I ain't never seen such a mean woman. Miss Caroline axed me and Topaz to keep an eye on her. Just a few more hours and she'll be out of our lives and I say good riddance."

Annie hoped Ruby would stay holed up in the nurses' lounge until Caroline came to work, but then Mrs. Whitman arrived with her demands to see the charge nurse. Ruby was the charge nurse until Caroline got there, so Annie didn't have any choice.

"I was coming ta—ta—to get you," Annie stepped back. "Wa, wa, we have a problem. Mrs. Whitman is here ta—ta visit. I said it's ta—ta—too early, but she says Caroline ta—ta—told her she could come anytime. She wants to ta—ta talk to the person in charge."

"Okay, I'll handle it," Ruby said, thinking that Helen was little and frail; it would be easy to strangle her. She would let Ian Whitman watch his devoted wife lose her life. Helen's body would fall across her husband's bed. Ruby would laugh as she injected him with the bubble of air.

The world would think he choked Helen to death and then died of a stroke himself. After all, Mr. Whitman had a history of violence. Look what he had done to Ruby's face just a few hours ago. With her thumb, she traced the crimson line from the lobe of her left ear to the corner of her mouth.

The day-shift nurses were too busy to wonder where Ruby was. Ruby would say she had gone back to the room to check on Mr. Whitman and found them both dead. Who could say differently? Not that fool Mr. Duncan; he didn't even know his own name.

* * *

At first it looked like the foyer was deserted, but when Ruby's eyes got used to the dim light she saw Helen standing by a tall artificial palm.

Her dripping umbrella was making a little river of water across the marble tiled floor. This annoyed Ruby.

"Put your umbrella out on the porch; you're making a mess of the floor."

Helen ignored the order.

Ruby went on in a harsh voice, "You are rather early to visit. Most of our patients aren't awake yet."

But Helen's early arrival worked to Ruby's advantage, so she added, "We'll make an exception this time; Caroline shouldn't have promised that you could visit anytime you felt like it."

Helen knew the way to her husband's room, and once she was allowed onto the ward she rushed ahead of Ruby who was fumbling with something in her pocket.

"It doesn't matter, let her have her way. It will be the last time." mumbled Ruby as she pulled back the plunger of the syringe, filling the barrel with air.

A second after Helen entered Ian Whitman's room; Ruby heard a loud scream followed by wailing. Annie, and the activities director, Victor, ran toward the sound.

When Ruby got into the room she could see that Mr. Whitman was dead. She pushed Helen aside and placed her fingers against his neck. There was no pulse and he wasn't breathing. "Get her out of here," Ruby indicated Helen, "and get the crash cart. This guy's a full code."

Annie pulled Helen out of the room. "No, no, no," Helen was moaning. "Ian, don't leave me."

"Call the doctor," Ruby yelled at Victor, and he hurried out to do her bidding.

Ruby didn't start CPR; she looked down at the contorted body and felt no pity. "You robbed me of a lot of pleasure by dying old man," she hissed. "Well, I'll collect it with interest from your darling wife and from your daughter and her baby."

Mr. Duncan watched with wide eyes, but said nothing.

When she heard the sound of rubber wheels and running feet in the corridor, Ruby shoved the back board from the head of the bed, under Ian's torso and began to push on his chest. The cart arrived. Placing an oxygen mask over his face, she continued the compressions, giving the ambu bag a squeeze at intervals, until the doctor showed up five minutes later.

"You can stop now," the doctor told Ruby. "You did all you could, but he's had another massive stroke. Get him cleaned up, and then let the wife come in. She can sit with him until the people from the mortuary show up."

"Date of death, 11/18/2001; time of death, 7:45 am; died of natural causes: stroke," he wrote on the death certificate.

Chapter Forty-five
Ruby

Even before Caroline took her coat off, Annie told her about Mr. Whitman's death. "We got him cleaned up and combed his hair. His wife is sitting with him." Annie didn't stutter when she talked to Caroline.

Caroline went immediately to speak with Helen. "Do you want to tell me what happened? Sometimes it does a person good to talk about their loss."

"I woke up and knew something was wrong." Helen said. "That's why I got here so early. It was like a cold hand gripped my heart and I just had to see Ian. They wouldn't let me on the ward. Finally that tall nurse with the dark hair was kind enough to let me in, and I saw Ian just lying there, all twisted up with his eyes and mouth open; I knew he was gone." She tried to smile, "It's what he wanted."

"Would you like to phone your daughter?" Caroline asked.

"No, I'm going to write her a letter. I don't want her to hear it on the telephone. Do you have paper and an envelope I could use? I think I have a stamp in my purse."

"Of course, I'll get it for you right away." Caroline thought it was an odd way to inform the daughter, but this poor lady was adamant about writing the letter. ~~Well, God bless her,~~ if that was how she wanted to do it; Carolyn wasn't going to argue.

* * *

> *My Dearest Medora,*
> *I haven't been much of a mother to you. I guess I just didn't know how. I don't remember my own mother or father you know...*

Helen paused and bit her lip; how odd her thoughts looked when she put them into words. Her plan was logical—the only practical action left to her. She bent her head and went on writing. When she was done, she folded the sheet of paper and sealed the envelope. She wrote Medora's name and address: Medora Schmidt, POB 24, Tamlin, Oregon, on the front of the envelope, and then searched through her wallet for a stamp.

When Caroline came in with the people from the mortuary, Helen gave her the letter. Two men in black suits zipped Ian's body into a black plastic bag and swung it, like so much dead weight, onto a gurney.

"I understand you've taken care of the arrangements, Mrs. Whitman," the tallest of the men said somberly.

She answered, "Yes, for me and my husband. We're both to be cremated and our ashes placed in the columbarium at my church." She stood at the door and watched the gurney disappear down the hallway.

"I'll be going now," Helen said.

"Do you feel up to driving? Perhaps you would like to call someone to come get you." Caroline thought Helen seemed unnaturally calm.

"My apartment is only a short distance from here and I prefer to be alone right now," Helen said. "Promise me you'll make sure the letter to my daughter gets mailed today," she added.

"Of course," Caroline replied. "I can call her if you like."

"No just make sure the letter gets mailed, and thank you for your kindness." Helen turned and left the room.

Caroline watched the pathetic little figure in the old fashioned polyester pantsuit march down the hallway toward the exit. Helen looked so lonely she made Caroline want to cry.

* * *

Ruby had already cleaned out her locker, and placed its contents: her extra sweater, antiseptic mouth wash, and her scrapbook of newspaper articles dating back to the death of her mother and Dr. Lockland in 1950, into a brown paper shopping bag. It was all done, and now she was walking out of the place where she had spent most of her waking hours for the last twenty years. It all seemed strange, and very final. She looked at her watch; it was a few minutes after nine.

Just as Ruby was picking up her purse, Annie came into the nursing lounge. "Miss Caroline asked me to-to—to give you this before you leave." Annie handed Ruby a gift-wrapped box. "It's a re ta—ta—tirement gift. Are you going to open it?"

"Not until I get home," Ruby answered. Who knew what the hell was in the box. She was pretty sure her coworkers hated her. They might have given her an empty box, or put itching powder or a stink bomb in the package before wrapping it. Maybe they spit in it—or worse. "Right now I have to get going. I have an appointment."

She planned to wait in her car until Helen came out, and then follow her. "Here," she handed Annie her Saint Elfreda Nursing Home keys, "make sure Caroline gets these." She grabbed the brown paper bag and stuffed the gift and her dry yellow plastic poncho into the top of it.

Luck was with Ruby. When she started down the corridor toward the reception area, figuring she might as well use the front door for her final exit, Helen came out of her husband's room. She also was headed for the reception area and the front door. Ruby caught up with her. "Sorry to hear about your husband. Were you and your husband married for a long time? By the way, where does your daughter live?"

Helen muttered, "Thanks," but didn't answer Ruby's questions.

"Ruby," Caroline's voice called.

Ruby turned, "I'm in a hurry Caroline."

Helen, head down, continued on, but Ruby hesitated for a moment and Caroline caught up with her.

"I'll walk up to the front with you. I want to put Helen's letter to her daughter in the mail tray." The effort of keeping up with Ruby's long strides soon had Caroline panting. "You sure are in a hurry," she puffed. "I just wanted to wish you good luck. Did Annie give you the gift? We all pitched in and Selina did the shopping; I think you'll like it."

They reached the receptionist's desk, and Caroline put the envelope in the mail tray. Ruby could see part of the writing on it: *Medora Schmidt, Tamlin...*, she reached her hand toward the envelope.

"That's private mail, Ruby. You've no reason to touch it. I thought you were in a hurry." Caroline's voice was sharp.

Ruby saw Helen pushing the heavy front door open. She had forgotten her umbrella by the artificial palm tree and the rain made dark splotches on her polyester suit, but she didn't seem to notice. As she walked toward her car, her hand groped in her worn purse for her car keys.

Ignoring Caroline, Ruby sprinted for the door and ran out into the torrent, not bothering with her poncho. She could feel the wet uniform sticking to her legs and chest, and had a momentary worry that the white material might become transparent when wet, but there was no time for such trivialities. Her car was parked around back in the employee lot. If she didn't hurry, Helen would get away.

The engine of the Crown Victoria started on the first try. Ruby nosed the big sedan around the main building and into the visitor parking lot. Helen seemed to be having trouble getting her car going. It was a rusty old Honda hatchback, nothing as luxurious as the Crown Victoria, Ruby noted with pleasure.

The engine of the Honda coughed and then roared to life. Dark smoke spurted from the tailpipe. Helen backed out of the parking place, changed gears and proceeded to the gate which creaked open. She passed through and it closed.

When Ruby reached the gate she waited impatiently for it to open again. Helen's car was disappearing down the lane; she was driving extremely fast. Once through the gate, Ruby pushed hard on the accelerator pedal.

"My God, I'm going sixty and not even gaining on that old car." She pushed the pedal to the floor and the big car leapt forward. Sixty five, seventy, she was beginning to catch up with the Honda. Helen would have to slow down to make the turn onto the main highway—but she didn't.

The huge tree stump with its sign loomed ahead. The old Honda put on a final burst of speed and swerved straight toward the stump, hitting it head-on. The hood of the car crumbled backwards pushing the steering column into Helen's chest, killing her instantly, but holding her erect in the seat.

The Honda continued moving; it bounced off the tree, and skidded sideways. The horn assaulted the quiet morning air with its continuous honking. Still traveling at a high speed, the Honda headed toward the Crown Vic. Ruby's mouth opened wide in a silent scream.

She saw Helen's eyes staring at her through the broken windshield. "She knows I have the ring," groaned Ruby and one hand went to the ring hanging on the chain around her neck. She held her other arm stiffly against the steering wheel in an effort to brace herself. The Honda rammed the driver's side door of the Crown Victoria. Ruby felt a sharp pain in her left arm and shoulder.

Helen's car came to rest five feet from the Crown Victoria and burst into flames. Ruby reached for the door handle with her good right hand, but the door was jammed. Her injured arm felt like hot pokers were being shoved into it. She undid her seat belt, lay on her back and kicked at the door with both her feet. It didn't budge.

"Come on, come on, it's going to explode." It was the gateman's urgent voice. Using a crowbar, he was able to pry the door open. He left his golf cart parked next to Ruby's car, and started running up the road

After wriggling out of the car, Ruby reached back in for her purse and the brown paper bag. Clutching her belongings, she hurried after the gateman.

The Honda exploded. Ruby stopped as if frozen to the spot. "Come on!" the gateman yelled over his shoulder. The Honda was now a ball of flames.

"She's trying to kill me. She wants to get back at me." Ruby sprinted forward.

The flames and heat from the Honda reached the Crown Victoria. There was another explosion. This one knocked Ruby to her knees in the mud. The gateman went back and tried to help her up, but she snarled at him like a terrified animal. He left her there, alone in the rain, and returned to his booth.

When the ambulance arrived, the EMTs found a woman kneeling in the mud. Her left arm dangled at her side and her right hand clutched a ring which hung from a silver chain around her neck. A large purse and a sodden brown paper bag were next to her. She looked dazed and was mumbling something about Helen trying to kill her.

"This is either a head injury or one for the psycho ward," the burly ambulance driver called to his helper.

Chapter Forty-six
Ruby

"I have a few routine questions to ask you." Detective Sergeant Mike Sullivan was doing his best to keep his faded black umbrella over his head while taking the identification from the pocket of his rumpled gray raincoat and holding it for the gateman to see. The worst of the storm had passed by, but the rain was still coming down steadily.

The night-shift gateman raised his bushy eyebrows and motioned the policeman into the booth. There were three stools in the little room. The day-shift gateman, wearing a badge which read *Derrick*, was busy setting up his log book and checking the gate controls.

"I've been on duty since midnight," the night-shift gateman's eyebrows formed a V over his nose when he complained. "The police officers responding to my 911 call asked me to stay and talk to you, but I'm beat and I don't know what I can tell you that I didn't already tell them."

"I'll be as brief as possible," Sullivan said, taking out a notepad and pen. "Name, age and home address?"

The gateman gave the information requested, spelling out his last name, "GOSTIARN, Zeke Gostiarn."

"Did you see the collisions, Zeke?"

"No, I didn't see the actual accident. I wasn't looking at the monitors just then." He decided not to add that he had been reading the sport's section of his newspaper at the time. "I heard a big bang and my booth kind of shook, and then there was a crash. The surveillance camera at the main road should show it all."

"I'm going to need that tape."

"I'll get it for you," Derrick said, and left the booth.

Detective Sergeant Sullivan wrote something in a notebook. "You said you 'didn't see the accident.' What makes you think it was an accident?"

"Well, it had to be…I mean what else could it have been?"

Sullivan made a note of this answer. "What did you do when you heard the 'big bang'?"

Zeke closed his eyes for a moment, remembering. "I came out of the booth; got into my golf cart, and drove down the road. It was still raining hard.

"Pretty soon I came upon the same two vehicles which had just gone past the booth a few minutes earlier—the old Honda with a visitor in it—and Ruby the night nurse in her Crown Vic. They were sideways in the road. The hood of the Honda was pushed into the front seat, and Ruby's side door was all smashed."

He stopped talking, clasped his hands together, and cracked the knuckles of both hands. Sullivan waited expectantly. Zeke resumed his story. "The Honda was on fire; I could still see the woman sitting there behind the wheel and not moving. I could smell her burning. God, it was awful. I'm never going to get it out of my mind."

Sullivan interrupted, "Were the vehicles in the same position as they now are?"

"Yeah."

"What did you do when you reached the vehicles?"

"I could see Ruby…"

"Tell me again, who is Ruby?"

"The night-shift charge nurse."

"Do you know her last name?"

"Naw, you'd have to ask Caroline the day-shift charge nurse for that."

"Okay, what did you do then?" Sullivan was writing rapidly.

"I could see Ruby inside the car, kicking at the damaged door. I was afraid the Honda was going to explode any minute, so I grabbed the crowbar I keep in my golf-cart for when the gate sticks. I pried the door of the Crown Vic open and dragged Ruby out. She reached back in and got her purse and a brown shopping bag. She was acting real weird saying stuff like, 'Helen wasn't destroyed by fire' and 'Helen wants to kill me'."

"Who is Helen?"

"I don't have the foggiest. I just kept trying to get Ruby to move away from the cars. Finally—I think—I heard two explosions one right after the other, and felt a heavy push against my back. My ears were ringing. Ruby fell to her knees. She was babbling and hissing and spitting. I couldn't get her up.

"My golf cart was in flames. I left Ruby and jogged back up to the booth to call for help. First I dialed 911; then I called up to the main building. Caroline, the head nurse came down, but she couldn't do anything with Ruby either. It took the ambulance guys and a couple of policeman to get her on the stretcher.

"God, I can't get the stink of that poor woman's burning flesh out of my nose."

Derrick reentered the booth and handed Sullivan the surveillance tape. "Thanks," Sullivan told him as he dropped the tape into a plastic evidence bag.

"I think we're about done here." He handed Zeke his card. "If you think of anything else call me at that number. I'll get your statement typed up and notify you when it's ready for you to look over and sign. Where can I find Caroline?"

"She'll be up at the main building," Zeke told him.

Sergeant Sullivan took a step toward his car, but turned back to say, "That nurse would be dead if it wasn't for your quick action. Getting her to safety when you knew the cars could explode at any second took a lot of courage."

* * *

Caroline showed Sergeant Sullivan into the nurse's lounge. It reminded him a lot of his office at police headquarters, and she reminded him of his mother. As she was handing him a cup of coffee, he noticed she wasn't wearing a wedding ring. He was still stinging from the divorce three years ago, but he wondered if—when the case was closed of course—he would have the guts to ask her out to dinner.

"Mrs. Whitman asked me to mail this letter to her daughter, but I thought, in light of what's happened, it might be important for you to see." Reaching into her pocket, Caroline drew out the sealed envelope with Medora's name and address on it.

"Why was Mrs. Whitman visiting her husband so early in the morning?" Sullivan had his book out again.

"She said she had a premonition. The lady was very wrapped up in her husband. He had been with us about a week and during that time she spent at least twelve hours everyday sitting at his bedside. It must have been a terrible shock to her this morning to find him dead."

"Dead?" Sullivan asked sharply.

"Yes, oh dear, you didn't know. He passed away early this morning. Mrs. Whitman was the one who found him. Our doctor said it was another stroke. Ruby tried to resuscitate him, but there was too much damage to his brain." She paused and took a sip of coffee.

"I offered to call the daughter for Mrs. Whitman—that's all they have—one pregnant daughter who lives in Tamlin. Her name and address are on the envelope." She pointed to the letter he held in his hand and continued.

"The people from the mortuary came for the body and I heard Mrs. Whitman say she had made arrangements for both Mr. Whitman and herself to be cremated. After the accident, I called the mortuary and asked them to hold off cremating Mr. Whitman until you say it's okay.

This nurse, Caroline, was a puzzle to Sullivan. Here she was collecting evidence for him like she thought something was rotten about the case, and yet she called the deaths "a stroke" and "an accident" She suspected something, Sullivan was pretty sure of it. He decided to probe deeper.

"What was Mrs. Whitman's state of mind when she left this morning?"

"She was calm, too calm. I offered to call someone to pick her up, but she said she wanted to be alone, and that she lived only a few minutes away. I thought it was odd that she didn't call her daughter. "

"What kind of a nurse is this Ruby, and what is her last name?"

Caroline hesitated before she said, "Ruby's last name is Kruger. She's worked here for a long time. This was her last night before retirement. It may be my imagination, but for about a month I've sensed that Ruby was upset about something. Maybe she was worried about retirement. I think nursing has been her whole life."

Sullivan was making notes in his book as Caroline talked.

"Does Ruby Kruger have a husband or children?"

"Not that I know of; she's a very private person."

Once again, Sullivan had the feeling that Caroline wasn't telling him everything. He said, "Thank you for your help. I'll have your statement typed up and give you a call when it's ready to be signed. If you think of anything else at all, please contact me," he handed Caroline one of his cards. "You've been very helpful. I'll ask the daughter's permission to open the letter, and the coroner will probably want an autopsy on Mr. Whitman's body."

As he was walking out the door a thought struck him and he took out his notebook again, "What is Mrs. Whitman's first name?"

Caroline thought for a moment and then replied, "Helen."

Chapter Forty-seven
Ruby

Ruby remembered screaming at the men who bound her hands and feet to the gurney and put the strap across her chest. "Helen can't be killed with fire. She's still out there and her eyes are staring at me. She's trying to get her mother's ring back."

They wouldn't listen to her. She felt the sting of a needle, and shadows engulfed her mind, moving from the outer edges toward the center. The gleam in Helen's eyes flickered against the encroaching darkness, and then was extinguished.

* * *

When Ruby woke up, she was still strapped to a gurney, but in a different place. This room was pale pink. There were no windows or pictures. She was wearing a white hospital gown and her belongings had disappeared.

Turning her head, she saw an open door leading into what appeared to be a hallway. A round-faced man, wearing a blue security guard uniform, was sitting just outside the door reading a newspaper. When he saw her eyes were open he called out, "Diane, she's awake."

"Okay," a woman's voice answered. "Don't go near her. She scratched and bit Ron and Cas when they tried to get her on the gurney.

I just finished patching them up and giving them tetanus shots. We'll have to test her for HIV and Hep spectrum. It took both of them and two police officers to subdue her. I'll let Dr. Beady know she's awake."

The security guard went back to his newspaper and Ruby closed her eyes again.

Helen had gotten the best of her for now, but she would bide her time. Helen's daughter and grandchild were as good as dead. When that task was finished she would be safe.

"Hello there," Ruby heard a cheerful voice say.

She opened her eyes and saw a diminutive man in a white lab coat standing over her. His pockets were stuffed with pens, pencils, a little flashlight, and stacks of index cards held together by rubber bands. A purple stethoscope with a rainbow bell was coiled around his neck.

"I'm Dr. Beady."

Ruby stared at him without speaking and he stared back for a few seconds. Then he said, "Do you know what today's date is?"

For the life of her, Ruby couldn't think of the date—not even the month.

"What year is it?"

Ruby shook her head "No."

"Do you hurt anywhere?"

Ruby nodded her head "Yes."

"I'd like to examine you. If I unlock the restraints will you cooperate with the exam? Remember, I'm here to help you, not to hurt you."

Ruby nodded her head.

"Louis, come in here," the doctor called.

The security guard put down his paper and ambled into the room. He stood behind Ruby's head as the doctor undid each of the restraints.

Ruby closed her eyes and tolerated the doctor's poking and prodding. Knowing that Louis was there watching made it about a hundred times worse. She flinched when Dr. Beady touched her left shoulder and moved her arm.

"I'd like to get an x-ray of your arm and shoulder," he told her. I also need the nurse to draw some blood for tests, one is for HIV. Do you consent to that?"

Ruby nodded her head.

"I'm going to start you on Ativan, which is a mild sedative, and some pain pills for your arm and shoulder. Are you allergic to anything?"

Ruby shook her head.

"I'm leaving a paper here for you. I've placed you on a psychiatric hold to give us a little time to evaluate your condition."

Ruby shook her head in a vigorous "no," but Dr. Beady, ignoring her protest, left the room. Louis remained standing just behind her head, where she couldn't see him, but could hear him breathing.

A nurse dressed in a blue scrub suit entered the room. She had a cup with pills in one hand and a cup of orange liquid with a straw.

"Hello Ruby, I'm Diane, one of the emergency room nurses. I have some medication for you and I want to draw your blood. I hope you'll cooperate with me, because the alternative is back into the restraints. This is the medication Dr. Beady ordered for you, Vicodin for pain and Ativan for anxiety."

She tipped the pills into Ruby's mouth and then put the straw to her lips so that she could drink the sweet liquid in the cup.

"Open wide and stick your tongue out," Diane said as she checked to make sure Ruby had swallowed the medication.

After the blood was drawn and x-rays of her arm and shoulder were done, a giant of a woman wearing plaid slacks and a green turtleneck sweater appeared in the pink room. "Hello Ruby, I'm Tina from psychiatry." Four keys hung from the ring attached to a pink coil around Tina's wrist. They jingled when she moved her arm. "I'm going to escort you to our locked unit. Dr. Beady will meet us there. Please remain on the gurney until we are in the unit. I don't want to have to put you in restraints again."

Two strong looking men dressed in white were waiting to push the gurney. Louis walked next to her. She could see him when she turned her head. His uniform was wrinkled and he smelled of sweat and tobacco. The medicine was making her sleepy. Things seemed out of focus, the edges of objects were soft and blurry.

Tina unlocked a set of double doors and the attendants pushed Ruby's gurney through. Tina waited for the doors to close tightly behind them before she opened the second set of double doors.

The two young nurses must have been waiting for her. They stared at her and one of them touched her hair. "We'll have to cut this before she applies the chemical treatment. It's completely matted," one of them said as she helped Ruby from the gurney.

"Do you mind if we cut your hair," the other young nurse asked Ruby. It's the only way we can get it clean. We've been battling an epidemic of head-lice and scabies, and so we have to wash everyone down with Quell insecticidal shampoo before they come onto the unit."

"Go ahead," Ruby's voice cracked. "I should have thought of that." Of course hair has germs and bugs. Ruby realized she had been walking around with stuff living in her hair; her eyebrows and body hair too. She decided shave all her hair off. That was the only way to be sure there were no bugs.

"Can I have a razor?" Ruby rasped. Her throat was sore from screaming at Helen.

"What?" the young nurse said.

"A razor—I want to shave my hair off—to get rid of the bugs."

"Oh, that's not necessary. I'll trim off the matted part and make it as neat and even as possible. We don't allow razors on this unit."

The two nurses stood just outside of the shower room while Ruby scrubbed herself all over. Before she could get herself completely clean they insisted she turn off the shower. They rubbed an ointment that smelled something like the poison spray used to kill ants all over her, except for her face. "Wait until the morning and then wash this off," they told her. They gave her a gray sweat shirt and sweat pants to wear.

"Where's my uniform? Oh my God, where's the ring I had on a chain around my neck and the bag of things that were in my locker, my scrap book, where's my scrap book?"

"Everything is safe. It's locked up in the patients' property room downstairs. You can get it when you leave," they told her, but Ruby wasn't so sure about that.

"I want my things!"

"Dr. Beady will be here to talk to you soon. You can ask him," they tried to sooth her. "We'll show you where your room is and you can rest until he gets here."

"I want my things," Ruby repeated, but she followed the nurses. She was afraid if she made a fuss they would think she was crazy and keep her there longer. Helen's daughter was in Tamlin. Ruby had a mission that couldn't be accomplished from a locked psychiatric unit, so she cooperated.

They gave her a private room. It was gray and square with no windows or closets. The single bed was covered with a faded tan bedspread. Although everything looked fairly clean, Ruby yearned to scrub the bed with disinfectant before she sat on it.

She paced the floor. The pain medication was wearing off and her arm and shoulder throbbed. Helen had caused all of this. Ruby knew she had underestimated her enemy, but no matter how many clever tricks Helen tried, she wouldn't be able to stop Ruby this time.

"Hello, may I come in?" Dr. Beady didn't wait for permission, but came into the room carrying a wooden stool. He put the stool down and sat on it. In his hand he held a clipboard.

"First of all, you've fractured your left shoulder. There's really nothing to do but keep it immobilized while it heals. I've ordered a sling for you. Is it hurting now?"

Ruby nodded, "yes".

"As soon as we are done here I'll ask the nurse to bring you another dose of pain medicine." The doctor scanned the papers on his clipboard. "I have a few questions to ask you. Do you know what day it is?"

This time Ruby knew the answers to all of his questions. Until he said, "'People who live in glass houses shouldn't throw stones.' What does that mean?"

He was trying to tell her something. What was it? And then she knew. It was rocks, not fire that would stop Helen. She looked over at the doctor. He was waiting for her to say something.

"I understand," she said.

"What do you understand?" the doctor asked.

"About using rocks instead of fire."

"Rocks instead of fire?" he repeated making it into a question.

"Yes," she said with finality and pressed her lips together in a straight line.

* * *

With the help of the tranquillizers and pain pills, the observation days passed quickly. On the last evening, Dr. Beady said, "Legally I can't keep you here any longer, but I would like you to stay a few more days."

"No thank you," Ruby answered.

"Where will you go?" Dr. Beady asked.

"The social worker helped me with a discharge plan. I'll get my belongings. The people from the car rental will pick me up here. The insurance company will pay for a rental car while I look for a replacement for the car Helen wrecked."

"I'm afraid you won't be driving for a while. It will be at least two months before you can use your left arm," the doctor said. "I'll ask one of the social workers to bring you a bus token and a schedule. The bus stops right out in front. A senior bus pass isn't very expensive. I think you should get yourself one."

Ruby glowered; senior bus pass indeed. Who did he think he was talking to? She wasn't an old woman and she resented being treated like one.

He saw the change in her expression. "Are you having any thoughts of hurting yourself or anyone else?"

Ruby shook her head "no," because she guessed that was what he wanted to hear. It was a little confusing. He was the one who told her about using rocks to get rid of Helen's daughter and grandchild. Of course she was thinking of hurting someone and he knew it. She would be leaving tomorrow, and she would never see Dr. Beady again and that suited her just fine.

Chapter Forty-eight
Ruby

Dr. Beady came to speak to Ruby early the next morning. "You will be discharged today. I want like to see you in my office in two weeks. I'm worried about delayed shock from the accident. I believe the trauma may have exacerbated an underlying anxiety disorder. You were definitely in the throes of a panic attack when I first saw you. I'll give you a prescription for enough tranquilizers and pain pills to last until our appointment."

He scribbled on a pad of paper, tore off two sheets and handed them to Ruby. "Take these to the pharmacy."

Trying to be polite, Ruby watched him closely. His lips were moving, but she had no idea what he was saying. She wanted to be out of there. As soon as she got home she would get rid of every bit of hair on her body and head. She had already managed to pluck out most of her eyelashes. It was torture to sit still and listen to Dr. Beady while bugs laid eggs and multiplied in the hair on her head and body.

The doctor stood up. He must be done. "Two weeks," he said.

She forced herself to smile. "Two weeks. And thank you for everything." She really was grateful to Dr. Beady for telling her to use rocks to destroy Helen and her pregnant daughter.

The nurse walked Ruby to the doors and unlocked each one for her. "Just show the people downstairs your armband and they'll give you your belongings," she said. "The gray sweat suit and slippers you are wearing are yours to keep. Do you have your bus token and schedule? Take the bus to the main terminal in Portland and be sure to get a transfer for Rosamunde, or you can buy a bus pass. Don't forget to pick up your belongings and medication."

Ruby smiled and said "yes". The nurse closed the door.

Ruby was free.

She started into the elevator, but thought of all the germs and diseases the people riding in there might be carrying. Luckily she was able to locate a set of stairs which descended to the ground floor. Her first stop was the pharmacy window where she picked up two bottles of pills.

Clutching the bottles in her hand, she found a restroom and went in. There was only one person in there, an elderly lady. Ruby waited until the lady finished washing her hands and went out. Then Ruby opened the pill bottles. She took two from each bottle, washing them down with tap water in her cupped hand. She waited for the medication to soothe her frayed nerves. It took about ten minutes for her to experience a sense of relaxation, and the accompanying feeling of wellbeing.

She remembered seeing a sign with an arrow pointing toward the patients' property room. She retraced her steps, found the sign and followed the arrow. When she showed the clerk her arm band, he produced a clear plastic bag with her name on the large tag attached to the top.

Sitting on a straight chair in the hallway, she sorted through the bag and located the chain with the ring. Once she had it around her neck again, she felt much better—more confident. Her purse was inside the shopping bag along with her scrapbook and the other things from her locker, and the retirement gift. At the very bottom of the plastic bag was her dirty, torn uniform. She put it into the trashcan, and thought about discarding the retirement gift as well. In the end curiosity got the better of her and she decided to take it home and open it.

She found razors for sale in the hospital gift shop and purchased three packages of five razors each. The hospital felt safe and comfortable. She put off walking out the front door into the gray drizzle.

Through the glass doors she could see people coming and going. She heard a siren wail. Traffic roared by and horns honked. She could see hundreds of cars in the parking lot. Anyone of them might belong to Helen. Ruby's hand sought the comfort of the ring.

She returned to the restroom and, disregarding the three other women in there, took two more anxiety pills and another pain pill. While she waited for the second dose of pills to take effect she washed her hands. Thirty minutes passed and people were beginning to give her odd looks. Although her hands weren't really clean, she went outside to the covered bus stop.

Waiting for the bus tested her courage. Several times she thought she saw Helen drive by. She hated to be near the crowd of germ-laden people at the bus stop, but she forced herself to stand very close behind a large woman. That way Helen would have a hard time spotting her.

When the bus pulled up and Ruby climbed the steps, she felt secure. Helen could ram her car into the side of the bus as many times as she wanted. No little car could hurt a big bus like this one. It was then that Ruby realized she would never drive a car again. Taking the bus was much safer.

* * *

The Portland bus terminal was big and busy, but Ruby easily found the ticket selling booth.

"I want a senior pass and, how do I get to Pine Cone Lane, just a mile before the turn-off for Saint Elfreda Nursing Home? I see a bus go right past my house everyday."

The ticket seller looked up and his eyes widened. He couldn't tell if it was a woman or a man standing at his window, one arm in a sling. The person was tall and concentration camp thin. The shoulders seemed exceptionally broad and the hands were big. "Do I say 'sir' or 'madam'?" he wondered.

Even the voice was androgynous, low and husky. The ticket seller had recently seen an old movie about cross-dressers. He recalled that men have Adam's apples and women don't. He stared at Ruby's neck—no Adam's apple.

"Yes ma'am, you want number 315. It makes the loop between the town of Rosamunde and Scappossa three times a day. The driver will let you off in front of your house; just tell him when you board. Number 315 leaves here in forty-five minutes. I can sell you a book of twelve tickets for fifteen dollars. That's probably your best deal since the month is almost over."

"Okay, give me the book." Ruby dug the money out of her wallet.

After putting her tickets in her purse, she headed for the restroom. She took one more anxiety pill and another pain pill, and then began washing her hands. Traveling was terrible for contaminating hands. All those people going to the bathroom and then touching doorknobs and walls, filthy! Ruby made a note to herself to wear rubber gloves the next time she rode the bus.

After glancing at her watch, she tore off four squares of paper towel. She dried her hands on two of them and put the other two over her hands so she wouldn't have to touch the door knobs in the station, or handrails on the bus. It was almost time for her bus. She looked all around after leaving the restroom and, not seeing Helen anywhere, she scurried out to the bus stop.

* * *

The bus driver stopped right in front of Ruby's house, just like the ticket seller said he would. Ruby was relieved to see that her house was still standing. With Helen on the loose, anything could happen. She searched in her purse for her keys, and unlocked the gate to let herself in.

"I bet David's been worried about me," she said to herself. "He expected me days ago. The last time I saw him I said I would have lots to tell him. He's probably been waiting and waiting."

By the time she walked up to the house from the road and got all the locks open, she was exhausted. There was David's freezer, but she was really too tired to deal with him and his petty demands right now.

"I have to get some rest," Ruby said. "I'll talk to you when I get up, David." She went into the bedroom; took two pain pills and two tranquilizers; lay down on the bed and pulled Gram's crazy quilt up to her chin. She was asleep almost as soon as she closed her eyes.

It was a restless sleep, filled with strange dreams of Helen's staring eyes chasing her in a flaming car. Ruby muttered in her sleep as she tossed restlessly in the bed. A scream woke her—it was coming from her own lips.

"I have to get a grip," she told herself. "I have to get organized." Her first item of business was to shower and shave. When that was done she put the gray sweat suit back on; gathered up the hair in a plastic bag and walked out to the road. She tied the bag securely and threw it into the road. The bugs wouldn't be able to find their way back into the house from that distance.

As she walked back to the house, she planned her day. She had three other items on her agenda. Opening the retirement gift box and doing something about David's germ-infested hair, but most important was to count her pills.

Procuring more medication might be a problem. She certainly wasn't going back to Dr. Beady and his talk about rocks. That man knew too much. It wasn't safe to ask him for the pills.

Then she remembered the weird old man at Saint Elfreda's. When the son brought his dad to the nursing home, he told them the old man had been getting tranquilizers from some doctor over by the bus depot, on Main Street above a liquor store. He said the doctor would prescribe anything if a person had enough money.

Ruby knew where the liquor store was on Main Street.

Once back at the house, she got the two pill bottles out of her purse, and reached under the mattress for several envelopes containing pills. The bottles from Dr. Beady were almost empty. She had needed a lot of medication to stay calm while traveling. The envelopes contained quite a selection of pain killers, tranquilizers and antipsychotics. She should have enough for about a week if nothing happened to upset her.

David was another problem. He had always been such a slob. Too bad, but she wasn't opening that freezer and let bugs from his hair out into the house. She would go to the store and get cans of soup and a can opener. He could have all the frozen dinners—the big hog.

A brilliant idea occurred to her, "I can get a plastic shower cap, some tape and a plastic sheet, too. That way I can cover David's hair and eyebrows with tape and the cap. I can tuck the sheet around him. That should keep the bugs in place. "She sighed happily, another situation brought under control by careful and intelligent planning.

Next she turned her attention to the retirement gift. She put on a pair of rubber gloves. After a moment's thought, she decided to open it out of doors, just in case. Carrying the box, she walked back down to the front gate. The plastic bag of hair was in the middle of the road, smashed flat.

She untied the red ribbon and lifted the cover of the box. There was a layer of tissue paper—that looked harmless—with something red underneath it. She folded back the paper and discovered a red sweatshirt. "Oh, how nice," Ruby exclaimed. "LOOK OUT WORLD, HERE I COME!" was emblazoned across the front in big black letters. "I really like it," Ruby said out loud. "They do care about me after all."

Chapter Forty-nine
Ruby

The room was cold, but she didn't notice. Sitting in David's chair with the remote control in her hand, Ruby dreamily flipped through the channels over and over again. Nothing held her interest, but that didn't matter. The pills gave her a pleasant disembodied sensation, and the TV noise and bright colors kept the house from feeling empty and lonely.

There was really no reason for her to feel lonely. She could always open the freezer and talk to David, but even though she had taped a plastic cap on his head; put tape over his eyebrows, and fastened a plastic shower curtain over his body, she was still uneasy about the hair bugs.

The image of David on the examination table wearing a paper gown and skimpy shorts was vivid in her mind. She had thought those swirls of blonde hair on his legs were so sexy. What a fool she was.

The hours drifted by, and she floated in and out of consciousness. It was hard to tell what was real and what was a dream; everything was so pleasant.

The room gradually darkened as late afternoon faded into early evening. Her nerves began to ping pong and she no longer had the agreeable suspended sensation. It must be time for more pills.

Coming back to reality was always painful, but it had to be dealt with. The highs from the pills were getting briefer; meaning she had to take the pills more frequently. In the bedroom, she lifted a corner of the mattress, and drew out two medicine bottles. Holding one in each hand, she gave them a shake. They were almost empty.

It was a good thing that tomorrow was Wednesday. She had a standing appointment with Dr. Cline on Wednesday. Meeting with the doctor was only the beginning. He would write out ten prescriptions for her: five for her anxiety pills and five for her pain medicine.

Ruby must go to the three pharmacies in Rosamunde and fill two of the prescriptions at each place. She still would not be through. Her next move was to take a bus to Portland and go to two more pharmacies.

The problem was, it wasn't enough anymore. She was going to have to ask Dr. Cline for six prescriptions of each medication and he might charge even more. She was already paying him five hundred dollars a week. Her Social Security only covered about half his fees, and then there was the pharmacy, a few groceries, the electricity bill and her bus pass. So far she'd been okay, because of the money from the automobile insurance company, but that was almost gone.

Sometimes she worried about what she was going to do when she ran out of money, which would happen very soon at the rate she was going. She considered a mortgage on her house, but couldn't seem to get organized to find out what was required.

She kept reminding herself to focus on her mission. Things weren't always going to so worrisome. Soon she would find a way to destroy Helen's evil children, and then her life would be perfect again.

* * *

Ruby always took extra care with her appearance on Wednesdays. She wanted to look attractive for her trip into town. This week she was wearing her red retirement sweatshirt, a pair of white polyester slacks, and her white rubber-soled nurse's shoes.

Her head and body had been shaved in the shower the night before. Now she folded a red and white bandana into a triangle and tied it over her head. The whole outfit was nicely coordinated. She was very pleased with herself. "Still beautiful at sixty-five," she commented to the mirror.

There were no clouds in the sky, but she rolled her yellow plastic raincoat into a small ball and placed it in her purse just in case. One never knew about the weather. After locking each of the four padlocks on the back door, she placed the keys in her purse and started toward the road.

She returned three times to check the locks and once because she thought she heard David calling her. Her mouth felt dry and her heart was racing. This morning when she woke up there had been only two pills left, the emergency ones she carried in her purse. She wanted to blame David, however she vaguely remembered getting up in the night and swallowing the contents of medicine bottles.

She had just finished locking the gate when the bus pulled up and stopped with a hiss of steam. After climbing on board, she held out her bus pass for inspection.

"Are you okay?" the bus driver asked, and then immediately regretted the question. He'd decided Ruby was a cancer patient undergoing chemotherapy. That would explain the lack of hair and emaciated figure, and the weekly trips to town. This morning she looked like death warmed over, all pale and sweaty. The poor woman needed to be in the hospital.

Ruby went to her regular seat in the back of the bus without answering the driver. Just an hour or so and she would have the pills she needed. "I can stand anything for an hour," she whispered like a mantra. Her teeth chattered and she couldn't seem to keep her feet still.

The bus turned on Elm Street and stopped in front of the Stone Oven Italian Kitchen. Ruby got out and began the four block walk to Dr. Cline's office. She stopped at the bank along the way to draw out $500, leaving a balance of only $52.30.

It seemed to be taking forever to cover the short distance, and she felt sick enough to lie down and die. No matter how bad she felt, she vowed not to give up until she had finished her business with Helen's nasty little pregnant daughter.

She made it to the liquor store, and went around back to the stairs in the alley. Holding the hand rail, she pulled herself, step by step, up to the second story. Dr. Cline's name was written on the office door in tiny black letters. She went in.

After adding her name to the list on the clipboard hanging on the wall, she plopped down onto one of the dirty plastic lawn chairs. She looked around. The place was crowded; a long wait was inevitable.

An elderly man sitting in a corner looked familiar. His mouth worked as if he were chewing a tough piece of steak. It was the patient from St. Elfreda's—the one the son had brought in. He must have somehow managed to be discharged. Oh dear Lord, what if he recognized her and tried to strike up a conversation.

She grabbed a sheet of advertising from the untidy stack of newspapers and magazines on the table beside her and held it in front of her face. Reading was too much of an effort so she closed her eyes. Time crawled by as she waited for the prescribed alleviation of her suffering.

She opened her eyes and peered around the advertisement sheet. Now it was only herself and the man from Saint Elfreda's left in the waiting room. He was staring right at her and talking to himself.

"Mr. Folgolbee," a heavyset woman called from the doorway. "Dr. Cline will see you next." The old man shuffled to where the woman was waiting for him. "Examination room B," the woman said as the door closed.

Ruby's tongue was sticking to the roof of her mouth and her nerves were so taut she thought she would scream. "Try to think of something else," she told herself and looked down at the paper in her hand. It was a real estate advertisement for property in Tamlin.

Tamlin! That was where Helen's daughter lived. Ruby looked at the paper more closely. Her vision was blurred but she could make out the heading, *Fern Schmidt Realty*, it said, *Let Us Guide You to the Home of Your Dreams.*

Schmidt—Medora Schmidt, that was the name Helen had written on the envelope. Ruby was afraid she would pass out. This was it—once again fate was on her side.

"Ruby Kruger...are you Ruby Kruger?" the heavyset woman was calling.

Ruby pulled herself together. "Yes, I'm Ruby."

"The doctor will see you now, examination room A," the woman said impatiently.

The closet-sized examination room contained two stools. Instead of sitting, Ruby stood trembling with the newspaper advertisement clutched tightly in her fist. She couldn't think clearly enough to formulate a plan, but she knew this was her opportunity. As soon as she got her medicine she would decide how to proceed.

The doctor knocked on the door and then entered the room. "How are we today," he asked. "We look a little pale and upset. Are we having a problem regulating our doses of medication?"

His long white fingers fastened on her wrist. "Hmmm...pulse is 150. Did we have too much week and not enough pills?" He smiled at her, "You are now at ten prescriptions, and that is apparently not enough. I can up you to twelve, but that will increase your weekly payment from five hundred dollars to six hundred dollars.

"I only brought five hundred dollars with me," Ruby told him. "Can I pay you the rest next Wednesday?"

"You know I can't do that," his eyes slowly made the trip from her face to her flat chest. He rested his hand high on her thigh. "I am willing to accept service in lieu of payment," he said in a business like tone.

Ruby had provided a service for him two months earlier when she was short on money because the check from her auto insurance company hadn't arrived yet. It had taken her weeks to feel clean again, and today she needed all her resources to complete her mission. She also needed her medicine.

"Just give me my ten prescriptions," she said, "and if I need more I'll come to the office on Monday or Tuesday."

"You know you can't do that," the doctor said mildly. "You are a Wednesday appointment—and that means Wednesday only."

Ruby felt her heart pounding in her ears. She had to have all her medicine; she had no idea how long she would need to be in Tamlin. "Oh, all right," she said, "but I'm in a hurry."

"Of course you are," Dr. Cline said gently.

Chapter Fifty
Ruby

While Ruby was completing her business with Dr. Cline, less than a block away, Detective Sergeant Michael Sullivan and Detective Jim Bayley of the Rosamunde Police Department were deep in discussion.

"It doesn't make sense," Bayley said as he hung up the phone. At thirty years of age, he looked more like a successful banker than a cop. He was a spiffy dresser, and the premature silver thread in his dark hair added a distinguished look. He had just finished a phone conversation with a frantic mother.

"Every few months the lady calls. She's a real nice woman, and I wish I could help her, but listen to this. Her son, her only child, is a strange duck. A while back, he writes his mom a letter on the sly saying that his wife is trying to kill him."

Bayley walked over to a small utility table jammed between two file cabinets, and poured himself a cup of inky black coffee. "So, about six months ago, I make a run out to the address on son's letter, a weird place in the boonies near Saint Elfreda's Nursing Home, to investigate. Here's this guy—like I say an odd duck—but happy as a clam. He just giggles when I ask him about the letter to his mom.

"I figure he's a nut case and the wife is almost as nutty as the husband. It was one strange place: no doors on the cupboards, no rugs or curtains, everything smelling of disinfectant and covered with plastic."

"Take away all the crazies and we'd probably be out of a job," Sullivan answered absent-mindedly. He had only been half listening. "I got a real puzzler going here, Jim. In November there was a death—natural causes—and a probable suicide at Mount Saint Elfreda. The thing is—it's triggered a lot of questions from relatives of other patients who died there recently."

There was a knock on the door, and Captain Jessie Jenkins, not waiting for a reply, entered. "I don't know what I did to deserve this," she said in her usual no nonsense tone. She was a short, muscular, woman with cropped hair and a hard-bitten face. "In the last fifty years Rosamunde hasn't had any major crimes; unless you count those two cold cases—the double poisoning and the house fire which took three lives—and they were never officially classified as homicides."

She pushed her glasses to the top of her head and stared at her two most experienced detectives. "I've been captain here for less than a year, and we go and have—what could be—a major crime wave at Saint Elfreda Nursing Home, of all places. The press hasn't picked up on it yet, but it's just a matter of time.

Bayley, whatever it is you're working on, finish it up in a hurry. I want you to help Sullivan with this can of worms. Find me the answers before the reporters ask the questions."

Sullivan helped himself to a cup of coffee and added three spoonfuls of sugar, ignoring his doctor's warning that he was borderline diabetic and needed to lose weight. After taking a sip, he made a face then held the pot toward Captain Jenkins.

She shook her head, and then went on, "As you know, we're getting calls—lots of calls—and most of them questioning whether the death of their family member at Saint Elfreda was from natural causes. The patients are old and sick, but just the same on the night of October 14th, there were four deaths in one night." She rubbed her eyes.

"They usually don't have that many in six months. The nursing home had an inordinate number of fatalities from mid October until mid November. Since then they've only had one death in over two months."

"So, a bunch of elderly people die in a short period of time. It could happen, Bayley said.

Sullivan replied, "It's just too many to be a coincidence—and something else—the head nurse, Caroline, is one smart lady. I'm sure she suspects there's something funny going on with their narcotic medications. She called me today to tell me she has the results of an in-depth audit and wants me to come out there."

"The situation is critical," Captain Jenkins went on, "we had a 911 call fifteen minutes ago. A man found his dad dead of an overdose not at Saint Elfreda's—in his own apartment—but the deceased had been a patient at Saint Elfie's two months earlier."

She held up a folder and took out the preliminary 911 report, glanced at it and continued. "The son talked about the dad getting too many narcotics both at the nursing home and from some doctor with an office over the liquor store by the bus depot."

Putting the folder on Sullivan's desk, she said, "There is a list in here of the phone calls from concerned relatives of people who died at the nursing home in October and November. Meet with the head nurse and then interview the relatives and the doctor over the liquor store." She started to leave, but changed her mind.

"Before you get started Sullivan, let's review what have you already have on the Mount Saint Elfreda suspicious death cases," she ordered.

In reply, he took a sheet of paper from his desk, unfolded it and taped it to the wall. "This is a list of all the staff. The check marks next to their names represent deaths that occurred while they were on the premises during the months of October and November."

"Only October and November?" asked Detective Bayley.

"During those two months there were fourteen deaths. Before then and since then the average is one death per month, nothing suspicious."

He took a pencil and drew circles around three of the names. "The night charge nurse, a janitor, and a nursing assistant, were all present when twelve of the fourteen deaths occurred."

He pointed to one name, "This night nurse—she was injured when the Whitman woman ran her car into the tree stump—and she was present at the time of all but two of the deaths. I've talked to Clyde Ferguson and Selina Short—the janitor and the nursing assistant—and their stories add up. I don't think they were involved, but I haven't been able to locate the night nurse. The only address anyone has for her is a post office box. She retired last month just after the Whitmans died. It seems like Ruby Kruger disappeared into the woodwork at the same time the death rate dropped off."

"Wait a minute," Bayley said. "The lady who keeps calling about her son David is named Kay Kruger. I don't know the wife's name. Maybe it's our Ruby. I have her address right here."

"Okay, stop at the Krueger house first. If you think you need a search warrant give me a call," Captain Jenkins said.

* * *

They had been sitting outside the locked gate honking for almost two minutes. "Looks like no one's home," Bayley remarked. "The wife came right out the last time I was here."

"Let's go on up to Saint Elfreda's and see what the head nurse has to tell us about the narcotic audit. We can stop here again on our way back. We don't have enough for a search warrant yet," Sullivan said.

* * *

Caroline's face was set in worried lines when she greeted them in the reception area of Saint Elfreda. "I'm just sick about this," she told them. "I had no idea; I blame myself for not watching closer. Come into the nurses' lounge."

She offered them a cup of coffee which smelled and tasted every bit as strong and vile as the coffee at the police station. "Here's what the auditors discovered." She placed a folder on the table. "Ruby signed out narcotics for patients who did not have them ordered; she miscounted almost every night so as not to show a shortage, and we have no idea how many patients didn't get their pain or anxiety medication because it went into Ruby's pocket." Caroline looked as if she was going to cry.

Bayley was surprised when Sullivan, usually so impersonal, reached over and patted her hand. "We'll need a copy of the report," he told her, and then said to Bayley, "This gives us sufficient cause for a search warrant. Give Captain Jenkins a call and ask her to get going on it ASAP."

As soon as Bayley left the room to make the call, Sullivan said to Caroline, "Don't be hard on yourself." He stood and started to leave, but turned back, "When this case is all settled, would it be all right if I called you—maybe asked you out to dinner?"

Caroline looked at him in amazement. The worry didn't leave her eyes, but she managed a smile, "I'd like that."

Chapter Fifty-one
Ruby

Bayley had just started to cut the lock on Ruby's front gate when the mailman pulled up behind the detectives' car. "Any problems?" he asked.

"Yeah," said Bayley. "It just occurred to me; there's no mailbox here. How did Mr. Krueger post his letter?"

"You mean the weirdo who lives here?" asked the mailman.

"Yeah," said Bayley, "I mean the weirdo."

"Well, a couple of times he flagged me down to give me stuff," the mailman paused—thinking. "Poor guy looked like death warmed over the last time I saw him."

"How long ago was that?" asked Sullivan.

"Geeze—months—quite a while," the mailman replied.

"Did he mail a letter at that time?" asked Sullivan.

"Well, not exactly." The mailman, looking slightly embarrassed, rummaged among the paperclips and gum wrappers in his ashtray. "Good, it's still here." He handed Sullivan the card David had given him.

"Looks like one of your cards, Bayley," Sullivan said, turning the card and trying to make out the faded scrawl on the back of it. He read slowly as he worked out each word:

Danger—Ruby wants to kill the man, the lady and the pregnant girl. She is trying to starve me. David Kruger.

"Who the hell are 'the man, the lady and the pregnant girl'?" Bayley asked.

"Why didn't you tell anyone about his card?" Sullivan turned on the mailman.

"Why should I? Do you see a stamp or a return address? I still can't make out what that scrawl says. The guy's loony tunes for Pete's sake," the mailman squirmed. "Listen, I gotta get on with my route. You need me for anything else, you know where to find me."

He drove down the road and stopped at the next mailbox.

"Listen Bayley," Sullivan said, "there's a chance that the man, the lady and the pregnant girl refer to the Whitmans. The daughter, I think her name is Medora, just had a baby. Radio into the station and ask the captain to make sure the girl's okay. Her brother-in-law's a deputy sheriff in Tamlin—Schmidt's his name."

Sullivan finished cutting the lock while Bayley made the call. The chain fell away and, after forcing the rusty gate open, they were able to drive up to the house. The front door was nailed shut; so they went around to the back.

"Look at that, four locks," Bayley said.

Sullivan pounded on the door, "Mr. and Mrs. Krueger, this is Detective Sergeant Sullivan and Detective Bayley. Open up, we have to talk to you." As he pounded he noticed the loose hinges and pointed to them.

"Those hinges won't hold; let's force it open. Put your shoulder to it," Sullivan instructed.

"I'll get the bolt cutters," Bayley replied.

Sullivan looked at Bayley standing there in his impeccable blue suit under his perfect gray London Fog trench coat and made no reply. Instead he raised his size thirteen boot and gave the door a kick. It would have fallen into the kitchen if not for the four padlocks.

Stepping into the room with Bayley right behind him, Sullivan called "Police," but there was no answer.

With guns drawn, the two men went into the living room and then the bedroom. The place was empty. "Okay," Sullivan said, holstering his gun. "Grab the kit out of the car, and let's get to work. We'll have to cut the lock off the freezer in the kitchen. Let's do the other rooms first."

They pulled on latex gloves, and started in the living room. "Not many hiding places for drugs here," said Bayley, turning the large reclining chair upside down and examining the bottom.

Sullivan whistled, "Look at this!" He was holding Ruby's scrapbook which had been lying on top of the TV. "It's nothing but obituaries. There must be a hundred of them. The first one is July 10th, 1950. It's the double poisoning—one of the cold case files," his eyes widened as he read. "The woman who died had a daughter named Ruby."

Bayley was standing beside him. "See if the other cold case—the house fire—is in there."

"Here it is, June 10th, 1957, and look there's her father's obit, and four obits for people who died in Sunny Hills nursing home—holy crap!" Sullivan closed the book, "Bag it up. We'll look at it later. The captain's going to have a fit. It looks like Rosamunde hasn't been as crime-free as we all thought."

Sullivan snapped some photos of the living room and drew a quick diagram showing the location of the scrapbook before it was placed in an evidence bag. Then they entered the bedroom where the tattered patchwork quilt was pulled up over a plastic wrapped mattress.

"What's in there?" Sullivan asked pointing the camera at a brown paper shopping bag in one corner. He crossed the room for a closer inspection, "Looks like we've found a damning bit of evidence against our doctor over the liquor store," he said.

He poured the contents of one bag onto the mattress. "Look at this, ten prescriptions for narcotics all written for Ruby Kruger by Dr. Cline on the same date. Ruby went to five different drug stores to fill them. Bag this up, while I snap a few pictures and do the diagram. Then you can start on the freezer lock and I'll radio the captain to have Dr. Cline and Ruby Krueger picked up."

* * *

"Why would anyone want to lock a freezer with such a heavy chain and padlock?" Bayley complained as he tried to figure out which would be easier to cut through, the chain or the lock. He decided on the chain and inserted his bolt cutters. His tool crunched through and the chain fell to the ground. He took a clean linen handkerchief from his breast pocket and wiped his forehead before lifting the lid.

"Sullivan!" His voice came out an octave higher than normal.

"Be right there." Sullivan hurried into the kitchen, "Holy shit!" he said when he peered into the freezer.

David's yellow face stared back from among frozen spaghetti dinners and loaves of bread. His lips were fixed in a perpetual scream. A shower cap was taped over his head and there was a piece of tape on each eyebrow.

"He's so damn thin. There's practically no flesh on him. Do you think he starved to death?" Bayley asked.

"I don't know," Sullivan replied, "but I'll get on the radio and tell Captain Jenkins we need a forensics team and the ME from Portland out here. The Captain will have to send a couple of uniforms to secure the place until the body and evidence are removed." He reached into the toolbox which served as their crime kit and tossed a roll of yellow plastic tape to Bayley. Tape off the crime scene and snap a few pictures of the kitchen and the body."

Sullivan spoke to the dispatcher, "Patch me through to Captain Jenkins."

"Jenkins," her voice was crisp.

"We got a body here," he told her. "In the freezer—pretty gruesome stuff. Can't tell whether he starved to death or suffered some sort of trauma. We need the forensics team from Portland and a couple of uniforms out here."

"You got it, and I'll issue an APB on the Krueger woman," Jenkins said. "If any reporters show up there don't talk to them. I'll call a news conference and issue a statement later this afternoon."

"Did you get in touch with Deputy Schmidt? He needs to keep a close watch on his sister-in-law and nephew until we make an arrest."

"I talked to Sheriff McBride, he said he'll get the message to Deputy Schmidt and personally check to make sure Medora and the baby are safe. He didn't sound too worried. I take it Tamlin is a small place where everyone knows everybody else's business. Somebody like Ruby Krueger would stick out like a sore thumb."

"I wish Sheriff McBride took this business more seriously. If the scrapbook is any indication, Ruby has already killed enough people to populate a town the size of Tamlin. I had to break the news to that young woman about her parents' deaths. I feel kind of responsible for her."

* * *

The drugstore was busy. Ruby sat on one of the three folding chairs reserved for people waiting for prescriptions and tried to keep from screaming.

"Ruby Krueger," your prescriptions are ready, the counter girl called.

Ruby blinked, for a moment she thought it was her mother behind the counter. She had almost forgotten that her mother had worked in this very drug store. It was here that her mother met Dr. Lockland. That was so long ago, and yet it seemed like just yesterday. She could remember everything: the little spurts of red juice jumping from the spaghetti sauce; the delivery boy; the sausage pizza, and her mother all dressed up setting the table with the good china.

"Mommy," she said tentatively. Several people looked at her, and then looked away when they saw how ill she was.

"Are you all right?" the counter girl, who really didn't look anything like Mommy, asked.

"I need my medicine," Ruby croaked.

"Well, young lady if you're Ruby then your medicine is all ready," the counter girl said in a fake jovial voice. "Don't get up. I'll bring it to you. Cash or Credit?"

"Credit," said Ruby, wondering how she was going to pay her credit card bills this month. So far she had managed by transferring balances among the six cards she had in her possession, and making minimum payments. Maybe she would get another credit card application in the mail.

"Thank you so much," Ruby said meekly when the girl brought the bag with the medication to her; took the credit card, and then brought Ruby the receipt to sign. The girl's condescending attitude was almost unbearable.

"I'd like to be the nurse taking care of her if she ever got sick," thought Ruby as she struggled to her feet. A wave of dizziness washed over her and she held onto the chair until it passed. Then, concentrating on putting one foot in front of the other, she tottered toward the exit.

"The things a person has to go through just to get the medicine they need," Ruby muttered as she left the drugstore. She sat on the bench at the bus stop and swallowed four pills from each bottle. Then she waited for the pills to work their magic.

As soon as she felt her strength and self confidence returning, she began to make her plan. First she studied the advertisement, and then she looked at the bus schedule. According to the schedule, the next bus for Portland would leave in two hours. That would give her enough time to fill prescriptions at the two other drug stores in Rosamunde.

Unfortunately, there would not be time to fill the remaining prescriptions in Portland. The bus to Tamlin was scheduled to depart just fifteen minutes after the bus from Rosamunde pulled into the depot. She would have to hurry to make it. There wasn't another bus to Tamlin until the next afternoon.

Book IV
Three Women

Chapter Fifty-two
Three Women

Medora locked the office and hurried to open the car door for the woman. "I didn't introduce myself; I'm Medora Schmidt."

The woman's trembling hand flew to the narrow silver chain around her neck. Clutching the ring which hung from it, she snarled," I'm Ruby—Ruby Kruger."

* * *

Ma Tom chuckled at Medora's attempt to communicate in Spanish. Then she forgot it and thought about dinner.

Vegetable soup would be good on this cold night. After chopping carrots, potatoes, onions, chilies and cilantro, she slid them from her cutting board into a heavy kettle. She added a can of chicken broth, a can of tomato juice, garlic powder, salt and pepper; then placed the kettle on a back burner to simmer.

Timmy was sleeping like an angel when she went to check on him. His fuzz of hair seemed to be turning more coppery every day. He was going to have unusual coloring: red gold hair and dark eyes. "*Mi nieto,*" Ma Tom whispered.

Next she went to make sure Papa Gus was okay. Since Charlie's death he spent most of his time in the workshop, slumped in his chair and staring dully at his tools. This afternoon he was pacing and rubbing his hands together.

"Goose, what is it? Are you ill?" She pressed the back of her hand against his forehead; he wasn't feverish.

"My dear, Charlie is very concerned about Medora. Will she be home soon?" he said in a surprisingly clear voice.

"Yes, Goose. You should try to take a little nap and when you wake up Medora will be here."

"No, Tomasina! Charlie says we must find Medora right away."

"She just called. She is fine," Ma Tom told him.

"You don't understand." His face took on a blank expression and he slumped into his chair.

"Goose…" Tomasina began, but the phone was ringing so she went to answer it.

"Hello."

"Ma Tom? This is Sheriff McBride. Is Ernest there?"

"How are you Sheriff? Ernest isn't here. He went to work on the roof of Charlie's barn. He might come by later."

"That explains why I couldn't reach him on the radio," Sheriff McBride said. "You asked how I am. Well I haven't been too good. Gout's acting up, and then I'm having trouble with my breathing—cough all the time—guess I should give up the cigarettes. What's a man supposed to do though? That young Dr. Lopez says beer is bad for the gout so I'm trying to cut back. Am I supposed to give up cigarettes too?" He paused to catch his breath, "On top of everything Doug's off on a fishing trip and I have to cover for him."

I'm sorry you are feeling unwell. I'll ask Ernest to bring you some of my vegetable soup. It will ease both your gout and your breathing."

"Thanks, I'd appreciate that," the Sheriff said, and then paused. "I don't know what's wrong with me. I almost forgot the reason I called. Tell Ernest I need to talk to him. Probably just a false alarm, but some female policeman from Rosamunde called. Wanted to warn us to watch out for Medora—something about a lunatic woman from up there and newspaper clippings or some such thing. Don't worry about it; just have Ernest call me when he gets a chance. Give Papa Gus my best." He hung up.

An icy prickling tickled the nape of Ma Tom's neck; she ignored it and rummaged in her cupboard for a plastic container. Ernest would probably stop by; he could take the soup to the Sheriff. When she lifted the lid from the pan, and reached for her wooden spoon, she became aware of her shaking hands and rapid heartbeat.

Standing completely still, she took a deep breath. One of the children was in danger; she was sure of it. Where were they? Ernest was working on the barn; Fern had gone to dinner with that nice young doctor, Enrique Lopez. Medora was with a client, and there was something strange about that client. "A woman of pain," Medora had said. "Some lunatic woman," Sheriff Mc Bride's words came back to her.

The woman of pain and the lunatic woman were the same person, she was certain of it. Why hadn't she listened to Gus? She called the Sheriff's office. The phone rang until the answering machine picked up. "You have reached ...." She pressed the end button.

Sheriff McBride's home number was in her book. With shaking hands she punched it into her phone. "Zitz, zitz, zitz,"—the line was busy.

She hurried to the workshop and threw the door open. Gus was still in his chair. There was no spirit behind his eyes. She shook him, "Goose, Goose, we must go to the cabin of Widow Weiss. You're right. Medora is in danger."

He was like a statue of living flesh and made no response to her urgent pleading. "Then I'll go alone," she said to the deaf ears of her husband.

Should she leave Timmy with Gus—no, it would be worse than leaving the baby alone. Who could know what Gus might do in his trancelike state? God forbid, he might burn the house down.

She took her black shawl from the hook by the door, went to the bedroom and wrapped the sleeping baby in it. Keys in hand, she carried Timmy to the truck. Medora insisted that he always be strapped into his car seat which was on the front porch, but there was no time for that.

The seatbelt slipped through a knot in the shawl. There—just as safe as the complicated car seat.

She drove down the long driveway. At the main road she turned in a direction she had never before traveled alone—away from town.

Rain came in spurts and it was necessary to use the windshield wipers. Prodded by a sense of urgency, Ma Tom had to force herself to drive slowly. The road was narrow. Signs along the way warned, "Danger—Sharp Curves" and "Slippery When Wet" and "Watch for Falling Rocks."

She glanced up at the boulder strewn mountainside, but decided it was best to pay attention to the road and the sharp curves. After all, what she could do if a rock decided to fall on the truck—nothing but pray.

* * *

Ruby Kruger certainly was odd. Why did she sway from side to side? And the way her feet shuffled back and forth ....

Are you sick?" Medora asked.

" You had brown hair the last time I saw you, Helen."

"Beg your pardon?"

"I mean, I need to take my pills."

"I have some water." Medora reached behind the seat for a bottle.

Ruby grabbed it from her, but didn't remove the top. Instead she examined it closely. Then she popped a handful of pills into her mouth, chewed before swallowing them dry and tossed the bottle into the back seat.

"Are you sure you feel well enough to look at the cabin this evening?" Medora asked. "Maybe we should go back to town." The woman looked sick and she was acting strangely. Her skin was gray and the whites of her eyes were the color of butter.

"Give the pills a minute to work and I'll be fine," she replied.

Medora considered insisting they return to town, but decided to continue to the Weiss cabin. She had to make the sale. This was her defining moment. If she was successful she could purchase Charlie's forty acres and build a little cabin, a legacy for Timmy when she was gone.

She took a deep breath, pushed the intrusive thoughts of death out her mind, and concentrated on the task at hand. The easement road to the Weiss property was clearly marked by the Fern Schmidt Realty sign. She signaled left before making the turn, even though there was no traffic.

"You can get a good deal on this property if you offer cash. You won't have to worry about the cost of mortgages and loans. It's an isolated location, nice for people who value their privacy," Medora said.

"Helen," Ruby said, "People in glass houses shouldn't throw stones."

"What did you say? Are you doing okay? You can see what I meant by remote," Medora thought the bumpy road was bothering Ruby. "It's beautiful here. And when we get to the cabin you'll see that you have a small private beach. Unfortunately, I haven't had time to get the ladder to the beach repaired, so we can't go down there today." As she slowed the Saturn, she added, "You might want to put in concrete steps; it would make the access much easier and safer."

A new pile of branches blocked their way. Oney was still up to his tricks. "The road is temporarily blocked," she continued, "but this is where I usually stop anyway. There's no place to turn a car around until tree stumps are removed from the clearing in front of the cabin. I'm glad the rain has let up; it's a bit of a walk from here."

Ruby slid out of the car with an agility that surprised Medora. The sick woman loped down the road toward the cabin. Medora followed at a slower place.

"It's perfect," Ruby muttered when she saw the storage shed. The clearing was littered with rocks, as was the hillside. Plenty of stones for her need, and afterwards, when Helen's body was locked in this little room; she would go back to town and find the rest of them—a girl and a baby. It was working out so well.

When Medora saw Ruby peering into the storage room her heart sank. The shelves were probably full of Oney's mason jars of moonshine. How could she explain that to the client?

"Would you like to see the cabin?" Medora asked, hoping to redirect Ruby's interest toward the A-frame building with the bright red tin roof.

"First, I want you to look in here." Ruby pointed.

Medora stepped through the doorway, but turned when she heard a man's voice shout, "Oh no you don't! That's Charlie's woman."

She caught a glimpse of Ruby's contorted face. A thin line of saliva dripped from the corner of her mouth and her lips were pulled back in a terrible smile. She had a baseball—sized rock in her hand. It couldn't be, but it looked as if she had been going to smash the rock into Medora's head.

Ruby threw the rock at Oney instead, and pushed the door shut with her foot, all in one motion. She shoved the deadbolt into place seconds before Medora, kicking and screaming, slammed herself against the heavy door

Oney was a small wiry man; he hopped out of the way. Jigging up and down in his filthy overalls, he chanted, "You let Charlie's woman out—that's Charlie's woman."

Ruby threw three more rocks. Oney easily danced around them. Then she noticed an axe leaning against a woodpile. She grabbed it and raised it over her head. She screamed and ran at Oney.

He saw her coming, her yellow eyes glowing. When he took a step backward his heel caught against a stump and he fell. As he desperately scrambled to his feet she brought the axe down. He tried to twist out of the way, but the blade caught his left arm.

The force of the blow threw Ruby off balance; she went down on her knees. Blood spurting from his arm, Oney sprinted into the surrounding trees crying, "Witch, witch, help, help."

Ruby, axe in hand, followed him at a run, but after a few yards she slowed down and then stopped. Her heart quivered in her chest and she couldn't seem to get any air into her lungs. She leaned against a tree, closed her eyes and slid to the ground.

* * *

It wasn't until turning into the easement road that Ma Tom realized no one knew where she and Timmy had gone. She should have left a note, but it was too late now.

She brought the truck to a stop behind the Saturn and got out. Using the shawl as a sling, she settled the sleeping baby into it and adjusted it around her shoulder.

As she was deciding what to do next, she heard a sound from the underbrush almost at her feet. She pushed the brush aside and called, "Medora?" But no, it was Oney, his overalls covered in blood from a pulsing wound on his upper arm.

"The witch with yellow eyes ...." his voice was apologetic.

"Oney, *pobrecito*," she exclaimed. "Who did this to you?"

"The witch with yellow eyes locked Charlie's woman in my storage shed," he said." I tried to stop her. I'm sorry...."

Ma Tom tore a strip from the edge of her skirt and tied it above the wound; the flow of blood slowed to a trickle. She told him, "When I return with my daughter, we will lift you into the truck and drive far away from the eyes of the witch."

"Go," Oney urged her. "Hurry."

* * *

When the door slammed shut, Medora was left in total darkness. The nightmare image of the crazed bald woman aiming a rock at her head was seared into her brain. She could neither believe, nor forget the thing she had just seen.

A man's voice had shouted a warning. It sounded like Oney; she had heard his voice before—at the Tamlin Cafe. She hadn't been nice to him, hadn't been able to stand the smell of him, but he was trying to save her. She hoped he would let her out soon. She pounded and screamed, "Oney let me out," over and over until her throat was so raw that hurt even to whisper.

A terrible thought assailed her. What if no one came to let her out? What if she was left here in this dark room for days, or weeks? "Maybe I'll start drinking the moonshine," she said and gave a hysterical giggle. A second later she reminded herself, "I can't lose it. I have to stay strong."

At first she tried singing to cheer her spirits, but her throat too sore. She couldn't focus on the Bible verses she had learned in Sunday school or the poems she had enjoyed memorizing. Finally she began to mentally build her cabin, and that activity not only kept her mind occupied, but also increased her resolve to survive. "I will live to build the cabin for Timmy," she declared.

* * *

Ruby opened her eyes and looked around. She had no idea how long she'd been lying there, but it was starting to get dark. She felt wrung out. It had been a long time, maybe days, since she eaten. Taking her pill bottle from a pocket she shook it—almost empty. She poured the remaining pills into her mouth. She was so close to getting Helen; nothing must stop her now.

Something rustled in the brush nearby. Leaning on the axe she pulled herself up and went to investigate. Through the trees, she could see a truck parked behind the red car. "What's that?" she screeched. "Where did that truck come from?" Tattletale Helen must have told on Ruby again. Her hand tightened on the axe and color suffused her pale face.

Something moved on the other side of the truck. "I hate you Helen!" she screamed as she ran.

"No, no, please!" Oney pleaded when he saw her.

Ruby raised the axe and brought it down again and again.

* * *

Too much time had passed. Where was Oney? What if Ruby returned first? A weapon—Medora needed a weapon. Her fingertips touched the shelf and she felt, what must have been, rat droppings. Acid vomit rose in her throat, but she kept searching, until she found a jar of moonshine. Well, it was better than nothing.

While she stood there, clutching the jar and waiting for Ruby's return, Medora heard the scurrying, squeaking sounds of rats. Little feet ran over her foot and a long tail brushed against her ankle. She opened her mouth to scream, but no sound came out.

* * *

She hadn't gone far before the weight of Timmy, even supported by the sling, made Ma Tom feel as if her back would break. She was bent almost double with pain by the time the clearing and the cabin came into view. She looked all around before moving out from the cover of the trees. The light was rapidly fading, but she could see that the dead bolt holding the door closed had no lock. That was good.

* * *

Medora heard scraping on the door and the sound of the dead bolt being pushed back. She closed her eyes; remembering Ruby's terrible smile, she raised the jar. A gust of wind, cold and damp as a grave, blew the door open.

Chapter Fifty-three
Three Women

Medora felt the jar slip through her fingers. It fell to the floor with a crash. Sharp splinters sprayed her ankles. Turpentine smelling moonshine drenched her shoes and stung the new little cuts. She kept her eyes tightly closed and covered her head with her hands. "Please…," she whimpered.

"It's Timmy and me."

Medora took her hands from her head and hugged herself. She slowly opened her eyes. "Is this really happening or is it a nightmare?" she tried to say, but her torn vocal cords wouldn't cooperate.

"Come," Ma Tom grabbed Medora's hand in a surprisingly strong grip, and pulled her into the trees. "Move quietly. The evil woman is near."

As they pushed their way through the undergrowth, Medora whispered, "Let me take Timmy. He's heavy."

Ma Tom put a hand to her throbbing back. "We are almost to the truck. It is best he stays with me and you will drive. There it is." She pointed through the trees. "First we must lift Oney." She guided Medora to where she had left him.

A shrill scream ripped from Medora's ragged throat. Oney was dead. The place where his face had been was an unrecognizable pulp.

"Get into the truck." Ma Tom said, but before either of them could move, Ruby, eyes wild, axe in hand, charged toward them.

"Get Timmy into the truck. Go for help!" Medora croaked. She grabbed a sturdy branch and poked at Ruby's chest and stomach, pushing her back.

Ma Tom ran to the truck, yanked the door open, and swung Timmy to the passenger side floor with a thud. She scrambled into the driver's seat.

Timmy was instantly awake and mad. His mouth opened wide; his head moved back and forth without making a sound. Then he began to wail.

Ruby shoved past Medora's branch. "Your baby's crying. I'll make it be quiet." She moved toward the truck. "Say bye—bye to your pretty little baby."

The locks clicked seconds before Ruby pulled on the passenger side handle.

It wouldn't open. She swung the axe toward the windshield. A hole the size of the axe head appeared. It was surrounded by cracked glass, but the windshield held together.

Medora grasped the branch tighter and rammed it into the backs of Ruby's legs, knocking her to her knees.

"Ta-dah," Ruby jumped to her feet, and held up two sets of keys.

"*Madre Dios*," MaTom prayed as she felt under the driver's seat for the spare key Papa Gus kept there.

Her fingers touched metal. With a shaking hand, she fitted the key into the ignition. The engine roared to life. She shoved the gearshift into reverse and careened backwards down the rutted dirt road. Timmy's screams filled the air as he bounced about on the floor.

Ruby, imitating the sound of Timmy's cries, ran after the truck.

Medora took that opportunity to conceal herself behind a tree. She peered out through the low hanging branches, and watched the rear end of the truck slam into a large pine tree. A second later, it surged forward—toward Ruby.

Ruby froze. ~~The truck was~~ almost on her when, with a screech of metal, the front fender collided with a tree stump and clattered to the ground. Wheels spun, throwing up debris. Unable to move forward, the driver reversed and drove backwards a short distance.

"Helen, no, no, no!" Ruby dropped the axe and disappeared into the forest.

Ma Tom stopped the truck and looked all around. "Medora," she called.

Medora hesitated. Could she make it almost 50 feet to the truck? Perhaps she could get to the axe, but where was Ruby? One more look through the branches and she would try to make it to the truck.

Too late, Ruby had the axe and was headed toward the truck. Ma Tom saw her, shifted gears and drove directly at her. Ruby skipped out of the way and the truck hit a tree trunk head-on. Ma Tom put the truck in reverse, stepped on the accelerator and once again backed rapidly down the rough road. This time she didn't stop.

The sound of the truck died out leaving silence in its wake. "Helen," Ruby called in a childish voice. "I won't hurt you. Come out and play."

* * *

Dark clouds obscured the brightness of the moon, and low lying stratus clouds produced an eerie fog that dampened sound and obscured vision. The rain was a slow steady downpour. Medora shivered, but she was glad of the dark cold weather. It hid her from Ruby. She pressed herself into the foliage.

The shivering got worse and her legs and feet tormented her with cramps. How long had she crouched behind the tree? It seemed like hours. Maybe Ruby was tired of searching for her and had gone away. Perhaps Medora could work her way to the main road and flag down a passerby.

She moved from tree to tree, making as little noise as possible. After a few minutes of this she realized she was too confused and too exhausted to continue. The night was so dark.

Medora found a mound of leaves and dead vegetation large enough to burrow in to. She was cold and tired. The leaves made a warm comforter. She closed her eyes.

.The sound of Ruby's strange childlike voice jarred her into alertness. "Helen, where are you? You shouldn't have told on me. I only wanted to borrow the ring."

. Medora panicked. She scooted back, instinctively trying to put distance between herself and Ruby.

"I hear you, Helen. I know where you are. One, two, three, here I come ready or not."

Medora tried to quiet her breathing. Heart hammering, she rolled to her hands and knees, and crawled backwards. Something grabbed her ankle.

"Boo! Gotcha' now—gotcha' this time," Ruby sang out.

Medora jerked free, jumped to her feet and spun around to stare into Ruby's grinning face. Putting her head down, Medora turned her back on Ruby, and ran. She thought she heard the thud of Ruby's feet behind her, but perhaps it was her own heart.

Crashing through the undergrowth, not caring if twigs tore at her face and arms, she ran. Her lungs felt ready to burst when she dashed into the clearing and saw the cabin and storage shed. "Oh, no," she gasped.

Seconds later Ruby was by the storage shed. She picked up a rock, threw it and howled with glee when it caught Medora under the left eye.

There was no place to hide, no way to escape, except maybe …. Medora remembered the rope ladder leading to the beach. The bottom section was gone and the two remaining sections were rotten, but anything was better than just waiting to be butchered.

Stones pelted her back and legs as she raced to the edge of the precipice. Dropping to her knees, she felt along the shadowy rocks until she found the ladder. She took a deep breath and began to descend— more sliding than climbing—the rope tore the skin on her hands but she didn't notice. The moon came out from behind the clouds; its light illuminated the cliff and the beach below. "Why doesn't someone come to help me?" she sobbed.

Up on top Ruby was hacking at the ropes. The axe was dull, but eventually the first section of the ladder fell away. By then Medora had reached the last step of the second section. She looked down at the beach. No one could fall that far and survive.

When the top section fell to the beach it pulled the second section, with Medora clinging to the last step, away from the face of the cliff and over the turbulent ocean inlet.

The stakes anchoring the section Medora clung to, driven into rock face of the cliff many years earlier, groaned and creaked, but held. Having reached its zenith, the frail contraption reversed direction and swung back toward the cliff. Medora hit the rock face with a dull thud.

For a moment she saw stars; blood from a cut on her forehead stung her eyes. She fought to maintain her grip on the frayed ropes. The ladder again began its outward journey away from the cliff; over white waves crashing on the rocks far below.

Hearing sounds above her, she looked up. Ruby, a dark silhouette, was balanced on the rim of the abyss. She was holding a rock; waiting for Medora to swing back into range before dropping it.

"I'm going to die. I used to think I wanted die, but I don't. Forgive me. Please God, I don't want to die. I don't want to leave my baby." The wind snatched the words from Medora's mouth and blew them into the universe.

She was still looking up at Ruby and the rock when she saw, what must have been a trick of the moonlight, something that looked like the shadow of a man.

Ruby whirled around. "The Spanish man," she screamed and dropped the rock. It bounced harmlessly down the face of the cliff. "No, no, don't." Ruby held her hands out in supplication.

Medora gripped the rope ladder and watched Ruby scrabble down the sheer face of the cliff, holding onto scrubby vegetation and bits of rock. "Keep away, keep away," she was saying.

The ladder again swung toward the cliff. This time Medora leaned back to cushion the blow. Her knuckles scraped across a jagged stone, but she was able to catch hold of a tuft of grass growing from a handful of soil trapped in a crevice. In this way she kept the ladder from swinging outward again.

Looking to her left, Medora saw Ruby's white rubber soled shoes sliding down the rocks, desperately seeking a toe hold. A twisted dwarf of a tree grew from a small rocky ledge an arm's length from the ladder. It was a risk, but …. Pressing into the cliff, Medora took a hand from the rope ladder and used it to guide one of Ruby's shoes onto the ledge.

Ruby's other foot found the ledge. She crouched less than two feet from Medora. The two women stared at each other.

"You saved me. I have a surprise for you." Ruby said pulling something over her head.

Medora shut her eyes, sure that Ruby was going to push the ladder and send her to her death. Instead, Ruby reached out and gently slipped an object over Medora's head. Medora looked down; moonlight glinted on a ring hanging from a silver chain.

"You can tell your mom I gave the ring back," Ruby said in her childish voice. "I just wanted to be your friend, but you told on me."

The rope ladder gave a creak as one of the bolts began to pull out of the rock.

"Your ladder's breaking," the child's voice said.

"I know." Medora whispered, and it was as if this was the most ordinary conversation in the world—an intimate little chat between two old friends. "I'll tell you a secret, Ruby. I thought life was too hard. I didn't want to live, but now I don't want to die. Isn't that strange?"

"Will you be my friend?" Ruby asked.

"Okay," said Medora.

"You can come onto my rock with me."

"I can't. There's not room for both of us."

Ruby's strong hands pulled the ladder, with Medora holding fast, halfway onto to the rock ledge.

"Your turn," Ruby giggled as she scooted off the other side. "Wheeeeeee…" She sounded like a happy youngster going down a slide.

Medora hauled herself the rest of the way onto the ledge and let go of the ladder before she looked down at Ruby's body sprawled on the rocks below.

Chapter Fifty-four
Three Women

Ma Tom couldn't stop shaking. How could she drive away and leave Medora alone with that woman? Poor little Timmy's cries tore at her heart. Tears streaked his red cheeks. He saw her looking at him and held out his arms.

"I can't pick you up, *mi hijo*. We must find someone to help your Mama.

The trailer, yes, we'll go to the trailer. If your *Tio* is not there, surely Carl will be nearby with his large dog, and there's a phone there. We will call for help."

She turned north, both hands gripping the wheel. Rain blew in the broken windshield. It drenched her, and dripped down the dashboard onto the sobbing baby.

Something was wrong with the steering mechanism. A noise from the under the hood, like Gus' grinding wheel when he sharpened her kitchen knives, hurt her ears and the stench of burning rubber wafting through the floorboards made her eyes water. Timmy was so close to the awful odor, but she had to keep going.

Screeeech—the scream of metal dragging—sparks flying—the truck bounced up and down but kept going. Through a shroud of mist she made out two mailboxes marking a private road. She slowed and twisted the wheel with desperate strength. The truck slid onto the muddy track. It whined and moved forward at a snail's pace. Ma Tom pressed the horn button so that it blared in a long continuous honk. A blast like twenty firecrackers all going off at once as the tires blew, and the steering wheel twisted out of her hands. The truck skidded sideways until the front tires came to rest in a shallow ditch.

She reached for her screaming grandson. Balancing him on her hip, she climbed down from the truck and ran toward the trailer.

* * *

Ernest had put his tools away and was getting in the van when Carl drove up. Lobo peered from under a tarp in the bed of the old truck. As Carl got out he said, "Nice steady rain."

"What are you and Lobo doing out in this weather?" Ernest asked.

"Provin' we don't have any sense," Carl said, holding up a six-pack of beer. "Have time for a quick one?"

"Sounds good," said Ernest. "Let me make sure my radio is on. Doug went fishing and Sheriff McBride is holding down the fort. I told him I'd be available if he needs me this evening. He's been kind of poorly; I don't like to think of him going on a call alone at night."

The two men sat in plastic yard chairs on the covered porch of the trailer with the dog at Carl's feet. "When's he going to retire?" Carl asked taking a pull on his beer. "Way it looks to me, you have all the responsibility of being the sheriff with none of the glory—or fat paycheck."

"He talks about it," Ernest took a long drink. "Ah—that's good." He wiped his mouth on the back of his hand, "but he hates to put himself on the shelf. I don't know what he'd do if he couldn't come into the office every day."

Lobo's ears twitched and he gave a "woof."

"Listen—I hear a horn," Ernest said. "Who could be way out here?" Beer in hand he ambled up the track. Lobo raced ahead, barking.

Carl put his open beer in the back of his truck next to the remainder of the six pack, reached for his walking stick and followed at a slower pace.

"It looks like Ma Tom," Ernest shouted and, dropping his can of beer, started to run. "What on earth," he said when he reached her. "You're soaking wet; so is Timmy." He took the baby from her. Timmy's cries turned into hiccups.

"What's happened?" Carl yelled as he hurried toward them.

Ma Tom began to speak in rapid Spanish, gesturing with her hands.

"Ma Tom, Ma Tom, please, English, please—slow down," Ernest said.

She took a breath. "*Una mujer loca*—crazy woman—she has killed Oney and now she wishes to kill Medora."

"Where are they? Does she have a weapon?" Ernest asked.

"What is this 'weapon'?"

"A gun, does she have a gun?" Carl asked.

"No, no gun—she has an axe, very big. You must go at once but you must take great care."

"Where?" Ernest asked.

"The Weiss cabin, in the woods, Medora hides from the crazy woman—now go."

"Carl, make sure they get home," Ernest said handing the baby to him.

"I should go with you." Carl said.

"I'll radio for backup from the Highway Patrol and Sheriff McBride. First take them," he gestured toward Ma Tom and Timmy, "to the big cabin. Make sure they're okay, and then meet me at the Weiss place." Ernest ran for the van. Moments later he sped by them.

* * *

Time passed, whether hours or minutes Medora couldn't tell. The clouds drifted across the moon and the rain continued. She squatted on the ledge afraid to move. Her legs, compressed by her weight, were numb. A Charlie-horse gripped her left thigh and she could feel cramps beginning in her feet. .She had to change her position.

She sat back on her buttocks and carefully shifted off her lower limbs. Then she held on to the little tree and stretched her legs one at a time.

Taking inventory of her body, she decided there wasn't a place that didn't have a good reason to hurt. Not only were her face, arms and hands covered with bruises, cuts and rope burns, but her engorged breasts were throbbing.

When was the last time she fed Timmy? Oh yes, at lunch. She had gone to the big cabin for lunch and nursed him. Ma Tom probably gave him a bottle in the afternoon. He must be hungry by now.

She was so cold and sleepy. Staying awake was torture; she forced herself to keep her eyes open. Random thoughts, almost like dreams, floated through her mind.

The Bible says, "Give thanks for all things." She should have given thanks for the rats. She'd love to be transported off the slippery ledge into that nice rat infested storage room. Her eyes closed.

She felt the hand holding the tree relaxing. She was so tired.

* * *

Despite the sharp curves and slippery pavement, and the quick call to the Highway Patrol, Ernest made it to the turnoff for the Weiss cabin in ten minutes. Once he was off the main road, he slowed and scanned the area for Medora or her assailant.

He pulled in behind the Saturn and decided to leave one door of the van ajar. If Medora was hiding nearby she would see the dome light and know he was near. She might be able to make it to the van and lock herself in.

Taking the Glock from the glove box, he checked the magazine, and slipped it into the pocket of his coat, then reached for his long black flashlight.

The Saturn looked purple in the flashlight's yellow ray. He swept the light in a wide arch around the car, and saw Oney's body. Ernest sucked in his breath, "Oney, poor little guy."

He shined the powerful beam into the trees as he walked toward the cabin, nothing stirred. Maybe Medora was hiding in the cabin or the shed.

He walked over to the storage shed, "Medora," he called, and heard something move inside. Gun in hand, he kicked the door open and pointed the flashlight into the dark interior. He saw three large rats on the nearest shelf, and heard more in the corners and ceiling beams.

"Oh shit," he said in disgust. "This place is infested with them." Something crunched under his foot and he turned his flashlight downward. The shards of broken glass near the door were still wet with moonshine. Someone had been there recently.

He dropped the Glock into his pocket and moved toward the steps leading to the cabin. "Medora—Maa-door-ah," he cupped his hands to his mouth and called.

Medora snapped awake. Was she dreaming or did she hear Ernest's voice?

Pushing herself back up against the face of the cliff she tried to yell, "I'm here Ernest. Ernest down here—Ernest." Her tortured voice came out in a croak.

* * *

Carl had Ma Tom sit next to the ruined truck. He put Timmy into her arms and draped his canvas jacket over both of them. "I'll be back in a jiffy," he told them, and then pointed at his dog, "Lobo—stay."

He jogged back to get his truck. "Son of a bitch," he said when his knee twisted and pitched him forward. Here he was, just like the night the tree fell on Charlie, handicapped by a bum knee—just like Nam— but he couldn't think about that. He had to keep control of his mind. No thoughts of Nam and no thoughts of losing Medora.

He took a deep breath and fought to stay calm. Ernest asked him to get Ma Tom and Timmy home, and he would. Then he would go to the Weiss cabin and see what Ma Tom meant about a crazy woman killing Oney—and trying to kill Medora.

He let the old truck idle while he settled Ma Tom and Timmy in the passenger seat, then he made a motion to Lobo. The dog jumped into the back and burrowed under the tarp.

As Carl drove toward the big cabin he thought of Papa Gus, and how he seemed to have lost his grasp on reality since Charlie's death. It was asking a lot of Ma Tom to take care of a baby and a demented old man in her state of shock and exhaustion.

"Do you think you can manage with just Papa Gus to help you?" Carl asked Ma Tom. She hadn't said a word since Ernest left except to tell him, "*Gracias*," several times.

She looked over at him, her dark eyes shining with tears. "You are a good man. You saved the lives of my daughter and my grandchild. Now you are willing to put yourself in danger again for us. You are like an angel to my family."

Timmy was dozing with his fist in his mouth. She brushed his red cheek with her fingers. "You must go fast to Ernest. Goose will take care of me and Timmy," she said.

He was relieved when Papa Gus came out on the porch and hurried across the clearing to the truck. Ma Tom placed Carl's jacket on the front seat and murmured another "*gracias*," as she handed the baby to Papa Gus. She leaned against her husband and they walked toward the cabin.

Giving a light "beep-beep" on the truck horn Carl waved and sped toward the main road. Fifteen minutes later he was turning into the Weiss property. He parked behind Ernest's van.

"Come Lobo," he called. The dog jumped from the truck, ran to Medora's car and began to bark. Following the dog, Carl shined his light on the ground and saw Oney.

He threw his head back and raised his fists. "Please God don't let us be too late."

Chapter Fifty-five
Three Women

Medora huddled close to the face of the cliff. The direction of the wind had changed; the damp tropical breezes of the early afternoon were now bitingly cold gusts from the north. Beneath the cliff, in the inlet, frenzied waves roared and dashed against rocky outcroppings.

She thought she heard Ernest calling her name, but it must have been a dream. No one was coming to save her, and she couldn't hold on much longer. Soon she would slide from the ledge and join Ruby on the rocks below.

If only she could see Timmy again. She never told Ma Tom or Papa Gus how much she loved them...sweet Fern...dear Ernest...Carl....

Carl—it must have been worse than this in Viet Nam, but he knew how to survive. What would he do if he were on this ledge?

An idea formed in her mind. He would tie himself on.

She didn't have a rope or a belt, but she did have her sweater with long sleeves. What could she tie it to? There was nothing except the little tree. It would have to do.

Getting the sweater off was tricky. She had to hold on to the tree with one hand, while, with the help of her teeth, she got first one arm, and then the other out. She was even colder than before, but cold was better than dead.

She poked at the sweater until she got one sleeve looped around the tree. Next, she pulled both sleeves around her waist and tied them together in a loose square knot. She pulled at the sleeves and was pleased to feel the knot tighten. When she relaxed her grip on the tree, the sweater held her in place. Her eyes closed and her chin rested on her chest.

* * *

Ernest heard Lobo's bark. "Over here by the cabin," he called.

"Did you find her?" Carl shouted.

"No, but they've got to be here somewhere. There's no sign of another vehicle, and where could they go? I have a feeling Medora and that woman are both hiding in the woods somewhere close by." He cupped his hands to his mouth, "Maa-door-ah."

Lobo ran back and forth with his nose to the ground. He gave a sharp bark, and then sniffed his way to the edge of the cliff.

"Call your dog back, "Ernest told Carl. " There's a vicious drop over there."

"He's on to something. We better take a look," Carl said.

"Be careful," Ernest swept his light in front of them as they walked across the clearing. When they reached the precipice he focused the powerful beam of the light on the beach far below.

She was caught in a crevice between two rocks. The outgoing waves pulled at her body, but the rocks kept her from being carried out to sea.

Ernest put his hands over his face and his shoulders shook.

Carl had seen it too—the body on the rocks. Something wasn't right about it. Medora always wore blue jeans—not white slacks.

Lobo put his head back and let out a yelp which ended in a siren-like howl. "What are you trying to tell us?" Carl squatted next to the dog and played the light beam over the rocky face of the cliff. "My God, it's her," he said when he saw a figure slumped on a small outcropping.

"What...." Ernest rubbed his eyes.

"Here...." Carl handed Ernest the big flashlight and retrieved his own smaller one from his pocket. "Shine your beam right about here."

He pointed with his light and Ernest did as he was directed.

"It's her! I'll get the mountain rescue kit from my van."

Carl gave Ernest the weaker light. "Turn off the big light so we'll have plenty of juice to work by when you come back."

Ernest raced down the track. He flung the door of the van open and pulled out a red duffle bag. Slipping the strap over his shoulder, he took off in the direction of the clearing at a run.

Hearing Ernest's footsteps, Carl switched the light on.

"I've got a hundred and twenty five feet of strong rope here," Ernest said, pulling gear out of the duffle-bag, "and two rescue harnesses. We'll fasten the rope to one of these stumps—probably that one." He motioned to a solid looking stump about three feet high and two feet in diameter. "I'll put on a harness, climb down there, and get the other harness on her."

"The Highway Patrol should be here any minute," Carl said.

"I know, I know," Ernest gave an impatient wave of his arm. "We can't get her up by ourselves, but I don't want to risk her falling off that ledge while we wait around."

"You're right. That wind is kicking up and the rain…I don't know how she's managing to stay on that ledge," Carl said.

"Help me with this. I've gotta get down there," Ernest dragged two coils of rope toward the stump as spoke.

Carl took them from Ernest and secured the shorter anchor rope around the stump. Then he uncoiled the long rope until he found the wrap of tape indicating the center. He attached the ring-like braking devise to the anchor rope and to the long rope using an Italian hitch knot.

Meanwhile, Ernest was getting into the harness, and making sure it and the rescue harness were properly attached to both the dead and the live ends of the rope. When he was satisfied everything was in order, Carl helped him slip the coil over his head. Both ends of the rope would be used in the descent. The live end went behind Ernest's right shoulder and under his right arm. He would move down that one. The dead end went behind his body and wrapped around his left arm twice. It would act as a brake.

In a crouch, feet firmly planted against the cliff, he backed over the edge and began to move downward at first slowly—push with the feet—let the live rope slip through his hands—push—slip—push—slip—he picked up speed—sliding too fast—in danger of losing control—he quickly pulled his left arm across his stomach. The rope bit into his arm; he slowed and then, heart pounding, he stopped next to Medora.

"I'm at the ledge. There's a piece of rope ladder here. I'm standing on it." Ernest called. "She's alive. She can't talk, but she looked at me. She knows I'm here."

As he was slipping one of her arms into the harness, he saw the way she had bound herself to a scrub pine with her sweater. When the harness was secured to the rope, he untied the sweater. He only meant to pull it free from the tree, but when he gave a tug the last of the roots tore away and little tree fell to the rocks below.

Holding Medora in his arms, he balanced on the ledge, and tried not to think of what would have happened if they hadn't found her. The little tree was all that held her, and it had been ready to give way.

"Are you okay down there?" Carl's voice was barely audible above the sound of the wind and rain.

"Okay down here," Ernest yelled back and Medora's eyelids flickered.

"Ernie, two Highway Patrolmen are here with me. Let us know when you're ready to be pulled up."

"Can you hear me, Honey?" Ernest asked Medora. "I'm going to turn you around so you're sitting on my lap—there. I'll have one arm around you and one on the rope. They're going to pull us up the mountain, and I'm going to use my feet to keep us from bumping into the rocks."

He pulled her to him, and reached for the rope. "Ready?" he asked and thought she nodded. "Okay, he called loudly. We're ready. Haul away."

"Oh, Ernest," she whispered.

"Can you hold on to me? I'd like to put both hands on the rope," he said.

"Yes," it was barely audible, but her arms tightened around him and she rested her head on his chest.

Up on top the men worked as a team. Ernest heard Carl's command, "heave," and the echo of the two Highway Patrolmen, "heave." As the rope tightened and pulled them up foot by foot, he pushed against the cliff with his boots. "Heave"—"heave," and they advanced. "Heave"—"heave," until they reached the top of the cliff, and Carl held out his hands and helped them the last few feet.

With Carl holding his arm, Ernest straightened up. Medora's legs were shaking. She leaned against Ernest and wrapped her arms around his waist.

One of the Highway Patrolmen tried to remove Medora's harness but she wouldn't let go of Ernest. She didn't say anything, just held on tight.

"See if she'll let you hold her while I get this equipment off, "Ernest said to Carl—and then to Medora, "Carl's here. We need to take our harnesses off."

She loosened her hold on Ernest, and Carl put his arms around her.

"Carl? Timmy? Ma Tom?" she croaked.

"Everyone's safe," he told her.

Ernest, removed his own harness, and then unbuckled Medora's. One of the straps brushed her cheek and she winced.

Carl touched the bruise under her eye. "We'll get you to the hospital and they'll help you to feel better."

She grabbed his sleeve and shook her head from side to side.

"You don't want to go to the hospital?" Carl asked.

She shook her head again and tried to say something. He put his ear close to her mouth and heard her whisper, "Timmy."

"She wants her baby," Carl told Ernest. "And I don't see any reason why not. It's a long ride to the hospital. We'll take her to the big cabin and call old Doc Clark or that new doctor—what's his name?

"Enrique Lopez," Ernest said. "He and Fern were going out to dinner tonight. Ma Tom or Papa Gus has most likely already called them."

"What's going on?" It was the booming voice of Sheriff McBride. "Why wasn't I notified of a problem? Had to wait to hear it from that smart-aleck new doctor."

"I'll fill you in tomorrow, sir," Ernest told him. "Right now, I'm going to take Medora home."

Epilogue
Medora

It's been four years since that terrible night. We each recovered in our own way. As soon as resilient little Timmy had dry clothing and a full tummy, he forgot the ordeal. Ma Tom's back never completely healed, but other than that, she, like Timmy, seems unscathed by the incident.

I don't sleep well; I have nightmares. I'm forever changed because of knowing Charlie and Ruby. I wear the silver chain Ruby gave me. Two rings hang from it: the old fashioned ring she took from my grandmother's house so many years ago, and the silver band Charlie slipped on my finger the day we were married.

The detectives, Sullivan and Bayley, came from Rosamunde to ask us questions a week or so after Ruby's death. "To tie up loose ends," they said.

They wanted to know about the shadow on the cliff, the thing Ruby called, "The Spanish man." I told them I believe it was Charlie's spirit.

Papa Gus and Ma Tom were quietly sitting on the couch. I was surprised when he said in a loud clear voice, "I'm sure Medora's right. After Charlie's death, he came and talked to me everyday in the workshop, but now he's gone."

Sullivan scratched his head and said, "I wonder how that's going to look in our report." They told us a little about Ruby—her childhood and her violent history—things they learned from her school records and scrapbooks.

After the detectives left, Ma Tom took me aside and told me the secret of Charlie's birth. She explained that without Mr. Seligman's brutal attack, she wouldn't have met Papa Gus; there would be no Charlie and no Timmy. She said. "In my lifetime I have learned that goodness can come from the ashes of evil. "

"And without Ruby, my parents would never have met." I said, beginning to understand.

* * *

I work for Fern part-time. Timmy is as at home in the real estate office, with his basket of toys, as he is in his own bedroom. On my days off I volunteer as a mentor for new mothers at Dr. Enrique Lopez's clinic. I love the work. Enrique says I should go to school and become a professional counselor. Perhaps some day I will.

Thanks to real estate sales commissions, Timmy and I now own Charlie's forty acres. We live in the three bedroom modular home I had moved onto the clearing where the trailer once stood. Carl calls it our "plastic house". He and Lobo are frequent visitors.

Charlie's furniture is still wrapped and stored in the lopsided barn. When Fern and Enrique were married last month, she asked if they could choose a few pieces for their house. Charlie would have been pleased.

* * *

On Valentine's Day, Ernest asked me to be his wife. I said "yes." We are spending our honeymoon getting ready for two sisters, nine and ten years old, orphans from Ma Tom's village. They are coming to live with us in our plastic house. We hope to adopt them.

Even Timmy helped paint the girls' room pale blue today. Tomorrow I'll paint fluffy white clouds on the walls, while Ernest and Timmy put glow-in-the-dark stars on the ceiling.

Timmy and Ernest are cuddled together on the couch, half asleep. When I sit next to them, Ernest says, "I'm completely happy."

I lean my head against his shoulder and whisper, "Me, too."